SHADOW'S HAND

The Shadow's Creed Saga
Volume One

Enjoy the adventure!

Noelle Nichols

Published by Phantom Ink Press

Text copyright © Noelle Nichols
Cover illustration and map artwork © Noelle Nichols

ISBN-13: 978-1-949051-01-8

Library of Congress Control Number: 2018947981

Noelle Nichols
www.noellenichols.com

Printed in the United States of America

For my Mom,
who always knew I would become an author.

The Shadow's Creed

A Shadow seeks peace within himself
and the world around him.

A Shadow stays true to his beliefs, letting
compassion guide his actions.

A Shadow does not condemn, searching
for the truth with unclouded eyes.

A Shadow does not take life, killing only
when no other option can be found.

A Shadow protects the innocent, using
his strength to aid those in need.

A Shadow does what he is capable of; no
more can be asked of him.

A Shadow serves until he is no longer able,
his life freely given to the people.

The Seven Virtues of the Shadow's Creed

Justice, Courage, Compassion, Honor,
Loyalty, Truth, and Strength.

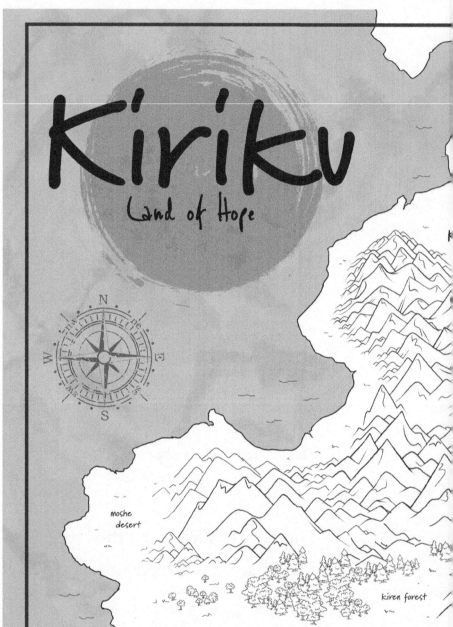

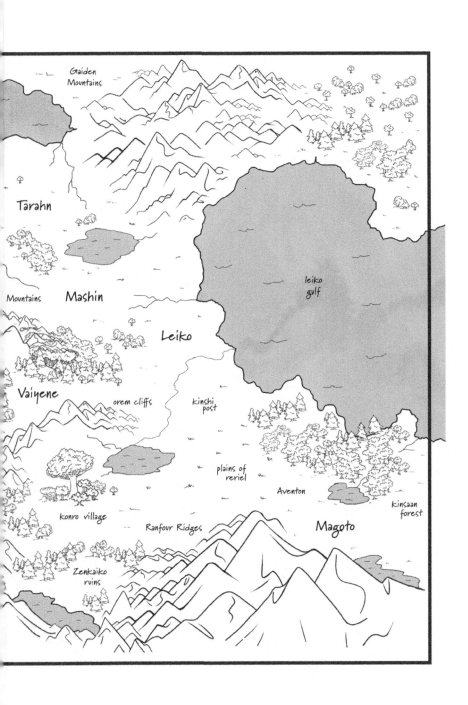

part one
KILO

chapter one
SHADOW MISSION

Smoke trailed across crimson skies. So much for an easy Shadow mission. I drew my staff from the leather holder affixed to my back and ran over the rickety dock. Water splashed onto the worn planks, dampening the fabric around my two-toed boots. The faint smell of smoke mingled with the fishy aroma of Leiko's ocean shore.

A little girl's shriek echoed from the town, sending a chill up my spine. Instincts and guilt quickened my pace. I abandoned my sister more than I liked—though not by choice. Like all Shadows, duty took me where my Phantom bid. Finae might be alone, but she was safe, under the protection of the Phantoms and Shadows. And that's all that mattered.

My penance was to protect those I could.

I wound between cottages that sat upon stilts, their damp wood eroding from the harsh weather. Despite the moisture in the air, smoke burned my eyes. I pulled the scarf up from around my neck and secured it over my mouth and nose.

The girl screamed again. She was close. I ducked under a low balcony, turning sideways down an alleyway to reach the street on the other side.

A tall, burly man had cornered a woman against a building. At her feet, a small girl balled her hands in the fabric of the woman's skirts. The girl was most likely her daughter. The woman brandished a broken piece of wood and swung at the man. He caught her arm, throwing her into the side of the building.

I held my staff against my side and charged, drawing the man's gaze. He grinned at me, confidence exuding from his walk. His smile widened as he unsheathed the sword from his belt. Without losing momentum, I thrust my staff toward the man. He stepped to the side, and I pivoted the staff in my hands, jabbing the end of the pole into his body. The man took the blow and lashed out at me. I jumped back, the sword tip catching the edge of my leather armor.

I kept my face masked from emotion. Any person who attacked another to feel powerful was neither honorable nor honest. I would need to watch out for his blackened ways. The woman and child were not close, but this man would use them against me if the opportunity arose.

A man without morals was a dangerous one.

I shifted my attention back to the man. He eyed the tear in my side. Behind him, the woman tried to pull her child to safety, but the girl would not move. Fear paralyzed her.

I shifted the staff in my hand as the man came at me, thrusting toward his knee. The direction of the man's sword changed, and I realized my error. I dipped my staff, blocking the sword from slicing into my stomach. The wood splintered, creating a large crack that ran along my staff. I pressed my lips into a thin line and kicked the man in the chest. His sword dislodged as he stumbled back. Before he could recover, I hit him with the heel of my staff and forced him to the ground, stomping on his sword hand.

The Shadow's Creed I was bound by required us to value all life, even someone as pitiful as this man. I took a breath and calmed the anger inside me. It wasn't my place to judge a man for a single deed. Though I doubted he had many redeeming qualities. Before I could contemplate further, I hit a pressure point in the man's neck to knock him unconscious.

I shifted the staff in my hand. The damage to it was severe, but the integrity of the wood still held. I would need to be wary of using it. I checked for danger before I returned to the mother and child. The little girl's eyes widened at my approach. She grasped onto her mother's skirts, pulling the fabric over her face.

They were shaken. Understandably so.

"T-thank you," the child's mother said, brushing a piece of golden hair behind her ear. I nodded and dropped to one knee, placing my staff on the ground. The little girl stared at me with eyes as blue as Leiko Gulf. I pulled the scarf from my face and set it around my neck.

Despite my intentions, I knew I looked no less threatening.

I smiled anyway. The girl reached out a cautious hand, touching the bond on my right forearm. Her mother reached to stop her, but I shook my head.

"Let her be," I said as the girl's tiny fingers traced the silver metal strands that wound around my arm. I had received my bond upon completing my Shadow training. Almost two decades now, I had served under the Phantoms. The bond was a symbol of pride among our homeland and across the lands of Kiriku. As a Shadow, I didn't want her to be afraid of me or who the Shadows were.

The girl finished tracing the metal encasing and withdrew her fingers. She raised her eyes to me. She didn't return my smile, but she seemed less afraid.

Somewhere behind me, a sound caught my attention, and I froze. It sounded like wood straining. A bow? I snatched my staff up from the ground and sprang to my feet, looking for the blur of an arrow. I pushed the woman back against the building. She jumped, startled. The arrow pierced my skin between the metal threading of my bond. I grimaced and pulled the shaft free. The girl shrieked from her place on the ground, and I ran at the man. My enemy fumbled with an arrow in his hand; his eyes darted between his trembling fingers and my approach. Horse hooves pattered behind me, and I caught sight of green banners and mounted riders.

General Mirai's men.

Allies.

I returned my full attention to the archer and ducked as an arrow scraped by my ear. Ignoring the momentary sting, I locked the staff behind the man's knee and swept him to the ground. The wind had been knocked out of him.

I scanned the men on horseback, and found General Mirai, his downturned eyes making him appear more approachable than status dictated. He wore light leather armor painted in various hues of green and gold. The rest of his men were not adorned with such fanciful coloring. In total, there were seven men on horseback. More would be in town.

Overhead, an arrow flew through the air.

I traced the curve of an arrow as General Mirai moved his horse closer. One of his men dismounted and attended to the man on the ground. "My men are sweeping the town. We can secure this part of the town and protect these two if you'd like to take care of the other archers."

I gave a sidelong glance at the mother and child. General Mirai would see to their safety. With his group, he would be able to ensure the townspeople were protected.

I nodded my agreement as another arrow flew overhead.

Fire burned on the arrowhead, but no smoke trailed behind. When it clattered against the stone pavement, I stooped to retrieve it, placing my finger on the arrowhead. The tip was cool, but there had been a fire in it before. How could that be? I discarded the arrow, focusing on the task before me—finding the archer. Speculations could wait. I wound between cottages, dodging a wave of people as they ran for cover. I paused and glanced up as another arrow shot through the air. This one, too, had fire on the head but was without a trail of smoke. Exhaustion did strange things to the body, but I was well within my limits. It was no illusion.

Something was not right.

At the edge of town, I crouched and inched forward. I kept my back bent, staying close to the ground, circling the archer's location. The area lacked vegetation. Some large rocks and dead flora spotted the field, but it did little to hide my advance. I sat back on the heels of my feet, behind an overgrown bush as something moved ahead. A cloaked archer raised an arm, the folds of the sleeve drooping to the elbow. Silver metal glinted around the archer's forearm.

Whoever this person was, they wore a bond. Hair rose on the back of my neck. Only the Shadows and the Phantoms wore bonds. Phantom Kural was in the town, and all the other Shadows were back home in Vaiyene, which was at least a three-day ride.

Who was this person?

I tensed, my hand shifting around my staff. A white mist rose from the person's bond, collecting in the archer's palm. A reddish hue permeated the smoke as it became more turbulent. The archer dipped the arrow into the flames. The arrowhead caught fire. When the archer picked up the bow, I stood, shaking the disbelief from my mind. The archer turned to me, relaxing the bowstring. They were shorter than I was, with slim shoulders. Their planted feet showed defiance at my approach.

The fire on the arrowhead still burned.

I contemplated my next move. If this person was using fake fire, her purpose was not to harm the townspeople. From this vantage point, aiming was impossible. Even a skilled archer would be firing at random targets. I kept my grip on my staff but did not raise it. I wanted answers, not to fight.

"Why do you wear a Shadow's bond?"

The person lowered their bow, the flame snuffing out as they exhaled. "You should be with your Phantom. There's no telling what he'll do this time."

A female voice.

She seemed exasperated at my presence.

Phantom Kural was one of the Shadow leaders. I had been under his command for almost a decade. He was in town picking up supplies as was our agreement with the town leader. I had not seen him since this morning before the raid started.

What was she implying?

Despite my unease, I kept the emotion from my face. There was no reason to give this woman leverage over me. From what I could see of her face, she had distinctive emerald-green eyes and high cheekbones. No one from the northern regions of Kiriku had green eyes. Few had the same pigment of skin as she did. They were characteristics of the Phia region, farther south than this town.

I kept my eyes trained on her. She did not hesitate with her approach. Her eyes narrowed at me. The bow in her hand posed no immediate threat. With my staff's reach, I would be able to disable her before she could reach me.

She stopped a few feet from me and reached out, touching the end of my staff. A thread of silver melted from her bond, snaking over her hand and fingers and into the splintered wood. I stood, dumbfounded. This woman created fire that was not fire, and she could also move silver from her bond and command it to move to another surface. It was…incredible.

Unnatural.

I had never seen anything like it.

When she pulled back, the splinter remained silver. I raised the staff to my eyes. The metal had filled the cracks. I brushed my fingertips over the surface, and a white mist puffed out at my touch. She had disarmed my usual quick battle wit by her unexpected kindness.

"Who are you?" I asked.

And why was she helping me?

She ignored me and walked back to the spot where her arrows lay on the ground. "Now that I've stopped my attack, the others will begin the final assault. Find your Phantom. He'll be in the forest, where the villagers won't go."

A group of cloaked riders burst from the edge of the town, their cloaks splayed in the wind, metal bonds prominent on their arms. I grew cold watching them—a chill of uncertainty. If they wore bonds, they would be mistaken for Shadows. The people—

the little girl—they would think we were the ones attacking the village. My throat went dry as I took a step back, away from the cloaked woman. I slid my right foot back, assuming a battle-ready stance. I did not sense ill-will from the woman, but the approach of her comrades demanded caution.

A Shadow was always ready.

One of the riders strode past me, the horse's ears pinned back. The stallion's tail swished in agitation as the others began encircling me. I drew in a breath and prepared myself for a fight—but they kept their swords sheathed. I held my stance, and the riders stopped. A black horse trotted through the circle, parting the others as it headed to the woman.

"We're done here," she said.

I stepped after her, cautious of the surrounding riders. "Wait. Tell me who you are."

She clicked her heels against the horse's side, saying, "Go to the forest." The irritation in her voice still there.

I gritted my teeth as her people fell into formation around her, heading south at a rapid pace. She knew something about Phantom Kural and why the raiders were here in Leiko. I wanted to pursue them, but my Shadow duty lay with my Phantom and the people. The townspeople's safety came first; finding Phantom Kural came second.

I put my fingers to my lips and whistled—long, then short. From across the field on the edge of the forest line, my white mare, Whitestar, trotted toward me. I reached my hand up and traced the hidden star in her fur. In the moonlight, a faint silver star became visible in her white hair. She nuzzled my neck as I fixed the staff into its holder on my back.

Little smoke rose from the town, and from this distance, it seemed only a single house had caught fire. I frowned, mulling over the situation. If the woman's intention had not been to burn down the town, what then had it been? What had she gained? I saw little motivation. In fact, based on her casual indifference to my arrival and her direct words about my Phantom, it almost seemed like she had expected me. Had that been her purpose? To warn me about Phantom Kural? Or had it been to spread lies about the Shadows, by assuming the bonds we wore? I bristled. We had worked too hard to let others ruin our alliances and blacken our good name.

Whoever these people were, they needed to be stopped.

I nudged Whitestar to the right, heading instead toward the smoke left in town. General Mirai's men gathered around a tall building near the docks. Flames engulfed the building. The fire billowed and wavered in the wind, overwhelming the remaining wood on the upper level. It wouldn't be long before the structure collapsed. Nothing could be done to save it.

General Mirai and his men held the line and kept the villagers back from the flames. Everything seemed under control. I would help out later with any casualties, but before doing so, I needed to confirm or refute the woman's words.

I guided Whitestar along the edge of the gulf near the Kinsaan Forest. Whispers told of how the people feared walking in the forest and refused to go there. Back in Vaiyene, we shared stories of a boy who had found himself lost in the caves leading into our village. He had never escaped, and his cries echoed to this day. The story kept children from exploring the caves and getting lost. It scared most, though it did encourage others, like me, to search the caverns for the truth. I never found any truth in Vaiyene's story, but the possibility something had happened to frighten the townspeople remained a possibility.

A gust of wind blew, dislodging a colorful array of leaves from the gnarled branches in the forest. Lack of sunlight caused trees to twist their reach, but these trees bathed in sunlight. It was unusual, but not enough to deter me from entering.

I dismounted and held onto Whitestar's reins, leading us inside the forest's edge. Pushing aside my cloak, I withdrew my light canteen. A tube sat inside, fixed to the center with sinew, containing oil to create a portable lantern. With a quick flick of a flintstone, the light brightened and surrounded us with a warm glow. The air smelled thin and dank. It wasn't the usual smell of decay, but a darker, fouler scent mingled with the forest's natural aroma. I stepped over a tree root, squinting against the meager light from my canteen, trying to navigate the maze of roots as they became twisted and overgrown. It had become too difficult to continue with Whitestar. I patted her side and commanded her to stay. Nothing seemed to be lurking, and she could take care of herself.

Birds no longer called in the trees. No animals or insects roamed underfoot. I remained patient, relying on my skill. I walked on the side of my foot, rolling from toe to heel to disturb the undergrowth as little as possible. Voices carried on the wind—at least two of them—the sound echoing off the twisted trees and forest canopy. I dimmed my light and tied it to my side, crouching and inching across the rotting leaves. The damp foliage softened my advance. Someone, or something, shuffled in front of me. I froze. My breath quickened as I reached my hand back to grasp my staff.

"The villagers are still cautious of us; we need to find some way to gain their complete trust," a male voice said. His tone was hushed but firm. "We've made steps to better your position, but we need more information."

"I've given you all the information I have."

The second voice I recognized. Phantom Kural. I shifted my weight and slipped behind a gnarled tree, trying to adjust and gain a better position. Who was he talking with?

"There will be consequences in Vaiyene should you refuse," the unknown man said.

My body tensed, and I suppressed the urge to intervene. I needed to know all the details. Phantom Kural had agreed to something, but what? And why was Vaiyene now under threat? The encounter did not feel right to me. Phantoms did not keep secrets from their Shadows. The mission was to set up a trade for fish oil to help get us through the winter. Or had that been a lie?

Metal scraped against metal in a flurry of movements, but I hesitated as I caught a glimpse of two metal bonds. One belonged to Phantom Kural, but who did the other belong to? In the dark, all I could see were the outlines of two silver bonds flashing in the darkness as they caught the scant sunlight. I pressed my back against the trunk of the tree, my distrust growing.

A white mist rose from one of the silver bonds. It snaked around the forearm of the bonded stranger as the man brought his sword up high over his head. Phantom Kural swung his axe, overpowering the man. The sword went flying, and Phantom Kural followed through with his movement, circling it above his head and lopping the man's head off. The body crumpled to the ground, and I slid behind the gnarled trunk.

My trust in Phantom Kural tore as clean as the man's severed neck. No matter the reasoning, I could not serve a man who chose not to obey the Shadow's Creed.

A Shadow does not take life,
killing only when no other option can be found.

Phantom Kural's life had not been in danger.

We could have questioned the man.

Unease choked my breath. Was it possible Phantom Kural had killed him so no one could ask questions? I tried to push the thought from my mind. It was not my place to question my Phantom, but this was not the Phantom Kural I knew. The man I served under would never...

I pressed my hand against my temple. First the woman and now Phantom Kural. What was the connection?

What was Phantom Kural's real purpose here in Leiko?

I needed more information before I confronted the others with what I had seen. If Phantom Kural had defected to the people masquerading as Shadows, it would be my word against his. I was a Shadow; he was my superior. None would believe my account.

I pushed myself onto my feet and stepped over a gnarled root, peering through the overgrown forest. Phantom Kural stood in a pool of blood, with his axe plunged into the ground. The severed head lay a few paces away.

Lifeless eyes stared back at me.

I began picking my way back toward town, keeping my movements slow and deliberate. Whatever had happened, I needed to find the truth.

chapter two
DOUBT & BETRAYAL

"**D**id something happen?" General Mirai asked, his sword unsheathed at his side. I eyed the blade. As a warrior himself, the general understood the strain of battle on a man's soul. Watching Phantom Kural behead an unarmed man had shaken the foundation I'd built my life on.

A Phantom never broke the Shadow's Creed.

Shadows did not kill.

The threat from the man in the forest warranted interrogation. What if he had been working with the woman with the bond? I would not be able to follow the connection now that she was gone, and the man now lay dead.

General Mirai shifted next to me. It was hard to speculate about Phantom Kural's motives with him near me. As if, somehow, his presence would expose my traitorous thoughts. I gave a sidelong glance at our long-term ally, my thoughts darkening as skepticism ate away at our friendship.

Was the general also involved?

At General Mirai's continued presence, I let out a long, drawn out breath. "Was there something you wanted?"

General Mirai chuckled, a smile spreading across his face. "I never thought I'd see the day you lost your composure."

He seemed amused by my irritation, which only irritated me further. I held my tongue, hoping if I kept quiet, he would leave.

He did not.

"Spar with me," General Mirai insisted. He glanced around and shifted the sword in his hand, lowering his voice. "I can't tell you here."

Curiosity stifled my annoyance.

I removed the staff at my back and followed him along the edge of the gulf. Mirai's men had erected a temporary camp on the border of Leiko. It was quite impressive. Small, tidy, and portable. Their accommodations were anything but lavish, but it served their wandering lifestyle. His men roared into laughter at some joke. They seemed more than content with their arrangements. The lifestyle did not appeal to me. My Shadow duties took me away from Vaiyene, but home was home, and I missed the camaraderie of my friends. We had trained for years together and had been friends long before then. We shared a bond only Shadows could. They were with me on most missions. In fact, being the only Shadow on this mission might have been the first sign something was amiss.

Shadows worked in teams.

I hadn't thought to question it before.

A group of men stumbled past us, their arms around one another's shoulders. Foaming liquid splashed lavishly from the mugs they held. It had been a long time since I had not been on a mission.

General Mirai pointed his sword at me, and my mind returned to the present. The waves of Leiko Gulf broke against a line of rocks near the shore. Water from the tide sloshed across the sand. I flexed my toes against the sole, digging myself deeper to create a solid foundation. Mirai adjusted his grip. He wielded a sword that required two hands instead of a sword that required one. It was an intentional switch to combat my staff.

"I have some information you'll find interesting," the general said as he extended his sword.

I gripped my staff near the end with both hands, waiting for the general to make the first move. "Have you told Phantom Kural about this?"

General Mirai lunged forward, and I knocked his strike away from my body, stopping my attack midway.

"I have not." He took a step back, lowering his sword, and giving me a nod to acknowledge the hit. "My trust in Kural has wavered. It's why I agreed to help on this mission."

I met his gaze and swung forward, but he blocked me. His eyes flicked to the silver filling in my staff. I slammed the end of my staff into his knee.

I didn't need him asking questions.

Mirai winced. I had softened the blow, but my anger got the better of me. I opened my mouth to say something, but he waved off my apology.

I'd sparred with Mirai before, but never with words. What did he know? I needed to know what he implied before making any decisions on how to deal with Phantom Kural. If his information was reliable, it would make confronting Phantom Kural easier.

Accusing a Phantom of misconduct would not be taken lightly, even with the general's evidence.

General Mirai's sword dropped to the ground, and he stepped closer to me, his hand withdrawing a letter from his pocket. The Shadow emblem was drawn on the paper: a black circle with a white crescent moon.

"One of my people found this on a body not too far from here. The dead man was wearing a bond on his arm. My men didn't recognize him as a Shadow."

I stared down at the emblem, my mouth dry. I stuffed the crude drawing into my pocket. Phantom Kural had gotten himself mixed up in something much bigger than himself.

"When was this person found?" I asked. I twirled my staff in my hands, then swiped at Mirai's side. Our sparring was for show, but the comfort of drills eased my mind.

The general blocked my attack. "A few days ago, but this False Shadow wasn't working alone. My men found three dead bodies following the first, all of which bore the same Shadow crest and silver bonds."

False Shadows. It was like a sword in my chest.

I swallowed a lump in my throat. The Shadows did not carry a crest. Nor did we wear it. Phantoms used the emblem on official messages, nothing else. Whoever these people were, their intentions were to be mistaken for Shadows.

But why?

"Did something happen with Phantom Kural?"

General Mirai stared at me.

I was bound by the Shadow's Creed to obey my Phantom. If I were wrong about Phantom Kural's involvement, about him being mixed up with these False Shadows, there would be consequences. General Mirai could testify, but the loyalty of the Shadows ran deep.

At least, it did for most of them.

"Kilo—" I met Mirai's harsh gaze. "Kural arrived back in camp before you did. His boots were stained with blood."

The image of the severed head and lifeless eyes of Phantom Kural's victim surfaced. I grimaced at the memory. I placed my right arm over my chest, bowing at the waist in Shadow fashion. "Thank you for your help."

General Mirai gave a slight bow in return and sheathed his sword. "I will keep you informed." He kept his voice low as he walked by me. "Watch your back, Kilo."

General Mirai still appeared loyal. I glanced over my shoulder, watching Mirai as his men gathered around him. They slapped him on the back and shoved a mug enthusiastically into his hand, inciting him to join them in celebration.

Until today, Phantom Kural had been someone I admired. It was the same affection General Mirai's men carried for him. Kural, along with the other two Phantoms, had trained me in the

Shadow ways. He had saved my life a few times, as I had saved his. For all my life, I had never considered myself anything but a Shadow. It defined who I was and what I dedicated myself to.

What if everything I believed in was wrong?

Was there some way Phantom Kural was protecting a life? Had I missed something? I wanted to believe in Phantom Kural—in the Phantoms—but all my mind could fixate on was a man who had killed in anger.

A man trying to cover his mistakes.

I closed my eyes and calmed the thoughts within my mind.

*A Shadow does what he is capable of; no
more can be asked of him.*

I had sworn to abide by the principles of the Shadow's Creed. While it didn't illuminate how to deal with Phantom Kural, I found some shred of comfort knowing I had fulfilled my duty.

I had done what I could given the situation.

Behind me, the sunlight disappeared behind the mountains, casting an amber glow that bathed the landscape in a deep orange tone. My heart darkened. The fire the general and his men gathered around became more appealing, and not for warmth. I left the water's edge, the merriment of celebration a more attractive choice than solitude. That much I knew of heartache and indecision. A man was better not left alone when his mind lay burdened with uncertainty. Better to live in the light than in darkness.

When I was within the fire's glow, one of General Mirai's men handed me a mug. He clapped my shoulder, sloshing the dark ale over the edge of the wooden pint.

"To the Shadows!"

I met General Mirai's gaze across the flames. He raised his mug in my direction, knowing as well as I, that tonight was not a night to celebrate the Shadows.

———

Thoughts of betrayal plagued my hard-won sleep. It was a cold night, but I enjoyed lying beneath the stars' light. My thoughts were quiet as the heat of dying embers warmed me. A twig snapped near me, and I closed my eyes.

The scent of old blood carried over to me.

Phantom Kural had returned.

I kept my eyes closed to better focus on Kural's voice. It was quiet, yet loud enough to make out his words. "I'll relieve you from your post."

General Mirai's men would not think it out of the ordinary to hand over the watch to a trusted ally.

After much rustling, the men settled into an adjacent tent. I inched around, trying to move without catching Phantom Kural's eye. He pretended to keep a lookout. As the minutes passed, I grew drained watching him, his gaze remained fixed on the barren plains of Phia. I was about ready to give up when he stiffened. An arrow landed at his feet, a letter tied to the shaft. He retrieved the note, and moments later crumpled it and tossed it into the flames. Embers flared up. Dark shadows danced across his face. Then he turned his gaze on me. I snapped my eyes shut and held my breath.

A hand shook my shoulder, and I pretended to wake as Kural's voice broke the silence.

"We ride for Vaiyene."

I bolted upright, knocking my staff near the edge of the fire. Phantom Kural's back was rigid. I snatched the letter from the coals, wincing as my fingers burned. Phantom Kural strode past, a fire alight in his eyes. The paper burned against my palm, but only when I was certain he was gone, did I uncurled my fingers.

I peeled the charred paper apart.

Vaiyene will burn.

All weariness of the day faded. Phantom Kural—no, just Kural—was no longer my Phantom. His betrayal was more than a mere blow to the ego. These False Shadows were a danger, and our people would be the ones to suffer for it

chapter three
FIRE & LOSS

S moke billowed from the Miyota Mountains. A dead weight
rested in the pit of my stomach as I spurred Whitestar into
a full gallop. Kural kept pace with me. His face showed no
emotion. I did not bother to hide my own anxiety—or anger. His
stupidity in getting mixed up with the False Shadows was careless.

Whitestar lost her footing as she scrambled over the rocky
terrain, and I lurched forward. I patted her neck and coaxed her
on, trusting in her abilities to manage the mountainside. The final
ascent to the caves into Vaiyene was the trickiest to maneuver.
Whitestar had much experience, as did I, but others would have
trouble traveling by horse or on foot. As it stood, our home's
location was a secret across Kiriku.

At least it used to be.

Kural was so tied up with these False Shadows that he had
lost sight of what was most important: our people.

Smoke blew over us, stealing my breath and contemplation. My heart wanted to push Whitestar faster, to get to my sister and our people sooner, but I needed to remain patient on the ascent.

I leaned into my horse's neck as we climbed the last ledge to the caverns that led into Vaiyene. A chill ran across my body, the dampness of the cave stiffening my muscles as we entered into the inner caverns. The horses' hooves echoed over the walls, their breathing a steady measure of our quick pace. I ignited the light canteen at my side, and a burst of light illuminated the small area around me. A light ahead ignited. Kural. His posture seemed unnaturally stiff. He held onto his horse's reins, his fingers clenching in irritation. Despite his involvement with the False Shadows, he was a Phantom. He cared for the people he'd endangered. I found some measure of sympathy inside me, but it remained fleeting.

Phantom Kural pushed his horse ahead, leaving the cave's darkness behind. I followed and took a deep breath, bracing myself for whatever lay in the valley below.

There was no preparing.

A wave of flames ravaged the eastern side of Vaiyene. The winds from the mountain peaks quickened the fire's reach. I clenched my horse's reins, the blood cold and numb in my veins. Screams echoed from the valley. I searched for an answer, for a reason—anything—but none came. Phantoms and Shadows aside, the people of Vaiyene were innocents, as were most people who were pulled into tragedy by their leaders. I gritted my teeth, anger replacing the chill. I'd never needed to worry about the safety of my friends and family before.

From my side, in a defeated voice, Phantom Kural spoke.

"Save as many as you can."

It was unsettling like he'd already accepted our people's fate. They were words of a defeated leader, of a broken man, and I hated him for it.

I brushed off my emotions as the screams penetrated my core. What I needed was a plan. This would be like participating in any other raid, battle, or ambush. If I let my emotions take over, they would paralyze me. Make a plan and stick to it. The Shadows would do what they could, and hopefully, it would be under the guidance of two capable and loyal Phantoms. I needed to meet up with them, but first I needed to ensure Finae was safe. Our parents had died years ago, and she had no one but me to watch out for her.

I turned Whitestar to the north and cut through the center of town. The smoke hung heavy and thick, collecting in the mountain valley.

I pulled my scarf over my face to filter the smoke.

Most of the flames here smoldered on the ground. This area must have been the first to catch fire. Nothing remained of the houses here. Nothing but the charred remains of people's lives. I swallowed hard as a wave of memories flooded my mind. This street was where the people gathered and said goodbye to the Shadows before we left on missions.

How many times had they lined the streets for me?

Beyond the emotional tie, navigating the empty streets left me disorientated. The trees, the houses, all of it, gone. All except—I turned to the mountain peaks. Something that could withstand the flames. Our home lay between the mountain peaks that led to the Reikon Tree.

Using my new sense of direction, I urged Whitestar into a gallop. Flames raged ahead as the buildings and trees here caught fire. The scarf around my face kept me from inhaling the smoke, but it did nothing to lessen the tears stinging my eyes. I squinted against the smoke and found a familiar outline in the distance. Fire obscured the balcony leading out from the second story, but the towering aspens still stood, though for not much longer.

I slid off Whitestar, fumbling with the drawstrings of my half cloak. When my fingers became steady, I undid the knot to my cloak and draped it across the saddle. A gust of wind blew cinders across my bare arms. From within Whitestar's saddle packs, I withdrew a thin length of leather and wound it around my palms. It wasn't much, but it would help.

"Finae!" I shouted from the doorway. There was no response. I drew in a breath. The faster I searched through the house, the better.

I rammed the door with my shoulder and steadied myself as the wooden door fell to the ground. Boards creaked overhead.

I did not have much time.

"Finae!" I yelled, coughing against the smoke.

No answer.

I ducked under a low-hanging beam as fire crackling overhead. Tears blurred my vision, and I fought to keep my eyes open. Through the smoke, I saw the outline of the metal staircase in the center of the house. I swore at my parents for their aesthetics. Though the stairs were helping to keep the house upright.

I stood at the bottom of the staircase and yelled again. "Finae!"

This time, I thought I heard something.

A scuffle.

I walked on the tips of my feet, skipping as many of the steps as I could. The staircase wobbled underneath me. I had almost made it to the top when a crack resonated beneath me. The stairs fell, and I leaped toward the smoldering beams overhead. My fingers curled against the heat, and I hissed as my flesh burned. I threw my elbows over the wooden floor, spreading my fingers and digging my nails as far into the planks as I could. Through the flames, I saw a body lying on the floor.

Finae.

I swung my legs behind me, drawing one knee up. I rolled onto my side and kicked myself forward with my other foot. My heart pounded in my chest as I pulled my body up.

The flames swayed at my approach.

"Finae!"

A gust of ash and debris flew over me. I shielded my face in my arm until it passed, crawling on my hands and knees. A large chunk of what looked to be the tiled-roof lay on the floor in Finae's room. At my approach, she shifted, and I struggled to breathe. A beam pinned Finae's leg. A collection of colors splattered across the floor. A glass bottle lay to the side. She had used the water from her paints to douse the fire. Her eyes welled with tears at my approach, and I closed the distance between us.

"I'm here now," I said, trying to keep the emotion from my voice. I bent my knees and wedged my hands under the beam. Soot stained the whites of her eyes, and she coughed against the smoke.

"Crawl out when I lift the beam."

The wood cut into my fingers as I hefted the beam. Finae struggled to move. My arms shook from the weight, but I held steadfast until she managed to maneuver her leg from under it. When she was free, I set the beam down and pulled her to her feet. I snatched a nearby rag and pressed the cloth over her mouth and nose, smearing blue paint across her face.

I smiled as the fire closed in around us. "Is anything ever not covered in paint?"

Her eyes lit up, and she stifled a cough. I tied the rag around her face and slid my arm under her shoulder. Part of the roof overhead collapsed behind us, shaking the floor and kicking up more debris. My eyes stung, but I kept them open.

I needed my sight to guide us to safety.

Finae coughed violently, and I held her against my chest. With the staircase collapsed, we had but one option. Finae was not going to like it.

"I need you to trust me." I glanced down at her as she huddled close. She didn't look up or acknowledge me.

I half-carried Finae to the edge of the balcony. Finae sunk down, covering her mouth as a fit of coughing overtook her. I left her and rushed through her room, into the hallway. I pried up a floorboard, finding a length of cord in one of our parents' many hiding places. I left the other assorted odds and ends, thanking our parents for their attentiveness. Though they were gone, they had instilled their preparedness in me. A habit that had served me well.

I returned to the balcony and wound the rope around the railing, pulling at the length of cord ot test its strength. It seemed sturdy enough.

I turned to Finae. "I'm going to tie you so you won't fall. Hold onto the rope, and I'll guide you down."

She looked at the rope, then the railing, her eyes widening.

"I-I can't."

I steadied her shaking hands. "Have I ever been wrong?" Her lips quirked at the edges, and I smiled.

"Have I ever let you get hurt?" I amended.

Her eyes remained fixed on the railing, and she took a step toward the edge. I caught her hand and stopped her.

"You don't need to look down. Everything will be fine. Here, look." I whistled to Whitestar and leaned over to make sure the mare was in place. The flames snapped, growing closer, but scaring Finae into action would not help. "Whitestar is waiting for you."

Finae chewed on her lip, then nodded. I began tying the rope around her torso and legs, moving her hands to the line at her chest. "Hold on here."

Finae took the rope, and I backed her up to the wooden railing. "Whitestar is waiting, and I'm right here. One leg at a time—there—that's it."

When both feet hit the other side of the railing, I grasped her shoulders and steadied her.

"Hold on," I reminded her gently. "Keep your eyes on me." The other end of the rope I wound around my waist in case I lost my grip. "Now, take a breath and a step down."

"Kilo, I'm scared." Her voice wavered.

I forced myself to smile and think of something to distract her. "Imagine our parents' faces. They'd be so mad at me for letting you repel off the balcony."

My words drew a smile from Finae. Our parents had been strict, but she had always enjoyed the moments I stole her away from their control.

A wooden beam fell, shifting the balcony underfoot. The rope dragged against my hand as I lowered Finae down. Blood stained the fibers as my skin blisters formed from the flames. The leather around my palms provided some protection, but it would be uncomfortable to hold anything for a while.

When the rope went slack, I rushed to the edge of the railing to see Finae waving from her seat upon Whitestar. Relief washed over her face. The balcony cracked. I threw my arms out to steady myself and walked backward, distributing my weight between both feet. Finae yelled from below, but I pushed her from my mind. I slid the rope closer to the house where it seemed more robust and jumped. My weight held for a moment, but then fire burned through the fibers, and I fell. Instincts took over, and I softened my knees and rolled onto my shoulder.

"Kilo, get out of the way!"

I scrambled to the left, and the balcony crashed down beside me, splintering into pieces. I stood and winced, moving my shoulder to make sure it was not broken. Finae's gaze fixed on me, and I shrugged off the pain.

I grabbed hold of Whitestar's reins, steering her away from the rubble. I had seen people lose everything, but I had never experienced it firsthand. When our parents had died, and Finae came under my care, this house had been a constant in the absence of stability.

Finae sobbed from her seat upon my horse. I wanted to say something, but what was there to say? Words would not bring back our home or stop the destruction of Vaiyene.

The same as words had never brought back our parents.

The rage of the fire pushed me into action.

I buried my emotions in duty, handing the reins to Finae. I whistled long and clear. It took a while, and it was distant, but a call returned. A few moments later, another answered. Both were too far away to pinpoint the exact location, but it did give me a general idea of where the other groups were.

"Take Whitestar and go east. The Phantoms' house is where survivors will take refuge. They'll look after you and bind your leg."

She would be safer there than where I was going.

Finae fell quiet, her eyes shifting to the flames. Her hands on the reins quivered. I moved to block the view. "I'll return as soon as I've done what I can."

She looked away, but not before I saw her frown. "Be careful."

Her voice was cold, and I hesitated. It was clear she wanted to say more, and I knew she wanted me to stay, but duty called me.

I couldn't take time to grieve for what we had lost. Finae knew this, having grown up around my Shadow father and me, but I knew it was a hard burden to bear—for both of us.

"I'll come find you when this is all over." I softened my voice and sighed. "I'm sorry. I know this isn't what you would like from your brother, but our people are counting on me." She raised her head, appearing surprised at my apology. She seemed a little less sullen, but the fact remained that I always chose my Shadow duty over her. The Shadows protected Vaiyene, and yet we could never be as diligent with the ones we love.

When Finae didn't say anything, the words fell from my mouth before I could stop them. "We'll make a new home."

It was an arrogant promise, and one that could take many years to keep, but I meant it. Finae's lips spread into a smile. She leaned over the side of Whitestar, and I raised my arms to give her a slightly awkward hug.

When Finae released me, I met her gaze. "Stay safe."

She straightened in the saddle and set out. I faced the flames in the opposite direction. The fire did not scare me, what did, was what I would find within them. I adjusted the scarf around my neck. Despite the haze in the air, my vision remained clear. The Shadows were an organization that supported Vaiyene. None of our work was visible to the villagers we protected. We secured alliances with other villages and towns, completed trades, or—like in Leiko—aided in the protection of the people when we traveled across Kiriku. But today, the Shadows would make a visible difference.

My heart swelled with pride.

This day our people would know who the Shadows were.

I used my renewed strength to keep my legs at a steady pace. Wind blew across my path, and when the soot and ash cleared, my heart sank. A few stalks of corn stood like torches against the darkened sky. The harvest was to be in a couple of weeks. There were still the root vegetables in the ground, but the loss would devastate Vaiyene; this close to winter, it would be hard to find another town with ample stores to trade.

I left the gardens and whistled as I ran, straining my ears to hear the location of the Shadows. When no one returned my call, I pressed deeper into the village, turning my path to the outskirts of the orchards. In the distance, people gathered before the storehouse. One by one, people ran into the buildings, returning with sacks of food reserves we had put away for the winter. They loaded the horses and sent them to safety, back to the gardens where the fire had already burned out.

A loud crack sounded, shifting the storehouse. A wave of dust burst forth. I covered my head from the onslaught of dirt and debris, rushing to join the others on the ground. Within the crowd, I spotted Syrane and Shenrae, my two best friends' children. They turned toward me as I drew near. Syrane loaded his bag of wheat onto the horse's cart and hefted up another.

"Where are your parents?"

Syrane and Shenrae exchanged looks, and I stooped down to pick up a bag of grain. Syrane dropped another bag onto the cart.

"Our mother is inside, helping to bring the grain out."

"And Zavi?" I asked, noting how Shenrae didn't meet my eye.

"He went to check the orchards," Syrane said. He threw his grain into the cart, the force of the bag slamming against the wood. I placed my bag next to his, and when Shenrae turned to follow her brother, I caught her arm.

"How long has he been gone?"

She glanced at Syrane's back to make sure he was busy and then met my gaze.

"Too long," Shenrae said, her voice low. "Syrane keeps telling me not to worry, but he was only to see what happened and relay information back. He should have returned by now."

I drew a deep breath and looked down to the east where the Phantoms' house was. Zavi would have taken that route, but it was not the shortest path. The quickest way was over the cliffs.

I gave Shenrae a reassuring nod. "I'll find him."

chapter four
A PHANTOM'S SINS

I curled my fingers around a gnarled tree root and pulled myself up and over the edge of the cliff. The grass here was overgrown and untouched. Many did not know the alternate paths through Vaiyene.

Few were as adventurous as I had been in my youth.

When the brush started thinning out, I quickened my pace and removed the scarf from my face, drawing in an unrestricted breath. Smoke still coated the air, but it calmed my nerves to be able to breathe freely. Ahead, the Reikon Tree split the sky with its branches. A few leaves floated and landed upon the lake that surrounded the great tree.

My feet squelched against the soggy grass, leaving muddy footprints behind. I came to the first vantage point overlooking Vaiyene and froze. The fire burned in the upper reaches of Vaiyene as well. As I came closer to the forest's edge, the air crackled at my approach. I lifted the scarf around my neck and plunged into the burning forest. Heat washed against me.

I whistled.

No response.

I turned to the north, staying on the edge of the forest, balancing speed with caution. I glanced down at the devastation below. A quarter of our peoples' homes were burned, and from what I could tell most of the fields. My gaze wandered the cliffside, something catching my eye. At the bottom, lying on a pile of broken rocks, was a man with blond hair.

Zavi.

I crouched to the ground, surveying the cliff for a place that would support my weight. When I was sure the path I had chosen was the best possible route, I swung my leg over, digging my hands into the rocks. I lowered myself down with one arm. A *craaack* broke above, and something fell. The cliff shook, and I held on. Gravel and rocks fell over the edge, pelting my shoulders and head. I flattened myself against the cliffside until the stones had passed.

I drew in a breath and recoiled as a weight slammed against my back, knocking me from my hold. I crashed into the rocks below.

I gasped for air, paralyzed.

The world faded in and out of view, and I closed my eyes against my swimming vision. In my mind, I pictured a tree, with strong, solid roots, and a trunk so large that the wind could not move it. I focused on the tree—on stillness—until the cliffside no longer moved. With a grunt, I shifted my weight and drew back my shoulders. I could no longer move my left arm, though I could see it underneath me. I flexed my right arm and managed to push myself up a hand span before I collapsed, pain flowing over me in waves. Moving my head to the side, I made out the smoking branches of an evergreen tree pinning me to the ground. I drew in a pained breath, the branches scraping against my back. They tore into my skin and seared my flesh. I pushed against the tree, my other arm shaking against the weight.

"Zavi! Kilo!" someone shouted.

The voice broke hysterically, echoing off the mountain peaks. I tried to identify its owner, but the more I moved, and the more I tried to figure out who the person was, the more my consciousness slipped. With one final effort, I pushed myself up, grinding my teeth as a thick branch wedged itself into my back. I cried out, fighting to stay conscious through the pain. I jerked to the side; the tree thudded beside me. I curled into myself and sat there, waiting for the pain to lessen.

Someone groaned near me, breaking through the misery.

I moved my neck, remembering something pressing I needed to do—something I had scaled the cliff to do. I squinted my eyes, focusing on a body on the other side of the ledge. Zavi.

Using my shoulder and the muscles in my side, I managed to shift myself into an upright position. The world flopped inside out, and I retched upon the rocks at my feet. I had tried to move too fast. A rush of heat passed through me, and I closed my eyes until the sensation was over. Using my good hand, I trailed my fingertips across the rocks to ensure where the mountain rested. I collapsed onto my knees and ground my teeth at the sudden impact against a stone. Zavi opened his eyes. A pool of blood stained his hair. With uncertain fingers, I touched the back of his head.

The bone was fractured.

He would not survive long with an injury like this.

"How bad?" Zavi asked, his words slurred. He blinked, and his eyes gazed off into the distance.

He was having trouble finding focus.

My throat tightened, and I tried to swallow. I couldn't bring myself to say anything. I sat down and shifted Zavi's head onto my lap. He groaned as I moved him but relaxed once settled. His skull had split where it impacted the stone.

Warm, wet blood soaked my shin guards.

I sat for what seemed an endless amount of time. My hands fingered the vial sewn into my robe, my duty pushing me into action. Zavi's breathing was slow, and the muscles in his face twitched with pain. If I gave him the poison, it would make his last moments painless. Would Mia resent me for expediting her husband's death? I pushed the guilt away and searched for another way. As much as I didn't want to believe it, the wound was fatal. Even prolonging his life at this point was cruel. Zavi shuddered and twitched, shivering as his life drained away.

"I'm ready."

His words were so quiet that I barely heard them. I almost wished I hadn't. Zavi's eyes fixed on mine. I wanted to fight him, deny the reality of the situation, believe there was a chance he would make it, but we both had seen battle.

We had seen death.

I glanced down at my hands, seeing blood staining my palms. When we first had begun to train to be Shadows, to save Zavi's life, I had killed. Now I would be taking the same life I had saved years ago. I grounded myself with Zavi's decision. He was a Shadow, and like all Shadows, he knew the price of duty.

This would be my last service to our friendship.

Using my teeth, I tore the vial out of the hidden pocket in my robe. I maneuvered the bottle into my working hand.

Zavi's eyes remained fixed on me as he struggled to find closure. His words were strained. "Mia? S-Shenrae... Syrane?"

"Safe."

I didn't hesitate. I didn't know if Mia was safe, or his children, but there were no other words I could speak.

Zavi shuddered against a wave of pain. I brought the vial up to his lips, steadying my hand while he struggled to drink the contents. Our first Shadow mission did not seem too long ago. How foolish we had been as Shadows. So carefree and reckless.

"Do you remember our first mission together, Zavi?"

His breathing slowed peacefully as his eyes closed.

A small smile crossed his lips, and I continued, trying to laugh through the tears. "Phantom Kural was so upset. I never thought we'd make it this far."

Zavi raised his arm, spreading his fingers out. I clasped his hand. "I'll look after them, Zavi. I promise."

He held on a few moments longer. My words eased his passing before his hand grew limp in my grasp. I lowered his hand to his chest and exhaled slowly, tears rolling down my cheeks. I raised my hand to cover my face.

Zavi's blood was on my hands.

Nauseated, I wiped what blood I could on the side of my pants. It was a small mercy I had found Zavi before he had bled out; he had not been alone. My father had died on a Shadow mission when I was younger. My mother had passed shortly after, from an illness she had contracted. Some speculated she had died of a broken heart. We all had known she would not pull through after my father passed. She had loved him dearly, more than she had ever loved Finae or me. Somehow, it didn't hurt as much as it did now.

Zavi was my brother—my Shadow brother, and I had failed to save his life. I drew in a breath and lowered his head to the ground.

I could look after those he had loved.

I owed him that much.

Emotion crippled my senses, but duty screamed louder. It was the solace—the escape—I needed to keep moving.

I struggled to stand. My strength bleeding out from the wounds on my back. I undid the threads to the hidden pocket in my sleeve and pulled out a small black pill. It was little more than an adrenaline rush, with minor numbing effects. Concocted from herbs gathered in the Miyota Mountains, all the Shadows carried them. We had been told to use it with caution. With overexposure, the pill continued to dull the senses. Emotionally and physically. I bit into the black pill, welcoming the bitterness. A touch of copper repulsed me. Whether it was Zavi's or my own blood, I didn't know. I focused on my breathing, embracing the mind-numbing effects of the pill as they eased my pain and gave me strength. I set my hand against the stone and pushed myself onto steady legs.

Zavi lay cold at my feet.

He would be buried and honored with the Shadows who had fallen. When Vaiyene was no longer in danger, the other Shadows would help me recover his body.

I reached my arms overhead, grasping a solid rock from the cliff. Pain no longer a factor. A slight tingling sensation trailed over the muscles in my back, where blood ran across the skin. I favored my left arm, surprised that I could still use it. When my hand grasped the edge of the cliff, I froze. The tip of a blade pricked the center of my neck.

I cursed myself for taking the pill. While it dulled the pain and allowed me to climb, it had dulled my instincts.

I should have noticed there were others above.

Hadn't someone screamed sometime before I reached Zavi?

I raised my eyes to see a figure standing over me, a cloak splayed behind them. Another person, shrouded in the same oversized black cloak, stood behind the first. Mia was held captive by the second, a blade at her neck. A trickle of blood slid down her pale skin.

I shifted my feet to take more of my weight.

"Who are you?" I asked.

To answer my question, the blade against Mia's throat pressed harder. It was blood, but nothing fatal. I wasn't foolish enough to lose my composure and cause her further harm.

Their intimidation would do nothing against me.

"You already know," the man replied. He lessened the blade's pressure against Mia's neck. "I saw you spying on us when your Phantom was learning his lesson back in Leiko. The Shadow will pay for the Phantom's sins."

The False Shadows.

My initial shock turned to anger as rage built up inside me. "Were you responsible for the man's death below?"

I saw no hint of humanity or honor in this man.

He enjoyed inflicting pain.

Mia and Zavi were innocent; our people were innocent.

At Mia's sharp intake of breath, I realized what I'd revealed. She had not known Zavi was dead. It was dark under the man's hood, but I thought I saw a glint of a smile.

"I think he slipped trying to get away from the fire," the man said, looking around at the flames burning my home. "Quite a fire, isn't it?"

I dug my hand into the cliff's edge, the rocks digging into my fingertips. "What do you want?"

He was close enough now I could make out his smirk. "Who have you told about your Phantom's dealings?"

To emphasize his power over me, he placed his boot on my fingers and pressed down. I continued to glare at him, grateful the drug blocked my pain. I needed to figure out what these men wanted. If either of my feet slipped, or my hand gave out, I would fall, and it was unlikely I would survive a second time. If I made a move, he wouldn't hesitate to push me off the cliff.

I had to play his game.

"I've told no one. In fact,"—an idea came to mind, my heart beating faster— "I was the only one who knew about how you killed people in Leiko and worked with Phantom Kural."

The man growled and turned back to his companion and Mia. In that split second, I vaulted up the cliff. My shoulder slammed into the man near me. He grunted as my full weight toppled him onto the ground. His sword clanged to the ground. Mia elbowed the man who restrained her, and she rounded on him, lashing out with her feet. I pulled back my good hand and punched the man, his hood falling to reveal a disfigured face.

I tried to pin him down, but with one hand, he pushed me off. I stood, my left arm dangling at my side. I needed an advantage. The gleam of the man's blade caught my attention, and I snatched it from the ground. The man's lip twitched, but he made no move to stop me. I adjusted my grip on the hilt, trying not to appear too hesitant with the blade. I had not wielded a sword since...

Killing to save Zavi.

Wielding a staff had taught me to use both hands in combat. It was a long, curved sword, not weighted for one hand, but the skill would come back to me. The memory of running a sword through a man's chest and blood dripping from my hands sprang to mind.

Zavi's blood was on my hands.

Would it forever be my shame?

"Kilo!"

My attention returned with Mia's warning, and I brought the sword up in time to block the man's first attack. A lopsided smile spread across the man's face as he jumped back and threw a dagger toward me. I adjusted the sword, and the blade clanged off the edge. Blood clouded my vision—the blood of the man I had killed years ago. The sensation of my sword embedding into his back ran through my arms. I shook off the memory, my breathing rapid.

This sword did not control me. I may have killed a man in the past with a sword's edge, but it had been to save a life. If I wanted to save Mia's life, I couldn't hesitate.

I focused back on the present.

The False Shadow had not moved. He was a tall man. Burly, with a decent amount of weight.

I could use his stature against him.

I held the sword at my side, sliding my foot behind and shifting my weight. The False Shadow moved, accepting my challenge. He grabbed his comrade's sword and ran toward me, his sword trailing at his side. When he was almost upon me, I shifted my weight and stopped the tip of his sword with the hilt of mine. I pivoted the sword, grasping it with my left hand. I grimaced at the pain, but my fingers curled around the blade, and I held onto it.

I sliced into the back of the False Shadow's calf.

Blood coated the blade.

The False Shadow tottered on one leg near the edge. I threw my weight against him, and he fell over the cliff. My shoulder crashed into the ground, my head dangling over the edge. The False Shadow's thud echoed through me. I rolled over and pushed myself up, glancing around for Mia. She lay on the ground not far away. I knelt by her side. Her breathing was shallow. I shook Mia's shoulders, but she didn't respond. I placed my fingers to her neck. The subtle beat of her heart assured me she was still alive, but I noticed a dagger had pierced her side.

It looked deep.

Two cloaked figures fought a short distance away. Both wielded long, curved swords and moved with the prowess of a trained warrior . Were they fighting amongst themselves? My mind grew unclear. I shifted the muscles in my back, wincing as my skin pulled the wounds open. The effects of the pill were wearing off. I should have replaced it before I left on my Shadow mission. The potency wore out over months. When had I last replaced it?

Someone cried out. One of the False Shadows sliced into their comrade's thigh, drawing a hidden blade and piercing their heart with the dagger.

I averted my eyes.

The remaining False Shadow turned to me, their footsteps heavy. They smelled of blood.

"A word of advice: let go of your Shadow's Creed," the woman said. "The world doesn't revolve around impossible morals. More people are going to die because of your weakness."

I ignored her comment as Mia stirred, and I took her hand. "Mia?" Her eyes fluttered, and a trickle of blood spilled from her lips. "I'm going to get you to Syrane and Shenrae. Hold on."

I held my breath as her eyes grew still.

I didn't blink until I saw her take a breath. While I could move my left arm, carrying Mia would be impossible in my weakened state. My head pounded as the pain began to overtake my will. How was I supposed to keep my promise?

Never had I felt so defeated.

First Zavi, and now Mia.

I jumped as a hand fell upon my shoulder. The False Shadow bent beside me and inspected the blade in Mia's side.

"I couldn't save her, but I can help you fulfill your promise."

Her offer of help was unexpected. I did not recall her trying to help Mia, but I had been preoccupied trying to defeat the other False Shadow.

A horse snorted beside me, and the False Shadow held out the reins to me. So clouded was my mind, I didn't even know where the horse had come from. I reached to take the reins, not fully aware of my surroundings. The sound of shouting in the distance stayed my hands. Voices drew near, some seeming familiar.

Shadows?

I pushed the False Shadow's hand away. "Go. It's the least I can do to let you escape."

My eyes focused on Mia's face. The rustling and pounding of the False Shadow's horse shook the ground as she left. Whoever she was, she was an ally, at least in some regard. While I could not confirm it, she had tried to save Mia. And her warnings about the Shadow's Creed, though barbed, may have been why I failed to protect my friends. If she were involved with the False Shadows, our paths would cross again. I could ask my questions then.

Right now, I needed to get Mia home, to Shenrae and Syrane.

I brought my bloody fingers to my lips. I whistled loud and clear. The world spun around me, but I squeezed my eyes shut, fighting to stay conscious until I knew Mia would be safe. My eyes unfocused, but the outline of the group grew larger, their horses shaking the ground at their approach. Riders dismounted. Someone stood over me. Their shape darkened my vision.

"Kilo, you damn fool."

Before I could form a reply, my consciousness slipped, and I knew darkness.

An inescapable sense of duty pulled me from blissful unconsciousness. With great effort, and against the pounding in my head, I opened my eyes and found the pain bearable. Looking up at the wooden ceiling, I recognizing the vaulted beams of the infirmary, waiting for my eyes to adjust. Someone had painted snow-capped mountains and thick pine forests on the wooden ceiling. I smiled. My sister must have been bored while she visited me. I rolled onto my side, grimacing as the bandages scratched against the wounds on my back.

A figure appeared at my side.

"How are you feeling?" It was Phantom Lunia. Her skin glowed in the moonlight coming through the large windows.

"How do I look?" I countered, smiling inwardly and trying to appear as if I were in little pain. For a Phantom, she was always very high-strung. I liked to ease her mind whenever I could.

She gave me a small smile. "I see you haven't lost your humor. Your sister refused to leave your side until I promised to watch over you. You can see she was quite busy."

Phantom Lunia gestured to the painting upon the ceiling, and she frowned. I chuckled, trying to control my amusement at her displeasure. Finae liked to be fully immersed with her creations. It helped calm her. Sitting around waiting for me to wake up would have made her restless. What intrigued me was how she managed to paint on the ceiling. Or when. I glanced up, twisting my head to gain a different angle. She would not have been permitted to hang from the beams. Had she painted it at night, or was there so much going on she had been alone?

My amusement faded as I tried to remember the events that led me here. I remembered falling off the cliff and being struck by a tree. It was how I had injured my arm. There were the fires and…

Reality came into focus.

Zavi and Mia.

Phantom Kural.

The False Shadows.

Phantom Lunia took a step closer, and I pushed the thoughts away, using the pain in my back to ground me in the present. I didn't want Phantom Lunia's condolences. Not now. I cleared my throat and assumed my Shadow demeanor. I could grieve later.

"How many people died?"

Phantom Lunia shook her head, her concern at my condition fading as she, too, assumed her role. Sometimes, it was easier to think of people as numbers and action as a strategy. I glanced down at my hands. The skin appeared red to my eyes.

Zavi's life would never be a number.

"Too many," Phantom Lunia said, raking her fingers through her hair. She paused, then locked me in her gaze. "What happened in Leiko?"

How did she know?

When I didn't answer, she prompted further.

"With Kural?"

I remained quiet, unsure of her ties to Phantom Kural and the False Shadows. How could she know without being involved?

I pushed myself up with my one arm and struggled to sit up. Phantom Lunia put her arms around me and helped me into a seated position. I grimaced, and she flinched. I waved off her apology before she could speak. Phantom Lunia couldn't lie. It was a hard trait to have as a leader. To me, it was a strength. To others, a vulnerability. But I needed to be sure of her loyalty.

"Where is Phantom Kural?"

She met my stare, and I read the answer before she voiced it. "Dead. We found Kural in the outskirts of town, near the gardens, with a brand upon his chest. It was the Shadow's symbol, but upside down."

She clasped her hands together, but not before I caught the slightest tremble. It was clear to me: the threat Phantom Kural had received, Zavi's death, and the mysterious False Shadow ally. Phantom Lunia knew nothing. Her apparent fear was enough to disprove her involvement. I hesitated, then berated myself for doing so. She was one of the Phantoms of Vaiyene. Hiding what I knew of Phantom Kural's participation would help no one.

It was time to gather our strength against the False Shadows.

I cleared my throat, ignoring the pain in my chest. "While in Leiko, I met a woman who warned me about Phantom Kural. They said he worked with the people who orchestrated the attack on Leiko. These same people set fire to Vaiyene. General Mirai called them the False Shadows."

Phantom Lunia grew pale, her voice wavering as she spoke. "This is a serious accusation."

Betrayal stung at my memories. I had looked up to Phantom Kural, trained under him, and all this time his loyalty had been to himself. It seemed the betrayal started—and ended—with Kural.

I constructed what I knew into a report. "These people, the False Shadows, are masquerading as our Shadow group. They wear bonds on their arms, and they now know where Vaiyene is."

Most likely Kural's intelligence.

I clenched my fist in my lap, wishing I could leave the wretched bed and infirmary. I wanted to act, to move, to do something—*anything*. It was then that I noticed the shift in Phantom Lunia's mood. Phantom Kural had been my superior and mentor, but to Lunia, he had been a friend. Someone she had relied on for strength. Her duties as a Phantom were to analyze and see the threat of the outside world. To protect all of us. The fault lay on her shoulders. Hers and Phantom Atul's. Three Phantoms looked over Vaiyene, and the Shadows served under them.

Phantom Lunia crossed her arms over her chest. "You are to speak of this to no one."

Though I did not like the idea, duty would bind my tongue, as it always had. "I understand."

I pressed my hand against my temples, the pounding in my head almost drowning out my thoughts. Almost. The effects of the drug I had used to climb the cliffs were taking their toll. The momentary burst of strength had come with a hefty price.

Phantom Lunia opened her mouth to speak, then hesitated. I closed my eyes, as if not seeing her emotion would lessen the blow. I couldn't use my Shadow duty to ignore reality forever.

"Kilo, Mia is…" She struggled to find the right words.

She was taking too long to get to the point. "Is she alive?"

"She doesn't have long."

The world darkened at the edges of my vision. I stared ahead, watching Phantom Lunia pick at a thread on her robe. She raised her hand, as if to place it on my shoulder, then decided against it. She gave me a slight bow instead.

Her fingers on one hand still ruffling her robe.

"You should get some rest," she said.

She was fiddling too much with her hands. There was more she was not telling me.

"What else happened?"

Phantom Lunia let out a long breath. "Phantom Atul died in the fires, as well as four of our Shadows."

This meant Lunia was the last remaining Phantom. Including me, there were eight Shadows left. I sucked in my breath and settled against the pillows, my head throbbing with the news.

"We'll convene later tonight and discuss what we will do. Try to get some sleep until then."

I stared at the ceiling and the depiction of the Miyota Mountains Finae had painted. The False Shadows knew where Vaiyene was. They knew the Shadows were weak. Never in our history had there been such a time. Our people would be shaken. And with so few people to help protect our village, were we even capable of defending ourselves? Sleep was a luxury we could not afford.

I flexed my back. There would be little I could do in this state.

Phantom Lunia's footsteps creaked against the wooden floor as she left the infirmary. My fighting spirit lay in wait, and I closed my eyes. Let the False Shadows come; I would be ready.

———

I struggled to focus, knowing this was Mia's last night. I dug my nails into the palm of my hand and peered down the long hallway for any sign of movement. Syrane and Shenrae were to notify me of any change in their mother's condition.

"Kilo?" Phantom Lunia prompted me.

I dragged my attention back to the meeting, reminding myself of the instructions I had given. At present, I could do nothing to help Mia. What I could do was to focus on protecting those we could.

Like my fellow Shadows, I tried my best to ignore the empty places around the table. The room had always seemed cramped, filled with books, scrolls, and Shadows, but today it was empty. The usual cheerful chattering had been replaced by vacant faces—an inability to process what had happened. Even though we had all experienced the same devastation, it seemed like a waking nightmare. At any moment, we could wake up.

If only that were true.

The scrapes on my back betrayed reality, making the ache of my body seem trivial. My real pain lay in the absence of my friends and regret of not being able to save them. If I had been sooner, would it have changed anything? I snuck a glance down the hallway, but there was no change. Could I have done more?

Phantom Lunia cleared her throat, and I noticed her watching me. She knew my thoughts were elsewhere. I disciplined my mind to focus on the present.

"We, as Phantoms, serve until we are no longer able to. Today we lost two great Phantoms. Danger has come to Vaiyene, and the need for strength in the Shadows is more pressing than ever."

I glanced around at those of us left, realizing this meeting was something more. We had not yet put the Phantoms to rest, and Lunia intended to choose their successors?

Becoming a Phantom was an aspiration of mine. I'd been a Shadow all my life, for almost twenty years, but I didn't want to become a Phantom under these circumstances. The weight of failing to protect weighed on my shoulders. It was more than the people of Vaiyene; I'd been unable to protect those I cared most about. Did I deserve to be a Phantom?

Phantom Lunia's gaze rested on me, and I knew it mattered little how ready I was. The time was now.

"Kilo, will you come forward?"

The wounds on my back stretched as I fought to stand. Blood soaked the bandages around my torso. Phantom Lunia moved to help me, but at my sharp glare, she stopped short. None of the other Shadows made to help me. Having trained with me, they knew my stubborn pride. It was petty, but my ego would not allow me to show weakness in front of my comrades. My body was broken, but my conviction remained strong. I had failed to protect my friends, but I would see their children live.

I steadied myself against the table and fought off a spell of dizziness. It was a great honor to become a Phantom, but already I felt as if I had failed. If I had seen Phantom Kural's defection sooner, could I have prevented any of this? Bitterness crept into my mouth, and I struggled to control my regret. Phantom Kural had involved himself with the False Shadows by his own volition. He had killed an unarmed man and forgotten his duty to his people.

I smiled to myself.

Phantom Kural's last lesson would be to teach me never to forget the Shadow's Creed. Never to forget our morality.

I swallowed my anger toward Kural and met Phantom Lunia's gaze. Had she any idea what turmoil ran through my mind?

"Kilo," Phantom Lunia began, "with your conviction and heart, will you bear the burden of leading the Shadows? Will you fight for Vaiyene and its people? Will you uphold the Shadow's Creed and become a Phantom the Shadows aspire to be?"

I looked around at my comrades. They were Shadows, yes, but like Zavi and Mia, they were my friends. We had trained together, fought together. Lived together. It created a bond none but the Shadows could understand. To protect them, I would need to take greater care, take greater precautions, to ensure we knew the False Shadows' intentions. Kural's wrongs, whatever they were, would be righted.

Vaiyene and my friends would not suffer again.

If the False Shadows needed someone to make amends for what had been done, I would become that person. I saw fear in the eyes of my friends, and I drew strength from their unease. Where they would falter, I would rise and become the leader they needed. It was my oath as a Phantom. I would find answers for my friends' deaths, not only for myself, but for Shenrae, Syrane, and the Shadows who stood alongside me.

For them, I would seek justice.

I drew in a breath and turned to address Phantom Lunia. "I am capable, and I accept the duties of Phantom."

Lunia smiled as her gaze sought out Asdar in the shadows. Throughout our Shadow training, and even now, Asdar was both my rival and friend. He had been with me in the worst times and challenged my strength and ideals.

He would make a formidable Phantom.

"Asdar, for your strength and determination, the same is asked of you. Are you capable of bearing this burden?"

He uncrossed his arms and pushed off the wall.

"I am, and I accept the duty of Phantom."

Lunia bowed to both of us. "Vaiyene thanks you for your service, as do we all. We returned the gesture, maintaining a small part of the tradition. "We will reconvene later as Phantoms. It seems there is somewhere one of us needs to be."

Phantom Lunia glanced over at me, and I spun around. Syrane stood in the hallway. He pulled his hand back, removing his fist from the hole he had made in the wall. His jaw tensed, and he turned to me. His now vacant expression nearly undid me.

Nodding my head to the Shadows and Phantom Lunia, I slid open the door and walked to Syrane. My heart clenched in my chest, and I put my arm around his shoulder. He leaned against me.

I raised my eyes to the wooden ceiling above us.

I hoped I had the strength.

Syrane sniffed beside me, and I walked him into Mia's room. The stuffy air suffocated my heart. It was dark and unsettling—so unlike Mia. Shenrae sat in a cushion beside the bed, asleep. I grabbed a blanket from the corner and draped it over her.

Mia rested on top of a white bed, surrounded by an abundance of pillows, with a woolen blanket draped over her body. If I had not seen the wound, she could have fooled me into believing she would live. I placed my hand on Syrane's shoulder and smiled at Mia, pretending it was an ordinary day.

"Would you like more light, Mia?"

It was subtle, but she nodded, a touch of a smile spreading across her face. As I pulled open the curtains, and light spilled in, it softened the room and splashing warmth across Mia's face. I knelt next to her bedside and took one of her hands in both of mine. Her hazel-green eyes sparkled at me. Syrane knelt beside his sister.

I opened my mouth but could not find words. How did one sum up a friendship? I squeezed Mia's hand instead and laid my head against our intertwined hands. What a beautiful experience we had as friends. We had grown up together, trained together, and experienced life together. When Zavi and Mia married, I had been happy, as it was I who had encouraged their friendship and love. They were perfect for one another and better because of it.

Shenrae sniffled in the corner, and I flinched from my thoughts. She was awake. I moved my gaze to her, tears threatening to break my composure. Mia would never see her children find their place in Vaiyene. What would they be sponsored for? Would they find a love like their parents had?

I tried to stop the thoughts spinning in my head, or at the very least to redirect them to something happier. I blinked away the tears.

"You never were good at goodbyes."

I returned my gaze to Mia. Tears flowed from her eyes.

I cleared my throat. "I suppose I'm not."

She laughed softly and shook her head. "Friends don't need to say everything with words."

Mia's grip weakened in my hands, and I folded her hands over her chest. Strength was leaving her.

"Take care of yourself, Kilo."

I swallowed against my tightened throat and commanded my lungs to keep breathing. I had to be strong for Shenrae and Syrane.

I extended my hand to Shenrae. She dragged herself off the cushion, wrapping the blanket around her shoulders. I turned to leave, but Syrane moved to block me. I wrapped one arm around Syrane, the other around Shenrae, and held them close. I kept my composure until I heard Mia's final breath, then lost all control.

———

A hand on my arm woke me. I blinked against puffy eyes and gathered my bearings. Moonlight spilled in through the open window. Sheer white curtains swayed in the breeze.

Finae knelt next to me. Mia still lay motionless in bed. Shenrae and Syrane were asleep in the chairs next to her bedside. They would take Mia tomorrow, her body burned alongside the others who had died in the fires. Her memory and her service as Shadow would be honored in ceremony.

I shifted and struggled to get up from the cold corner. I didn't remember falling asleep on the floor. Finae slipped her arm under my shoulder, and I sucked in a breath, my wounds protesting. With Finae's help, I stumbled into a walk, working the stiffness from my legs.

She closed the sliding door to Mia's room and turned to me, her voice quiet. "I'm glad you're safe."

I rubbed my swollen eyes, guilt coating my words. "I'm sorry I didn't find you earlier; Mia and—"

Finae shook her head. "I'm just happy you're safe."

We walked through the hallway of the Phantoms' house. The sliding doors closed on either side. The house was a sanctuary for the people and a place for the Shadows and Phantoms to gather. Tonight was the first time people had taken shelter here.

I glanced down at Finae, hesitating before I said the words, "I've become a Phantom."

Finae slowed, and I held my breath, hoping she would understand. My Shadow duties had taken me away from her. Now that I had become a Phantom, the responsibility on my shoulders would be even heavier. When Finae looked up at me, her smile was genuine. She put her right arm over her chest and bowed at the waist, in Shadow fashion.

"I always knew you would become a Phantom." She straightened, a smile still on her face. "Congratulations."

Relief washed over me. I knew Finae was mad at me for leaving sometimes, but she knew how much being a Shadow gave me purpose. Being a Phantom was what I always wanted. It was who I was. Now I needed to prove myself worthy of the title.

When we passed the infirmary, I grinned. "I liked your addition to the vaulted ceiling. It always was a little too dull for my taste."

Finae laughed and covered her mouth, stifling the sound so as not to wake anyone. "You should have seen the look on Phantom Lunia's face."

I smothered my amusement. I could imagine.

Finae was withdrawn, but a free spirit. If I believed she would become a Shadow, I would have told her not to anger Phantom Lunia, but there was still plenty of time, and the role did not suit her. She was too young to worry about being sponsored or how she would contribute to Vaiyene. She was taken care of by my status as Shadow, now Phantom, and would continue to be provided for until she was of age to pursue her own duty. For now, I wanted her to enjoy her childhood—as much as she could with times as they were.

Finae stopped at the edge of a room and led me inside. Two cots were inside, covered with thick blankets and bedding. "I helped Phantom Lunia prepare all the rooms. This one's ours."

In the corner of the room, were a few paintbrushes and mashed up berries and leaves for makeshift paint. A dirty jar of water sat at Finae's bedside. Even after losing everything, she continued to stay true to herself. She might have been proud of me, but I was more so of her. The fire and fear of danger did nothing to her bright personality. She was making the best of the situation, even though she was hurting. Her painting was like training for me. It stilled her mind from the overwhelm and made the darker days easier to endure.

I sat on the edge of the cot closest to the window, the brisk wind blowing over me. Finae hummed to herself, fiddling with a paintbrush in the water. She unrolled a scroll and stared at the blank canvas.

"Do you want me to grind the ink for you?" I asked.

She hated that part the most.

She grinned. "Yes, please!"

I slid to the floor, taking the ink stick between my fingers. Placing a drop of water into the grinding stone, I scraped the ink back and forth, not surprised when Finae leaned to dip her brush in before I had finished.

It would be one of the last quiet moments for a while.

Moonlight did little to brighten the somber atmosphere. Raindrops rippled the lake's surface, reflecting a few stars in the night sky. The Reikon Tree stood vigilant. It's strong roots twisted over the mountainside, splaying into the lake's depths. The original Phantoms of Vaiyene had designated this place as sacred because of the tree's tenacity and endurance in such a harsh environment.

Here was the final resting place of the Shadows. A Shadow's weapon—and their spirit—remained to watch over Vaiyene. They were the foundation of our people. The Phantom's Oath and the Shadow's Creed demanded a person's life be given to the people. I found solace knowing that a Shadow's life meant so much. True strength could not be acheived through desire alone. One had to understand the meaning of loss and pain to even scratch the surface of the word. It was a fool's strength that guided most people, but a deep-rooted purpose was at the core of the Shadows, especially the Phantoms. That purpose resonated with me. I'd lost so much, and yet I felt a greater sense of purpose than I ever had.

The people of Vaiyene looked to me now.

Shenrae and Syrane stood on either side of me, their parents' swords in their grasp. Unlike my hands, Zavi's and Mia's remained untainted in their Shadow duty. They had never borne the offense of killing.

Shenrae's hands trembled as she struggled to hold her mother's sword steady. Ten short years ago, I had carried my father's sword in the same procession. I rested Phantom Kural's axe against my leg and held out a hand to steady Shenrae's hands.

"Your parents were proud of you and always will be. Draw strength from your memories and the love they had for you."

I kept my eyes fixed on the tree, respectfully ignoring the sobs coming from either side of me. Tomorrow, Syrane and Shenrae would climb to the lakes above the Reikon Tree, where they would wash their parents' swords in the pure waters. It was symbolic of cleansing the spirit and releasing the duty set upon a Shadow's soul. It was a tough climb, but the ruggedness of it gave loved ones closure. Once released from service, those left behind would return the swords to the Reikon Tree. The Shadow's service and sacrifice would be remembered, forever a part of Vaiyene.

The Farewell ceremony for the Shadows was poetic and pure. Each Shadow received their bonds in the lakes above and returned to the Reikon Tree in death to complete the cycle.

Down below, at the edge of the lake, Asdar began the procession. Lunia stood at the base of the tree, clad in a ceremonial black and gold robe. She held a lit candle in her hands. No parting words were spoken. The villagers bordered the lake, standing on the shores with candles of their own, their solidarity a show of quiet support.

Asdar carried the axe of Phantom Atul across the waters. He, too, wore the Phantom's colors. For brevity's sake, we passed on the traditional ceremony of Phantom Ascension. The robes would be enough to let the people know the identities of their new Phantoms.

Quiet murmurings broke out as Asdar waked across the lake. A hidden pathway made of pebbles and rock lay beneath the water's edge. His movements were slow and intentional, drawing awe from the crowd. When he had crossed the waters, he paused before Phantom Lunia and bowed to the Reikon Tree, setting Phantom Atul's sword upon the moss-covered rocks. He knelt upon one knee, his right arm across his chest. He paused to give respect to his predecessor. He rose and stood next to the tree. The procession continued as two sons strode across the lake, each carrying the sword of his father. They knelt and joined Asdar.

I glanced down at Shenrae and Syrane, giving them a reassuring nod before they took the first step across the water. They walked side by side, and I could not help but see their younger selves. Years ago, Zavi and Mia had brought them here to show them the Reikon Tree and explain to them what it meant to be a Shadow. I held the memory dear. I would never forget their excitement and wonder at the tree and the life of a Shadow. At that time, they had both wanted to become Shadows. What path would they choose now?

Shenrae and Syrane bowed to the tree and placed their swords upon the rocks. Shenrae fell to her knees and began crying as she laid her head next to the blades.

I wrapped my fingers around Kural's axe, remembering the image of blood on the blade and of the man's severed head lying on the ground. The memory was vivd in my mind.

Death was part of life, but the Shadows believed we were not judges of the world. The life of every person was sacred—even those who did wrong. They still had a purpose, a family. Naïve as it might be, and as difficult as it was sometimes, I wanted to believe that to be true. Sparing a life was honorable, dutiful, and it showed a kindness not often found in the world.

Taking a life burdened the soul in unexplainable ways. It changed a person, haunted them and made them cold to the world. How many nights had I woken up feeling the warmth of blood as it slid over my hands? I had exchanged my sword for a staff long ago, and I did not intend to rescind the decision.

A calm settled over me as I renewed my will to protect our people. I stepped onto the lake's surface, the dense fabric of the Phantom's robe dragging across the waters. It was impractical as everyday garb, but it would bring hope to the people. They needed it now more than ever.

My eyes drifted to the people on the shore. Vaiyene was a small town of a couple of hundred people. I knew all by name and possessed a fondness for each person. I couldn't see their eyes from this distance, but the weight of their gazes lifted me up.

I drew in a deep breath.

The pure waters lapped at my indiscretions, and my mind turned back to the Shadow's Creed.

> *A Shadow does not take life, killing only*
> *when no other option can be found.*

I had killed to save Zavi's life. I had sworn never to use a blade again.

> *A Shadow does what he is capable of; no*
> *more can be asked of him.*

I had failed to save my friends, but I vowed to watch over their children.

> *A Shadow serves until he is no longer able,*
> *his life freely given to his beliefs.*

I wanted to create a peaceful world for my sister, Shenrae, Syrane, and all those who depended on my strength.

My feet touched the solid earth, and I paused at the base of the Reikon Tree, bowing low. Five blades rested upon the moss and rocks. Four Shadows and Phantom Atul, all worthy of respect and remembrance. My fingers were numb around Kural's axe handle. None would know of his misdeeds: about the fire, or about the man behind the Phantom's mask. I gritted my teeth. If not for Kural's actions, all of them would have been alive.

Out of the corner of my eye, I saw Phantom Lunia shift her weight. She had forbidden me from telling anyone, but I was no longer bound to her. I was of equal rank and had a say in how to handle matters in Vaiyene.

A Shadow does not condemn, searching
for the truth with unclouded eyes.

I looked down at the bond on my right forearm. I, too, was not a perfect Shadow. Even before I had ascended to Phantom, perfection stretched beyond my reach. Phantom Kural had not been a perfect Phantom, but he had sparred with me, taken me on missions. He had played some part in who I had become. If the people knew, it would cause panic. They would no longer trust the Shadows, and they too would share my doubts about who we were as a people. Would I have been better off not knowing about Phantom Kural's failure to the Shadow's Creed? The knowledge made me stronger, brought me closer to the truth, and made me realize where my morals stood. But our people did not need to bear the burden of uncertainty. Their lives were simpler and more peaceful without that knowledge. A Phantom's duty was to protect the people—by more than physical strength.

I chuckled inwardly as I contemplated hiding the truth. My father had always said a Shadow's hand was most effective when it remained unseen, hidden from the people's view.

I never understood what he had meant—until now.

It would be my first act as a Phantom.

I laid Phantom Kural's axe upon the stone and bowed low. Kural had done what he believed was best. He had fulfilled his oath as a Phantom, and I could not fault him for that.

I straightened and joined Asdar and Phantom Lunia at the base of the tree. From within the folds of my robe, I retrieved a candle and lit it from Phantom Lunia's flame. Those who had carried the weapons across the lake brought one of their own, lighting it from one of the three Phantoms. When Shenrae and Syrane ignited their candles, their eyes were red. As they turned to leave, I managed to speak, though my voice was ragged with emotion. "Stay here."

Asdar and Lunia exchanged glances. It was not customary for any to stay with the Phantoms, but Lunia gave a nod of approval. I wanted to be there for them when they placed their candles beside the swords of their parents.

They needed someone.

I met each persons' gaze and each nod of the head as they accepted me. Their hopes and dreams, their desire for peace and safety—it was a heavy burden, but I could carry it. It was why I had joined the Shadows. Now that I was a Phantom, nothing restrained my ambition for Vaiyene's future.

I met Finae's smile. Pride shone in her eyes, warming my heart. I wrapped her in my arms and held her tight. My friends were gone, but there were still a few I cared for.

Finae lit her candle and placed it on the ground, respectfully bowing to those who had lost their lives. When Phantom Lunia and Asdar left, I drew in a breath, letting it out slowly. I attempted a smile, trying to be strong for Syrane and Shenrae. I knelt upon the ground and placed my candle between Zavi's and Mia's swords. Their children joined me, putting their candles in the cracks of the rocks. I covered my eyes with my hand, placing my fingers over my eyes to hide my tears. When I removed my hand, I looked at the mark on the back. The scar was as prominent as it had been seventeen years ago. Zavi, Mia, and I, on our first Shadow mission, had burned ourselves with the tip of a blade. It was little more than a triangular imprint, but the mark showed our ties.

As long as I lived, I would carry them with me.

"Did you ever notice the marks on your parents' hands?" I asked, my voice steady. "We were about the same age as you when we branded ourselves with a metal knife."

I stood, offering Shenrae my hand and nudging Syrane with my foot. "There's a place not too far from here, where I used to go with your parents. We should talk."

I met Finae's gaze over Shenrae's head. She gave me a small nod, understanding. I would meet up with her later.

We left those who lingered, circling the Reikon Tree and stepping between the swords, lances, and other weapons of the past Shadows. Their souls were at peace now, but their protection remained. It was the unspoken strength of the Shadows.

One never truly was alone.

Leaves fell onto my shoulders, and I brushed them off, the fresh air bringing peace to my steps. The Reikon Tree was a sight in any season, but in winter, giant icicles hung from the branches, catching the sunlight and casting rainbows across the frozen waters. I had brought Finae here many times. She had wanted to capture the image on canvas, but I had stopped her. Sometimes the only way to experience something was to make the journey for oneself.

The climb brought back memories. Good ones. Memories of times past, and by the time we made it to the overlook, peace had returned to me. Shenrae and Syrane trailed behind me, trudging solemnly through the decaying leaves. I climbed onto the boulders overlooking the Reikon Tree and sat down on the edge of the rocks.

"This is what your parents fought for." My words were quiet as I looked down at the charred remains of the once green valley.

Shenrae and Syrane were old enough to understand a Shadow's burdens upon their family, but I needed to do what I could to bring them closure. My heart was still numb from everything that had happened, but it was warm enough that I didn't wish to cause them unnecessary pain or worry. No one had told them why their parents had died—or how—or of the real motive behind the attack.

I wrestled with the consequences of doing so.

If our places were reversed, I would appreciate the truth. But, they were young, impressionable, and Syrane did not have control of himself. Anger would give them purpose, but it would destroy them. The Shadows never sought vengeance. Their parents would not have wished for it either. But knowing Syrane and his temper, if I did not guide his emotion, it would turn him to a darker path. Zavi had struggled with rage in his younger Shadow years.

Syrane and Shenrae waited for me to continue.

They deserved the truth.

"There's a group impersonating the Shadows, called the False Shadows, who are responsible for the fires." I kept a close watch on their reactions. "I found Zavi at the bottom of a cliff. He was injured after a fight with one of them. I was there for him in his last moments."

Syrane's jaw tightened at the news, but I continued. They both needed the whole truth, as much as I knew of it in order to draw their own conclusions.

"Mia was captured by the False Shadows and fought against them. The injuries she received after fighting them were fatal. If one of the False Shadows had not intervened, she would have died before I reached her."

I hoped they grasped the complexity of the situation.

"A False Shadow gave me aid, once in Leiko and again in Vaiyene. I don't know why, which is why discretion is necessary. I tell this to you because your parents' deaths were part of something bigger than the Shadows. Those responsible are not all wicked. There's more than hate at work."

I waited, analyzing the weight of my words. Syrane's muscles were tense; anger emanated from him. He possessed Zavi's restraint, but it would not take much more to break it. When it did, he would lash out. His target would be the False Shadows.

I stood up and faced both of them. My hands were relaxed at my sides, my expression, and my stance calm. "Do not think thatI am not angry with how your parents died. I don't approve of involving innocent people. It was not your parents' or even Vaiyene's fault in any of this. None of this should have happened."

I took a breath and pressed my fingers to my temple. "Even so, your parents would have given their lives to save both of yours. It was their duty to protect you and ensure you had a choice for the future."

I clapped my hand on Syrane's shoulder. "We will not seek vengeance against the False Shadows." At my words, Syrane averted his eyes, and his muscles tightened under my grasp. I gripped his shoulder, bringing his attention back to me.

"I will find justice for them, Syrane, for both of you."

I let him go, hoping I had reached him. As a Phantom, I possessed more authority to make a change, but I would not go against our morals. I would not kill the False Shadows, nor would I track them down to make them suffer for their actions. Vengeance blinded a man. I had vowed to protect life, not take it.

Syrane was upset. Shenrae was harder to read. Her emotions were more withdrawn, much like Finae's always were. What she thought, I couldn't begin to speculate. Instincts told me she would find her own way to deal with the loss of her parents. She had Mia's compassion.

Words would not be able to take away their pain, nor did I want to take the pain of their parents' deaths away. Loss was part of what made the Shadows strong. It was what drove us and guided us to protect.

Still, I suffered from my own guilt and failure.

"I'm sorry I was not able to save them," I said.

"We know—" Shenrae's voice broke, but she struggled through the words. "If there was a way…"

Syrane drew in a breath, his hands clenched at his sides. "We don't blame you. We know you did everything you could."

He finished his sister's words. It was something that needed to be said before we could move on. I swallowed the guilt. Zavi and Mia would not have blamed me.

I had done all that I could.

I turned back to the Reikon Tree. My friends' strength was now part of the Shadows who had fallen.

"In time, the pain will lessen, and you'll be able to move on. It is the Shadow way. Draw strength from your parents' love for you."

My gaze remained on the Reikon Tree.

Their strength was in all of us.

chapter seven
A PHANTOM'S DUTY

"We need to repair our connections and strengthen the goodwill with the surrounding villages," Phantom Lunia said, spreading out a map of Kiriku on the table in the command room.

Food was our main concern.

I rubbed my eyes and tried to bring my mind to the present. The long day had muddled my focus. "How much would you estimate we saved?"

"Perhaps enough to last us through half the winter."

Asdar snorted from the opposite end of the room. He leaned against the wall, his arms crossed. "If this winter is a short one. There's no telling when the last snowfall will end this year."

"We can hunt in the winter to supplement our grains," I said as I walked around the table, scratching at the stubble on my chin. "The Shadows will not be able to make it down the mountain, but we can expand our hunting grounds to the upper regions."

Prolonged snow would threaten our food supply, but the longer we were buried in snow, the longer we remained safe from an attack. The more snow this winter, the better.

Asdar glared at me. "Most of our Shadows capable of such a feat are dead."

I let out a breath, rubbing my temples.

Phantom Lunia sighed. "We will need more than what we can hunt. A fifth of our people died in the fires, but we still have a couple hundred to feed."

I stopped circling the table and leaned over the map. There were at least another few weeks before winter would be upon us. It would be even longer for the villages farther south or closer to the gulf. Leiko's fish were always plentiful, but it would be risky returning so soon. Would they even consider a deal with the Shadows anymore? With the False Shadows using our name for their own blackened purpose, our allies might see us differently. Even if the fire had not happened, Vaiyene would struggle to survive without our trade agreements. At least a third of our supply came from across Kiriku, centered in the eastern region of Randaus.

Had the fires not been enough to satisfy the False Shadows?

Did they have to threaten our alliances, too?

There were no other options. We needed to do something, and Leiko was our best chance, albeit the riskiest. I could stop along the way and try and forge new alliances as a secondary plan. I rolled my shoulders. The wounds on my back were healing, and my arm had healed enough. It would be best to avoid fighting if I could, though I could use the staff with one hand if needed.

"I will head to Leiko and stop in the villages along the way."

Phantom Lunia frowned. "You're hardly in a position to do battle if you run into trouble. Take someone with you."

I opened my mouth to reply, but Asdar beat me to it. "There are none to spare. We need our remaining Shadows to strengthen Vaiyene's defense and train new Shadows."

I nodded. "I agree with Asdar, Phantom Lunia—"

"Lunia now, Kilo," she interrupted with a smile. "We are equals."

Heat rose in my cheeks, and I floundered to regain my thoughts. "It will be easier to travel alone anyway. We don't know how far the False Shadows have tarnished our name. For now, I'll travel as discreetly as possible. No Phantom robes, nor Shadow garb—with my bond covered."

Lunia always held the well-being of the Shadows above everything else. I appreciated her concern, but we could no longer avoid danger.

"We need to find people who can help us rebuild Vaiyene—those who are sponsored as builders and architects, as well as bakers and butchers," Lunia said as she crossed the room and picked up a weathered book from the shelf. She opened the spine, turning the pages with care. Her fingers ran down the pages, searching. It was the book of Vaiyene's people. Inside was a list of every person in Vaiyene, each listed with their family and what they were sponsored for.

"Our top priority," she continued, "is to figure out food preservation and a way to handle rations."

The affairs and menial tasks of keeping the town running had been her duty for as long as I could remember. I glanced over at Asdar, who eyed a group of younger villagers outside of the windows. He did not look our way.

"I will train those who are capable of joining the Shadow ranks."

Lunia breathed out a sigh of relief and sat on the edge of the table, her back hunched over. We each had our burdens, but rebuilding the town, and easing our people's fears would be the hardest. It would not be easy to rekindle the people's spirits, but it would be pivotal to the restoration.

"Thank you both for your quick actions," Lunia said. "If we're all agreed, I'd like for us to implement our strategies within the day. You are both welcome to stay here again or move in, as you are now Phantoms. Many of the people have opened their homes, taking in those who have lost their own, so there's plenty of room."

Asdar bowed and took his leave, saying nothing to either Lunia or me. I smiled and turned to Lunia. "He'd rather sleep in the training grounds than here."

Lunia laughed and covered her mouth as Asdar paused and turned at the end of the hallway. I caught a glint of amusement in his eyes before he walked away.

Finae wasn't going to be happy I was leaving, but perhaps I could arrange for her to not be alone.

"I will try and convince Finae to stay here," I said. "She gets lonely when I'm gone."

It would ease a little of my guilt to know she was not alone. Lunia's smile faded. "She is always welcome here."

I bowed before leaving and walked down the hallways, peering into the room we had been staying in. I wasn't surprised to find it vacant. In the corner, a piece of paper lay on the wooden floor. Small bowls arranged beside it. They were empty.

I sighed. Finae never did stay put, and I had a feeling I knew where she had gone.

———

Finae bent over as she sifted through the debris of our burned home. Soot covered her hands, her face, and her clothing. There were even long streaks of black in her blonde hair. I closed my eyes against the scene. I would always fail Finae as a brother.

Despite my efforts, I always abandoned someone for my Shadow—now Phantom—duties. Not only Finae but Shenrae and Syrane. Staying in Vaiyene would be ideal, but if I stayed, they would die of hunger. I preferred their hatred.

A clatter startled me from my musings. Finae panted as pieces of soot fluttered into the air and wood settled to the ground. She coughed, then began gathering something from the rubble.

The rest of her collection of paintbrushes.

I brought Finae brushes from all the places I visited on Shadow missions. She kept a few with her at all times, but her collection were burned in the ruins of our home. Painting was her passion, but more than that, the brushes served as a tangible reminder that I was always with her.

A half-burnt plank cracked under my foot.

Finae jumped at my approach.

"Kilo!" She hid the brushes behind her back, her face flushed. "I didn't know when you'd return, so I figured I'd keep myself busy."

"Are any of them salvageable?" I walked over the wooden planks, mindful of my balance on the uneven pile. Her eyes welled up, and she held them up for me to see. The handles remained intact, but the bristles were gone. I wrapped my arms around her, drawing her close.

"I know the boys tease you for caring so much about painting, but I love your work."

Her talent did not fit into the traditional paths of sponsorship in Vaiyene. One day—if she chose that path—I would convince the other Phantoms of her worth. We needed other weapons to bring hope to this changing world.

Not everyone needed to wield a blade.

I held her at arm's length and looked into her puffy eyes. She smiled and made to throw the brushes back into the rubble, but I stopped her. "I know you use the back of our chopsticks to smear paint." She glared at me, and I chuckled. "You can still create beautiful work from these, but I will bring you back some proper ones."

Her smile faded as her gaze returned to the devastation.

"I can't believe it's all gone."

Her shoulders slumped, her happiness dimming before me. She would no longer find comfort here. I had grown up in this house the same as she had, but even when our parents had still been alive, it had never felt like home to me. Riding a horse, pitching camp, coming home after a Shadow mission to see Finae—that was my sense of home.

Finae's sense of home was this house, and now it was gone.

"I'm sorry I'm always gone so much. I know it must be hard waiting for me to return."

I had never taken the time to get to know her everyday life. Now I never would. Tears poured down her cheeks. How lonely she must be.

She wiped the tears with the back of her hand. "I know what it's like for you, what it was like for mother and father as well. Duty calls you. I don't like it, but I understand it."

Her words cut into me as truth could. I'd had the thought plenty of times before, but it hurt more now that the words were spoken. I could not be with her, but I could find someplace where she would feel welcome and give her a purpose.

I tried to keep my tone light. "Phantom Lunia said you could stay in the Phantoms' house. You can help rebuild Vaiyene while I'm gone."

Finae graced me with a genuine smile. "I'd like that."

I smiled in return.

Finae shivered beside me. I removed my Phantom robe and draped it over her shoulders, laughing as it dragged against the ground. She raised her arms and laughed as well, the folds making her appear three times her size. It dwarfed her as it hung from her small frame. A gust of wind rustled the folds of the robe.

I inhaled deeply. The air was cool and damp; earthy undertones hinted at the coming of snow.

Time pulled at my mind, stealing the joy of the moment.

"I don't know how long I'll be gone this time, Finae."

Her arms deflated at her sides. It was subtle, but I didn't miss the shift of her heart. As much as I hated leaving, there was nothing that could be done; it was the burden of my duty.

chapter eight
MASHIN

Nightwind came to a halt as a shadow passed over us. Dark-feathered birds circled overhead. I grimaced, drawing the scarf over my nose, my stomach already anticipating what was to come.

Scavengers.

It seemed the False Shadows made it before I did.

I rubbed Nightwind's neck, for my comfort more than his. Before I had left Vaiyene, Asdar had found me in the stables and offered his black steed to take on my journey. I had accepted his kindness. Finae cared a great deal for Whitestar, and it would give her something to look after while I was gone.

I slid to the ground, my boots squishing into the sodden earth. Moisture dampened the air, not from rain but from the pools of blood. I let go of Nightwind's reins, taking the staff from the leather holster on my back as I crept past the first row of houses. Decaying corpses leaned against both sides of the streets, their slack bodies positioned as if waiting for someone to discover them. Eerily, it reminded me of coming home from a Shadow mission—where the people lined the streets to welcome us home.

The connection quickened my heart.

They were mocking me, the False Shadows.

My mind searched for a reason. What was the purpose? Slaughtering an entire village, even for some twisted sense of revenge, held no meaning. Mashin was a humble village, a mere dozen or so cottages made of stone and thatched roofing. They didn't even trade with any other village.

I forced myself to analyze the situation as Shadow training had taught me. Evaluate what has happened, nothing more. It lay deep in my nature to analyze, to sympathize with the victims. It gave me the will to save even the lowest people from death. But empathy would do nothing for me here. Unless I had been present the moment the False Shadows had come, I couldn't have helped them. There was no one left to grieve.

Except for me.

I knelt down in the mud next to a body. I no longer cared to keep the blood from my hands. Whatever purity I had gained from Vaiyene and the Reikon Tree had long since washed away. Bile rose at the back of my throat, the stench of decay penetrating through the scarf around my nose. It had been at least a day, maybe two, since they had been slaughtered. The skin was limp, the limbs swollen, and a touch of green tainted the once pale flesh. If the temperature had been warmer, I wouldn't have been able to recognize the body as female.

The woman looked to be the same age as my mother would have been—had she been alive—around fifty summers. Her eyes stared lifelessly ahead. I shifted from her vacant stare, calming my emotion. Death had glazed her eyes and frozen her mouth in a grimace. A muscle in her jaw protruded.

She had seen death coming and had faced it.

I closed her eyes with my hand and glanced over at the next victim. It was a man, younger than the woman, but age still creased his freckled skin. His face was stoic, proud.

He, too, had faced death with honor.

A glint of metal directed my next move. The intricate silver threads of a bond encircled a young boy's forearm. As I approached, his expression seemed twisted in terror. Burns mirrored the metal threads. I turned his arm over and leaned in closer. A scar ran from his wrist down to his elbow, topped by a few silver beads.

The bond had been soldered together.

I set the boy's arm across his body and stepped back. The bonds were not real Shadow bonds, but imitations as I had suspected. True Shadow bonds were forged in a cavern, above the Reikon Tree. I remembered vividly the silver pools and the moment when the metal climbed onto my arm.

Overhead, a raven beat its mighty wings. A black feather came loose, fluttering through the air and landing in a pool of blood. Scavengers served a purpose in the world, though I did not like the idea of its feast today.

More wings beat above me.

I placed my fingers to my lips and whistled long and low. Nightwind trotted to me, scattering the ravens, but not before one of them left with a villager's eye.

So much death, and for what purpose?

Had it really been for revenge?

I inhaled the bitter air. Something needed to be done with the bodies. They would never find peace if I abandoned them. Some people outside of Vaiyene buried their dead, but I couldn't afford that much time, and my arm had not healed enough for the strain. I needed to move on, but seeing the dead mistreated made me hesitate. I'd never met these people, but the will to see them sent off from the world weighed on my conscience. What if it were my friends who had been left to be eaten by scavengers? I would hope someone would take the time to preserve their dignity in their final moments. Being able to live with my choices was not a question but a necessity. I could not live with myself if I walked away. I would give myself until sundown; then I needed to move on. The False Shadows could slander our name, but they would never break our will. The Shadow's Creed was the heart of the

Shadows, and even those who were not Shadows carried the same basic principle of compassion.

The easiest way would be to burn them, as we did in Vaiyene. I knew nothing of these people's customs, but I had a feeling their spirits would not mind.

I cracked my back and rolled my shoulders, whistling for Nightwind to follow. Propped against one of the houses, next to two dead bodies, was a shovel and a rake. I lashed them together with strips from an old burlap sack I gathered. On the threshold of a cottage, I hesitated. Taking from the dead did not bother me—Shadows were taught to be resourceful—but it did bother me to enter a place untouched by tragedy. Back in Leiko, raiders had gained resources from their pillaging. The people there were used to misfortune, as living there came with a risk. But here, the people of Mashin cared only for the length of the sun and protecting their meager harvest.

I brushed the sentiment aside, trying to ignore the glasses of water on the table and the curtains cut by an unsteady hand. The table legs had been hand-carved. A grandfather too elderly to work the fields? At the back of the house, in the corner, were two small cots. Two children. I pulled the pelt from the bed and returned to my work, finding comfort in having something to do with my hands. I slashed holes in the fur and tied it to either end of the litter's poles. Once finished, I tied the ends crudely to Nightwind's saddle and dragged a body onto the frame.

I stood up, a bead of sweat on my brow.

I didn't know which house belonged to this man. It was an odd thought, but it bothered me nonetheless. It would be best for the deceased to be in their own homes, but there was no way for me to know.

I led Nightwind to the door of one of the cottages, transferring the man off the litter and pulling him into the center of the house. I repeated the gruesome process until all the bodies were inside the cottage closest to where they had laid dead. If I noticed a resemblance, I laid the people together. When I had finished, I pried a wooden floorboard loose and wrapped the end with strips of cloth. I doused the end of my makeshift torch and ignited the end. I watched the flames and let the emotion of the moment engulf me, feeling the pain of the innocent lives lost.

I left the first building, watching the fire grow in intensity as smoke spiraled into the sky before I set fire to the rest of the village.

Mashin was no more. The fire, like the crystal waters of Vaiyene's lakes, would cleanse the people's spirits.

I mounted Nightwind and nudged his flanks with my heels.

I did not look back at my handiwork.

chapter nine
TARAHN

On the horizon, a spire of rock and mortar jutted into the sky, cutting the rising sun in two. I dismounted as the multi-colored roofs of Tarahn came into focus. It was the first town on my journey to Leiko—one I had never been to—and one where I hoped the Shadow name still held meaning.

I shed the cloak from my shoulder, rolling it and stuffing it into my saddle packs. It was too Shadow-like for any who were familiar with the way we dressed. The possibility of being associated with the False Shadows was too risky. From within another saddle pack, I withdrew a roll of bandages, wrapping the linen around my bond. Hiding who I was made me angry, but I couldn't risk an adverse reaction to my being a Phantom for the sake of my pride.

Tarahn possessed a military force, and from what I had heard from Phantom Kural on a former Shadow mission, their strength was formidable. Best to put ego aside and observe.

I led Nightwind toward the town and assumed an air of a tradesman. The trick to infiltration was to exude unshakeable confidence; if you felt you didn't belong, people picked up on your uneasiness. In Shadow training, we had sometimes been given a new identity to assume, to boost our confidence and open us up to new possibilities when on missions. It had seemed juvenile, silly even, but I now realized how much that training had prepared me to be a Phantom.

A crowd formed on the edges of the town. It was early—too early for the number of people wading through the gates. I didn't recall Tarahn being a marketplace where people came to sell their wares.

Had something happened?

Nightwind snorted in outrage as I led him through the crowd of people. His feisty spirit reflected my anxiety, and I stayed close to the black stallion's side. His sheer size parted the wave of people as they gave him space to maneuver.

I gave my own snort of outrage.

At least they respected a horse, if not a Phantom.

Ahead, an iron gate stood in place by way of two long metal stakes thrust into the ground. On either side were watchtowers. An assortment of colored stones decorated the stonework. Above, two guards kept a watchful eye on the flow of people.

Were they watching for the False Shadows?

I adjusted the bandage around my arm and kept my eyes focused ahead, elbowing through the crowd. The stench of sweat and foul breath suffocated me, and I struggled to maintain a quiet impatience to get where I needed to go. Inside, my heart was out of rhythm. Bodies pressed against me from all sides, jostling my arms and increasing my panic. Even the watchtowers seemed to close in around me. It wouldn't be too much longer until I was through. I forced myself to breathe at a steady rate, regaining my hold on my emotions. I breathed a sigh of relief when the wall of people dissipated. Nightwind and I drew no particular attention from the guards. I didn't stop to choose a path. Instead, I followed where most of the other people went. As much as I hated being in the crowd, wherever they were going, they headed there for a reason.

I was here to experience the moment, as were they.

Whatever that moment was.

I loosened the staff tied to Nightwind's torso, taking in the strange architecture of Tarahn's buildings. Of the three current Phantoms, the one with the most experience outside of Vaiyene was me. Any information I gathered on the lifestyle here could be useful later. Even if I was uncomfortable, I needed to be diligent, starting with the seemingly mundane details.

Starting with their apparent love of color.

The same decorative stones of the guard towers were present in the rest of the town's architecture. It created the perfect backdrop for a colorful array of people and their equally flamboyant clothing. To Vaiyene's standards, the wild colors and patterns were unusual, but it did give the atmosphere a lively exuberance. Unlike Leiko's bustle of fishing and trade, this town's energy seemed richer and fuller. The people could express themselves how they liked, and the town flourished because of it.

It was a promising start. If Tarahn was this well-off, perhaps they would not be fooled by the False Shadows.

Nightwind and I pushed our way into the center of town. The crowd butted against us as people gathered in circular rows around a raised stone platform. Asdar's stallion snorted his impatience, giving a steely eye to a balding man who ventured too close. I pulled the reins tight and eased us into a corner, cooing instinctively to calm the horse's anger. A smile spread across my face. It was too bad Nightwind's master didn't calm as easily.

A tall, lean man, clad in full battle armor, strode across the platform, flanked by two guards. This was the commander of the military force, possibly the lord of the town. He removed his helmet, and a mess of brown hair flopped onto his head. The guard at his right turned his head toward me, focusing on Nightwind and me as if he knew we didn't belong. I gave him a slight bow from the waist, turning my hands out at my sides, palms up, to show I meant no harm. He gave me a small nod in return and gazed back toward the murmuring crowd.

"The situation is under control," the commander said, projecting his voice over the noise of the crowd. "We have not learned why the man came to our village, but rest assured he will be dealt with. We will find the answer to his actions."

I bristled at his words. Had a False Shadow come?

Nightwind bumped the back of my head, and I reached up to stroke his muzzle. When I returned my attention to the stage, the same guard who had noticed me whispered into his commander's ears. He glanced over at me.

"Guards have been stationed throughout the town for protection. Once we find out more, I will inform you. If any of you see anything out of the ordinary, do not hesitate to find one of my guardsmen."

The commander nodded to the guards and stepped off the platform. The crowd parted to give him space as he strode in my direction. I resisted the urge to grab my staff. Neither the guards nor the leader reached for their swords. I wouldn't be the first to draw a weapon.

A gong clanged from the north.

Both guards and the commander spun around, drawing swords from their belts. Horses stampeded from the opposite end of the marketplace, scattering the crowd in all directions. People screamed and fled, impeding the guards trying to act against the mounted riders. Masks covered the riders' faces, but the silver bonds on their forearms were worn with pride.

At last, I had a chance to prevent their destruction.

I drew my staff, and the guards rounded on me. The bandage around my forearm slipped, and a piece of my bond was revealed. I held my ground, focusing my attention on the commander. He stood at the same height as I and had familiar downturned eyes.

His resemblance to General Mirai was uncanny.

The commander's eyes glanced at the bond on my forearm. His eyes scanned my two-toed boots and the light canteen at my side before his gaze rested on my face. He turned, addressing the guards. "He's a Shadow. Turn your attention to the False Shadows."

Did he know about the False Shadows? It was a term coined by General Mirai and had not been used outside of the Shadow ranks. Had General Mirai told him about the False Shadows?

I cut off my speculations and mounted Nightwind, gripping my staff with one hand as we wound through the panicked crowd.

The commander yelled from behind me. "Form up!"

He and his two guards moved to either side of me. Together, we created a line of four against the six oncoming False Shadows. We would see if he was as skilled as the general.

One of the False Shadows unsheathed a sword and swung it into the crowd. I placed my staff into the holder at my back, letting go of Nightwind's reins. He would follow the formation of the other horses without my direction. Grabbing my bow from Nightwind's sidem I nocked an arrow, taking aim. It flew, hitting the False Shadow in the shoulder. They didn't drop their sword, but it did stop the next swing. The injured man fled down a side street.

One down.

The five remaining False Shadows split as I readied another arrow. The town guards each pursued one rider, their commander stuck to my side. I squeezed my knees together, letting Nightwind know to keep his path. Another False Shadow cried out as a sword sliced into his side. Judging from the spurt of blood, the wound was fatal. I winced. He could have had valuable information, and even if he knew nothing, he did not deserve death—even if he did not respect life. I threw my bow over my shoulder, exchanging it for my staff. With my heels, I spurred Nightwind toward the two remaining False Shadows. Tarahn's leader lifted his sword above his head. It was an offensive attack that wouldn't spare a man's life.

It was General Mirai's form, but with none of his mercy.

A woman screamed as Nightwind ran past her. Her cry rattled my senses as a False Shadows charged her. I guided the black stallion with my knees, pushing him with my right leg to go left. Vaiyene flashed in my memories, and I heard the screams of our people in the fires. I saw the False Shadow's snide face after he pushed Zavi over the ledge and the grin of the man. I remembered the sting of regret from not being able to save Mia.

Would I have been able to save her if I had killed?

Resentment boiled within me, and I tightened the grip on my staff. Nightwind picked up speed without my direction, sensing my emotion. My staff rammed into the False Shadow's chest. The momentum knocked him from the saddle, and he crashed to the cobblestones below. His leg bent at an unnatural angle.

I allowed Nightwind to form up with the others, eyeing the False Shadow as he writhed on the ground. The woman they had tried to kill had escaped. Most of the villagers had fled, leaving the area open. No more innocent lives would be lost.

Two False Shadows remained.

I guided Nightwind to the right, bringing him around. Two False Shadows charged the town leader from either side. I spurred Nightwind faster and loosened my grip. The end of my staff made scant contact; the False Shadow slid off the saddle. His foot caught in the stirrup, and he dangled as his horse fled the battlefield. Without the adjustment, my staff would have crushed the man's lungs. I pulled back on Nightwind's reins, slowing him down and calming his adrenaline-fueled haste. In a contest of mounted combat, the staff's ability to kill couldn't be matched. If I'd met the man with my full strength, with a harder wood than my chosen staff, I wouldn't have been able to spare his life.

Whether it was my emotion or Nightwind's, I would have to be more cautious. The stallion sensed my unease.

I hadn't been in the right mind since Phantom Kural.

Tarahn's commander charged the final False Shadow. Swords clashed. Then he pulled back, swinging his sword over his head and bringing the tip of his blade across the enemy's neck. The False Shadow clutched at his throat, kicking his horse and fleeing the scene. I signaled Nightwind to go after him, but the commander blocked my path.

"He will either die from blood loss or, like the cowards they are, take his own life."

I narrowed my eyes, balancing my staff across Nightwind's saddle. As if to answer my question, Tarahn's leader jerked his head to the side, and I looked where he indicated. A froth of bubbles cascaded from the False Shadows' mouths. The whites of their eyes had turned a ghastly shade.

"We've been trying to capture one of the False Shadows for quite some time." The commander dismounted and wiped his blade. "They'd rather die than accept mercy." He met my gaze, a wry smile touching his features. "Which is why I didn't bother trying to spare his life in your company."

I watched the guard close the eyes of the False Shadows, and the commander motioned for me to follow, leaving the guards behind to deal with the bodies.

"My brother told me about you. The Shadow who refuses to kill. Or, to be more precise, one of the Shadows who refuse to kill. Honorable, considering how the False Shadows have slandered your name."

"We all have our ideals." I kept my tone neutral, not sure yet what to think of this man. "You're General Mirai's brother?"

He nodded. "Kefnir."

"Kilo."

"Ah, so a Shadow no more then. A Phantom." Kefnir watched me with interest. "Our information network is quite good. We know more about the False Shadows than even you."

I blinked a moment of exhaustion away, trying not to let the information he knew unsettle me. Between the battle today and taking care of the dead the day before, the corners of my mind were foggy. I didn't have my usual judgement of character in this worn state, though I knew to be cautious around him.

I recalled the earlier commotion. "Have you captured any of the False Shadows?" My mind struggled to keep all the information straight. I should have slept more.

Kefnir met my eyes. "This morning, we did capture one alive." He scratched his head, his eyebrows were drawn together. "He seemed quite different than the others, which might explain why he didn't take his life."

As we made our way back to the platform, the gong rang out, this time higher in frequency. A few braver townspeople opened the shutters to their homes, their inquisitive gaze following our path. I picked at the bandage over my bond.

Kefnir spoke under his breath. "Unwrap the bandage around your arm."

I looked at Kefnir sharply, not sure what he had planned.

"I don't want my people attacking those who have done nothing because of what they perceive. That causes war, of which I do not wish to take part in."

A pacifist. The ideal aligned with the Shadow's Creed. He was more like General Mirai than I had initially judged him to be.

I unwrapped the bandage from my forearm, not solely because of Kefnir's words, but because I needed to see the damage for myself. What did the people think of the Shadows?

Someone hissed, their words lost, but the tone carried to me. They feared me. On the outside, they appeared angry, but I was confident it stemmed from their uncertainties.

I kept my hands relaxed on Nightwind's reins. If I wanted to make a real difference for my people fix the damage caused by the False Shadows—and Phantom Kural—I needed to be willing to take risks. I drew in a breath. I would be able to use their fear in my favor if they did turn on me.

A man paused to let us pass. He extended his arm to stop his wife and two small children from walking farther. Kefnir waved his hand, a small smile on his face. The man's features softened, and he relaxed. Kefnir's people trusted him.

Trust that deep was not easily given.

Kefnir reached the platform in the town center, dismounting and motioning for me to do the same. The guards now flanked both of us. People ventured out of their houses, trickling into the square. They raised their fingers to point at my bond. I shifted on my feet, uncomfortable under their gaze. If they felt threatened, they would riot against me. I kept my face emotionless, not letting them see how shaken I was.

"I swore an oath," Kefnir said to the crowd, unsheathing his sword as he held it in his palms, "to protect this town and all who live here. With this sword, I promised to defend all of you. I have kept that promise. Dangerous times are upon us, and our enemy seeks to blind us from the truth, and draw us into an unjust war."

I eyed Kefnir's sword, not sure of his intentions.

His words were raw as if he were talking to a friend. His lack of separation between ranks made the people trust him.

Kefnir lowered his sword to his side and set his other hand on my shoulder. "This is Kilo, Phantom of Vaiyene. He protected you today. The ones who attacked are known as the False Shadows. They are imposters, wearing the same metal casing you see on Kilo's arm. I caution each of you to think before you judge someone as your enemy by appearance alone."

The whispers of the crowd stilled, but they didn't cease their stares. Would they listen? Could war be avoided, or would the False Shadows force our hand?

Kefnir cleared his throat and sheathed his sword. "Together, we will defeat this enemy and bring peace back to Tarahn and all those who live across Kiriku. This is the Land of Hope, and we will fight to defend it."

The crowd cheered. Kefnir left the platform and turned north, motioning for him to follow me. His unexpected show of allegiance to the Shadows humbled me.

"Thank you," I said.

Kefnir was General Mirai's brother, but I had not expected him to defend the Shadow name so publicly. It was a risk to his people, opposing the False Shadows as such.

Perhaps the Shadow name still meant something.

Kefnir waved his hand dismissively, leading me down the windy cobblestone road to a guardhouse made of grey stone. On one end, a guard tower stood, a tall metal spire jutting into the sky—the same spire I had seen from the edge of the town. If I squinted against the sun, I could make out the guard standing next to two brass gongs, each the size of a man. The entrance towered over our heads in an archway of stones. At our approach, the guards pulled open the door, exposing vaulted ceilings. Natural light spilled in from the windows, ushering rays of light onto an enormous wooden table. There was space for at least three dozen men.

A guard greeted Kefnir with a slight bow.

"We have the room ready, sir."

The guard led us down a darkened hallway, and through a maze of twists and turns, until my usual good sense of direction could no longer keep its bearings. The air was stale and cold. I kept my eyes focused on the bobbing of the guard's lantern, trying to keep my senses attentive. I couldn't even spread my arms out; the walls were so close together.

Kefnir gripped the door handle. "Let's get this over with."

His words warned me seconds before I entered the dim room. It was lit by a single lantern hung from a chain. The room's dankness darkened my mood. In the center of the room, a young man stood, his hands tied over his head.

Kefnir slammed the door behind us, and the man jumped. A rope had rubbed the skin near his wrists raw. He was thin, scrawny even, and too young for such treatment. A blindfold covered his eyes. If he had not been held up with rope, I wasn't sure his legs would have been able to hold him.

His hair was black as night, and his skin was darker than that of the people in northern Kiriku. He looked to be about the same age as Shenrae and Syrane. Barely a man by Vaiyene's standards.

"Do you know who I am?" Kefnir asked.

The man said nothing.

Kefnir circled the man. His footsteps drummed against the stone floor as he continued his interrogation. "I'm the man whose village you have attacked for no reason. Answer me, and I'll let you live. Or, if you prefer, you can take your life."

Kefnir glanced at me, stopping before the man, and I waited for him to continue. I did not care for his method of questioning.

"We'll start with an easy question. What purpose does your group serve?"

My heart quickened.

When the man didn't answer, Kefnir drew a dagger from his belt and closed the distance between them. My eyes flicked to the blade, and I intercepted Kefnir, grabbing his arm to stop him. He yanked his arm back and glared at me, but I ignored him. I inspected the man from up close. A bruise swelled on the right side of his chin. His breathing was erratic and shallow. I took a step closer, and the man trembled.

False Shadow or not, he did not deserve this.

I reached for my own dagger belted at my hip, and I cut the rope tied to the ceiling. The man's legs gave out, and I put one arm around his torso to steady him. When his legs were stable, I untied the blindfold and stepped back. His emerald eyes met mine. Then he found where Kefnir stood against the wall.

I had undermined Kefnir's authority, potentially losing Vaiyene an ally, but the choice had been the right one.

I couldn't stand back and watch him torture this man.

I stepped in front of Kefnir, turning my back to him, gaining the young man's attention and showing my trust in Kefnir. The will to protect pushed me past my exhaustion, sending a surge of adrenaline through my veins, which sharpened my mind. Even if Kefnir was angry, we both wanted the same thing. If we were to be allies, he would have to abide by my ideals.

"What is your name?" I kept my voice even and my body still. Kefnir didn't move behind me. "I ask you to cooperate, for both our sakes. I've defied Kefnir, and if you give no answer, I will be forced to allow him to do what he wants to make you talk."

Judging from his ragged appearance, his torn clothing, and his bruised cheek, this man's trust would be hard to earn. But I had to try. I stepped closer, keeping his gaze on me and away from Kefnir.

"I promise you will not be hurt anymore, but to ensure that I need your cooperation." The man's gaze fixed on the dagger. I dropped the blade and kicked it away, spreading my hands out to the sides.

"I am Phantom Kilo of Vaiyene—"

The man's eyes snapped to me. "You're part of the Shadows."

I smiled, my wit returning in full force. "And you're one of those who impersonate the Shadows." The man flinched at my words, and I regretted my sharp tongue. Anger had got the better of me. I could almost feel Kefnir's smirk when the man remained quiet. I tried to picture Syrane's stubbornness and quick temper. How would I speak to him?

I kept my face neutral, showing none of the annoyance caused by the mistreatment of Kefnir's men. He was a False Shadow, but I did not believe he was evil at heart. I'd waited to see a False Shadow, and now that I had, it almost disappointed me. I found no hatred in my heart. He was young and afraid—and easily influenced. It didn't make him a bad person, merely misguided. I knew nothing of the circumstances which had put him here, but I was willing to give him a chance.

If what Kefnir said was right, he had not tried to kill himself upon being captured. I needed to find the reason why before Kefnir's patience ran out. Could I reach him by showing him the compassion of a Phantom?

I held out a hand to the man. "Let me see your hands."

The man stared at me, unmoving. That much I had anticipated. I bent down, pulling another dagger from the inside of my boot. I drew the blade from its sheath and extended the hilt, glancing at the ropes that still bound his wrists together.

"You can either cut the remainder of the ropes or cut me with the blade. The choice is yours."

The man's eyes widened, and he reached out a hesitant hand, eyeing me to see if it was somehow was a trick.

I kept my eyes focused on him, my intention to find out who he was as a person. I cleared my throat, keeping my tone casual. "A False Shadow pushed my friend over a cliff not long ago. I wasn't able to save his life."

At my words, the man paused and lowered his arms, averting his gaze. He let out a long breath.

Regret?

Or was he beginning to see his position as futile?

"While I was trying to save him, his wife fought against the False Shadows. She died, with her children at her bedside."

It was subtle, but there was a slight shift in the man before me. His shoulders hunched over. There was a desire to live, but he felt defeated. I didn't believe he was happy being a False Shadow. I flipped the blade around and grabbed his wrist. His eyes jerked to me, his muscles rigid. I cut the ropes around his wrists, freeing his hands.

"Despite what you may think, I don't hate you. I thought I would, but now that I've seen you, all I see are the two children whose parents died at the hands of the False Shadows. The same sadness is in your eyes. You don't have to be one of them. We can protect you."

I held the man's gaze, hearing Kefnir shift behind me.

"Ikaru," the man said. "My name is Ikaru." Exhaustion ringed his eyes, and he swayed unsteadily on his feet. I reached out a hand to steady him. Some people were capable of taking another's life; others were not. I didn't believe he was capable of killing anyone.

I glanced at Kefnir in the shadows.

"Ikaru has the protection of Vaiyene. I would ask you and your guards to treat him as such."

Kefnir stepped into the light. His eyes narrowed as he tilted his head and observed Ikaru. "Are you sure that's wise, Kilo?"

Ikaru was scared and without direction. Syrane and Shenrae were no different. They, too, would be struggling to find their purpose, their place in the world. If circumstances had been different, this could have been Syrane. Whatever circumstances this man had found himself in, they were what had driven him to be in the False Shadows. Not the desire to kill or to hurt.

"I will take full responsibility for him."

We needed him to trust us. Every ally we could turn to our side would be invaluable. Ikaru would be able to help us understand our enemy. Befriending him was the first step, but more than that, I wanted to give him a chance.

I walked Ikaru to the edge of the room. Kefnir didn't speak but paused before he pulled the door open, nodding to the guards on the other side. I breathed a sigh of relief and let go of Ikaru, nodding to reassure him Kefnir would uphold his end of the bargain. Ikaru took a step, stumbling on the first stair. He threw his arm out and caught himself, bracing his body against the wall before he forced his leg onto the next step.

Kefnir addressed the guard. "Lead him upstairs and provide him with food and water."

I started after Ikaru and the guard, but Kefnir threw his arm out to stop me. His palm hit against the stone wall. "I don't like to be undermined."

He clenched his jaw as he fixed his eyes on me. There was anger behind his calm demeanor.

I held his gaze. "I understand. However, I won't forsake what I believe. That man that *boy* was scared, and we both knew it. Intimidation will make him hate you." I watched Ikaru's hobbled journey up the steps, still seeing Syrane in his place. "I have a feeling intimidation is what's driven him to be where he is today. Kindness can go a long way."

At the very least, I would provide him with safety before he made his own choice about the False Shadows. Or before he was no longer able to. Kefnir removed his arm from my path, the edge of his lip twitching. "My brother was right about you. The Shadows are an interesting group. Different than most. I hope you're able to maintain your idealism in this new world. God knows we need it."

I followed after Kefnir, steadying myself against the wall.

It was a changing world, one where the consequences of our actions would be invisible to most people. Though I felt grounded in who I was, the thin line between right and wrong weighed on my mind. One misdeed could affect all of us. Not only the Shadows but all those who lived across Kiriku. We needed to keep our eyes unclouded and seek the truth.

And that started with Ikaru.

Chapter ten
IKARU

"The False Shadows," I said, leaning one arm on the table, "what is their purpose?"

Ikaru broke off a piece of bread and sighed before he met my gaze. "I will answer your questions, but first I must warn you. Word of my capture will spread. Hitori will do whatever it takes to make sure I don't have the opportunity to talk." His eyes shifted to the door. "I wouldn't be surprised if a group is already on their way."

I exchanged a glance with Kefnir, who shrugged. "My men are patrolling the area as we speak. If the False Shadows are coming, we'll know."

I turned back to Ikaru, forcing myself to be patient. "We're not afraid of the False Shadows."

"You should be."

He didn't know who we were, and already he doubted our abilities. I swallowed my anger. My ego did not depend on a boy's impression.

I kept my voice even. "Who are the False Shadows, Ikaru?"

Ikaru took a bitter gulp from his mug and set it down sharply, the liquid sloshing inside. "The False Shadows are a group of people whose sole purpose is to cause ruin across Kiriku."

His response was almost comedic.

The thoughts of a boy.

"Why?"

"To draw the attention of the Shadows."

My pulse pounded in my ears, the anticipation drowning out everything around me. Nothing mattered but Ikaru and me.

"What are the False Shadows trying to hide?"

Ikaru hesitated, and Kefnir's fingers inched toward the dagger at his side. His patience was running out.

"A dangerous ability."

I looked over at Kefnir. He seemed skeptical.

"What kind of ability?"

I thought back to Leiko and the female False Shadow, the one who had given me information about the False Shadows. The flaming arrows—I never had figured out what they were.

Were they related to this "dangerous ability"?

Ikaru still hesitated, and I shifted, my mind following the thread. "Back in Leiko, there was a woman, a False Shadow, who used arrows whose flames were an illusion. Some of the arrows did real damage, but not hers."

Ikaru let out a breath and swirled the mug in his hands. "We call it the Skills. It's the power of deception as well as the manipulation of energy."

Even as someone who had witnessed the Skills firsthand, Ikaru's description sounded convoluted at best.

But it was something.

Kefnir pushed away from the table and stood up, his arms crossing over his chest. "Show me."

Ikaru glanced at me, alarmed.

I shrugged. "I'm curious to see myself."

I moved away from the table and stood next to Kefnir, not sure what to expect. Ikaru didn't have an arrow. Were there other ways to use the Skills?

"There's no precise methodology," Ikaru said as he walked away from the table, mug still in hand. "We're still learning how to use the Skills."

I wanted to tell him to get on with it, but diplomacy held my tongue. "Whatever you're capable of is fine."

Ikaru nodded and focused his attention on the mug in his hand. We stood in silence until I noticed a small change. The metal handle began to glow. It was dull at first, but the light soon grew in intensity. Ikaru's breathing became slow and rhythmic. His muscles relaxed as he channeled this mysterious power. The Skills seemed to have a calming effect on him.

"Now fire," Kefnir said, his voice low but commanding. I jabbed him in the ribs to keep him from breaking Ikaru's focus. A small flame flickered to life, growing inside the mug with rapid speed. When the fire grew as big as a man's head, Ikaru took his other hand and placed it into the flames.

I moved my hand into the fire, and the flames bent around my fingers. It put off no heat, and yet it was indistinguishable from a real fire—at least by sight.

Kefnir stuck his hand into the flame. "Remarkable."

Dangerous.

With the False Shadows' quest for vengeance against Vaiyene, how long would it be before they would use it against us? I glanced over at Kefnir. How long before they came for Tarahn? I frowned, watching as Ikaru allowed the flame to sputter and die. What else could this power do? It couldn't only be an illusion. No, there was something much darker to this power. Why else hide it? Instincts warned me the False Shadows were distracting us for a reason.

If that really was their purpose.

Kefnir crossed to the window, his gaze focused on the town outside. "How long have the False Shadows possessed this power?"

Ikaru put the mug on the table. "Not long. A short time before the False Shadows were formed."

A season, maybe less.

"We need to act now," I said. Before the power was misused. I withdrew a thin map from the folds of my robe, spreading it onto the table. "Where are the False Shadows? Who is their leader?"

Ikaru walked to my side and inspected the map, pointing to a town bordering the gulf. "Hitori will be at Leiko when the moon is full."

Hitori—the leader of the False Shadows. Ikaru feared her, as he did the False Shadows. I refolded the map and returned it to my robe, ignoring Kefnir's eyes upon me. The name mattered little to me. The journey to the gulf would be at least a four-day ride, if not five, which left little time to prepare.

"Under the circumstances, it would be best if you were to accompany me, Ikaru," I said, turning to him. The color drained from his face. "I can protect you from Hitori, but I will need your cooperation and knowledge."

Ikaru stiffened, his eyes scanning the windows and the doors. His eyes were distant when they returned to me.

"You don't know what she is capable of."

The hollowness in his voice stirred a rage inside me.

I didn't know Hitori, but the fear inside Ikaru sickened me. Not Ikaru's fear, but the master who controlled the False Shadows. How many of the other False Shadows were afraid to stay true to their own beliefs because Hitori held power over them?

Kefnir's eyes trailed me as I paced the room to regain control over my emotions. Even Shenrae and Syrane, children of Shadows, would hesitate to follow me into enemy territory.

Kefnir returned to the table and sat down, leaning back against the wooden chair. "What has been your role in this, Ikaru? What have you gained from the False Shadows?"

"My life."

Ikaru's face showed no emotion, his manner was once more withdrawn. He traced his finger over the edge of his mug. "It's the same for most of the 'False Shadows,' as you call them. She knows our weaknesses. We have no choice in the matter, so we do what we must."

I pushed my fingers against the bridge of my nose.

Blackmail. Threatening the lives of those you cared for, threatening one's own life—there were countless ways to take a man's life away from him. No wonder he feared Hitori.

Kefnir moved to the end of the hall and summoned a guard, then returned to speak to Ikaru. "Phantom Kilo and I need to discuss a few matters. Stay here and don't go into town."

Ikaru nodded as he sank down into a chair. "I understand."

Kefnir left the hall but guilt stayed my departure. Ikaru was surrounded by horror and anger, and yet he refused to be like the other False Shadows. The will to live stirred inside him. If he could overcome his fear, he would be able to stand against Hitori and end her power over him.

Someday, I hoped to free him from that fear.

I clapped Ikaru on the shoulder. "You should be proud of the courage you displayed today. I promise you, I will put a stop to Hitori."

Ikaru didn't respond to my words, but his melancholy would pass. The longer he stayed away from Hitori, the better. In Tarahn, Kefnir would be able to look after him. I wouldn't force him to follow me. Enough people had been telling him what to do.

Whatever he chose to do this time, the choice was his own.

I had given that sliver of hope back to him.

———

Kefnir stretched out on a stone bench, lying upon his back. His eyes focused on the clouds overhead. "What brought you to Tarahn? It was no coincidence you came when you did."

Water trickled over a small waterwheel. I inhaled, catching the light fragrance of lavender from the bush growing beside the stream. The slow trickle of the water soothed me.

Was it only today I had arrived in Tarahn?

I rubbed the back of my neck, easing the tension from my shoulders. "Vaiyene was attacked by False Shadows. They set the fields and our homes on fire."

Upon my arrival, I had worried about what kind of man Kefnir would be, but he seemed a reasonable man. From what I'd seen of his town, his capabilities of providing aid were substantial. His honesty and open nature would make asking for supplies an easy matter.

Kefnir pushed himself onto his arms.

Weariness coursed through my veins, and I sank down onto a stone bench next to Kefnir.

"They burned most of our crops and food reserves." I plucked a leaf from the bushes beside me and twisted it in my fingers. Were the leaves in Vaiyene gone now? I let the blade go, watching it fall to the ground.

"We lost many people, and I fear, even with rationing, we will not survive the winter. Phantoms Lunia and Asdar are rebuilding quarters for the people to live in, as well as training more Shadows. My charge is to find provisions for our people."

"When do the mountain passes close?" Kefnir swung his legs over the bench and rested his elbows on his knees. "It has to be soon."

Unpredictable mountain weather made estimations tricky.

"A couple of weeks before the snowfall," I said, hoping my approximations were correct. "Another to make it impassable by cart."

"Tarahn's harvest was plentiful this year. We will be able to provide what you need. In addition to food, we also have a rich supply of furs and oil. Would that be sufficient?"

I breathed a sigh of relief, crossing my hand over my chest, but before I could finish, Kefnir waved his hands at me.

"No formalities."

A twitch of amusement pulled at the corners of my mouth.

"I've been beaten to death with it growing up. Even my brother is a stickler for it. I've tried explaining it to him, but"— he shrugged—'habits are habits'."

I chuckled at his frustration, suspecting General Mirai knew how much titles and courtesies annoyed him. Which reminded me. "You wouldn't happen to have some paintbrushes, would you?"

Kefnir raised an eyebrow at me.

"I have a little sister who was devastated after the fires. It would mean a lot to her if I returned with replacements for her brushes."

A smile spread across Kefnir's face. "I'm sure we can find something in town to brighten her spirits." Then he chuckled, fixing me with a considering gaze. "So, even a Phantom worries about such matters."

I met his smile. "Even a Phantom."

"When will you leave?"

I inhaled another deep breath of lavender, taking a moment to assess my own capabilities. Time was limited, but I was at my limits.

"Tomorrow, before nightfall." I could afford one night to clear my mind and the day to prepare. If Hitori would be in Leiko, I could not miss the opportunity.

I was looking forward to meeting her.

chapter eleven
LEIKO

On the edge of Leiko, I stripped down to my inner robe and wound a piece of cloth around the bond on my forearm. My leather armor was snug against my skin. While not the perfect disguise, it would allow me to blend in at the local marketplace and overhear any gossip about Hitori and the False Shadows without drawing too much attention.

Last time, I'd been welcomed as a Shadow. I wasn't sure how I would be received this time. It was not too long ago the False Shadows had appeared, but already I tired of following them.

But today I would find their leader.

One step closer to putting an end to all of this.

I wrinkled my nose; even this far from the docks the stink of fish hung heavy in the frigid air. The smell clung to my clothing and penetrated my skin. I held Nightwind's reins as we walked down the wet, muddy streets until the ground became stone.

White canopies lined the streets. Vendors called out their offerings as people bustled about with baskets and carts. As in Tarahn, the people parted at Nightwind's approach, and I stroked the black stallion's neck, grateful for his company and size. I leaned back against Nightwind's side as two kids barreled past me, swinging sticks in their hands. They stopped a few paces away from me, and the boy lunged at the girl. She clacked her stick against his, giggling and making quite a show of mock swordsmanship. From the other side of the marketplace, another child ran toward them a black cloth draped over his head. He brandished a stick, and they scattered, squealing in mock fright.

"The Shadows are coming! Run!"

A shiver crawled up my spine. Were the Shadows a game amongst children? All the years of training, all the hard work, and pain, all the Shadows who had given their lives to protect peace— all of it for nothing. I swallowed my bitterness and reminded myself: not all people feared us. General Mirai and his brother both saw merit in the Shadows. They believed in us and continued to trust us. Still, the game disturbed me. If I didn't find some way to put an end to the False Shadows, the children's game—their fear—would spread.

It was enough to make me question myself.

Would I ever be able to repair the damage?

Even if somehow, I managed to remove Hitori from power and put a stop to the False Shadows, would we be able to regain the respect we had lost?

In Vaiyene, children also pretended to be Shadows, but they did so out of admiration. This was a mockery.

My weariness grew, and I sought out a quieter place in the marketplace. I avoided eye contact with as many people as I could. The lie they lived grated against my mind. They were being tricked, manipulated, and their hate misdirected. Could they not see it?

The children's screams rattled me. Even as they disappeared into the crowd, their mirth continued to echo inside me. All this had begun outside of my control—with Phantom Kural's foolishness. But I had forgiven him for his failure. I'd become a

Phantom and accepted the duty to right my predecessor's wrongs. Holding onto my anger did nothing but cloud my judgement.

I breathed in and brushed the anger from my mind.

My eyes trailed over intricate metal workings, dried herbs, and an assortment of glassware in the marketplace. A few tables down from where Nightwind and I browsed was a vendor specializing in clothing and fabric accessories. I picked up one of the tunics. The quality surprised me. The fibers were soft like rabbit's fur, much different than my functional, often scratchy, Shadow garb.

I selected an indigo robe and exchanged coins with the woman. Back in Vaiyene, the Phantoms sponsored individuals, giving them a sort of allowance for their daily tasks. Silver coins were given to Shadows upon acceptance into the ranks. Our people did not have much need for more than what our people created, and if they did, the Phantoms and Shadows secured the transaction through trade or exchange of coin in the neighboring towns. Vaiyene's coins were different than the ones they used in Leiko, but I carried a collection of all currencies.

"A perfect choice, sir," the grey-haired woman said, pointing at the color. "It goes well with your eyes."

She seemed kind. I could imagine her sitting in front of the fireplace, spinning the thread and cutting intricate patterns for her clothing. Her passion lay in creating beautiful garments, and it showed. I wouldn't hesitate to sponsor her as a seamstress.

I put my arms through the tunic. The sleeves were long, baggy even, but it made me appear more like the people of Leiko. It also added an extra layer to conceal my bond. I meandered to the next booth, bending to look at an assortment of wooden flutes. In the booth adjacent were paper kites modeled after various fish from the gulf. I picked one up, inspecting the details of the fins and protruding eyes. Finae would have loved these. But something so delicate would be destroyed as I traveled.

The marketplace showed how much Vaiyene could grow. We were content as we were, but once I ensured safety for our people, I hoped to expand Vaiyene's economy and bring a new era of prosperity. Being forced to leave Vaiyene and travel did give some insight into certain possibilities.

The False Shadows had opened my eyes in that regard.

I stopped before a table laden with an assortment of blades. The vendor, an older man with a long, scruffy beard, shuffled over to me. Deep wrinkles cut into his face around his mouth, and his mud-brown eyes were sunk deep into his face.

Hard times had left their mark.

His eyes focused on me, and when I went to pick up a blade, he jumped at me and caught my arm. He pushed up the sleeve and bandage around my forearm to expose my bond.

He smiled, revealing a missing tooth. "That's quite the craftsmanship you have there."

I yanked my arm away from him and looked around to see if anyone had noticed. People moved about their business. I returned my attention to the man, pulling down my sleeve to cover my bond. He must have caught a glint of my bond when I put the robe on.

I was about to walk away from him when he spoke.

"It's like the ones I make."

He picked up a blade and a sharpening stone, seemingly pleased he had regained my attention. The man struck me as eccentric and entitled. Never a good combination. I pulled Nightwind's reins, blocking myself and the man from people's view.

I leaned closer to him and said in a low voice, "What do you know about the Shadows?" I kept my hand at my side, poised to grab my staff if necessary.

The man's grin spread. "I know there are a lot of people pretending to be one these days." He looked at me a moment, then declared more loudly than necessary, "You're not one of the pretenders."

I kept my emotions in check, but my heart quickened.

Who was this man and what did he want?

The man's voice dipped, causing me to lean in. "I've been commissioned to make those whatcha-ma-call-its on your arm there for Shadows, though I have to admit, the design on yours is much more intricate than the ones I make."

He seemed happy to ramble to himself about matters. He scratched his beard and kept his eyes on me. "Are you here to find the ones pretending to be you? They haven't arrived."

He knew too much.

It was risky talking to him in such a public place, but if I tried to remove him, I had a hunch he would make me regret it. I checked the booths closest to us. The marketplace seemed too loud for anyone to hear our conversation—unless he yelled again. I gambled on his knowledge being worth my time.

"What else do you know?"

The old man dug his finger into his ear. "You'll have to be more specific, son. I know a lot about a lot of things."

I resisted the urge to indulge him and prolong his self-ramblings. He'd already informed me Hitori, and her False Shadows were not in the town. I hesitated. But what if he knew more?

The old man began nodding his head, his focus on me while he rolled a strand of hair between two fingers. "I have many years of experience. My father taught me how to smith, and his father taught him. Lots of work goes into each one."

Picking up one of his blades, I turned it over in my hand. The silver material seemed similar to my bond.

Who was this man?

"Is there a specific place where you get your materials? I'm sure an exquisite blacksmith like yourself uses only the highest quality metals."

"Quality metal is of highest concern."

This was worse than talking to a child. I stifled my annoyance and waited for him to continue. I set down the knife as the man blew air from his lungs.

"I can't tell you that. A blacksmith is as good as his metal."

He seemed almost outraged at my request, yet tickled enough to continue our conversation. My tolerance of him waned. I met all kinds on my Shadow missions, but this man was…unique.

"If I told you where to find it, everyone would be making them. It requires certain procedures to be put into place, certain qualities that need to be preserved or else the whole thing doesn't work. I traveled a long way to find it. In old ruins, far away from everyone. Don't think many go there..."

I left as the man started descending deeper into his madness. I didn't have time to sort through his ramblings.

"They should be here soon!" the man yelled after me, realizing that Nightwind and I were no longer in the front of his booth. When I didn't acknowledge him, he shouted even louder.

"The people you're looking for should be here soon!"

I gave a few curt nods, excusing Nightwind and myself from people's paths as they turned, trying to find the source of the commotion. I cursed him under my breath as we left the marketplace. If he were sane, I would have asked who commissioned him to make the bonds, but I already suspected it was Hitori.

Who else could it be but the False Shadows?

The specific type of metal he used interested me. Why would the bonds he created need to be made of a particular metal? Wouldn't any silver metal do? It was the ramblings of an aging mind, but the detail intrigued me. He knew valuable information, but I didn't have the patience to deal with him further. Mia could have coaxed it out of him. Her quick mind—or Zavi's—would have tricked it out of the man. They were a great team.

I sighed and pushed a touch of sadness away.

Nothing seemed out of place in Leiko. In fact, it seemed a level of calm had settled over the town. The fishermen on the boats were out in the gulf, the marketplace bustled with business, and everyone seemed to have their job to tend to. I turned down the street to where I had met the False Shadow. Where the woman with the fire arrows that were not real.

The twisted outline of the forest came into view.

I stopped.

Hitori had not even had to create a place where people wouldn't go; they had already done it themselves. I turned my feet in the opposite direction, walking alongside the ocean's shore, away from the town and its people. The chatter of crowds turned into the crash of waves, and the familiar unsettling feeling came over me as I drew closer to the forest's edge.

An innate sense that something was wrong.

The memory of Phantom Kural cutting the head from the False Shadow sullied my perception. It hadn't been right for him to do so, but I now understood his position. Being a Phantom was not an easy burden.

I left Nightwind inside the entrance of the forest, draping his reins over a low tree branch. If it were possible for him to come with me, without making noise, I would have taken him.

The sunlight dimmed as I picked my way over roots and fallen trees, and I lit my canteen at my side. Overhead, birds fluttered, beating their wings as they moved from one tree to the other. The atmosphere remained dark, but knowing animals did not avoid this place lessened my unease.

Trees bent away from the main road, and I glanced up, surprised to see a thin lining between the tree limbs—as if the branches themselves did not want to touch one another. A mangled tree, twisted in gruesome curves, blocked my path. It was large, wider than my arm span and had deep cracks in its bark. Its limbs were finger-like.

My foot caught as I approached, and I tripped. I steadied myself against the trunk. A white mist dissipated at my touch.

The Skills?

I glanced down. What I'd tripped over was no tree root; it was soft and husky. I bent down and ran my hands over the loose dirt. A piece of canvas stuck up through the earth. I pulled on the edges.

It didn't budge.

I moved some of the dirt away, piling it to the side, then I planted my feet and heaved. A portion came free. I kicked more dirt away and gave one final pull. The sack came loose from the ground. The bag was almost as tall as I was.

I bent down and placed a dagger against the fibers, splitting open the sack and recoiling as I did so.

A human corpse stared back at me.

Wrinkles were creased in his forehead, and his mouth hung open in a strangled scream. At the corners of his mouth, maggots weaved in and out of small holes, gnawing on the rotting flesh. I looked away, bile rising in my throat.

What had Ikaru not told me?

When I regained my composure, I scanned the surrounding area, my chest tight. None of the dirt seemed packed. A sense of dread settled in my stomach, and I swallowed, my hands trembling as I knelt to the ground. I brushed aside leaves. It wasn't long before I uncovered another canvas sack. I pulled it free from the earth. The size and weight of the bag were equal to the first. Another person lay inside. I didn't need to open it to know. However, answers might lie hidden inside. Holding my breath, I sliced through the fibers. Another man. His face, too, was frozen in terror.

It was the same as Mashin.

A massacre of innocent people.

I sliced open another bag—another man, his face formed into a grimace. I unearthed another—a young woman. When I pulled the fifth bag from the earth, resolve left me and I fell to the ground beside the small cloth burden. It was not even half the size of the others. Inside was a little girl, her eyes frozen in agony.

What horror had these people seen?

I calmed my racing heart, each strangled breath a reminder that I possessed the power to stop whoever had done this. The girl couldn't have been older than seven summers. I tried not to think about what had happened to her family—or if any of the people I had unearthed were her family.

I started to close the sack, then noticed something glistening. I reached a hesitant hand inside and pushed the bag away from the girl's arm.

A bond was wrapped around her right forearm.

Why?

If the bonds were supposed to make the False Shadows look like Shadows, Hitori should have known a child would never have been allowed to join the Shadow ranks.

I laid the child back down and stood, at a loss.

There was nothing I could do for them.

I feared they would never find rest here, but I couldn't move them without raising the townspeople's suspicions. I could not afford to bring more doubt to the Shadow name. There was nothing I could do for them. They would be buried and forgotten.

My heart grew numb, my mind protecting itself from the pain. Hitori's actions held no purpose, no justice, and no sense of honor. She killed without thinking. How could one stop such a person?

My focus drifted to the tree, and I maneuvered my feet through bodies half-hidden amongst the forest floor. I avoided the patches of soil that seemed loose and disturbed.

I needed a moment to think and assess.

When my back touched the tree, the ground quaked beneath me, and I struggled to keep my focus on anything. My vision became too blurry to pick out detail in the darkness. I squinted, the vague outlines of trees coming back into shape. The corpses I'd dug up had disappeared. In their places were holes, dozens of them, if not hundreds. I peered into one of them, expecting to see bodies, but the hole had no end.

I took a step back, trying to navigate the crumbling earth.

A bloodcurdling scream echoed through the forest, and I covered my ears with my hands, squeezing my eyes shut. Even so, the scream shook me. When at last it faded, I removed my hands and found them shaking. Terrible pain in my chest squeezed my heart, making it difficult to breathe. A figure, whose face I could not see, dragged the girl—the same one from the cloth sack—near the base of the gnarled tree. I tried to reach her, but for every span of distance I covered, I came no closer.

The figure threw a man to the ground. The man hugged the girl, yelling words I couldn't hear. Over and over the figure shouted, and over and over the man pleaded, until finally, the person held a blade to the girl's neck. The man stopped his pleading and held out his hands, a white mist spiraling from them. His hands became blackened, and another figure stepped forward, placing a bond upon the man's arm. The skin of the man no longer turned black, and the mist he called forth rose around him, gaining in strength and force. Trees swayed as a strong breeze howled overhead. The wind whipped at my face, and I threw up my arms to protect myself as a tree crashed. It shook the ground and scattered leaves and fragments of wood in all directions. I stumbled, losing my footing as a scream pierced my heart. I fell and withdrew my fingers from the bark, coming back into my mind with a start.

I shuddered at the memory, staggering away from the tree.

It was a memory—I was sure of it—but how was that possible?

I drew in a ragged breath, rubbing my fingers together. A thick red substance coated my fingertips. Sap? I smelled the sticky resin. There was a distinct scent of iron, similar to blood. I wiped the material on my cloak and backed away further, grasping the folds of the robe by my chest. The grip of terror had seemed so real like the one screaming had been me. My vision unfocused, and I blinked, staring at the leaves and dirt and…dead bodies.

I averted my gaze, regretting my decision.

There was no peace to be found in this place.

I struggled to breathe against my tightened chest and closed my eyes, blocking out my surroundings and escaping inward. Not even the birds' calls were welcome to me now. I sought the memory of my friends, of Zavi and Mia. Though they were gone, our experiences together always grounded me when peace was out of reach. I turned my hand over to look at the mark we had branded into ourselves during our first Shadow mission.

Something cracked in the forest, drawing me back to reality, tearing me from my heart's desire. I reached for my staff and backed up, wanting to take the fight away from the gnarled tree. Whatever power it held—if it really was infused with the Skills—I needed to protect its memories. If I could assess the memories, I could find out what had happened here.

Phantom Kural was dead, but the consequences of his actions remained. Defeating the False Shadows and Hitori would be easier if I knew what the original offense was.

If this tree could tell me…

Movement in my peripheral vision awakened my instincts, and I pivoted on my foot. The snap of a tree branch confirmed I was not alone. I swung my staff, meeting my attacker's sword. I sidestepped and disengaged, seeing another person emerge from the trees.

Dual combat had never been my strong point.

I watched the man from afar. He looked down at the ground, picking his way over the bodies. It was the advantage I needed. I sprang to the left, rushing the man as he stepped over a body. His footing was uneven; one foot was upon a root, the other on unsteady dirt. I thrust my staff at him, and he attempted to block it, but he could not bring his sword up in time. I struck him, and he fell over the root. He scrambled away, limping as he pushed himself up. I held my staff near the center of my body and twirled it, lashing out at both my opponents to keep them at a distance. A third figure, shorter than the other two, walked into the clearing.

Was one of them Hitori?

"I want him dead. Now." The last person said.

They seemed likely the leader.

Before I could figure out if my assumptions were correct, two more False Shadows came from the forest. Swords were in their hands. A soft glow came from the exposed bonds upon their arms. The hair on the back of my neck rose.

Were they going to use the Skills against me?

Ikaru had not mentioned different uses for the Skills, nor had he alluded to the extent to which the False Shadows could use the power. He seemed frightened of their abilities, but did I stand a chance against them?

I shifted onto one foot, twisting my torso as I brought my staff over my head, sweeping at the man closest to me. He fell to the ground, and I slid my staff back, jabbing behind me to catch the other man's hand. He recoiled, almost dropping his sword. I turned to face the woman. Near her, the sword in the man's hands glowed.

A red hue circled the blade.

The sword looked normal, but the hint of red made me uneasy.

I glanced behind me.

Two people closed in from opposite sides.

The woman stood back, her arms crossed over her chest. She held no weapon. One was either concealed, or she preferred others to do her fighting. There was a possibility she could not fight herself, though I found it hard to believe Ikaru would fear someone afraid of getting their hands bloody. I sprang into action, twisting my staff over my head, keeping the men at a distance. They closed in around me. I needed to give myself more room. The man on the right seemed unsure how to fight against me, and I pressed my advantage. He swung at my staff with his sword, and I blocked him.

A novice mistake.

I thrust low and broke his ankle.

The first rule of combat taught in Shadow training was to strike your opponent, not their weapon. The second rule was to strike where you could disable. If this had been a one-on-one battle, knocking the man's sword from his hand would have been sufficient enough to disable him.

Fighting for one's life changed the stakes.

I drew in a deep breath, slowing my heartbeat as I turned my attention to the remaining three. Two moved back, and the one with the glowing sword advanced. I didn't question their reasoning. I swung my staff, and the man brought his sword up to meet it. His sword sliced through my staff.

I withdrew.

How was that possible? The blade should have cut into the staff, not broken it. Certainly not sliced through solid wood. I remembered the fire on the arrows and the red hue around the man's sword. Fire?

I shifted my weight between my feet. I needed to fight the False Shadow without connecting with his blade. Which meant I couldn't defend. I needed another angle and fast. I scanned the area, my eyes locking onto the sword next to the man whose ankle I'd broken. Panic gripped me, but I forced it down. There was no other way. I thrust my staff into the holder on my back and snatched the sword up, running into the forest. My fingers tightened around the hilt of the blade.

A memory of blood flashed before my eyes.

Swords did too much damage, but if there was no other weapon I could use against this man...so be it. Regret would not kill me. People were counting on me to protect them, and I would not compromise their safety because of my aversion to the blade's killing edge.

The man using the Skills chased after me, and I leapt over a fallen tree. When my foot landed on the ground, I used the momentum from my jump to swing the sword around with both hands. The man's eyes widened, and he stumbled, stopping before the tree. He barely brought his sword in front of his chest to block me. I disengaged, lashing out at his knee. He swung his sword to meet mine, sliding his blade up my sword's shaft close to the hilt.

The heat from the blade singed my skin.

He was burlier than I, with broad shoulders and more mass. It gave him more strength behind his attack, but he couldn't cut through the sword's metal. The Skills didn't seem to affect the sword as they had my staff, but he still needed to be kept at a distance. Already my hand blistered at the sword's proximity.

If I could defend myself, I could survive.

Survival was all that mattered.

The other two men appeared in the distance, and I lowered my sword, holding it out to the side as I ran deeper into the forest. The chase would create distance and allow me to fight them individually. I kept my eyes on where I was going, trusting my feet to adjust to each obstacle. I weaved through the forest trees, jumping over rocks and squeezing through narrow gaps in the forest. I chose the quickest route, not the easiest. When I found a dense, overgrown place in the forest, I stopped and rested. I took deep breaths to regain control of my breathing. Other than the wind overhead, I heard nothing. Experience had taught me to stay cautious even when the danger had seemingly disappeared. I continued on, though not as quick as before. A short distance away I found a better location. One where I could hide. I parted the branches of a thick grove of trees and slipped inside, ducking down.

There I waited.

Moments passed, and my breathing returned to normal.

A shift in the leaves caught my attention. The forest was too quiet for anyone to sneak through it. I held my breath as tree branches shuffled behind me. A boot stepped close to my hiding spot. I lunged at the person, grabbing his legs and knocking him to the ground. He dropped his sword into the dirt next to me, breaking his fall with his hands. I scrambled on top of him and used my weight to pin him to the ground; his sword in my hand.

"Don't move," I said, pushing the flat of the sword against the back of his neck. I eased off the pressure, and he coughed for air, turning his head to the side. He struggled, spitting out a mouthful of leaves. His eyes flicked behind me, and I rolled away, ducking under an arrow shot at my back.

I scrambled to my feet. "Tell your friend not to release another arrow, or I'll kill you."

A mocking smile spread across the man's face. "You wouldn't kill a person, would you?" A trickle of blood ran down his neck where I'd held the blade.

He didn't seem bothered by it.

The sword grew heavy as my heart did in my chest. The False Shadows knew how to defeat us. The Shadow's Creed was my greatest weakness. His mocking smile sickened me, and I gripped the sword tighter. I took a breath and smiled, regaining my focus.

"You're right; I won't."

I threw the sword to the side, grabbing my dagger and throwing it at the archer upon the rock. In an instant, I'd drawn my staff and rammed it against the man's head. He fell unconscious as an arrow embedded itself into my shoulder. The tip pierced my leather armor, and I ducked to the ground, picking up a rock before I scrambled up the hill. Before the man could nock another arrow, I threw the rock at his head. The man dodged, and I slammed against him, falling on top of him. The arrow embedded itself deeper into my arm. I ignored it and put my hands around the man's neck. I pushed harder, and he gritted his teeth. His face turned a sickly blue. I released him, standing up and kicking his weapons over the edge of the rocks. These False Shadows were far more persistent and skilled than the ones I had encountered before.

Hitori must keep those loyal and strongest at her side.

I pulled the arrow from my shoulder and turned to see the man reaching into the folds of his cloak. I stomped on his hand, eliciting a cry from him. A small black pill rolled from his hands.

Was his will to live so little?

It sickened me.

They might pretend to be Shadows, but they were nothing like us. A Shadow owned their failures with honor and worked to right them. I pressed my boot into the center of his chest. "If you want to die, at least make your life worth something."

I reached down and pulled the hood from the man's face, surprised to find he was much younger than I'd imagined him to be. A scar ran from the top of his face down to his chin.

"I've taken one of your comrades into my protection," I said, trying to gain a feel for his thoughts on being in the False Shadows.

The man spat on the ground.

"What reason do you have to help your enemy?" A toothy smile spread across his face. "You're as weak as your morals."

His words stirred something in me, confirming my previous feelings about the Shadow's Creed being a weakness in their eyes. However, I refused to sink to his level. He was defeated, and I would not kill an unarmed man—no matter how arrogant he might be. I would not fail like Phantom Kural had before my Phantom duty ended. Even if this man didn't listen to reason.

"You may feel that you are giving your life up for a noble cause, but let me tell you, what you are doing is in vain," I said, keeping my voice flat from emotion. "You're nothing but a tool in the grander scheme. One your leader is too cowardly to pursue alongside you."

The man's eyes narrowed, but he said nothing.

"Your leader does not even fight amongst you but instead commands you like a frightened child. Tell me, what worth do you find in a leader who refuses to fight with you?"

"She's more of a leader than you'll ever be," the man responded. "Unlike you, she has a spine."

He lunged at me, and I jammed my staff against the side of his head. He was nothing but a fool set on the illusion of a noble cause. I was even more curious to meet this Hitori woman. If she could convince fools to give their lives for her, I wanted to judge her worth for myself, though she already did not have my respect. A leader who refused to fight alongside their men was no leader.

"Do what you will," I said, leaving the man. If he crawled back to Hitori, so be it.

I turned in the opposite direction, back to the area with the dead bodies and where I thought Hitori to be. At least, I thought it was the same direction. Gaining my bearings in this forest was impossible. Even the damned forest, without sunlight and warmth, shredded my composure. Of all the people who could have impersonated the Shadows. Nothing but a coward. My vision wavered then, and I stumbled over a downed tree. The shapes of the trees melded together, and it became hard to distinguish one from another. I squinted my eyes and tripped over something on the ground. Someone shouted behind me, and I scrambled to my feet.

My hands began to sweat, and my heart beat with intense pain.

The arrow had been poisoned.

A crunch of leaves made me jump. I could no longer see anything in my peripheral vision. Sensing someone's presence, I swiped in an arc. The end of my staff smacked into something too hard to be human. I tried to pull back, but a hand caught the end.

"Call to your horse. There's little time." The pressure released from my staff and the dark blur of an outline moved. Someone pushed something into my hand. "Drink this."

When I didn't move quick enough, the same person took the vial from my hands and pressed it to my lips. I hesitated, then drained the contents, a dribble of liquid sliding down my chin. There was little point in poisoning an already poisoned man.

"Who are you?" I sputtered.

A fog on my mind disoriented me.

"Someone tired of saving your life." The woman dropped something into my pocket. "Drink this when you wake up next. You're going to need it."

I heard her words and tried to engrave them into my memory, but her voice already became distant. The poison had taken hold of me. She shoved me headlong, and I almost dropped my staff, stumbling as my feet plunged into a stream. I had not heard the trickle of water.

"Follow the stream," she said as she left. "I need to lead them away."

"Wait—" I turned, but I knew she was gone.

My vision faded. Before, I'd been able to differentiate shapes, but now even colors were a blur. I placed my staff into the water and followed the edge of the stream. I whistled long and low, trusting that, whoever the woman was, she would have told me if it were not safe to do so. I faltered and fought to continue onward. My staff gave me some sense of progress, though I didn't know if I was moving away from or toward danger.

If the False Shadows found me now…

Something nudged against my back, and I whipped my head around. It was subtle, but I could make out a musky smell. I raised my hand, and the wet nose of a horse touched my fingers. I trailed my fingers down the horse's neck, fumbling at its reins.

"Nightwind?" He pushed his face against my chest. I groped for the stirrups, finding it an impossible feat to orient myself. Nightwind stood still, watching me with wide eyes. I imagined him laughing at my feeble attempts as his master would.

With utmost faith, and nothing less than a considerable amount of trust, I jumped onto the stallion. I slid my leg unceremoniously over his girth. I dug my hands into my saddlebag, cursing as my fingers brushed against everything but what I wanted. With much exasperation and with my last remaining thought of clarity, I pulled out a length of rope and tied one end around my torso and the other around the saddle.

Darkness edged into the reaches of my mind. I dropped the reins and wound my fingers into Nightwind's mane.

"Go home," I mumbled as the world faded into darkness.

chapter twelve
CONSEQUENCE OF ACTION

Garbled noises in the distance disorientated the world around me. A rhythmic rocking made it hard to gain any semblance of balance. I opened my eyes, my vision a slurry of blurred colors. Shapes moved past me. I was moving then but to where? I brushed my hands over short hair smelling of musk.

It calmed me, like a familiar scent welcoming me home.

My fumbling fingers found a rope tied around my chest. I tried to move my body without success. It seemed the knot had been tied while I was in a state of impairment. Knot tying was a fundamental Shadow skill. This could not even be considered a knot.

The blurs of color became too much. I closed my eyes against the onslaught, inhaling the crisp morning air as I tried to steady the sloshing in my head.

At some point, I became aware of a voice upon the wind. I ignored it, trying to focus on figuring out where I was and what had happened, but the voice was incessant, and I focused on it.

It seemed important to do so.

The voice seemed familiar like I'd heard it recently.

"Kilo," the voice shouted again, "slow your horse!"

Hoofbeats mixed with Nightwind's rhythm. I turned my head, opening my eyes to see if my blurry vision had passed.

It had not.

Instinct reassured me this man was not an enemy. Despite not being able to see him, I placed my hand on Nightwind's neck and whispered, "Whoa, boy. Easy. This man is a friend."

My words came out cracked, but the muscles in the great steed's neck relaxed as he slowed his pace. He panted heavily, and guilt panged me. While I'd been unconscious, he had taken me to safety. Wherever safe was. "Thank you, friend." I couldn't tell if the thought was spoken or not, but I dutifully stroked Nightwind's neck to reaffirm the sentiment. The stallion came to a halt, and I wobbled in the saddle.

A hand steadied me.

"Why didn't you stop?" A man asked in an annoyed tone. I tried to form words, but my voice would not cooperate. The man tried again, his tone softer. "Do you know where you are?"

I licked my bloodied lips. "No, I can't see anything. I can't even recall who you are." My voice cracked. Even squinting, it was hard to make out the outline of a person before me. "I was poisoned."

The man swore and shouted orders to someone else. I pressed my hands against my head to try and dull the pain.

"You look as if death is upon you."

The voice clicked into place. There were only a few people who would talk to me like that. I didn't have much sense of time or direction, but I knew I was not in Vaiyene. The air smelled different.

"Kefnir?"

"Yes, it's me," he said rather shortly. He began tugging at the rope around my waist. "You're lucky one of my people saw you before your horse took you past the town. If he hadn't run to get me, we would never have been able to stop you. Even so, it was a mad chase to catch up to you."

I stiffened in the saddle as the ropes grew tight around me. I heard the ching of metal being drawn before I felt a dagger gnawing at my bonds.

"Remind me to ask you the next time I need something tied."

I chuckled to hide my growing panic. I must have blacked out from the poison on the outskirts of Leiko. It was a four-day ride to Tarahn. I was fortunate to have woken up at all.

With the straps cut, and my movement unrestricted, I started to sit up, then vomited over the side of the horse. I clutched the saddle as the world sloshed around.

"Take it slow. You've likely not moved in a while."

I groaned and eased my muscles from their stiffness. I sat up again, slower this time, and managed to keep the sickness at bay.

"I'm going to take you into town. Can you stay upright?"

"I think so."

I didn't know for sure, but it seemed the expected answer.

Nightwind walked slowly, then transitioned into a normal gait as Kefnir urged him on. I placed my hands on the stallion's neck for support. My head rattled as we neared the noise of town, and I found my grasp on reality slipping.

Kefnir touched my arm, and my head jerked up. "It's not too much farther. We're at the northern entrance so not many will see us."

I appreciated his words, but my mind couldn't form a picture of the town. It was an odd sensation, not being able to see. Humbling, considering Kefnir offered his aid without complaint. It was almost as if I could trust him like I would a friend

Nightwind plodded under me. I kept my eyes shut, knowing the motion and blurring colors would make me sick. If my vision did not return, I would not be a Phantom for long. I tried not to allow myself more thoughts on the matter. Thinking about what-ifs did nothing but bring unnecessary worry.

"Don't the Shadows often use poisons in their arsenal?" Kefnir asked, breaking the beginning of my downward spiral. I heaved a sigh of relief at the distraction.

"They do." I kept up with Kefnir's thinking, thankful for something else to concentrate on besides my misery.

"Would anyone in Vaiyene know of an antidote? Or be able to identify the exact poison?"

"It's no poison I know of, and I've studied and been exposed to many over the years. Any poison that causes blindness is usually a temporary effect. At least, the ones we use are."

The effect should have worn off by now.

I shook my head and continued, keeping my thoughts factual. "Besides, if it were one of the ones we use, the effects would be lessened. I have somewhat of a tolerance."

That part of Shadow training had not been fun.

"A pity. I hoped to expedite your recovery by sending for someone in Vaiyene." Kefnir sighed beside me and came to a stop. "I'll have one of my men look after your horse. Do you think you can walk?"

I took a steadying breath as I shifted one leg over the saddle. Kefnir put his hand under my elbow as I slid off Nightwind. My legs almost crumpled under me as I hit the ground. Kefir held me up until my legs found their strength. I tripped over a cobblestone, and Kefnir bore my full weight.

"I've meant to fix that. Sorry. I should have warned you."

I grunted; my throat still scratchy.

"We're in front of my house. There are two steps."

I tried to picture a house, but all I managed was the effort to keep my legs moving. I lifted my foot onto the first step and hefted myself up, then stepped onto the other. When we crossed the threshold, Kefnir led me a few paces more. The slight breeze and the sun's warmth left me.

We were inside then.

"You can recover in my room since it's on the bottom floor."

"Thank you. I didn't know when I met you I would be such an inconvenience."

Kefnir chuckled and removed my arm from his neck. "I'll let you rest on the bed. It'd probably be best if you stayed upright, at least for a while. We'll get some water and food into you before you sleep. If you think you can manage."

Kefnir placed his hands on my shoulders and guided me. "Back up a little bit. There you go. Now slowly. We don't want you losing any more fluids, especially not on the good rug."

My legs hit the edge of the bed, and I sat down. Every effort was excruciating. Kefnir began fussing with the laces of my boots. When he pulled them free, I dragged my legs up, and something fell from my pocket.

"What's this? It's some sort of vial."

I held out my hand, and Kefnir placed it into my palm. The surface was textured, with small bumps along the surface. I tried to recall how I'd come by it. Someone in Leiko had given it to me.

"I was given it before I lost consciousness." I opened my eyes for the first time since Kefnir had come to my rescue. I could just make out the shape of my hand, and the nuance of a vial. Kefnir's blob of an outline wavered beside me.

I let out a slow breath.

The world had stopped spinning.

"Do you think it's an antidote?" Kefnir asked.

I unstoppered the vial and raised it to my nose. There was a pungent, earthy smell to the mixture, with slight hints of charcoal. I swirled the liquid, the memory returning to me. The woman in the False Shadows had made me drink the same liquid in Leiko. If there was a chance I could regain my eyesight, I would take it.

I smirked. "Only one way to find out."

Before Kefnir could reply, I tipped the vial at my lips and drained the contents. I grimaced at the bitter concoction, becoming aware of the beating of my heart. I couldn't see Kefnir's face, but I imagined the look of horror that would be on it. That, for what it was worth, brought me some morbid respite.

If I was going to die, I did not want my last thoughts to be of how I had failed to protect Vaiyene.

Should I have given Kefnir a message to deliver if I did die? I shifted on the bed and stilled my mind, holding onto the Shadow duty that brought me comfort. I was strong for the people I protected. Blind or not, it would change nothing. Even if my sight did not return, I was still a Phantom and would serve my people. It was my duty after all.

Kefnir cleared his throat. "I'll get you some water. Would you like some food as well?"

"Water and food would be appreciated."

Kefnir's footsteps receded, and the sound of water trickling came from the other room. When his steps returned, I extended my hands, taking the mug. I curled my fingers around the surface and brought the cold liquid to my lips. I sipped it gingerly, cautious of taking in too much at once.

A tray of what smelled like fresh bread was placed on the bedside next to me. My stomach sickened at the thought of food. Kefnir scraped a chair across the wooden floor. His outline plopped down into it.

"Did you find anything in Leiko?"

An image of the young girl with the bond on her arm flashed before my eyes. Her contorted features and haunted eyes burned into my mind.

"I found bodies, Kefnir." I held onto the mug with both hands as the memory faded. "And a girl with a bond on her arm. Dead, of course."

There was no reply.

I wasn't sure if Kefnir waited for me to continue or not, but the images kept appearing before me. I reached for the bread to find something else to occupy my mind—even if vomiting was the alternative.

"I haven't heard anything about this." Kefnir bent over, his head sinking into what I imagined to be his hands.

I pressed my fingers into my temples and tried to remember what had happened. Vague snippets remained in my memory.

The bodies.

The gnarled tree.

The Skills.

None of which made any damn sense.

I slammed the mug down, and water splashed against my leg. "There's a reason the False Shadows are putting bonds on people. At first, I thought it was to impersonate us, but there's more to it."

It frustrated me that I couldn't see Kefnir. What was he thinking? Did he even believe what had happened? Without the ability to perceive how my words were interpreted, I felt naked in the conversation. If I could see one facial expression, I would feel more at ease. I drew in a breath. My thoughts made no sense to me, but maybe Ikaru could clarify what I'd seen.

"I'd like to speak with Ikaru. See if he can explain things." When Kefnir did not respond, my stomach sank. "What happened while I was away?"

Kefnir exhaled. "Shortly after you left, Ikaru snuck out. We still don't know how he accomplished it, but somehow he managed to slip my guards."

He had made his choice then. I had offered Ikaru sanctuary, but he had chosen to go back to Hitori. We had lost our one link to the False Shadows. There were questions I had not gotten to ask him.

A door creaked open, and a draft caused me to shudder. Heavy boots clopped across the wooden floor. Kefnir's blurred outline stood up to meet the newcomer. They conversed in hushed remarks. The newcomer left, leaving Kefnir standing before me.

"A letter came for you at the Kinshi Post."

I frowned. Anything sent to the Kinshi Post would be a desperate effort by the Phantoms to reach me. I took it from his hands and turned it over, running my fingers over the wax crest to confirm it was the Phantom's. Although Hitori could fabricate it. The Kinshi Post, however, was secure. As long as Kefnir's man was still his own, the information could be trusted.

I handed the letter back. "If you wouldn't mind."

The envelope crunched as Kefnir broke the seal.

"Return to Vaiyene. We believe the grain sent was poisoned. Your sister has fallen ill. Asdar."

I stopped breathing.

Finae had been poisoned?

And our people?

Of all the times to be in this useless, crippled state...

"What grain was he suspecting to be poisoned?"

A twinge of suspicion crept into my mind, but I dismissed it. Kefnir would never have poisoned the grain. It would have been easier to kill me than transport poisoned grain across Kiriku to Vaiyene. Besides, he would never involve innocents. He cared too much for his people to inflict pain on others.

One other person knew I had spoken with Kefnir in private. I kept the anxiety from my voice. "When did you send the grain to Vaiyene?"

"As soon as you left for Leiko."

"And when did Ikaru go missing?"

Kefnir swore and slammed his fist against a wooden surface, knocking something over that broke on the floor. It was a theory at this point, but Ikaru knew Kefnir and I had talked. If he had been able to slip away from Kefnir's guards, he could have spied on us—and I had offered him protection!

I needed to get home.

I stared into the flames and blinked, making out the details of the fire. Kefnir's face was not as blurry as it had been either. I swung my feet over the edge of the bed, and Kefir put his hand on my shoulder to stop me.

"You're in no condition to go anywhere."

"I must." I brushed his hand off my shoulder. "There's no time to sit around. It will take me almost three days to make it back to Vaiyene."

"Neither you nor your horse is capable of that journey. While I understand your sense of duty, Vaiyene would rather have a late Phantom than a dead one."

I dismissed his words and pushed myself onto my feet. "My sight is returning. I can heal on the way to Vaiyene."

I took a step, and my vision turned upside down. Kefnir steadied me and pushed me back against the bed. The antidote might have been working, but poison still weakened my body. Even my short attempt to stand had drained my energy.

I couldn't ride in this condition.

"I'll leave in the morning."

Kefnir grumbled under his breath. "If you wish to think you will be leaving, you are free to. I will make preparations regardless."

I looked over at the bread on the platter and picked up a slice. I needed to get home to Finae and make sure Syrane and Shenrae were safe. I forced down a mouthful of bread.

I would get to Vaiyene or die trying.

chapter thirteen
RESOLVE

My fingers ached, and my grip on Nightwind's reins weakened despite my efforts to hold on. I'd managed to convince Kefnir to allow me to leave through persistence, or as he called it, "my stubbornness and damned pride." Kefnir had threatened to break off the alliance he had begun with Vaiyene if I died before making it home. I doubted he would, but it added to my desire to return alive.

It was the third day since I had left, and Vaiyene seemed impossibly far away. I had taken it slower than I liked, for my sake and for Nightwind's. It would take another day, maybe two, if we pushed ourselves. The landscape was still blurred by my damaged vision, but Nightwind knew the way. I was grateful for his eyes and will. Without his stamina, we would never have been able to leave when we did.

I owed Asdar for his kindness.

I drew in a breath and stared through the blurry landscape to the west, where Finae's fate remained uncertain. My fingers tightened around Nightwind's reins.

———

I fell off Nightwind, steadying myself against his flank as I emptied the remaining liquid in my stomach behind the Phantoms' house. My hands trembled at my sides, and I clambered down the hallway, trying to remember which room we had stayed in many nights ago.

Sliding open the last door, I peeked inside, my knees almost buckling underneath me. I saw the paintbrushes on the ground and rushed inside. I knelt beside Finae's bedside, relieved her coloring seemed normal. She slept peacefully. Tears sprang to the edges of my eyes.

She was well.

I meandered back down the hallway and into the council room. In the hearth, a fire smoldered. Almost extinguished. The feeling seemed mutual. I blew against the flames and threw another log onto the fire. It wasn't that cold, but the action occupied my mind.

Footsteps approached, and I lifted my tired gaze. Lunia's face paled; her voice trailed off when she caught sight of me as if she didn't believe I was real.

"Kilo?"

My body was weak, and my vision spotty, but I had made it. Asdar stepped out of the shadows, into an area in my vision where he appeared less blurred. I pushed up off the floor, staggering as I did so.

My head began to spin.

Asdar frowned as he drew closer. His expression was neutral. "You look on the edge of death."

I hoped to get to more important matters and avoid their inquisition as to my health.

"What have you found out about the wheat?"

"It was sent from Tarahn, and anyone who ate it fell quite ill." Asdar crossed his arms and glared at me. "Whoever agreed to help you did quite the opposite."

I stiffened at the remark and fought to keep my voice level. "I assure you, Kefnir did not poison the grain he sent."

"Did you do anything or just forsake all of us here?" Asdar spat the words at me. "Your blind faith in people clouds your judgement. You made that mistake as a Shadow, Kilo, and you continue to make it as a Phantom."

His eyes were unrelenting in his unwarranted attack against what I'd accomplished. "This isn't Shadow training anymore. More than the lives of your friends are at stake."

"I will vouch for his character on my life," I said evenly, closing the distance between us. "Your mistrust in people keeps them away. Who would come to help you if ever you needed it?"

Lunia sank into a chair. Her hands wound through her long silver hair. "Enough. If we can't rely on one another, we will all fail. Our people need hope right now more than anything. Besides…" She pointed to a small scrap of paper lying on the table. "We found this within the last bag of grain. There's more to whoever poisoned the grain than simple hate."

I picked up the note, my hands clenching the edges of the worn paper. It was the symbol of the Shadows, with letter scribbled underneath.

This is just the beginning.

I crumpled the note and threw it back onto the table, my nails digging into my palms. This would be the last time the False Shadows threatened Vaiyene.

"The False Shadows are behind this."

If Ikaru was the cause, I would kill him myself.

"What proof do you have of the False Shadows' guilt?" Asdar's nostrils flared at me. He would rather believe one of our allies had sabotaged us. He'd always been a fool when it came to people.

"Because," I said, drawing out the word. I pointed to the note on the table, my hand steady. "This is a threat to Vaiyene, aimed at me for trying to stop the False Shadows. For trying to repair what damage was done by Phantom Kural."

Out of the corner of my eye, I saw Lunia stumble to her feet. "Kilo, don't. There are some principles we must protect."

I ignored her. I was done protecting Kural. I was done lying and not taking action. I was done letting the False Shadows get the best of us. Protecting Kural's reputation meant nothing to me. Besides, Asdar was a Phantom now; he deserved to know. Whether he decided to do more with the information than I did, it was up to him. I'd made my decision when I became a Phantom to conceal and protect his image for the people's sake.

"This all began with Kural, the man both you and I looked up to." I met Asdar's gaze without flinching. "He aided the False Shadows, and when he couldn't give them what they wanted, he killed them. The fires in Vaiyene happened because of him. His weakness to protect our people. Stop destroying the allies we have, and help me do something!"

I took a long, deep breath and broke the silence that had followed my declaration. Both Asdar and Lunia shrank back at my anger. What did they know about anything outside of the village?

"This is much bigger than Vaiyene," I continued, finding my anger had not dissipated. "We need to do something before this threat grows, and we are unable to stop it."

I wanted to round on Asdar for his attack earlier, but I bit my tongue. It was not in his nature to restrain himself. He needed to gain a level of restraint he had lacked as a Shadow, as I needed to become less trusting. I wanted the truth—the whole truth. I knew a portion of it, but there were pieces still unclear to me. What was the purpose of the False Shadows? The Skills seemed to be the center of it, but what did Hitori intend to do with them? It was the missing piece I was most uncertain of, and what I feared the most.

Lunia finally spoke, her face pale.

"Before anything else, we need to protect Vaiyene."

I shook my head. "The way to protect our people is to stop the False Shadows. If we don't make the first move, they will come again, and next time we will not survive the encounter."

"We don't have enough Shadows to do so," Asdar said, his breath heavy with irritation. He began pacing the room, his hand on the hilt of his over-sized axe. "We have no choice but to be patient. Snow will soon begin to fall, and it will prevent a direct attack on Vaiyene. No one can make it over the mountains."

"If we give Hitori the winter to train her False Shadows, we won't be able to defeat her." I paused, composing my thoughts. He and Lunia didn't know. "She possesses a power with infinite possibility."

Asdar and Lunia exchanged glances.

"What power?" Asdar asked, his eyes narrowed.

I shook my head and fought off a wave of dizziness, bracing myself against the table to stay standing. The poison was impeding my action and clouding my mind. My head throbbed, so much so that it was hard to know what to say and in what order.

I sat down into a chair, putting my hand against my temple. "I don't know the full extent of it, but it's some sort of manipulation of energy. It's all I found out from the False Shadow."

"And where is this False Shadow?"

I cursed myself and Asdar's quick wit. The damage had already been done. "He escaped."

"You didn't restrain him?" Asdar's voice became a building torrent. "What were you thinking?"

I met his glare and fixed my jaw. "We had an agreement—"

Asdar cut me off. "And what did he do? Stab you in the back? Tip off the False Shadows about our whereabouts and tell them the Phantoms are weak? He used you to get the wheat inside Vaiyene. He used you to poison our people. Finae became ill *because of you.*"

I struggled to keep my voice even. "What should I have done?"

"Killed those who threaten us."

The resolve in his voice left no hesitation.

Everything we had trained for, the ideals and morals we believed in as Shadows, how could he forsake them? To throw away what we trained for—lived for? Were the False Shadows capable of destroying what we stood for as Shadows?

Were we that weak?

I shook my head, trying to still my thoughts.

"You don't mean that."

Asdar met my gaze. "I do."

Out of all the Shadows, Asdar was the only other to have taken life. I'd struggled to forgive myself ever since killing to save Zavi's life. I could not even hold a sword without feeling the life of another in my hand. How could I take a life intentionally? Did Asdar not feel remorse for the lives he had taken?

Lunia stepped between Asdar and me. She seemed unbothered by our exchange. "Perhaps rest is in order. This latest attack by the False Shadows caught us off guard." She lifted her gaze to Asdar. "Be mindful of your words."

Asdar's jaw tensed against the reprimand.

Not killing was what separated us from the False Shadows. While I couldn't deny it would make things easier, the cost would be too great. I glanced down at my palm, remembering the dead I had encountered. Could I have saved them if I had killed?

I lifted my head. My hands fisted at my side. "I burned the village of Mashin to the ground."

Lunia and Asdar snapped to attention; Lunia's mouth gaped.

"The people there were slaughtered by the False Shadows. I found more dead in Leiko, hidden in the forests. Both times, our Shadow bond wrapped around people's arms. I can't turn my back on the innocents being slain across Kiriku."

Lunia sighed, dragging her eyes to me. "We need you here in Vaiyene. Your place is here."

Could she not hear me?

People were dying because of the Shadows—because of us.

I turned to Asdar. His face was a perfect mask. Given his earlier comment, I expected a word in my favor. When he offered none, I tried to keep the plea from my voice.

"Asdar?"

He was silent, his eyebrows furrowed. When he finally answered, he would not meet my eye. "You can't forsake our people to deal with the affairs of others. Our people here are threatened. In the springtime, our Shadows will possess the fighting capacity to put an end to the False Shadows."

I swallowed my disappointment. Spring would be too late. If my conscience allowed me to forget all the people across Kiriku, I still couldn't agree to their lack of action. The Skills were dangerous, and after encountering Hitori's closest followers, Ikaru's words of warning were beginning to sink in.

I didn't know what Hitori was capable of.

None of us did.

I could stay in Vaiyene and hope we would be able to gain the strength needed to defeat the False Shadows, defeating Hitori when we felt "prepared." Or, I could pursue Hitori myself and learn about the Skills, striking when Hitori seemed vulnerable. Finae was in Vaiyene, as were Syrane and Shenrae. A part of me screamed to stay here, to protect our people and close my eyes to the outside world—but my instincts screamed louder. If I didn't find a way to defeat the Skills, our Shadows would die. Vaiyene would burn, and innocent people across Kiriku would be killed. Asdar might have been the weapons master, and I did not doubt his ability to train Shadows who could fight, but the Skills would never be defeated through combat alone.

If I let the Shadows confront Hitori, they would die.

I would not let that happen.

The Shadows were more than warriors. Asdar would train the Shadows for one purpose—to kill. The ideals of the Shadows were shifting. The Shadows, and the creed we lived by, meant too much to me to allow that. I needed to act now and prevent more bloodshed. I needed to find a way to ensure the Shadows would be able to remain as they were: peacekeepers.

I had to take the chance. Whatever it took.

I blinked away the outlines of Asdar and Lunia as I stumbled to the door. "I must follow what I believe in."

"Stop."

I glanced over my shoulder at Lunia. Her gaze was fixed on me. "If you leave, your title of Phantom will be forfeit. You will no longer be welcome back in Vaiyene. You will be disgraced and discharged from the Shadows for abandoning your duty as a Phantom."

I'd never heard Lunia speak in such a tone. Her calm, almost meek nature hid her inner strength. We shared a love for Vaiyene, but we believed in different methods to save our people.

My hand hovered at the door.

I closed my eyes, an image of Shenrae and Syrane fighting the False Shadows appearing in my mind. Their eyes grew cold as blood trailed down the swords in their hands. I would not allow Zavi and Mia's children to become mercenaries who killed.

Asdar and Lunia couldn't comprehend the threat the Skills posed. As I had doubted Ikaru's words, they too doubted mine. The power of the Skills was too abstract, too new, to elicit fear.

My fingers slid between the door and its frame.

I would do what needed to be done to protect those under my care and ensure the Shadows stayed true to the creed I believed in.

I could live no other way.

I leaned against the wall, trying to steady the pounding in my head. While my conviction was firm, my body betrayed me. I drew in a few deep breaths. The pain dissipated as I made peace with my decision. I had to do what I believed was best. To protect those I cared about, I needed to leave Vaiyene. They would not understand, but in time, hopefully, they could forgive me. Shoving off the wall, I rounded the corner and entered Finae's room. I couldn't abandon Finae. Not this time.

"Kilo, you're back!" She sprang up from her painting, and my eyes fixed on the Miyota Mountains. The picture was half-finished, but I would know those peaks anywhere. Finae followed my gaze and smiled. Would I ever see them again?

From inside my tunic, I pulled out a small package held together in the middle by a thin ribbon. Finae's smile widened at the gift. She undid the ribbon and squealed with joy at the array of paintbrushes. Her happiness brightened my spirit.

I let out a heavy breath.

Finae's face fell. "What is it?"

I met her eyes. I hated how it was always like this.

"I fear I've made a decision that has already changed your life. I hope you'll forgive me for it."

Finae didn't say anything. Her eyes dropped to her painting, and she bent over, swishing one of her new brushes in a clear glass of water. I watched the white swirls mix with the water—so like the coloring of the Skills.

"I have to leave Vaiyene." I swallowed and forced the words past the emotion choking my voice. "I don't think I'll be coming back this time."

Finae dropped her paintbrush into the water, placing her hands on the ground as she stared up at me.

"What do you mean?"

Dizziness tugged at my mind, and I sat on the bed next to her, patting the space beside me. Finae joined me, her displeasure at doing so apparent by her slow movement.

"To do what I believe is right, I need to leave Vaiyene. I've discovered a new threat. Asdar and Lunia don't understand the potential dangers."

Finae frowned, rubbing her hands in her lap.

"Why can't you come back?"

"The other Phantoms don't agree with my decision." I fumbled for an explanation. Asdar and Lunia held their own beliefs. There was nothing I could have said to change their minds. "As a Phantom, I must do what is right, even if others do not agree."

The freedom of being Phantom meant I could choose to follow my beliefs. However, if two of the Phantoms disagreed, Vaiyene rules dictated a Phantom either abide by the decision of the others or leave. I'd heard stories in Shadow training of Shadows going "rogue," but I couldn't recall that ever happening. I had thought it was a way to scare us into obedience.

I smiled inwardly. A rogue, huh?

Finae twisted her hands together. She was young—fourteen summers—too young to be considered for sponsorship. Lunia would allow her to remain in the Phantoms' house, but Finae would not be happy. That was not what I wanted either. We were all that was left of our family, but was it selfish of me to even consider taking her?

Was she too young to decide for herself?

She deserved the opportunity to choose regardless, and whatever she decided, I would support her. I struggled with the words, then slid off the bed and sat on the floor in front of her.

"Would you come with me?"

She met my eyes and stared at me. Did she understand what I was asking of her? I opened my mouth to repeat the question when her face brightened, and a smile spread across her face.

"Do you mean it?"

While I didn't completely like the idea, it seemed the best option. Finae spent too much time alone. I didn't want her to grow up without someone to look after her, without someone to explain to her what was happening in the world. Her friends were few, if any, and our parents had died years ago. She was a solitary person, preferring to spend time by herself, but I knew the spirit inside of her felt trapped.

"I don't know if I will ever be allowed to return, and if you leave with me—"

"I want to go with you," Finae interrupted. She stood and began picking up the brushes from the floor, plunging them into a glass of water to clean them.

I let out a sigh of relief.

Yet she must understand the full implication of leaving with me. "It's going to be dangerous, Finae."

She began tidying her paints and grabbed a sack from the corner of her room. "Do you believe what you're doing is right?"

I blinked, not expecting the question. It was a wise question— one beyond her years. I'd been too busy to notice that in the span of a few years, she had grown. She was no longer the same girl mourning the loss of our parents.

"I believe it's what I need to do. Whether it is the right thing to do, there's no way to know for certain."

Finae straightened. "Then I believe in you."

Her words were simple but sincere. I couldn't help but smile at this bittersweet moment. Vaiyene was our home, but to protect it, we had to be exiled from the place we loved. Finae possessed a heart both kind and patient. If there were more people like her, I was certain we would not have been faced with this choice.

Finae turned to look at me, a balled-up pile of clothing in her hands. "What are you going to tell Shenrae and Syrane?"

I groaned, not bothering to hide my frustration. Being a Shadow was hard; being a Phantom was much more so. If I hadn't been chosen to be a Phantom, how much different would my path have been?

I turned around and stood in the doorway of Finae's room.

Shenrae and Syrane needed to know my reason for abandoning them. A letter would be a cheap replacement for a proper farewell, though it would be the easiest option. I couldn't bring myself to walk away from them, and I didn't want them to remember me in such a way.

"When you've finished packing, get Whitestar ready." I took a step and hesitated. One horse would not be enough. "Get a second ready. One unclaimed by the Shadows."

I glanced back to see Finae's eyes widen. She nodded her understanding. If I were to be a rogue Shadow, I might as well start by stealing a horse.

I found Shenrae and Syrane in the storehouse, sorting through the sacks of grain Kefnir had sent. The air was dusty, but I could see the damage from the fire was not enough to have burned down the building. It seemed sturdy enough to last the winter.

From afar, Shenrae and Syrane seemed to be enjoying themselves. They laughed at some comment spoken between friends.

They would be fine without me.

Still, I hesitated before crossing the distance. A deep sense of loss slowed my steps. I would miss Syrane and Shenrae, as I would also miss Vaiyene. Shenrae spotted me first and waved me over. She propped the sack in her hand on its end and stooped down next to it. Her fingers pointed to the thread holding the bag sewn in place.

"The ones without the X-stitching are the ones that have been tampered with by the False Shadows."

A slight weight lifted from my shoulders.

Not all of the grain had been poisoned.

Syrane hefted a bag from a cart and placed it into a pile on his left. "These are all the ones safe to eat. Shenrae noticed the stitching. She's got an eye for detail."

I placed my hand on her shoulder. "Well done."

She smiled, her grin spreading from cheek to cheek. I glanced behind me as unease settled over me. Asdar walked into the storehouse. He caught my eye but said nothing as he began helping carry the good grain into the storehouse.

"I need to talk to both of you."

Syrane and Shenrae exchanged glances but followed without any hesitation. I took them away from the storehouse, leading them into a grove of birch trees. A few leaves clung to the branches, providing spotty seclusion. It would have to do.

I swallowed, my throat dry.

All I could do was be honest with them.

"I've chosen to leave Vaiyene."

They both opened their mouths to speak, but I raised my hands to stop them. "Please, let me finish. This is not easy to say."

Whether it was the break in my voice or the affection they held for me, they quieted. I didn't look away from Shenrae or Syrane, but glanced from one to the next. "As a Phantom, my oath binds me to do what is best for Vaiyene. The other Phantoms have forbidden me to pursue what I believe is best. The penalty for disobeying the others is exile from Vaiyene."

It was hard to get the words out, but I persisted. "I'll no longer be a Phantom or even a Shadow. I've chosen this, and I believe it's what I must do."

Tears rolled down Shenrae's cheeks. Syrane's eyes focused behind me; he clenched his hands into fists at his sides.

Was his anger toward me?

"I'm sorry."

They were quiet. If Syrane was indeed angry with me, I'd rather he threw a punch at me than refuse to meet my eye. At least Shenrae's emotions were easy to read this time. I sighed and glanced around, getting my bearings. An idea came to mind. It would take Finae a while to pack for herself and get the horses ready, and we had a little time.

"Come on," I said, leaving the trees and heading toward the Phantoms' house. I would have to be careful to avoid Lunia, but it was something I could do for them.

The two of them plodded along behind me, their pace less than enthusiastic. We moved in silence, taking the back trail that led to the gardens surrounding the Phantoms' house. Hidden in the cliffs, between two boulders, was a cave. I hadn't been there in many years, not since first joining the Shadows, but I doubted anyone else had found the spot. I crouched down at the edge of the trail and watched for any movement. The Phantoms' house was large, spanning in a U-shape across a field surrounded by trees. None moved on the wooden deck.

Syrane bent down next to me. "What are you looking for?"

"Phantom Lunia. I'm not sure how she'd feel knowing I'm with you." A child-like smile spread across my face. While my words were serious, the nostalgia of being younger and sneaking around with Zavi brightened my mood. Now I was here with his children.

"The trick about sneaking is"—I glanced back at Shenrae—"to walk with patience and skill."

She seemed less than impressed with the prospect, but Syrane's eyes twinkled with mischief. I stood up, motioning them back and placing one foot in front of the other. "There's something called the fox walk, or as your father called it, 'the sneaky foot.'"

Shenrae laughed and covered her mouth, glancing around to see if anyone had heard her. She was getting into the spirit.

"Your mother thought it was a silly name, too."

I gestured back to my foot, raising it up and pointing at the outer edge. "This is the blade of your foot. To execute the sneaky foot, you need to rock your foot onto the blade and then set your foot down."

I shifted my weight onto my back foot and placed the blade of my other foot down, rolling it slowly onto the sole. "Like this." Syrane jumped into step beside me and copied my move.

"Not bad for your first attempt," I remarked.

The sober atmosphere that had been present earlier had dissipated, and I desperately wished there was some way I could keep the smiles on their faces. Syrane and Shenrae practiced for a few moments more while I rechecked the Phantoms' house. It looked clear. I waved my hand, returning Shenrae and Syrane's attention back to me. We kept low to the ground, crouching as we moved across the loose stones and grass, climbing under a branch and disappearing into the thick pine trees. Pine needles crunched underfoot, releasing a fresh scent into the air. Syrane and Shenrae kept close to me, mimicking my movement and prowess. I envied Asdar. He was going to be able to teach the next generation of Shadows.

I hoped he understood the honor.

I held back a prickly branch for Shenrae and nodded toward a crack in the cliffside. "It's in there."

The cave was smaller than I remembered, but it was large enough for all of us—if no one stood up. My distaste of tight spaces turned my breathing ragged. I shook the light canteen at my side, awakening the flame within, and navigated my way to the back of the cave. I ignored the rocks scratching my hands and brushed off the shards covering the wooden chest. I pulled it free and pushed it into Syrane's hands. He looked at me, confusion on his face before he slipped his fingers over the metal latch.

"In our youth," I explained, "your father and I weren't the best Shadow trainees."

Shenrae leaned close to Syrane as he opened the box. Inside were two daggers, both still in perfect condition.

"One night your father and I stole a dagger each from our Shadow fathers. We hid them here, near the Phantoms' house in the middle of the night. We swore one day we'd return to uncover them."

We could never have known how important such a boyish act would be. Syrane and Shenrae each took a blade in their hands, drawing the daggers from their sheaths. The light from my canteen reflected in the daggers' metal.

"They're yours now."

"Thank you, Kilo," Shenrae said, turning the blade over in her hands. She touched the hilt with her finger, tracing the silver metalwork and sapphire inlays.

I led them out of the cave, calming my emotions for what was to come. It was time. I looked from one somber face to the other, trying to picture their smiles as I embraced each of them. They were so young, but they were also Zavi and Mia's children, which meant they were strong.

"I will put an end to the False Shadows and return peace to Vaiyene."

Out of deep respect for the Shadow's Creed, I crossed my right arm over my chest and bowed to the ones I would leave behind.

"It is my deepest regret that I will not be able to guide you through life. I believe whatever path you choose, whatever choices you make, will lead you to happiness. Fight for it. Protect one another. Live."

Tears beaded the edges of my eyes. I was doing this for the two of them, as their parents would have.

"Will we never see you again?" Syrane's words were scratchy.

I couldn't bear the thought.

I had always considered Syrane and Shenrae to be as close to my heart as Finae—as close as blood. I didn't know what the future would bring, but I needed hope to guide me through the darkness. I wanted to believe it was possible.

"I will find a way to return."

Somehow.

part two
SHENRAE

chapter fifteen
SPONSORED

I knelt at the base of the Reikon Tree, my mind unclear. Snow meandered around the great tree's branches, falling in light mounds around me. Snowflakes covered the fur cloak that lay across my shoulders, but I didn't bother to brush them aside.

My parents' swords rested in the ground after Syrane and I had purified the blades in the alpine lakes. The snow made their final resting place seem peaceful. Beautiful even. We had come here often as children—Syrane, my parents, and me. My mother had told us about the Shadows of old and their will to protect us. About how they had sacrificed themselves to protect others so that we might live peacefully. My father had told us tales of their own journey and of the people they had helped along the way. I'd listened to their stories, gaining a sense of wonder that my parents stood for something greater than themselves. Even in death, their spirits continued to watch over Vaiyene.

I didn't know how to describe it, but being under the Reikon Tree brought me peace, like the Shadows themselves, wrapped me in their protection.

It was a sense of peace beyond my understanding.

From a young age, the Shadows had been my idols. Now, on the verge of deciding what path I would take, I remained unsure. Would I even be able to become a Shadow?

I leaned forward and brushed the snow off my parents' swords, letting my fingertips trail over the wrapped hilts. Would I be able to uphold their names? I rocked back onto my knees and looked up through the twisted branches at the overcast sky. I pulled down the scarf from around my nose and let the snowflakes melt on my skin. I blew out a cloud of breath. When I was young, I used to read through the Shadow's Creed, pretending I was a Shadow alongside Syrane. We had recited the creed together, created fake Shadow missions, and established mock villages. I smiled at the memory. I'd almost forgotten. Back then I had been so sure.

Now I hesitated.

Why?

What bothered me the most was not knowing what to do. Was I making the right choice asking to become a Shadow? Would I disappoint my parents because I was no good? These thoughts— and countless more—had been swirling in my head since Kilo's exile. If he had still been in Vaiyene, my thoughts on the Shadows would have remained untouched. I might have idolized them as I once had. But the Phantoms' actions made no sense—turning their backs on the threat that loomed...

It was not Shadow-like.

And if even the Phantoms were afraid, what made me think I could do better? I pushed myself onto my feet, the blood tingling as it recirculated through my legs. I cut off my thoughts before they ran away too far. "One decision at a time." My mother had always patted my head as she said those words.

Syrane and I were on our own. We had decided to become Shadows to stay together and to find our place in the world. It seemed as good a choice as any. I had no natural talents. I couldn't create anything with my hands. Even how to grow wheat was beyond my understanding.

But I knew how to be a Shadow.

Our parents had raised us by the Shadow's Creed and instilled our belief in it. While my understanding of the creed was through their eyes, one of the principles demanded a person stay true to one's self and be loyal to those they loved. Becoming a Shadow alongside my brother would be the first step in upholding the teachings passed down to us.

I ran my hands through my hair, digging my fingers into the side of my head. I wish I knew if it was the right decision.

––––––

I rubbed my hands together to warm them, glancing around at the bare trees surrounding the Phantoms' house. I hadn't seen Syrane, but I was sure the Phantoms had sponsored him as a Shadow.

Now it was my turn to ask for sponsorship.

Phantoms Lunia and Asdar ambled in my direction, their heads together as they discussed something I couldn't hear. Years of stress had turned Phantom Lunia's hair gray long before age should have touched her features. Even Phantom Asdar seemed to have succumbed to stress of late, or maybe it was the dim lighting of the moon that made the lines under his eyes appear much deeper.

When they drew closer, Phantom Lunia spread her arms and gave me an awkward hug. I appreciated her gesture of comfort, but she was part of the reason Kilo had been exiled—for reasons I still didn't believe. I kept the anger quiet and buried it deep.

Both Phantoms wore their ceremonial robes of rich black and gold. An oversized hood rested upon each of their shoulders, revealing a golden lining. I hadn't seen either in their robes since Asdar and Kilo had ascended to Phantom. The robes symbolized the Phantoms' strength and protection. I drew some comfort from the small measure of the tradition they kept, even if one of the Phantoms was absent. Even if the current Phantoms didn't think so, in my mind, Kilo would always be a Phantom. It was bittersweet, and I tasted the bitterness in my mouth. Young people requested to be sponsored when they became of age. Kilo had been like a second father to both Syrane and me. With our parents dead, and Kilo gone, the importance of the milestone seemed weakened—but it remained a necessary one.

They would have been proud.

I swallowed the emotion and tried to keep my back erect, as my father had taught me to do in the presence of the Phantoms.

"I regret that we are not able to give you the proper setting for your request," Phantom Lunia said. Her voice was weary from exhaustion.

Asdar's eyes settled on me. His giant axe was affixed to his back. He never went anywhere without it.

"Plead your case, Shenrae."

I flinched at his words. His desire to get this over with was not subtle. I snapped my feet together, put my right arm over my chest, and bowed at the waist. The Phantoms returned my gesture.

"I wish to be sponsored as a Shadow of Vaiyene."

They exchanged glances, and when they returned their eyes to me, they didn't seem surprised.

Phantom Lunia held my gaze. "What makes you want to be a Shadow, Shenrae?"

I gathered my thoughts, choosing the one appropriate for the situation. Instinct? Was that a valid answer? I looked over at Asdar, and my thoughts escaped me, fading before I even began speaking.

Already, he doubted me.

Asdar's eyes narrowed and looked me over.

"The Shadows do not seek revenge."

I shook my head, finding my voice. "I don't want revenge. I understand my parents' duty to Vaiyene and their desire to protect the village. They raised me by the Shadow's Creed."

Lunia smiled at me, revealing the dimples in her cheeks. "A fitting answer for one of Zavi and Mia's children."

Her warmth washed over me, and I relaxed. My response had been acceptable.

"What can the Shadows do for you?" Asdar asked.

I said the first thing that came to mind. "I want to stay with my brother, but more than that…" I hesitated under Asdar's gaze. Would he find my reasoning too childish?

Lunia gave me an encouraging nod, and I swallowed.

"More than that, I think the Shadows will help me find my place in Vaiyene. If there's something else, I'd be better suited for, please tell me, though I don't think I'd be good at anything else. My parents and Kilo found purpose in the Shadows, and I want that more than anything."

To my surprise, a faint smile appeared on Asdar's face. The left side of his lips twitched up, and he exchanged a knowing glance with Phantom Lunia.

"They are one and the same."

Lunia chuckled. "Though in much less eloquent terms."

I frowned, not quite understanding the exchange, but the Phantoms seemed in favor of sponsoring me.

Phantom Lunia still wore a smile on her face. "You have spirit, Shenrae. Your parents would have been proud of you."

"Shadow training begins tomorrow." Phantom Asdar gave me a low bow and handed me a single silver coin. His slight smile disappeared as he strode away. His voice carried on the wind. "Sunrise, tomorrow. Don't be late."

I closed my fingers around the coin's edge and drew in a relieved breath. Lunia kept her eyes on Phantom Asdar's back, then returned her attention to me. "He's not as cold as people think. You'll be in no better hands than his during Shadow training."

Her gaze turned toward the north, where the remains of burned houses stood. "These are difficult times to be in the Shadows. Even outside the Shadow ranks, you would face dangers your parents never experienced."

I opened my palm and looked over the silver coin, forcing my apprehension aside. Being in the Shadows allowed me to do something about that danger. I would rather risk my life and do something than pretend we were safe.

"There's not enough silver in the world to repay you for what you've lost. A Shadow's sacrifice can never be repaid."

The silver coin sparkled in the dim light of the moon. The death of my parents didn't seem far enough away to consider putting a price on their lives. They had died protecting what they loved.

It was all anyone could ask for.

Phantom Lunia picked at her robe and smoothed down the wrinkles on the front of it. "I've gone too long without sleep." She cleared her throat and trailed back to our earlier conversation. "Asdar sees something in you. Not even your brother was sponsored by him."

I smothered a smile. So Lunia had sponsored Syrane.

Phantom Lunia bowed to me.

"Welcome to the Shadows, Shenrae."

Even though she had warned me about the dangers, being sponsored as a Shadow seemed right. The Phantoms' approval meant they, too, believed I could become a Shadow. My parents and Kilo had lived by instinct, following what they believed in without fear of consequence.

I wanted to live the same way.

chapter sixteen
THE FIRST DAY

I gave up trying to sleep. Instead of lying in bed, I climbed to the training grounds behind the Phantoms' house to try and satisfy my restlessness. So far, it hadn't worked. It almost seemed my mind grew more restless being closer to the arena.

What would Shadow training be like? What weapon would I choose? How long did it take to become a Shadow? I indulged in a few thoughts before my restlessness overwhelmed me. To still my mind, I tried picking out and counting the wooden targets that hung in the trees below.

I hadn't found very many targets before voices interrupted me. I slid off the jagged rock pile and clambered down the side of the training area, spotting Syrane. Torey walked beside him. When we were younger, her family had often invited us over when our parents were away on Shadow missions. I smiled at their ambling gait and animated gestures. I wished I shared their enthusiasm.

My mind remained more nervous than excited.

"Shenrae!" Torey gave me a hug. "We missed you at breakfast. How long have you been here?"

My stomach grumbled in response. I'd forgotten to eat again. "I couldn't sleep, so I figured I would explore the training grounds before everyone arrived."

Syrane smiled at me. "Are you ready?"

I shrugged. "A little nervous."

"You'll be fine."

Syrane meant well, but no words would comfort me. I needed to act and experience the training for myself before my nerves would calm. I let Torey and Syrane follow behind me as I took the first step across the dormant grass. The training arena was large, with different areas and obstacles in each quadrant. Hanging from trees in the distance were the wooden targets I'd been counting earlier.

Torey bumped into me, giving me a small smile. "Don't feel bad for being nervous. Everyone is."

Syrane walked to my other side. "We're all on equal footing."

I drew in a steady breath as the others began arriving. They were right. We all trained to be Shadows for the first time. There was no sense worrying myself over something that had not happened. I glanced around at our new comrades, taking note of those who had chosen to become Shadows. Including me, there were nine of us gathered in the center—six males, three females. I'd gone through basic training with most of them. Circling the edge of the arena were seven more. The bonds on their arms distinguished them as Shadows.

Syrane noticed my gaze. "They're probably here to help Phantom Asdar with training."

I nodded without paying much attention, looking around for Phantom Asdar. My fellow trainees seemed as confused as I was, though more patient and less worried. The Shadows were stoic, their gazes focused outward, toward the forest surrounding us.

A peculiar feeling settled over me. The Shadows' gazes seemed too intent, even if they were standing guard. Their muscles were too tense and rigid.

They knew something was going to happen.

I scanned the area, trying to find something amiss, but nothing seemed out of the ordinary. A rush of wind blew past me, and I spun around as an arrow embedded itself into the ground a few paces away. It quivered upon impact, and another bolt struck the ground—this time to the right—almost hitting one of my comrades in the foot. The Shadows sprang into action. They drew their swords and rushed off into the trees. I spun around and moved to the side. An arrow skimmed my arm.

Torey pulled on my arm. "Move!"

I stood my ground, watching the arrows with keen eyes.

Syrane pushed me from behind. "You're a standing target. We have to move."

I ignored him as more arrows hit the ground. Each time, they missed their mark. No one had that bad of an aim. I hadn't even moved. It was an orchestrated attack.

"They're not trying to hit us," I said, studying the forest. Torey and Syrane exchanged glances but stayed at my side.

A movement in the trees caught my attention—not on the ground but in the treetops closest to where we stood. I raised my hand and pointed, locating the archer hidden in the pine needles.

The arrows stopped.

Phantom Asdar dropped from the treetop and strode to meet Torey, Syrane, and me. When he was a few paces away, he gave me a small nod.

"Well done."

The Shadows emerged from the trees with bows slung over their shoulders. The Shadows-in-training began trickling back into the center of the arena. A few of their stares lingered on me as they walked past to form a circle around Phantom Asdar.

I shied away from their gazes, trying to keep my smile modest.

"See, nothing to worry about," Syrane said, clapping me on the shoulder.

Maybe I did stand a chance as a Shadow.

"Shadows," Phantom Asdar said, his voice raised so they could hear him, "train amongst yourselves outside of the arena."

While the Shadows left, Phantom Asdar fixed his full attention on us. "That was your first test. I wanted to know how you responded to danger. One of you displayed the correct response."

Phantom Asdar paused and caught my eye before continuing.

"Before we proceed, I would like to make one thing clear. If you do not like my methods, you are free to leave. If you don't have the spine to stick to your commitment, you are free to leave. You've all chosen to be here—don't forget it."

As if to conclude his speech, he stopped in front of a wooden box. "Difficult times are ahead of us. None but the best will become Shadows."

My apprehension returned in full force. I stifled the panic, clinging onto my one validation: Asdar had chosen to sponsor me. It meant he believed in me.

Phantom Asdar waved his hand at the box. "Choose your weapons. I want to assess your abilities before we begin with foundations."

One by one, the others picked their wooden weapons. They shifted them in their hands, testing them out. Some knew what they wished to fight with, while others took a few practice swings. Syrane gave a long wooden sword a test, swinging it crosswise in front of him. Our father had fought with a longsword.

It suited Syrane.

Torey also chose a sword, though hers seemed much less bulky and thinner than Syrane's. Most of the others picked swords. I saw the appeal. When I thought of someone who protected, I, too, pictured a sword in my mind. I reached out an unsteady hand and wrapped my fingers around the hilt of a sword. It was longer than expected—and heavier. Much heavier. It seemed awkward to hold, but I didn't know the proper grip or form to be able to judge a sword. I placed the wooden sword back in the box. Kilo fought with a staff. I had asked him his reasons once, but he never had answered. He had said it was something better left in the past. I'd respected his desire not to tell me, but I could have used the advice. Compared to the sword, it was lighter, and it fit more natural in my hand. That seemed as good of a reason as any to choose it.

When I found my place with the others, Phantom Asdar held out a wooden battle axe. "Form two lines and face your opponent."

Asdar stood at the opposite end of my line, giving everyone a partner to spar with. I shifted my hands up and down the staff, my heart beating out of rhythm.

"Those to the east, you will be defending."

Everyone shifted around me. Why hadn't I thought to prepare for this? My original thought was to blunder my way through, stabbing and slicing, but blocking was a different matter. How did one block with a staff? I peered down the line, trying to analyze what the others were doing. Most had spread their feet wider than their shoulders, with their weapons away from their bodies. Some even shifted their weight from foot to foot. I tried to mimic their stance. I held onto the staff with one hand, losing my focus as Syrane gestured a few places down from me. He waved his hand at me, then gripped his sword with two hands as if it were a staff. I adjusted my grip to mimic him.

He nodded his approval.

"Prepare yourselves. Wait for my mark."

Asdar's voice brought my attention back to my opponent.

Meyori faced me, her bushy brown hair standing out in all directions. She was the same age as me, though I didn't recall too much about her besides her harsh tongue. She hadn't yet insulted my lack of experience. Being unkind had never stalled her tongue before. I pushed the thought from my mind and focused on the staff in my hands. I drew in a breath and tried to recall any advice given to me by my parents or Kilo.

None came.

I shifted onto my left foot and gripped my staff. My muscles tensed, and when Asdar shouted the release, my eyes instinctively closed, and I thrust out in front of me. My opponent's wooden blade collided with my staff. When I opened my eyes, Meyori's nose scrunched up at me.

"You'd think you'd be better at this, being the daughter of Shadows." Her screeching voice remined like a raven's.

I let Meyori's insult bounce off me, though the barb stung. I wanted to make my parents proud. I already knew they would be cringing at my poor display. Meyori shifted her sword, and I brought my arms back toward my chest. Asdar shouted his next command before she could speak further.

"Prepare to attack!"

Again, I snuck a glance down the line at the others and slid my right foot a few inches in front of my left. I balanced my weight and grasped my staff with two hands.

I visualized swinging the staff up and over my head, into Meyori's head.

"Attack!"

I swung the staff with such force that I lost my balance and tripped into Meyori. She pushed me off in disgust, as if I were infected by some disease, and stormed off in a huff of rage.

Heat rose to my cheeks, and I stared at the ground, trying to ignore the snickers.

Asdar cleared his throat. "Switch opponents. Quickly now."

I stayed, staring at the ground. Meyori cursed under her breath as she moved down the line to find a more competent opponent.

"I'm sure our parents had stories of when they failed." I looked up and caught Syrane's smile. He stood in front of me and held his sword out. "They were Shadows, but they weren't perfect, Shenrae. Don't let them discourage you."

That was easier said than done. Syrane at least had some idea of what to do. Meyori's irritating voice continued to screech down the line. I turned to glare at her and caught Asdar's gaze. I forced myself to breathe in and out. He seemed to be assessing my next move. I adjusted my grip and faced Syrane.

She could insult me all she wanted, but I wouldn't quit.

"Those on the east, prepare to defend yourselves."

Syrane gave me an encouraging nod. I adjusted my hands on my staff and met Syrane's blow. He didn't use his full strength, but I moved in time to block a strike to my side. We continued for the rest of the day, shuffling through opponents and nursing our aching muscles. We broke throughout the day, to relax both our minds and bodies. Asdar led us in some stretches while we rehydrated and ate. It was not until the sun passed behind the mountains that we stopped our training.

He strode down the line, his wooden axe at his side. "I've seen what I needed to. Well done today. We'll continue tomorrow at first light."

I let out an exhausted breath, grimacing at the tenderness in my back. My fellow trainees began shuffling away. Most seemed to have gained at least a few bruises.

"What a day." Syrane paused beside me, rubbing his arm. A large welt rose from his arm where the flat of a sword had hit him.

Torey limped up behind Syrane. She looked tired but gave me a smile, her eyes wandering over the bruises across my body. "I'm starving."

I laughed at her unexpected response. I half-expected her to give me some sort of pep talk about tomorrow being a better day, or how we had promising futures as Shadows.

Syrane turned his attention toward me. "You'll get better. Today was to gauge everyone's abilities. We'll be starting with foundations tomorrow."

Syrane and Torey had fought today; I'd done nothing but flail my staff around, trying to keep myself from getting hurt. The others were already better—much better. I hadn't thought I would be the worst in the group. I swallowed the resentment and returned his smile.

"Let's get something to eat," I said.

Torey's face lit up, and she and Syrane began chatting about the first day. I let them walk ahead of me, not entirely sure being a Shadow would be any better than what I'd endured today.

I sighed.

Tomorrow was another day.

chapter seventeen
SHADOW LIFE

"Some people don't know when to quit."

I shifted my ankle and winced, ignoring Meyori's comment and the sneers of two Shadow trainees next to her. It'd been a full cycle of the moon since we started training. I'd managed to dodge her sword, though my ankle was tender from a somewhat awkward attempt to evade her. Each day, my fellow trainees expected me to quit. And each day, I refused. I wouldn't give them the satisfaction. They could sneer and chide all they liked. Competing against them to be the best didn't interest me, though I knew it frustrated them—I was here to become a Shadow, not to inflate their egos.

I dragged my staff in the dirt, using it to offset my weight as I walked to the Phantoms' house. Torey spotted me from across the arena and made her way over to me. She glanced down at my ankle, and I sighed.

"Meyori again?"

I shrugged off the comment. The green roof of the Phantoms' house appeared in the distance, and I held my staff at my side as we drew closer. Syrane waved at us from under the wooden archway. He held out his hand and helped me up. I saw his gaze, but he restrained himself from asking about my ankle. I appreciated it. We walked down the wooden deck, my footsteps thumping out of rhythm. A damp mist rolled over the wooden beams, coming from the towering waterfall of the high peaks. Shimmering in the fog, a rainbow caught the last of the sun's light.

Most of the Shadows-in-training had gathered already, seating themselves onto large cushions at the edge of the balcony. Phantom Asdar and Meyori were missing. I exchanged glances with Torey and Syrane. Asdar came around the corner, carrying a basket full of leather canisters. He set them down in the middle of the deck. The Shadow's light canteen.

Syrane nudged my elbow with his, but I ignored him. Despite not wanting to let Meyori get to me, her jeers nonetheless had stolen my enthusiasm for the day.

"Today I'd like to offer each of you your first piece of Shadow gear; as a reward of your progress and hard work. This light canteen contains an oil that is easy to light and is a pivotal part of our everyday gear. We use them for illumination purposes, but the canteens can be used for long-distance signaling—which I will go over at another time."

Phantom Asdar picked up a canteen and ran through the names of the different parts, showing us multiple ways to light the oil, as well as how to extend the life of the flame and how to diminish it in a hurry. When he had finished with his explanation, we each grabbed a light canteen from the basket on the table. Syrane handed me one, grabbing a second for himself. It was much lighter than I'd expected, with a smooth, almost paper-like texture to the exterior. A light fragrance of oil leaked from the canister.

I curled my fingers into the sides of the leather.

This was proof that one day I would be a Shadow.

"I would like to congratulate you on making it this far. I mentioned not all of you would become Shadows on our first day. Meyori is no longer welcome among our ranks. Working as a team is a critical part of being a Shadow. I will tolerate nothing less."

I raised my eyes to see Phantom Asdar's gaze on me before he turned his attention to the others.

"The Shadows will be working with you tomorrow, on strength and recovery. Take the rest of the day off and return tomorrow ready for more training."

I kept my back straight as I forced myself up from my knees, ignoring the side-looks and hate from the others. They blamed me for Meyori's expulsion from the Shadows, though the blame lay on her own shoulders. I clenched my fists at my sides and pushed my mind where I needed to focus—on becoming a Shadow.

Curiously, Phantom Asdar had not retracted my sponsorship. As Phantom, the right was his, but his hesitation in doing so made me wonder. Why?

He had rejected a talented trainee in favor of keeping me.

Combat was no strength of mine. It was not self-pity but fact. I had hurt myself more than any of my opponents, and with the False Shadows lurking at the edge of everyone's minds, the Phantoms needed warriors—not some girl who couldn't swing a staff without unbalancing herself.

"A Shadow finishes what he starts."

It was something my father had always told Syrane and me, and they were words I'd engraved into my heart. My commitment to see the training through, and to figure out if I had what it took to be a Shadow, pushed me to continue.

Until I could no longer lift my arms, I would continue to swing my staff. I had to. Survival depended on a person's strength, and I was working to find mine.

Asdar stood in the center of the arena, his arms crossed over his chest. The early morning light backlit his features, and I shifted around him to keep him in full focus. We had learned about using our position to gain the advantage over our opponent. I smiled to myself; His choice of using the sun more than illuminated the point.

"To become a Shadow, you must experience firsthand what it is like to be a peacekeeper of Kiriku," Phantom Asdar began, as the last of the trainees put down their weapons. "I will be taking three of you outside of Vaiyene."

There were gasps around me as my fellow trainees jostled one another to get a better position in the circle. It would be the first time any of us had been allowed outside of the village.

I smothered my excitement. Asdar would take those talented in combat. Other than Meyori, none had left Shadow training—which meant there were seven others more capable than I.

Asdar continued. "Syrane, Torey, and Shenrae, you will accompany me to the village of Koto. The rest of you, continue your drills and head home early. Get some rest. Tomorrow, the Shadows will lead the drills in my place."

Syrane and Torey both grinned at me, and I couldn't help the smile from widening across my face. My first Shadow mission! Asdar motioned for us to follow him, and we fell into line. As we cut through the gardens and bamboo groves to the Phantoms' house, a sense of pride welled up inside me. I paused before stepping onto the wooden deck. Our parents had been Shadows their entire life, frequenting the Phantoms' house. While I'd not been training for long, my life already seemed to hold more of a purpose than it had before. Or perhaps it was the certainty that came with a fixed routine.

Was this what my parents had found in the Shadows? Assurance?

Phantom Asdar walked under the wooden archway, leading us inside the U-shaped Phantoms' house. On either end of the main entrance, the hall split in two. Sliding doors had been created from multiple pieces of wood, with paper inlays inside the gaps. My eyes drifted upward to the rafters that mimicked a canopy of trees. It reminded me of starlight breaking through cloud cover. We entered through a sliding door into a large, open room. A table large enough to seat the Shadows and Phantoms was placed close to the ground. Kilo had sometimes referred to it as the command room, though I believed the correct Shadow terminology was the council room. The Phantoms didn't command but offered counsel. The Shadows kept peace outside the village, offering themselves for hire to those who needed our services, doing things such as guard duty, peacekeeping, assisting with alliances, and helping with agricultural issues like farming and disease.

I ran my finger across a row of books settled into a large bookcase that lined the walls of the room. It was a library spanning across every imaginable topic—knowledge the Shadows were trained in. On the wall, a map of Kiriku hung, with "Land of Hope" scrawled underneath. My eyes trailed over the detailed mountains and landscape, following the curves of ink to the Miyota Mountains. Nestled in the mountain peaks, hidden in a valley, lay our village. The Shadows kept hope alive for Vaiyene. In the middle of that struggle, Kilo stood between us and the False Shadows.

When spring came, would we be ready?

Phantom Asdar laid out a scroll on the table, placing rocks on the edges of the paper to keep it from folding in on itself. The map centered on the western regions of Kiriku—Randaus, where Vaiyene and many other towns and villages were located.

Asdar pointed to the north of Vaiyene, to a town called Koto. "We have a long-standing contract with Koto for root vegetables. They're not a large village, but they do have a sizable field to replace some of the tainted grain."

I stared at the map, trying to memorize the details of the land, not taking for granted Phantom Asdar would guide us back to Vaiyene. It seemed a test he would likely employ. One I wanted to be prepared for.

"We leave at midday and should arrive well before nightfall. We'll spend the night and get a sense of the people there and their opinion of the Shadows. It will be a short trip, but one that will give you some experience and insight into what being a Shadow means. Any questions?"

It seemed a simple enough mission.

When neither I nor the others said anything, Asdar rolled up the map. "Go then, prepare, and meet back here at midday tomorrow. Even though this will be a short trip, prepare yourself for every possible outcome, as a Shadow would."

———

Four horses whinnied at our approach. Asdar appeared from inside the stables, carrying a large canvas pack. He slung the bag over his stallion's back—Nightwind. The horse's name carried almost as much weight as his master's.

"Once you become Shadows, you'll pick your own horse and raise it from a foal. This will strengthen your bond. It will become the animal you use for your missions." He gestured to the other horses. "These three are not bonded with anyone. Their temperaments are mild and suitable for even unskilled horsemen."

My ears burned at the remark.

Was Phantom Asdar directing the comments at me? I stifled my annoyance. Unlike combat, my mother had taught me how to ride at a young age.

The young chestnut mare watched me with interest, ears pointed in my direction. I held up my hand and took my time in approaching. When the horse pushed her muzzle into my hand, I breathed easier. I transferred my pack onto the horse, cinching down the straps, ignoring Asdar's watchful eye. He could critique my combat skills, but my horsemanship needed no work. Phantom Asdar chuckled and grabbed the reins of his black stallion, leading it away from the stables. I pointed my horse after, falling into his rhythm of movement as Syrane and Torey scrambled to tie their packs and catch up to us.

Rays of light warmed my skin with the promise of good weather. It eased my mind—a simple mission down the mountain and back up, a taste of what was to come.

We traveled down the main dirt road that wound from the Phantoms' house and into the residential area. The last remaining leaves floated down from tall aspen trees overhead. Snow had fallen in Vaiyene overnight, but only a few patches had not melted. Our journey through the village was silent, but it was not an uncomfortable silence. It was filled with respect for the moment.

A villager came to a stop as we continued down the main dirt road of Vaiyene. He stepped off the path, his gaze trailing after us as we led our horses past him. Though we were not Shadows, more people began to line the road, their gaze focused not on Phantom Asdar but on us. I dropped my eyes and tried to avoid eye contact. It made me uncomfortable like somehow, the weight of success was greater under their gaze.

"Safe travels, Shadows!"

"Good luck!"

"A speedy return!"

Not long ago I'd been part of the crowd, bidding my parents and the other Shadows good luck on their journeys. I breathed in unevenly, feeling tears on the edge of my composure. This was a moment our parents would never see. I blinked away the tears.

A young girl, no more than four, ran into our path. She grinned, her chubby arms held against her chest.

"Good luck, Shadows!"

She tossed a pile of snow into our pathway, the flakes glistening as they covered our path. She giggled at the sight and skipped back to her mother's arms.

"Shenrae?" Syrane asked, disrupting my tears.

I shook my head and tried to remember what we'd been talking about, but all that remained was a sense of loss. A gaping hole that seemed impossibly large.

"Our parents would have been the first to wish us luck."

I glanced back, surprised to see a smile on Syrane's face. He didn't meet my gaze. Instead, he looked out over the people gathered, as if he could see our parents in the crowd. Of course, he knew what I was thinking. He felt the same way.

"They're watching over us, you know. Our parents' swords are among all the Shadows of old."

A hand touched my shoulder. Torey had guided her horse next to mine. "I know it's not the same, but you and Syrane have always been like a family to us."

She pointed into the crowd. Torey's parents and two younger brothers waved at us, their excitement growing as they noticed our attention. I nodded, a tear escaping my control. It wasn't the same, but we were not alone.

Someone waited for our return.

I didn't know each of the people who gathered, but I knew of them. I'd seen them, walked with them, grieved with them. Was that what becoming a Shadow meant? Looking out for their safety as well as my own? They gathered not for Phantom Asdar but for us. The realization gave me a sense of what I stood for. I knew the theory behind being a Shadow, but this was the first glimpse of tangible proof that a Shadow stood for something significant.

Something more than a silver coin.

Vaiyene's people needed me. I wasn't the strongest, nor the quickest, but I would do what I could for them.

It didn't seem too bad of a life.

The procession slowed as we neared the end of the village. The people waited. They would continue to do so until we mounted and started into the caves that led outside of Vaiyene.

Asdar came to a halt and swung his leg over his black stallion. His shoulders were pushed back, his back erect. His very posture seemed to affect those gathered. With his knee, he turned his horse and faced the crowd. He put his right arm over his chest and gave a short bow to the people. They cheered. Asdar's words were rough, but he knew what he was doing. He made a good Phantom.

I glanced back, focusing on the intense gaze of the crowd. It almost seemed as if they held their breath—waiting—until we mounted and began our journey. Torey and Syrane smiled at me, and I put my hand on my horse's saddle, unease at the edge of my mind

If I were a better Shadow, things would be different.

I didn't want to let them down.

I drew in a deep breath before I lifted myself up and swung my leg over my horse's saddle. I forced myself to sit tall and proud—as if I were worthy of the people's admiration.

The entrance to Vaiyene's cave system lay ahead. The giant maw of the cavern's edge was vast enough for us all to ride through mounted. A hollow wind blew from the depths, sweeping a cascade of snow across us. My hair whipped around me, and I tied the shoulder-length mess at the top of my head with a ribbon.

Phantom Asdar disappeared into the dark caverns. I held my breath as excitement bubbled within me. When I was very young, Syrane and I had snuck into the caves. Our parents had berated us for it, saying it was a dangerous place. They had forbidden us to go there again. Their words and the stories about the boy lost in the caverns had frightened me, but I was no longer afraid of the stories people whispered.

I wanted to find my own truth.

At my side, I unstoppered the light canteen. I brought out a small slab of flint and stone and lit the wick.

Crystals caught the glow from my canteen and glinted as we passed under long stalactites. Tiny droplets ran along the edges of the sediments, their scent reached throughout the cavern air. It smelled like rain and reminded me of sitting under the wooden pagodas in the gardens; Syrane and I had gone there often as children. If it rained hard enough, the raindrops pattered like drums on the stone pavers.

I inhaled, savoring the memory.

Glancing around, I realized I'd forgotten to make a note of which turns to take.

I had a lot of work to do with my Shadow discipline.

Dust danced before my eyes, reflecting the rays of light from the outside world. I raised my arm to shield my eyes as we emerged from the cave. We walked amongst the clouds, the area covered in white fog, but I could see a horse and rider stopped ahead.

Phantom Asdar's figure was almost imperceptible in the mist.

I moved my horse beside him, and Torey and Syrane fell into place beside me. A grin spread across my face. We were about to go where few had the privilege of going.

My heart yearned for the change.

chapter nineteen
KOTO

"When we reached the bottom of the Miyota Mountains, the air seemed less heavy around me like a weight had been lifted. Over the past few weeks, I'd progressed little in my Shadow training. It had affected me, making me doubt myself more than I already did. Phantom Asdar's request for me to join him on this mission had somehow renewed my conviction.

Today I would prove my worth to be in the Shadows.

We kept the horses alongside the river, as there was no road down into the valley. Carved into the incline of the mountain, a few houses had been set at the base of the valley. At the opposite end were rows of tilled dirt and fields of rice paddies. From the looks of it, a small portion of the area still bore vegetation. A thin bridge connected a dirt pathway from the field to the village. It was the first road I'd seen outside of Vaiyene.

What kind of place would Koto be?

Excitement stirred in me, but my nerves clouded it. A pain in my stomach made me regret snacking at our last stop. I needed to calm down. If I didn't overthink and dwell on what could go wrong, my nerves tended to dissipate. It was something I desperately wanted: peace of mind. My parents had always seemed at peace, as had Kilo. How did they do it?

Phantom Asdar raised his hand, and we dismounted. He pulled his horse close, his eyes narrowed, scanning the valley ahead of us. "Put your light canteens away and keep your furs and cloaks drawn closed. We do not dress too different from those in the village, but they've seen me carrying my light canteen. If they see yours, they may associate you with me. I'd like a chance to see what they think of Vaiyene without one of its Phantoms asking them about it."

Syrane snuffed out the flame from his light canteen. "Are we traveling separately?"

Phantom Asdar nodded. "I'll meet with the village head, and the three of you can follow. Take note of anything out of the ordinary. If they have a problem with me here, there will be gossip." He turned his eyes back to the village. "Stay together. I'll come to find you once I'm finished."

Before I could come up with a question or even a plan, Asdar was already leading his horse away.

"He's never very clear with his orders," Torey said, expressing my sentiment. "I guess he expects us to figure it out as we go."

I laughed, though without humor. Asdar must have trusted us enough to not supervise us. We did have some training in how to act in new situations. Best to apply them.

Syrane adjusted her horse's saddle packs and took a breath. "Well, I suppose we should start heading down? Make use of the remaining light."

I glanced up at the sun and guessed that we had a few solid hours left in the day. We were not too far from the road into Koto, but if anyone saw us coming from this direction, they would know we had come from Vaiyene.

"We should join the road up there on the ridge." I pointed to the hill to our left, where the road began to wind down from the mountain. "That way, if anyone sees us, they'll think we're travelers from somewhere else."

"Good idea," Syrane said, already turning his horse around. "This is our first mission, so we should be cautious."

My heart quickened as we drew near the village. What kind of people lived there? No travelers came to our home. I'd never met anyone I didn't already, in some way, know.

On the horizon, a man appeared, barrels strapped to either side of his horse. We had dismounted to give the horses a break. We were vulnerable. Torey and Syrane had real blades with them, and I had my wooden staff strapped to my horse's side, but I tensed as he came closer. Did people here greet one another? What should we say? What if he knew we were from Vaiyene? I took a breath and calmed my thoughts, trying to rationalize my fears. To him, I bet we appeared as travelers heading toward rest after a long day.

"Good afternoon, sir," Syrane said. "How fares the road ahead? We were debating among ourselves if we should continue or seek shelter for the night."

The man cleared his throat and shifted his lips, moistening them with his tongue. Freckles dotted his nose and cheeks, with a few light wrinkles around his mouth. There was a touch of gray in his beard.

"There's been little snow these past weeks; you should be safe to continue if you choose to." He pulled his horse to a stop next to Syrane. "Though if you've never been to Koto, they are quite a friendly village. Small, but friendly folk, always willing to help, even in these times." His eyes became unfocused, and his smile fell. "Even in these times, there are still good people."

Syrane exchanged glances with Torey, and then his gaze meandered to me as if debating what to do. I kept my focus on the man. His words implied he had heard of the False Shadows, perhaps even met them on the road himself.

"We should get going," I said. "I think we'll take your advice and stay in Koto for the night, then continue east. We're traveling to Tarahn to stay for the winter."

At the mention of Tarahn, the man's eyes snapped to me. His hand went to his head as if he were fatigued or dizzy. "I would travel with caution if you're heading east. There have been rumors of raiders and people being attacked on the roads."

The man fussed with the cap on his head and mumbled under his breath. "A man never used to have to worry about leaving his home for some potatoes."

"Thank you for your time," Torey said, giving the man a big smile. "We wish you a speedy—and safe—return home."

The man waved us off. Both he and his horse ambled away, the barrels of potatoes swaying. I hoped he made it home safe.

We continued our wandering pace into Koto, taking the time to cool down the horses. The houses we had seen earlier had been created with intricate stonework. Age had darkened the stones, which contrasted against the clambering vines that sprawled across the surfaces of the houses. If it hadn't been the start of winter, the vines would have almost made the village disappear into the mountainside. A woman and a man walked toward us. They dipped their heads in greeting while they strode along, continuing their conversation about some game they had played earlier. They didn't question us as travelers.

We crossed another bridge, one pieced together with stone. I ran my fingers over the surface, marveling at the patience it must have taken to fit each stone into place.

"Shenrae, come on."

I looked up to find Syrane and Torey already on the other side of the bridge. I hastened to catch up with them, berating myself for getting sidetracked by something as mundane as a bridge.

People gathered in the road ahead. A pile of lumpy sacks seemed to be the center of their attention. Someone pushed a tottering cart of potatoes between them, the cart digging tracks in the damp earth. The vegetables, which seemed to be potatoes, were divided into piles and slung into canvas sacks.

The potato packers looked up as we drew near, and one of them moved to meet us. "Are you part of the group from Vaiyene?"

His eyes traveled behind us as we slowed our pace.

How did he know?

"They are," Phantom Asdar said from behind us. I glanced over my shoulder, and he gave us a curt nod before he handed his horse's reins to Syrane.

"I've finalized discussions with Iena. She should have sent someone over with numbers."

Something behind Phantom Asdar caught my eye. A man wandered between the houses. His clothing was dark and earthy, quite similar to the Shadows' garb. He kept to the shadows and glanced around as if checking to see if anyone noticed. A glint of silver flashed from his forearm.

Was that a bond on his arm?

"Shenrae?"

I shook my head and lifted my head to see Asdar's gaze on me. His eyes widened when I turned to him; then the emotionless mask concealed his expression.

He bowed to the people packing the potatoes.

"Will you excuse us for a moment?" They nodded and hurried to help with another cart coming in from the field. Phantom Asdar hissed at us to follow him. When we were far enough away that the field hands couldn't hear us, Asdar rounded on me.

"What did you see?"

I hesitated. What if I was wrong and I had not seen a bond? What if I was right?

I swallowed and met Asdar's gaze. "There was a man who seemed like he didn't belong. He avoided the villagers, and I thought I saw a glint of silver on his arm."

Torey's and Syrane's eyes widened behind Asdar.

"Was it a bond?"

I swallowed, my heart racing. "I think so."

"If what you saw is correct," Phantom Asdar said, ushering us farther away from our horses and the villagers, "this mission is going to be far more than what I wanted it to be."

We had been training for such a short time.

It was too soon for this.

Torey called out, and I spotted the arrow as it flew overhead. Smoke trailed behind the shaft. It struck the dried vines covering the buildings.

Phantom Asdar whistled, but his horse was already almost upon us. He fixed us in his gaze. "I will not command you charge into battle with me. Protect the villagers."

Asdar threw himself onto Nightwind, and the giant stallion reared. The eyes of the beast matched the man's spirit. He didn't stop as he spurred past the farmhands, saying something to them that made them flee. Without realizing it, I found myself running alongside Syrane and Torey, back to the horses. Before I could even catch my breath or grasp the full weight of what was happening, Syrane and Torey were mounted.

I stood paralyzed at my horse's side.

Torey moved her horse next to mine and nudged me with her leg. "We're in this together. Stay close and breathe."

Syrane brought his horse to the other side of me. "We'll take the lead. It might not be as bad as you imagining it. Remember the stories our parents told us? About their fear as they rode into battle, and how they always felt better knowing they fought for something important?"

My vision of the houses around me became unfocused, but I drew in a steadying breath and mounted my horse. Our parents had always said that, in the moment, their fear disappeared. They only thought about saving as many lives as possible.

To them, it had always been about protecting.

"Phantom Asdar does not expect any of us to fight," Syrane said as he surveyed the scene. He brushed his cloak back, touching the hilt of his sword. "Stay here and help the villagers get to safety."

Torey reached out and placed her hand on my arm. "You don't have to come with us."

They both kicked their horses into a gallop, and I watched their blurry outlines as I struggled to breathe. Their forms disappeared into the burning village. Smoke already rose from three of the buildings. They were stone houses, but the flames began to spread across the dried vines, leaping from one building to the next, climbing onto everything not made wet by rain or melted snow. I closed my eyes, but that didn't shield me from the cries of the people—or from the memories of Vaiyene burning around me.

What would happen if I were as hopeless on the battlefield as I was in Shadow training? I fisted my hands to stop them from shaking. I had never given up before.

This was no different than a drill.

I drew in a few deep breaths and recited the first lines of the oath the Shadows swore when they ascended from training. Even though I was not yet a Shadow, I knew the words because of my parents.

> *I will be strong in the face of my enemies, though I do not know the outcome. I will do what I can, not what I must, for there are others who depend on my strength.*

I urged my horse into action, unhooking the staff tied to the saddle packs. I held it close and remembered the demonstrations Kilo and the Shadow group had performed at a festival.

> *A Shadow protects the innocent, using his strength to aid those in need.*

Torey and Syrane, as well as Phantom Asdar, were my comrades. Though I didn't know what help I could offer, I would regret not putting my strength to the test.

I would regret abandoning my brother and my friend.

I had to try.

I held my breath as I rode through the smoke and past villagers shoveling dirt onto the hissing flames. I peered through the haze, trying to pick out where Phantom Asdar headed. Smoke stung my eyes, and I led my horse without any direction, trying to think where Asdar would lead the False Shadows.

He would lead them away from the village.

I pulled on my horse's reins, directing her toward the last of the houses and into the field. Nightwind's black form came into focus through the smoke. I clicked my heels against my horse when I saw Asdar facing down a rider on horseback. Nightwind reared as the rider drew close, lashing out with his front legs. The False Shadow, fell from his saddle. His horse bolted as Syrane and Torey fell into formation around Asdar.

Two more riders came from either side. An arrow trailed across my vision, embedding itself into the fallen man's chest. Phantom Asdar looked up and spotted me.

"Find the archer!"

The downed rider clawed at the arrow in his chest, gasping for breath. Another arrow embedded itself in his body, close to the first.

He stopped moving.

I heard Phantom Asdar's voice like a whisper carried by the wind, muffled and distant. My focus remained on the man with two arrows in his chest; blood and foam trailed from his mouth.

"Shenrae, move!"

I jerked my gaze away from the man, instinct taking over as Asdar's voice broke through my daze. I kneed my horse to the mountainside. The archer would search out cover, and this field had no place to hide. I directed my horse up the western slope, untying one of my saddle packs. Shifting its weight, I positioned it in front of me to help block my chest should the archer see me coming. My horse struggled against the steep mountainside, and I leaned forward, trying to help distribute my weight into a better position. I kept my gaze ahead, looking for any sign of movement. When the terrain leveled out, and thick evergreen trees surrounded us, I brought my horse to a stop and waited. A few of the thinner trees creaked and swayed, their leaves chattering overhead in a gentle breeze. Underfoot, the forest floor cushioned our movement.

I slid off my horse, walking on the blade of my foot, as Kilo had taught us the day he left. The sneaky foot.

My lips twitched at the name.

A flicker in the trees ahead made me freeze. My heart pounded in my ears, and I waited, not daring to do more than breathe. When nothing else moved, I raised my foot, rolling it onto the sole. Leaves rustled and echoed through the trees, and I glimpsed a figure in the forest. His shoulders flexed as his elbow pulled the bowstring back, aiming at me. His bond glinted in the light filtering through the trees. He let loose the arrow, and I flattened myself against a tree trunk, the arrow tearing into my cloak. My heart pounded in my ears, and I tightened my fingers around my staff, dropping the horse's reins as I scrambled for cover. I couldn't hear anything but the sound of my heartbeat. I tried swallowing my panic, but the crunch of leaves made my heart pound harder. Sinking low, I crept around a tree branch. A fallen tree blocked most of my view, but with my free hand, I steadied myself against it, thankful at least that my balance enabled me to move without making too much noise.

There was a crunch from my right—then another.

I turned my focus away from anything but the sound of leaves crunching and the progress of my pursuer. Closing my eyes, I imagined where the person stood. I loosened my fingers around my staff and shifted its weight and position. The man took another step, and I leapt out from behind the tree, swinging my staff low to the ground. It slammed against the man's ankle, and he jumped back. I flew at him, my staff pinned at my side. I collided against his chest, breaking his bow with my momentum. We fell to the ground, and I landed hard on my elbow. My arm stung, and I rolled to the side. Using one hand, I reached to grab my staff, but he was too quick. He yanked it from my grasp and pushed against me. I tripped over a jagged root, hitting the ground hard. I curled into myself, drawing my knees upward as the man pulled a dagger from his belt. He tossed my staff to the side.

I huffed and eyed the blade, pushing myself away from the man with my legs. He grabbed the front of my robe and placed the dagger to my neck. Hot liquid slid down the side of my throat.

He was going to kill me.

The thought surfaced in my mind as my instincts kicked in. I lashed out, kicking with my feet, growling as I lunged for my staff. The blade cut into my shoulder. My fingers curled around a rock beside me. The man's teeth flashed through his curled lips as he recovered, and I smashed the rock into the side of his head.

He stumbled, and I snatched my staff before running.

I zig-zagged through the forest, no longer thinking about being quiet. I needed to put distance between us. Asdar had been running us through agility drills, having us stretch our muscles and perform exercises to increase our speed. It wasn't the most glamorous part of training, but it seemed to have paid off.

I slowed my pace and dug my fingers into an expanse of rocks, hoisting myself up to a better vantage point. When I pulled myself up and over the edge, I knelt and scanned the forest.

Something moved in the trees.

I squinted and tracked the movement, distinguishing four legs and green saddle packs—my horse. I breathed deeply, trying to calm my heart to a sustainable pace. If I could reach my horse, I could escape the archer.

Was it worth the risk?

I watched the area from where I'd come, taking slow, deliberate breaths. I waited. My horse wandered farther away, but the man didn't seem to be following me.

Before I lost sight of my horse, I clambered down from the rocks and peered around the trees. My horse's ears perked up, and I clicked softly to her. She turned her head, and I reached out my hand as she pressed against my open palm. I laid my head against her flank and reached up to touch the cut around my neck. When I removed my fingers, they were stained with blood. My arm ached from where I had fallen on it, but other than the cut on my neck, I'd survived my first encounter unscathed. The horse's ears swiveled, and I undid the bow tied to the saddle packs. I withdrew an arrow from the quiver and fumbled with the bowstring, trying to make my movement minimal. The uncanny sense of someone watching me made my skin crawl.

A branch snapped, and I whirled around, releasing my arrow without a target. The arrow embedded itself into a tree, quivering at the impact.

Nothing moved.

Had I imagined someone watching me?

I shivered, unease settling over me. An animal could have snapped the branch, but would an animal make my skin crawl? I pushed a strand of hair back from my face and let out a long breath, affixing my staff to the side of my horse. I kept the bow in my hand.

I followed the sun's path, trying to find a sense of direction. The day was almost over, and I needed to make it back to the village before the light disappeared. Already, the sun's light waned, casting long shadows. My horse shied away from the path, and I placed my hand on her neck, looking around for whatever made her anxious. Hidden among the decaying leaves, not too far from where we stood, a man lay with a dagger in his chest. A froth of bubbles spilled from his mouth. I didn't remember many details about the archer, but this man seemed comparable in size. A flicker moved to my right, and I raised my bow as a figure receded into the forest, the gleam of a bond on their forearm.

My heart quickened, but the person continued to move away and soon disappeared. I lowered my bow and urged my mare forward, turning north, into the slope of the mountain. Below were the fields of Koto.

I hoped the others had fared better.

chapter twenty
THE SOURCE OF STRENGTH

Syrane, Torey, and Phantom Asdar stood around a dead man's body. All of them looked up at me, except for Syrane. My stomach sank. Why would Syrane not meet my eye? As I drew closer, nothing could shield me from the harsh realities of Shadow life. A man lay on the ground; an axe protruded from his split spine. Blood soaked the earth.

I glanced between Syrane and Phantom Asdar. Despite the lack of emotion on his face, I could sense his irritation. He grasped the hilt of the axe and pulled it from the man's flesh. I shuddered and closed my eyes as the wound gushed blood. The squish of flesh being dislodged from the axe made me cringe. My head became light, and I fell as my knees crumpled beneath me.

Phantom Asdar caught me with one hand and steadied me. His face became blurry as dark circles appeared in my vision, and I lost consciousness.

I awoke to Torey holding my head off the ground. My head lulled as I came to. Blood still oozed from the man's wound, pooling around his chest. I averted my eyes as bile rose at the back of my throat.

It hadn't been a dream.

"Phantom Asdar killed the man to save Syrane's life," Torey said under her breath, moving her hands under my arms.

I dug my feet into the wet earth and looked around until I saw my brother. He noticed my gaze and yanked his horse's reins and started back to the village; his anger flared up as he stormed away. The Shadows didn't kill. Though saving another Shadow's life was an exception, but Syrane would have a hard time accepting it even so.

Torey started after him.

"Leave him," I said, watching Syrane's rigid body trudge away. It was best to let Syrane deal with his emotions before trying to reason with him. Talking to him now would do no good. I swallowed, a foul taste in my mouth. Of all the reactions I could have had, did I really have to blackout in front of Phantom Asdar? I dragged my hands across my face. What kind of Shadow passed out? I blew out an exasperated breath.

"I guess we were disappointments today," I said.

Torey shrugged. "Even Phantom Asdar was not prepared for this. I don't think he expected anything."

She was right, but I had to prove my strength on this mission. I swallowed the emotion, trying to bring my mind to the present.

"Where did Phantom Asdar go?"

Torey gathered the reins from her horse. "To try and smooth things over with the village head, to make sure she knows we weren't behind this attack."

Before the attack, the villagers had not been afraid of us. With any luck, that hadn't changed. The timing of the False Shadows' attack seemed no coincidence.

Torey handed me the reins of my horse, and I kept my hand on my horse's side. A few whispered as we walked back into town, but the people soon returned their attention to smothering the remaining fires. As we had no bond to identify us as Shadows, it was unlikely they would place blame on us.

Down the dirt road, Phantom Asdar and Syrane spoke to a woman dressed in red. She had a thick fur coat upon her shoulders, and her brown hair was braided down her back.

"We'll get to the bottom of these attacks," Phantom Asdar said, his eyes flicking to Torey and me. "In the meantime, we offer you our aid. Do not hesitate to ask for what you need. We will be leaving tomorrow afternoon if all goes well. Until then, we are at your service."

The village leader nodded and drew in a shaky breath, clasping her hands in front of her. "Thank you for your protection. I don't know what we would have done without you."

She held up her hand and dipped inside the house behind her. When she returned, she handed a pile of linens to Syrane. Asdar put his right hand over his chest and bowed at the waist. When he straightened, he glanced at Torey and me.

"Tie the horses and come with me."

We followed Asdar back to the edge of the field. He entered a small shed and grabbed four shovels from within before leading us back to the man he had killed.

"Only under one circumstance do we kill: to save one of our own, or another in danger. I want the three of you to remember this day. If there's anything to learn from this experience, it is that we grow strong to protect the lives of others."

Phantom Asdar fixed his gaze on Syrane, who stood staring at the body on the ground. I placed a hand on Syrane's shoulder, but he shrugged off my touch. He needed more time. This was the same way he had reacted to our parents' deaths.

Despite knowing this, it still hurt.

Asdar cleared his throat and returned my attention to present matters. He handed me a shovel. "One deed does not define a life. The duty of a Shadow is not to pass judgement but to ease pain where he can."

I took the shovel and glanced down at the man at our feet. It could have been Syrane. My hands grew cold. This was what it meant to be a Shadow. Like Kilo had said, like Phantom Lunia had said, and like the man on the road had spoken—these were difficult times. One where our survival was uncertain.

Metal scraped against the earth, and I flinched. These False Shadows were, in a sense, our enemies, and we didn't know their reasons for the attack. How did we know we were justified in our actions? I lifted my gaze to Phantom Asdar. Wasn't his order to not pass judgement a judgement in itself? A request to withhold hate and treat everyone with the same care for life as we wished for ourselves? In Shadow training, he seemed cold and uncaring, but Asdar embodied the Phantom spirit the same as Kilo.

Torey nudged my arm, and I realized that Asdar and Syrane were now wrapping the dead man in the linens given us by the village leader.

"We should help them," she said.

I nodded. We grabbed the other linen sheet from the ground and began arranging the man's arms against his body. His eyes were still open, and I kept my gaze averted as we worked. Asdar bent down next to me and closed the man's eyes.

"Help your brother transport the body. I'll finish here. There's an area of land on the eastern slope, bordered by trees with an iron fence surrounding it. Iena, the village leader, is allowing this man and the other to be buried there."

I bent to the ground and picked up the feet of the man Asdar had killed—the man who had tried to kill Syrane. Together, Syrane and I lifted the man into one of the farmhand's carts. I guided the cart while Syrane pushed it over the bumpy terrain, the wheels thudding against the earth. Silence hung between us. Even if Syrane had wanted to talk, I wasn't sure what words I would have said. Emotion seemed beyond either of us.

Syrane's face remained vacant, his eyes dull.

My own body felt numb from emotion.

Syrane slowed the cart as we approached the edge of the iron fence. The area was small, with rocks used as markers. We laid the man on the ground and stood out of the way of Phantom Asdar and Torey.

Asdar caught my gaze. "Bring their swords."

I went back to the field, and Torey joined me in the search. A mixture of hoof prints and footprints smashed down the tilled earth beneath our feet. The gleam of metal shined in the mud, and when we made it back, Syrane and Phantom Asdar had already dug a substantial pit. We set the swords aside and picked up our own shovels. Out of the corner of my eye, I glimpsed a few people on the edge of the village watching us. A chill in the air crawled up my spine. I shivered. The sky had clouded over, and the ground was almost frozen. We chiseled away in silence.

When at last we had dug a hole deep enough to ensure the men's safety from vermin, my hands were blistered. I pulled the edge of my cloak around myself and tucked my hands inside to hide them.

My parents had once told me of the pits where some people buried their dead—"graves" they had called them. It was different than our own custom, but the sentiment remained the same. Even though the men had tried to kill us, they were still people, with a family or someone they loved.

Phantom Asdar bent on one knee, the other supporting one of his arms. His eyes were closed. After a few moments, he opened his eyes. He placed the swords over the men's chests, then began covering the bodies. Once the graves were covered, Phantom Asdar straightened, his mouth pressed into a thin line. His usually straight back bore a slight curve. His attention turned to Syrane.

Syrane's face was as ghostly as the dead.

Phantom Asdar placed his hands on Syrane's shoulders and shook him. "Loss is what makes us strong. Those of us who have been the cause of death are the ones who can grasp the full burden of being a Shadow."

Asdar grabbed his shovel and walked away, leaving the three of us in front of the gravesites. Up until this point, I had thought I knew what being a Shadow was, but my heart had not known the pain. I glanced over at Torey and Syrane. I didn't want to lose either of them. Would I have killed to save Syrane like Asdar had? I looked down at my blistered hands. Since starting Shadow training. Bruises lined my legs and arms and spanned across my entire body. I'd been cut, bruised, and beaten, but I'd not felt the fear of almost losing someone I loved, of someone dying when I failed to save them.

Syrane would never forget this day, but neither would I.

Torey looked up at me from the ground.

"We're in this together," I said, repeating her advice.

Torey smiled, and Syrane finally met my gaze. A deep sadness remained in his eyes, and he seemed unfocused like he was staring at something we both couldn't see. Syrane had lifted me up, encouraged me throughout my life. I couldn't recall a single situation from our childhood when the roles had been reversed.

It was my turn now.

"Next time, we'll be better prepared," I said, the words seeming foreign on my tongue. I didn't know if I believed it, but it was what Syrane needed to hear.

Syrane grabbed his shovel and pulled it from the ground. "Asdar is the strongest person I know, and even he was shaken. We're on the verge of war. We don't know if there even will be a 'next' time."

The hostility in his voice made me recoil. He seemed to listen to Asdar, but my words were hollow. Meaningless.

"We better head back," Syrane said, as he slung the shovel over his back. "Anything could happen."

———

Syrane stood in the distance, his face in shadow. A man ran at him with a sword raised above his head. I yelled out a warning, but it was too late. The man's sword sliced into Syrane's back, and blood dripped onto the barren ground.

I bolted upright, waking from the nightmare. Sweat beaded my brow, and I took a few deep breaths, glancing at my companions. No one was awake. We'd been on one mission, and already both Syrane and I had almost died.

Phantom Asdar and Torey slept beside a large mound of potato sacks. I crept across the floor, tiptoeing so as not to wake either of my companions. I grabbed my long, fur-lined cloak and slipped outside. Syrane sat on an old water barrel, sword propped against his chest, surveying the night sky. The moon was nearly at path's end. Morning would come soon.

"You're up early," Syrane said, not moving his gaze.

"I thought I could relieve you so you could get some rest." I hesitated, trying to gauge his mood. "Or I could keep you company."

It was half-true, though the root of the situation was my concern. Unlike me, Syrane was not used to being a failure. Asdar had killed to save his life because Syrane had failed to protect himself.

What could be going through his head?

Syrane stayed silent.

I crossed my legs and leaned against the water barrel. Syrane would talk when he was ready, if he felt like it, or not at all. I respected his choice, even though it frustrated me. I sighed and turned my gaze skyward. Stars twinkled in the almost-morning sky, with dark hues of blue changing to a lighter, more muted tone.

Syrane stood and unsheathed his blade.

"I knew being a Shadow would test my limits, but I didn't think I'd have to be rescued by Phantom Asdar the first mission."

I stretched my legs out and looked up at him. "It could have happened to anyone."

Syrane grasped the handle of his sword and twisted it in the moonlight. "The worst part was, I froze. The man charged with his sword, and I choked. I couldn't move. We practice every day, but for some reason, I couldn't bring myself to raise my blade against him." Syrane lowered the sword and sighed. "I was afraid, paralyzed by the thought of the man's sword running through me. If Phantom Asdar hadn't been there…"

"I'm sorry I wasn't there," I said as Syrane returned his sword to its sheath. "I still trust you to protect me."

Syrane gave me a small smile, and relief flooded through me. He worried me when he became withdrawn. It was an irrational fear because he always came around, but the longer he took to speak to me, the more anxious I became.

I inhaled, enjoying the crisp morning air and the crickets chirping around us. Every once in a while, an owl would call somewhere in the distance, adding another voice to the morning ambiance. Soon the crickets would be silent, and the birds would migrate to warmer weather.

A creak from behind startled us both. Phantom Asdar gave us a sidelong glance as he pushed the door open. His eyes were calculating as he looked us over. He moved in front of us, his cloak catching the wind before he sat down, facing us. He crossed his legs and propped his head up with one of his arms.

"I'm surprised neither of you has confronted me about Kilo." His eyes moved with interest from Syrane to me. I held my breath, not sure where he was going with his comment.

I met his gaze. "I didn't know it was a discussion."

He laughed wholeheartedly, then sat at attention after he had recovered. "It's not, but I expected it nonetheless." He grew serious, amusement leaving his tone. "How you must despise me for playing a part in his exile."

His tone seemed too casual to be speaking to us. Syrane and I both thought of Kilo like a second father. Rank didn't separate us, but Asdar was our Phantom, our superior and leader. His casual words and posture seemed to give off a different atmosphere than when he conducted training sessions.

What was he getting at?

Syrane caught my eye. He seemed as confused as I. After everything that had happened, I didn't care to surmise his intentions.

I took a breath. "Phantom Asd—"

Asdar held up his hand to stop me. "Speak to me as if I were not your Phantom. Kilo never held back. Neither did your parents. I don't wish to train mindless Shadows."

I tried not to glare at him. If he wanted me to speak honestly, and without holding back, I had no problem with it.

"Kilo was forced to leave because you and Phantom Lunia were too afraid to go after the False Shadows. He's the one trying to protect us. All we're doing here is hiding."

Heat rose to my cheeks as Asdar's gaze became more intense. He seemed bothered by my words, but he always was hard to read.

Had he expected me to say something else?

Asdar shifted his gaze to Syrane. "And you?"

Syrane tightened his hand around the hilt of his sword. "Training will never prepare us. How can we defeat an enemy we know nothing about?"

Bitterness lay heavy on his voice. It was tone I'd never heard before. It pained me to see him hurting.

Asdar kept his head on his palm, watching us both, seemingly deep in thought. "How much did Kilo tell you?"

I hesitated and glanced over at Syrane, who shrugged. "Enough to know he left to pursue the False Shadows against yours and Phantom Lunia's request. He said the False Shadows were not all bad."

Asdar turned his gaze eastward—to where Kilo had left to track down the False Shadows. "And therein is where strength will be found. Kilo's weakness is the Shadow's Creed, which I'm sure by now he's figured out himself. Now that he's no longer a Phantom, he's free to bring about his own justice, without any consequence but his own moral judgement."

The Shadow's Creed was his weakness? Like Kilo, both my parents had lived their lives according to it. It had brought purpose to their lives, as it now brought strength into mine.

Phantom Asdar returned his focus to me. "As far as the Shadows are concerned, Kilo is away on a mission in the east. Whether he retains or forfeits the title of Phantom depends on what he chooses to do. To be exiled requires two Phantoms' consent."

Syrane drew in a breath. "Kilo only thinks he's been exiled."

Asdar stood, a ghost of a smile on his lips. He removed the axe from his back and propped it against the rain barrel before he leaned against the house, arms crossed.

"Now get some sleep."

I pushed myself up from the ground and followed Syrane back inside, my movement slow. Kilo was still a Phantom, and he didn't know. While I was glad to know Kilo's exile from Vaiyene was false, Asdar's tone was ominous and vague about why Kilo knew nothing of his exile.

What did Asdar know that we did not?

"Shenrae."

I stopped and glanced back at Phantom Asdar.

He held out a small vial to me. "The False Shadows use poison on their blades. Be sure to clean your wound with this. Let me know if an infection develops."

I took the vial and raised my hand to the scarf covering the cut on my neck. How had Asdar known? I gave him a slight bow before I followed Syrane into the storehouse.

When I lay down, instead of feeling relieved at Kilo's exile, my mind raced with a single question.

Why?

"There will be no more Shadow missions until spring,"
Phantom Asdar said, his arms crossed over his chest
as he stood before the Shadows and trainees. Syrane
mumbled under his breath in an agitated tone. He shifted in his
chair, his hands clenched in his lap under the table.

Yesterday had shown us how inexperienced we were, but
hiding in Vaiyene would not give us the experience we lacked.

We wouldn't be prepared for an attack.

"As we all know," Asdar said, continuing his report, "Kilo is
gathering information about the False Shadows. He's made new
alliances in the eastern quarter of Randaus and is progressing
from there. He's gathering information we can use when the time
is right. In the meantime, we'll continue training in Vaiyene
and—"

"We're going to sit by and do nothing?" Syrane's eyes were on the table. The anger in his voice was subdued but apparent. He didn't mask his displeasure with Asdar's choice.

Asdar had told us not to treat him as a Phantom.

Phantom Asdar's lip twitched, but otherwise, he didn't react. "As hard as it is for me to sit back and admit it, we are unprepared to fight the False Shadows. You of all people should understand this."

Syrane flinched and swallowed the rest of his words. He leaned back against his chair, the desire to argue, gone. If he wanted to debate Asdar further, he seemed to have lost his will.

Asdar's words cut deep, but they were true.

"A dead Shadow is worth nothing," Asdar said, his eyes sweeping over all of us. "Our priorities will be strengthening our ranks and preventing any more losses. Winter will provide us with time. In the spring we will need to lead Vaiyene with unmatched strength."

Phantom Asdar gave a curt nod to Lunia and stepped away from the table. He leaned against the wall, his arms crossed. His mood seemed to have soured at Syrane's outburst, which didn't surprise me. Asdar was a fighter. His decision to remain in Vaiyene rested solely on our lack of ability. If we'd been stronger—if we had been capable Shadows—we would have been helping Kilo with the False Shadows.

Phantom Lunia rose and took a deep breath before speaking. "Thanks to this last mission, we believe there is enough food for the winter."

I breathed a sigh of relief. Some good news at last.

"We're making good progress rebuilding. If the weather stays mild, we should be able to get our people into their own temporary places. After the snows melt, we can begin setting permanent houses and replanting areas the fire devastated."

Phantom Lunia clapped her hands in front of her. "Thank you all for your hard work."

The meeting concluded, and the Shadows and trainees filed out of the room. Syrane didn't even glance at me before pushing away from the table and storming off.

I remained, wringing my hands in my lap.

Phantoms Asdar and Lunia talked in hushed tones in the doorway. Asdar noticed my gaze, and his eyes studied me for a moment before his focus returned to Lunia.

Why had he agreed to sponsor me?

The question resurfaced in my mind. Phantom Lunia had said he saw potential in me but did I belong in the Shadows? Back in Koto, my fear had paralyzed me. I'd hesitated to follow Asdar into battle, and when confronted by the False Shadows, fear had made me forget my Shadow training. I'd survived through instinct.

How had Kilo and my parents become fearless?

What was their secret?

I drew in a breath. Was I holding my comrades back? I cringed at the thought. Even if it were true, our parents had instilled a belief that we must finish what we started, but what if my persistence hurt the Shadows? Should I quit because I was the weakest?

"Is there something you wanted to ask me?"

I startled from my thoughts and jumped to my feet. Phantom Asdar stared down at me. I peered around him, noticing that Lunia had left. Heat rose in my cheeks, and I met Asdar's eyes.

"W-why did you sponsor me?" I blurted the question out, regretting the words as soon as they had passed my lips. Phantom Asdar stared at me with level eyes, and I tried not to shrink away from his gaze.

"You wanted to become a Shadow, didn't you?"

"That's it?" I frowned. "Everyone who asks to be sponsored as a Shadow gets to be a Shadow?"

Asdar chuckled and sat on the edge of the table. "Everyone can try to become a Shadow, but not everyone will. I told you that the first day of Shadow training."

I remembered Meyori's dismissal, but I longed for an answer. I wanted to know why Asdar had sponsored me. Wouldn't a weapon's master be able to tell if a person was suited for battle?

Asdar walked over to the sliding doors of the council room. "Why do you want to be a Shadow, Shenrae? You've experienced your first mission. You struggle with combat skills in training. You were hurt by the hands of a False Shadow. You've almost lost your brother. What is it that keeps you here? What are you fighting to prove?"

I pressed my hands against my head, trying to sort through my emotions. What *was* I fighting to prove? That I would not be beaten? That my life was worth something? That in some way I was as strong as my parents had been?

None of those answers seemed right.

It was more than that.

Simpler.

I didn't want Syrane or Torey to die. I wanted to become stronger, so next time I could save Syrane. If Torey froze, I could be the one to protect her. I needed to become strong so no one else in Vaiyene would lose the people they loved. If I could possess the strength, I could make sure the people I cared about survived. Asdar, Lunia, and Kilo—they were only three people. They couldn't be everywhere at once, and with so few Shadows, it would be hard to defend against an attack. Even though I was frightened of battle, not being there to save Syrane or Torey scared me more. The False Shadows were formidable, but did any of us know how powerful they were? Was our training for nothing if we froze in battle?

If Kilo would willingly leave to pursue the False Shadows, the situation was grimmer than the Phantoms let on. Everyone knew how precious Vaiyene was to Kilo. To become Phantom had been his dream for as long as I could remember.

Asdar knew.

It was why he had pushed Kilo to do what he needed to. Being stuck in Vaiyene as a Phantom did nothing to solve the problem.

I removed my hands from my head. I needed to become strong. I needed to be able to stand against the False Shadows, and to do so...

I needed Phantom Asdar's help.

I drew in a deep breath. "I want to learn how to fight so I can protect Syrane and Torey." Asdar glanced over his shoulder at me. I placed my right hand over my chest and bowed low. "Can you train me to be a better warrior?"

Long moments passed.

Did he not believe I could?

I remained as I was until I saw Asdar's sandaled boots draw near. I lifted my head, and Asdar nodded. "I will try. Tomorrow morning, before dawn in the arena, we'll begin with the *very* basics."

———

I knelt on the ground with my head in my hands. Why had I asked Asdar for one-on-one training? My stomach was in knots. If I couldn't figure out how to improve my combat skills by Asdar's hands, it was impossible. I wasn't cut out for it. I was a failure.

I dug my fingers into my scalp.

This was ridiculous. I had to stop thinking like this.

Torey and Syrane had both tried to teach me how to fight, how to anticipate moves, how to watch a person's body language, but even though I saw it, my reactions were never fast enough. I couldn't grasp how to counter what I saw and translate action in a real-time situation. I groaned and dug my nails into my palms. At this point, all my thinking was robbing me of any positive outlook for my training. I would never improve if I didn't try my best. I rocked back onto my feet and stood, grabbing my staff from the ground.

Phantom Asdar met me halfway in the arena; his gaze trailed down to my staff. "No weapons today."

I rested the staff against an outcropping of rocks and returned.

"Your reactions are terrible, and your defense is weak at best."

I almost balked at his way of saying hello, but I was the one who had asked for additional training. He'd taken time away from being a Phantom to train me. I should be grateful I was getting this opportunity.

"You can scrape by with defensive moves, but you'll fall apart when there is anything requiring skill." Phantom Asdar held his arms up in front of his body. "Mirror what I do."

I raised both my arms. How was this going to help?

Phantom Asdar swatted at my arms. "With strength. Think of it as a sword. You need to keep it sturdy to deflect anything and forceful enough to do damage."

I straightened my arm and tensed my muscles.

Asdar nodded his approval. "Keep your arms up and block me. Protecting yourself is foremost in combat."

He brought back one of his arms to his waist, then punched it. Each action was deliberate and slow, allowing me to analyze each movement. When his fist drew near my chest, I moved my right arm and blocked him with my forearm.

"Good. Again."

He brought back his left arm this time and punched at me. I moved my left arm to block. We did this a few times before he nodded and took a step back.

"Now I want you to strike, and I'll defend against your attack."

I pulled my right arm back and fisted my hand.

"Keep your fist up, like you're going to elbow someone." I frowned and adjusted my grip. I punched out, and Asdar blocked me.

"Straighten your fist, or you'll break your wrist."

We went over the same process a few more times until the routine of it became ingrained in my mind. Then we switched. He went through the drill, and I countered with attacks. Each time, we did it a little bit faster.

After a few more rounds, Phantom Asdar nodded.

"We need to work on your footwork, your balance, your speed, and your focus. The staff is a good choice for you. Because of its reach, you have longer to react. If you can become quicker, it will be easier to catch your opponent off guard and disable them before fatal blows are exchanged."

A few Shadows had begun to trail into the arena. I glanced over at them, noticing their judgmental looks.

Asdar cleared his throat. "You need to let go of your apprehension of them. It's holding you back."

Two of my comrades began talking together, their eyes passing over me before they giggled. I frowned. Were they laughing at me? Asdar hit me in the shoulder with a staff. I jumped to attention and looked around, wondering where the longer staff had come from. Mine still rested against the rock outcropping.

"Kilo used to train with this staff. Its reach will allow you to keep your opponents at more of a distance." He spun it in his hands and stretched it out toward me. "He'd be happy for you to have it."

I wrapped my fingers around the staff and weighed it in my hands. It was heavier than the one I'd been using for training, but it did possess an extended reach.

"You'll have to work on your strength, or you'll become more of a liability than you already are. The weight will unbalance you until you are accustomed to the difference. Kilo no longer uses such a sturdy staff—to lessen the power behind his blows—but you could use the extra bit of weight."

I smiled to myself. It wouldn't be a gift if there were no backhanded insults. I bowed at the waist in Shadow fashion, with my right hand over my chest.

"Thank you." I meant it.

Phantom Asdar gave a small bow in return and headed toward the crowd that had gathered. He paused after a moment and glanced back at me. "I'm not as talented as Kilo is with the staff, but I can show you how to wield one better than mindlessly flailing it about." A thin smile crept onto his face. "As amusing as it is to watch you attempt it, now that you're willing to learn, I will teach you what I can."

I didn't know whether to be upset or happy, but Asdar didn't wait for a response. He moved into the center of the arena, and my fellow trainees trailed after him.

Over his shoulder, he shouted back at me.

"And a word of advice—stop caring!"

I frowned.

Stop caring about what?

My fingers trailed over the wooden staff in my hands, picking at the leather Kilo had wrapped around the center. It was worn from training, but it was sturdy.

I started after Phantom Asdar, to the center of the arena.

Syrane's and Torey's glanced over at me, as they walked into the arena. For the first time, my enthusiasm at training matched their own.

chapter twenty-two
A NEW PATH

"Keep your back straight," Phantom Asdar said as he paced beside me. "Bring your right leg out farther and balance your weight between both feet. Keep your staff on your shoulder. Now strike."

I swung my right arm high over my head, following through in an arc. After almost two weeks of dedicated training with Asdar, the staff seemed less awkward in my grasp.

"Keep your elbow straight at the beginning of your strike."

I drew in a breath and brought the staff up to rest on my shoulder before executing the move again. A rush of air rustled the grass beneath my feet. Phantom Asdar nodded. He held his staff with one hand, rolling his shoulders to loosen his muscles. He circled me, and I kept my eyes trained on his movement, waiting for the moment he would strike. When his left leg fell out of rhythm, I brought my staff around.

Asdar swung his staff to block me.

I turned on my back foot, shifting the staff in my hands as I brought it up across my body. Asdar moved and blocked me. A bead of sweat was on his temple. I was winded myself, but there was progress in my speed and ability.

"Your left arm is weak. You need to practice more with your less dominant hand. It won't take long before your enemy spots your weakness."

I shook out my arms, shifting on my feet.

Asdar set aside the staff and drew a sword from its sheath. The sword was the most common weapon—and the one I trained against most often. After running through the same drills so many times, the staff was beginning to become second nature.

Asdar shifted his stance. Usually, his weight was distributed between each foot, but he was beginning to favor his left ankle. That was his weakness. If I could trick him into thinking I hadn't noticed his slight limp, I might have a chance of beating him.

I slid my right foot out and swung my staff in a circle toward Asdar's side. He shifted his weight and swung his sword up to block me. At that moment, I shifted the staff to my other hand and struck Asdar's ankle. He sucked in a breath as the wood connected. Then he gave me a nod, acknowledging the hit.

He seemed happy. "This will be our last training session."

I held my staff loose at my side, disappointed.

Phantom Asdar sheathed his blade. "And look, your comrades have witnessed your victory."

I spun around to see most of the Shadows-in-training on the edges of the arena. Even some of the Shadows watched me. Torey brought her hands up close to her face and clapped. Syrane gave me a smirk.

I returned their smiles. I hadn't even noticed them.

"Walk with me," Phantom Asdar said, his voice quiet. He led us back to the Phantoms' house and toward the gardens. When we reached the stables, he stopped. A black stallion had been turned out in the pen. It wasn't Nightwind, but one very similar.

"He's from Nightwind's lines. He doesn't have a name yet, as he's still young and not bonded. If you can handle him, he'll serve you well."

I reached out my hand and was met with a derisive snort. I laughed. The stallion was every bit as friendly as Asdar.

"You'll need a good horse," Asdar said by way of explanation. "Kilo would never forgive me if I let you leave Vaiyene without one."

"But I thought the Shadows weren't leaving…" I trailed off, and Asdar crossed his arms over his chest. Letting me have a horse seemed an unusual gesture. He fixed me with a look I couldn't identify. He kept his emotions masked intentionally.

Lately, it had become easier to read him.

Why was he cautious?

"We will not be going on any Shadow missions. Taking three of you outside Vaiyene when you were unprepared was foolish of me. I will not risk the lives of our Shadows or those in training, but," he opened the pen of the black stallion, "I have taught you everything you can learn here."

I opened my mouth to protest but lost the will to argue at Phantom Asdar's pointed stare. I was improving and was ready to fight for the chance to continue to be a part of the Shadows. I'd worked too hard to be dismissed. Asdar led the stallion out of the pen, and I waited impatiently for him to continue.

"You will never be a warrior in the same sense your brother or your parents were, or in the same way as Kilo."

"But, I've—" The words died out as Asdar continued.

"I knew this when I sponsored you as my Shadow. There's a man we work with regularly. His name is General Mirai, and he holds similar ideals to the Shadows. He'll be able to train you better than I am capable of."

My heart sank. I'd just started to look forward to our training sessions. Now I was being sent away. Asdar rubbed the horse's muzzle. Was I that bad of a Shadow? Over the past few months, I had begun to trust Phantom Asdar more. He'd taken the time to train me, and even though his words were rough, his actions betrayed his care for my training. He intentionally went slow, explaining each move and countermove until I was able to mimic them. Sometimes repeating them more than once until I grasp the movement.

I sighed, not bothering to hide the disappointment in my voice. "If you believe that is what's best."

Asdar was quiet, giving my own mind time to wander. A sudden sinking sensation darkened my mood, as heavy and as dark as the emptiness I'd felt at my parents' deaths. Our training would end, and I would be away from Torey and Syrane and their constant reminder of why I was training to become a Shadow.

What if something happened to them while I was away?

What if I was not there to save them?

Asdar cleared his throat. "If I didn't respect General Mirai, I would not consider it."

I reached out my hand, and the black stallion pressed his nose against my palm. I tried to feel excited at the opportunity, but my attempt was unsuccessful.

"Vaiyene is going to need more than warriors. I'm a warrior, Shenrae; I can't teach you the finer aspects of the Shadow's Creed, or how to navigate this world. Those answers you'll have to find on your own, and to do that, you need to go elsewhere."

I ran my hands down the stallion's muzzle, letting him get used to my touch. Tears threatened to break my composure, but I fought them back, placing my hands on either side of the horse. Asdar set his hand on the stallion's shoulders to reassure him as I hoisted myself over his back. I curled my fingers into the horse's mane. He didn't seem to mind being ridden bareback. The Shadows were given horses when they ascended to being full Shadows. I was not yet a Shadow—was this Asdar's way of an apology?

"Greymoon," I said, my eyes still on the stallion.

Asdar nodded his approval at the choice of name. He was quiet. Then his words made reality inescapable.

"I will escort you to Tarahn, where General Mirai is waiting. We must leave before the snowpack is impassable."

His eyes surveyed the sky. "As it is, we're taking a risk."

I tried not to think about it. "How long will I be there?"

"Winter will make it impossible to return. I do not think even Kilo could make the journey home. When spring returns to these lands, you will return to Vaiyene."

I slid off Greymoon and patted his neck; his nose nuzzled against my shoulder. "Thank you," I said again, swallowing my tears. At least I would have one friend. Asdar bowed to me and left me with his stallion—my stallion.

"Well, Greymoon, it's just going to be you and me."

———

I hated saying goodbye. Something about it felt so final, definite, and unsure. The death of my parents was still fresh in my mind. Which made this no easier. Regardless, I needed to say goodbye no matter how hard it would be. If I didn't make it back, at least they would have received a proper farewell to remember me by.

I waited both patiently and impatiently— impatiently for it to be over and patiently because I didn't want it to be over. Until I said goodbye, part of me could deny it. Saying goodbye meant I would not get to see my brother and my friend for quite some time. Saying goodbye meant, for the first time, I would be alone. I pressed my hands over my eyes and sank down onto the balls of my feet, staring at the burned remains of my family's house. Idly, I drew circles in the ash with my fingers. There was no going back. My parents and home were gone, and as much as I wanted it to be so, things would never be the same.

Rubble shifted behind me. Torey smiled as I glanced over at her. She walked as if nothing was amiss as if today was not possibly our last day together.

I was going to miss her.

When she was within arm's reach, she wrapped her arms around me and hugged me tightly. "I'm so happy for you. This will be such a great experience."

I wished I could have been as confident as she was.

The finality of Asdar's order still shook me. Even though the experience would be worthwhile, training in a new place with new people didn't appeal to me. My place was here, with Syrane and Torey. I needed them. Time seemed short of late like somehow every moment counted. If we possessed such a short amount of time, wouldn't it be best to spend it here? Where I belonged?

"Shenrae?" Torey's smiled wavered as her eyebrows knit in concern. Had she asked me something? Before I could ask her to repeat herself, Syrane's ungraceful trudging drew my attention. His arms wrapped together, squeezing an oversized bag. He stumbled over a wooden beam while trying to make his way through the rubble. Torey rushed to help guide him.

"What did you bring all the way out here?" I asked.

Syrane dropped the sack and grinned at me. His face was splotchy with dirt. "Open it."

From his boyish grin, I knew whatever was inside would draw a reaction from me. I walked over and opened the sack, peering inside. I covered my mouth and laughed.

"Potatoes?"

I picked one up and turned it over in my hands, glancing up at Syrane. His grin grew wider. Torey stared, dumbfounded, back and forth between the two of us.

"Ever since Shenrae was little, she's always loved potatoes. If I didn't know her, I would say it borders on obsession. We ate them so much when we were younger, our parents almost forbade her from asking for them."

I rubbed away a bit of dirt from the potato in my hand, tears welling up in my eyes. Such a silly thing to bring as a goodbye gift.

"I didn't know if they would have any in Tarahn." Syrane hesitated, then continued. "Anyways, I thought it would be a nice reminder of home on your journey. Potatoes are hard to come by these days."

I blinked back the tears and stood. I looked from Torey to Syrane and tried to find words. I wanted to know they were going to be safe. Nothing was assured anymore, but I wanted to forget about that for now. I did my best to adopt Torey's carefree nature and settled for something simple to express myself.

"I'm going to miss the two of you."

Silence descended between us, and I looked down at the sack of potatoes. I wouldn't be taking it with me.

"Didn't your parents and Kilo have marks on their hands to remind them of each other?" Torey gave me a wry smile and pulled a dagger from inside her boot.

Our parents and Kilo had possessed an unbreakable bond. After experiencing Shadow training, I was beginning to understand how important they'd been to one another.

Syrane nudged my arm, jostling me from my thoughts. "It was a mark they branded into themselves on their first Shadow mission. What do you say, Shenrae? We're fabled to do great things because we're the 'children of Zavi and Mia.' Might as well follow in their footsteps, right?"

Torey smiled. "Guaranteed greatness."

And it would be a way to remind us we were not alone.

I liked the idea.

Syrane swatted Torey's dagger away and drew his own from the belt at his hip. The blade caught the light. He held out the hilt, tilting the edge to expose the decorative crest etched into the metal handle. It was the one Kilo had given us.

"Let's get a fire going," Torey said, rubbing her hands together. "Our feast awaits!"

I eyed the bag and groaned.

I hoped Syrane and Torey had brought more than potatoes.

Torey began gathering a pile of salvageable wood we could use to build a fire. I started after her, but Syrane blocked my path.

"You're going to be fine."

I met Syrane's gaze. "I know."

It didn't make leaving any easier.

Syrane gave me a lopsided smile and began helping Torey transport wood into a pile. I pulled out a small flint stone and swept brittle pieces of wood into a mound. When the kindling caught fire, Torey began leaning the planks of wood against one another, blowing at the smoking flame to spread its reach. Before long, the light illuminated the area, warming an otherwise bitter night.

Syrane and Torey prepared the boiled potatoes, digging out some dried meat and fruit from the packs we all wore as Shadows. Considering the rations for the winter, it was nothing short of a feast. When we had eaten, we all stood around the fire, flames casting dark shadows onto our faces. The smoke blurred my vision of my companions, but I thought I saw tears in Torey's eyes.

I cleared my throat, not wanting to descend into tears myself. "Shall we?"

Syrane wrapped a cloth around the edge of the dagger's blade and knelt next to the fire, holding the hilt as close to the flames as he could. The hilt's edge glowed a crimson red, and Syrane turned around, looking between Torey and me. At Torey's hesitation, I held out my left hand.

"Hurry," I said, wrinkling my nose against the oncoming pain. Syrane pressed the blade against the back of my hand, and I gritted my teeth, hissing as metal seared my flesh. Syrane pulled the knife away; blisters had formed at the edges of the mark.

I raised my eyes at Torey. "It was your idea."

"I know." Her eyes watched Syrane as he heated the hilt back up in the flame. "I'm not very good with pain."

She held out her hand, and I placed my hand around her wrist to keep her from flinching. When the dagger's hilt pressed against her skin, she closed her eyes and let out a soft whimper. I took the knife from Syrane. The metal turned red in my grasp, and I stared into the flames. We'd completed our first Shadow mission and encountered the False Shadows. We'd survived. I twisted the dagger in my hand, evenly heating the metal before standing and pressing the blade against the back of Syrane's hand. He didn't flinch. I left the metal against his skin for ten counts before I set the dagger on a rock to cool. I flexed my hand and winced as my skin stretched over bones. The mark was an inflamed wound, but it mattered little to me what it looked like.

The sentiment it served eased my mind.

We sat around the fire, in the place where Syrane and I had grown up, burning the last reminders from our old life. Earlier it had made me sad walking among the ruins, but I realized this was the beginning of a new part of our journey. We would do what we needed to grow strong enough that our past mistakes and shortcomings would be behind us.

We were Shadows together, and that made us strong.

———

Grimacing, I loosened my grip on Greymoon's reins. The skin was still inflamed from the previous night. The brand seemed to be healing well enough, though the timing was somewhat inconvenient. I would be riding for quite some time, and I didn't have a good sense of Greymoon's manners to give him free rein.

If Phantom Asdar noticed my lack of grip, he said nothing.

We didn't take the main path leading out from Vaiyene. Instead, Asdar led us on the high trail, at the edge of the village, into the forest and through the cave system that doubled as Vaiyene's entrance and exit. Asdar stopped at the overlook on the outskirts. I paused beside him, looking out over the sweeping peaks and the valley below. Somewhere next to the river lay the village of Koto. Much farther to the east, across Kiriku, Kilo searched for the False Shadows.

A calm settled over me.

My ability with the staff was passable. I would never become a staff master, but I would be able to hold my own.

I could defend myself against the False Shadows.

I could survive.

If Asdar thought General Mirai would help with my training, I would accept the challenge and do my best. I moved my fingers, stretching the burned skin. Even if Syrane and Torey were away from me, I would carry them with me—like Kilo, and my parents always had.

I placed my hands on Greymoon's sides and threw my leg over his back. I situated myself in the saddle and adjusted the reins over his neck.

"Are you prepared?" Asdar's gaze was fixed on me.

I drew in a breath. "I am.

part three
KILO

chapter twenty-three
KILO'S JUSTICE

"He was there again." Finae tapped my shoulder, and I glanced back at her. She pointed down a darkened pathway between two vacant buildings constructed of metal. A man meandered in front of us with a cart full of unrefined ore, humming as he went about his business.

"Not him," she said, exasperation in her voice. "Of course, the moment I point him out, he disappears."

I put on a smile for Finae's sake. "Keep an eye out."

I knew we were being followed. We had been for quite some time, but I didn't want to worry Finae by confirming her suspicions. The False Shadows wanted me dead. I knew that much. What concerned me was why they hesitated to make a move against us.

With Finae traveling with me, I was more cautious of danger. Like the False Shadows, I was biding my time. Finae still refused to carry any weapon to protect herself. I'd worked with many people with varying degrees of self-defense on Shadow missions. My sister was the first who had refused to carry anything, even for show. Her innocence made me hesitate.

I wanted to keep my distance from our enemy.

A drop of water fell from the shingled roof overhead onto Finae's head. She flinched as it hit her, scowling at the raindrop with unabashed anger, jumping over a puddle of mud to try and stay some manner of clean. It was moments like these I would treasure. It was selfish, but Finae brought a touch of joy that had been missing from my life for too long.

I watched, amused, as she walked on the opposite side of the street to avoid the muddier sections of the road. Here in Aventon, the tangy odor of lead and minerals hung heavy in the air. The people here had grown accustomed to it, but my eyes stung from the sulfuric acid stirred up by the recent snowstorm. I had refused the offer to stay in the town because of the irritation. Finae had mentioned it when we first arrived, but she seemed too distracted to complain.

I shielded my eyes from the sun and judged the distance from the horizon. It was almost mid-morning, about time to meet our contact.

"Let's head to the center of the village."

I scanned the crowd and turned into the center pathway, between the rows of old, rickety buildings made from metal sheeting. Rust stained the edges of the buildings, showing off the age of the small mining village. The buildings were no longer occupied—too much of a safety concern—but the town's history remained. It brought me comfort. Here was a place where tradition and history were respected.

The crowd parted around me, but Finae struggled to keep up. She pushed past a few of the villagers, regaining her position at my side. She mumbled something under her breath, but I didn't shift my attention from the person who still followed us. Out of the corner of my eye, I saw the figure disappear, and I raised my voice. "We don't want to keep our contact waiting."

Finae raised an eyebrow but humored me and trotted to match my pace. We circled a large brass statue of the original founder.

Raindrops reflected the shimmer of minerals in a colorful array. Finae gasped at the display, admiring the collection. If the False Shadows hadn't been following us, I would have liked to let her spend a few moments with her paints. I knew she was dying to bring them out, but I worried about an ambush.

I jostled through a tight cluster of people, bumping elbows with a few of them before doubling back around and veering off in a new direction. I coaxed Finae through a darkened alleyway, between an inn and a tavern, emerging almost in the exact place we had begun.

Finae rolled her eyes at me. "Very funny."

I flashed her a smile before I started in the real direction of our contact, the diversion's true purpose was lost to her. Finae saw my deception as a jest, but my actions were a statement—I know you're following us, and I'm prepared. I knew of the False Shadows' movements, as they knew of mine.

We were close to Magoto, where Hitori was.

The False Shadows would strike; it was no longer a question in my mind but a waning timeframe. A cart bumped into view on the crowded street before us, and I nudged Finae. Together we pushed through the crowd to meet Orin, the village blacksmith. His cart was to be delivered inside Magoto's walls. The last cart until spring. None but those with a solid reputation and necessary wares were allowed inside Magoto.

Not even Orin could enter, but his wares could.

It had taken me almost two weeks to win Orin's and the other villagers' trust, but little by little, they had welcomed us into their humble lives.

Orin's face lit up as we approached. His long gray beard flowed down his chest and over his sizeable potbelly. Two large mules plodded ahead of him, pulling the oversized cart through the middle of town.

"Come, let us start our journey," Orin said, gesturing to the cart with both arms. "You can ride in the back or walk beside it. The back is rather cozy, but up front"—he winked at Finae—"you get to sit beside me. The view's not too bad either."

Finae grinned at the man and laughed sheepishly. It warmed my heart seeing Finae grow more comfortable around people. She'd never been allowed outside, save for rudimentary training. It was due to our parents' overwhelming fear they would lose her, as they had our late brother. Even after our parents' deaths, Finae didn't leave home, turning instead to her paintings for comfort. I shrugged when she looked back at me. She seemed to be enjoying herself on this trip. I needed to take her to Tarahn, to show her the kites and all the colorful people there. She would be inspired, but Finae enjoyed herself despite not being shown extravagance. Her innocent nature humbled me. She had no want for anything. To experience life—and paint—were her simple desires.

Orin stopped his mules and helped Finae up onto the wooden seat at the front of the cart. She flashed me a smile and sat, plopping her hands in her lap. I grabbed the side of the cart and hoisted myself over, settling myself on top of an old weathered crate that squeaked under my weight.

I scanned the town behind us, watching for shadowed figures in the alleyways.

On the horizon, there was a lake. A subtle mist had settled upon the waters, brushing across the top of the lake with a quiet grace. Yellow and orange aspens lined the edges of the water. Winter had not yet touched these lands. Vaiyene's mountain pass would already be packed with snow, closed to both Finae and myself.

Not that we could go back.

I forced myself to be in the present, with Finae. If faced with the choice again, I would choose to leave Vaiyene the same.

My conviction was as sharp as the day I had left.

Red leaves capped a few of the trees, and they rustled in the distance. The late-autumn atmosphere was hard not to appreciate. While this region's beauty was not the same as that of Vaiyene, it possessed a unique charm of its own. The closer we drew to Magoto, the more I laughed at my initial impressions of where the False Shadows lived. Even as old as I was, it was still easy to think of them as monsters hiding in the dark. If I were to ask Finae to paint where she believed the False Shadows lived, would she create a landscape where the sun did not reach? Would volcanoes dot the horizon, with magma flowing down into the village and the False Shadows sacrificing their own people's lives? I rested my head on the back of the cart, amused. Nothing was ever that simple. The simplicity of youth had faded from my life long ago.

My gaze returned to the fading village of Aventon. A figure on horseback headed in our direction. They were persistent. I would give them that. I kept an eye on the direction and speed of our unwelcome companion, finding them of no concern at their current distance. I pulled a small journal from inside the pocket of my robe and found a blank page, scribbling out a rough draft of the landscape and direction we traveled. One day, I would compile all my notes and drawings for Vaiyene's records. The Phantoms' knowledge of the southern regions of Kiriku was sparse.

I took my duty seriously even as a rogue.

I raked my hand across my face, taming the hairs that had come loose in the wind. I held a chunk between two fingers. The color had faded. To conceal our identities, I'd dyed both Finae's and my hair completely black, to fit in with the people who lived across Phia. The False Shadows had made it easy to concoct a fitting story for ourselves: the wandering siblings—the last survivors of a small village, devastated by the Shadows. I leaned against the back of the weathered cart and twisted my shoulders, trying to find a comfortable position.

Orin's voice carried on the wind: "I thought we were done for, but my brother jumped out from the bushes, a sword in hand. I was about to punch him—for scaring me, you know—but something rustled in the forest behind him, so I held off."

I could picture Finae's wide-eyed expression, waiting for the conclusion to the epic tale. Orin thrived on Finae's enthusiasm.

"And a boar came out of the bushes and nailed him right in the buttocks!" Orin leaned back, chuckling as he delivered the punchline to his story. The cart shifted as he moved.

Finae's laughter drifting back to me.

I smiled.

Orin continued his story. "To this day, my brother doesn't mess with me. You see, the world has a way of coming around if you're not nice to people."

I inhaled, enjoying the clean air and peace of travel.

It was a good moral to the story, though the tale itself made no sense. But not every story needed to be grounded in reality. I stifled a yawn. The rocking of the cart made it difficult to stay alert. I looked out across the barren landscape through half-lidded eyes, listening to Orin as he began his next tale.

———

Wheels lurched underneath me, and I bolted upright, grabbing my staff as we bumped across the tall grass. Orin's weight lifted from the cart, and I shook off the residual fatigue from too little sleep. Small white mountains were on the horizon. I rubbed my eyes, and the mountains became intricately placed white structures nestled against each other. Two stone guard towers flanked the edge of the wall surrounding the town. Unlike the lake we had passed earlier, this is what I expected from the False Shadows.

Isolation.

Walls were built to keep people out or to keep them in.

Both seemed applicable.

Finae scrambled out the front of the cart, and I helped her into the back. She crouched beside me, and we moved the canvas tarp over us and secured it to the metal posts on either end of the cart. I tried to ignore the stifling sensation of the tight space.

Orin stepped into the cart and peered in at us, his long beard waggling. His kind eyes passed over us.

"Once I reach the gate, the guardsman will take the cart. You're on your own after that."

I nodded, striving to maintain my diplomacy and composure.

"Thank you. I will find some way to repay your kindness."

My palms grew clammy as Orin adjusted the tarp and placed a box at the end of the cart to hide us. He gave one final smile before darkness enclosed us.

"Good luck," Orin said, his voice dampened by the tarp.

The cart sank as he settled himself into it. Once again, the cart bumped as it made its way back onto the dirt road. Particles of dust settled in through the side of the tarp. I forced myself to take long, calming breaths against air heavy with metal. I'd been on worse Shadow missions than this and had been in tighter spaces. I closed my eyes and tried to find other thoughts to occupy my mind, but all I could think of was the suffocating air and how loud my breath seemed to be.

"Are you okay?" Finae touched my fisted hands, and I dragged myself to the present. I furrowed my brow and realized my knuckles were white around my staff. I loosened my grip and forced my hands to relax.

"I'm not a fan of tight spaces."

"Do you think there will be paintbrushes in Magoto?"

I tried to smile, knowing she was trying to help me think about something else. I played along as best I could. "We can look, although I'm not sure how the economy works here." Nor was I sure we wanted to risk such an interaction.

"Do you think I could make a brush out of my hair?"

I frowned, not sure if she was joking or not. "Mom did say you had hair like a horse."

I couldn't see her face but imagined my comment drew at least a smile from her. Our family had not been the most loving, but some memories I still cherished.

Orin pounded on the cart to silence us.

A rough voice shouted in the distance.

"Halt! That's close enough."

Something scraped against the wooden cart.

"I'm under orders from Hitori to bring the final supply of metals for Magoto," Orin shouted in response. His voice was gruff and calm, and his experience in dealing with the guards was evident in his speech.

"In exchange for the wares," Orin droned on over our heads, "I am to receive my usual payment."

There was silence, then a screech and a low, grating noise.

"We were told to expect you."

Finae placed her hand on my shoulder, and I took a deep breath, forcing my mind to focus on the conversation. I needed to read the situation without error. A fight would alert others of our arrival. If possible, it would be best to sneak in, but if there was going to be a fight, I needed to gain the upper hand.

Finae's life depended on it.

"Your payment," the guard said. Coins jingled in the exchange.

We pitched forward, and I pressed my face against the edge of the cart and squinted through the cracks.

"I'll be back by week's end to retrieve the cart," Orin said. "Do me a favor and keep it inside until then. Don't want any bandits scuffing up the wood."

He was a good man and smarter than he appeared. I appreciated the effort, even if they did unload the cart right away. He had even agreed to watch our horses until we returned.

The cart clacked over the stone bridge. Metal screeched, and I shuddered as the sound crawled through my skin. The gate shut tight. I drew a mental image as the cart continued into Magoto, recalling my Shadow training. Right, left, another left and a straight line. As the cart slowed, I reached out a hand to Finae. No matter what happened, her safety came first. Heavy footsteps approached the cart—from the sound of it, at least two pairs.

"Hitori will want these to be documented and carried inside the stronghold before sundown."

"We'll never have enough time," the second voice said with a groan. "What's the rush? It's not like we need the metal to make swords tonight."

"Stop complaining, Borin." The first man chuckled. "It's always something with you, isn't it?"

I shifted my weight and held my staff in hand. It was difficult to maneuver into position in such tight quarters, especially without moving the tarp above us. A hand gripped the edge of the tarp and began untying the ropes farthest away from us. I sank low; ready to spring the moment the tarp lifted.

"Hitori and her group have arrived," a woman said, her voice low and commanding. Her footsteps were much lighter than those of the two men. I hadn't heard her approach. "I suggest you report at once. She's in a bitter mood today, so I wouldn't delay."

I held still, my breath caught in my chest.

One opponent was better than two.

"Go," the woman said. "I will tend the horses and summon some of the guardsmen to help unload the cart."

Two pairs of boots scuffled across the pavement. I strained my ears until I could no longer hear their tread upon the stone. They would be turning around a corner. Based on the sound of the woman's voice, she was by the right corner of the cart. I shifted my weight and was about to spring into action when the woman spoke.

"You can come out now."

I froze. Had this person seen my movement, or was she talking to someone else?

"I've been tracking you," the woman continued, untying the restraints to the tarp. "I know you've both seen me."

Finae drew in a sharp breath.

The woman removed the box at the front of the cart, though it was not much of a view—white stone upon more white stone. I peeled a portion of the tarp back and stood, revealing myself.

"And you can put your weapon away," the woman said. The hood of her cloak rested on her shoulders. Her raven hair blew in the wind against skin darkened by the sun. Her cheekbones were high against her green eyes—traits of the lower regions of Kiriku. Her arms were crossed over her chest. She was well into adulthood, but not too old for age to slow the body.

"If I planned to kill you," she said, exasperation heavy on her words. "I would have let you die in Leiko."

"You're the one who gave me the vial and helped me escape."

"You should have figured it out sooner. The others would have killed you and your sister."

Her words chilled me. Even though she seemed to be on our side, I did not like her knowing Finae was my sister. I brushed off my apprehension and placed the staff back into the holder on my back. I jumped down from the cart, offering my hand to help Finae down.

"Who are you?"

"Rin, one of Hitori's tools, or my favorite term, one of the 'False Shadows.'" She made no effort to hide the resentment underscoring her words. She was neither fond of Hitori nor of being in the False Shadows.

"Why do you keep saving me?"

Rin stroked the horses' muzzles and met my gaze.

She didn't hesitate. "I need you alive."

I waited for her to elaborate, but Rin turned to tend to the horses. I wouldn't be getting any answers, at least not here. Which was for the best. Finae glanced at me, and I shrugged. Whatever Rin wanted, I would listen. She held the answers to countless questions, and I needed her cooperation, if not her help.

Rin unhitched the horses and put them inside the stalls behind us, motioning for us to follow her. She led us to a small wooden shed in the corner by the stables. The door squeaked and almost fell off its hinges as she opened it to retrieve two black cloaks identical to her own.

"Put these on. It's a large enough town to go unnoticed, but it'd be better if we conceal your identities as best we can."

Finae glanced at me for permission, and I nodded. Shadow training taught to acclimate to your environment. We had shed our old clothing after leaving Vaiyene, but if Rin was offering us the opportunity to blend into the False Shadows, it would enable us to move undetected. We put on the cloaks and followed Rin down a narrow road that led to the lower level of white stone houses. The stones here were deteriorated. Large chunks were missing from the structures, the outsides seemingly burned from a fire.

Stone did not easily crumble, nor did stone catch fire.

A cold breeze cut through layers of clothing and chilled to the bone. The cold was nothing new to me, but this cold crept inside of me, making it hard to breathe. I pulled the cloak away from my neck to get more air. Rin stopped before a house chiseled from stone and motioned us inside. It was dull, mundane at best, and the walls were an off-white gray—like everything we had seen so far. Two wooden chairs and a bedframe sat in the corner. It was stark, dark, and empty.

There was no warmth in this town.

I waited for Finae to settle inside before my attention snapped to Rin. She watched me, a hint of amusement on her lips.

When she didn't speak, I prompted her. "Why me?"

"I need someone with influence and strength to kill Hitori. Her rule here is nothing more than tyranny."

My eyes flicked to the door as if guards would appear at her words. I shirked off my apprehension and met her words with honesty. Her use of the word "kill" was too casual.

"You seem quite capable." I glanced at the sword belted at her hip. "You only need to gather people of similar mind to make a change."

Rin chuckled without humor. "None of the people in this town have the spine. I would take up arms myself, but I'm a mere tool to her. If she got even a whiff of my plans, she wouldn't hesitate to kill me."

My eyes narrowed. "And why do you think I can help you? I may be a Phantom"—was a Phantom—"but there's only so much power I possess." And I had not even been able to save my own people.

"I know what you saw in Leiko," Rin said, her voice void from emotion. "Innocent people are dying because of Hitori. You wouldn't have come this far into the southern lands of Kiriku, to Magoto, if you didn't want to see this through to the end."

I couldn't deny her words.

I sensed no ill will from her, but prudence demanded disinterest until I gained more of a sense of her character. Even though she had saved my life, getting involved with another town's problems did not align with saving Vaiyene—no matter how many people they had killed.

She continued as she crossed over to the window. "You can stay here while you're in Magoto. No one lives in this sector anymore, and I doubt anyone will notice the smoke from a fireplace. There are other things on the people's minds."

I nodded, glad for the shelter. That much I would accept. The stone floor and walls would be chilly, but at least it was safe. Safe as it could be.

Rin glanced out the window, then turned her gaze back on me. "I will return tonight with some supplies, as well as information. Stay low until then."

Finae slipped off her small bag and began digging through it. She inspected the hearth and the cast iron pot hanging from a metal rod. Rin made her way to the door, then stopped beside me, a strange look in her eyes.

"She has Skill Poisoning as well?"

I frowned. "Skill Poisoning?"

Rin shook her head. "I'll explain later. There's a meeting I need to attend. If I'm absent, Hitori will become more suspicious of me."

I shook my head, trying to digest the encounter. Rin surprised me on more than one account. She was very forward, but we did share a common goal: we both wished for Hitori's removal. I undid the staff at my back. The silver repair Rin had placed there in Leiko gleamed in the darkness. I wanted to know more about Hitori, the Skills, and whatever this "Skill Poisoning" was. Coming here at been a risky move; we had to make the most of it.

Finae pulled out her sketchbook and grabbed a black charcoal pencil. She flipped to a new page and began recording our journey. Our meeting with Rin seemed not to have phased her. I knelt next to the fireplace and pulled a log from the pile of wood next to the stone hearth.

"Are you going to kill Hitori?"

I flinched at Finae's words and raised my head, but she didn't pause to look at me. I had always encouraged her to speak her mind, even if the subject was sensitive. I broke a rivet of wood off from a log of wood and tossed it into the hearth.

"You know the Shadows and Phantoms don't kill."

I unstoppered the light canteen at my side and fed the small, thin piece of wood inside. When it caught fire, I placed it under the stack of wood in the fireplace. Sitting back on my feet, I looked over at Finae. Why would she have asked that?

"Rin seems like an interesting person."

I nodded, sending Finae a careful look. "Even if she's helped me in the past, it doesn't mean she's not dangerous."

Finae seemed content to drop the subject, losing herself in her sketching. I watched the flames come to life in the hearth. Hitori's guilt was undeniable. She had killed dozens, if not hundreds of innocent people. Death carried out by her False Shadows rested on her conscience. Whether she felt remorse was a different matter. Justice would find her. I would make sure of it—as soon as I weighed the cost of lives against her own.

I brought one knee up and rested my elbow, sinking my chin into the folds of my cloak. Finae sketched without care or worry. Her judgement of Hitori was simplistic and absolute, with no room for error. Bad people deserved death—only good people were allowed to live—but life was more complicated than that.

I watched the flames with unfocused eyes, analyzing the play of light and dark across the cold stone.

The False Shadows killed.

Their transgression: taking innocent lives. However, more than a handful of them had been forced into being False Shadows and killing to protect those they loved. Were they to be charged with the same justice as Hitori? With Finae's absolute judgement, some would say yes. Others, no. It mattered how a person executed their own personal judgement. When did we make exceptions to the rule of life and death?

If I had never taken the time to listen to Ikaru, I would have believed all the False Shadows were evil. The Phantoms were trying to paint the picture this way.

It simplified life, made decisions easier.

Sometimes I missed it, although I had never been a Shadow who blindly followed orders. It was why I'd questioned Phantom Kural's murder of an unarmed man, and why I'd questioned him before I was even a Shadow. Never mind his involvement with the False Shadows. What had given Phantom Kural the right to take that man's life? Dealing in absolute justice lessened the burden of consequence, but it did not mean the answer was the right one. The root of evil lay in a man's choice—or lack thereof. Whether the False Shadows realized it, they decided to follow Hitori's orders. Their position was not easy for anyone, and I did not blame them for choosing to save the lives of their loved ones, but it remained their choice.

An exchange of one evil for another.

I held my palm out before the firelight, seeing the blood of the man I had killed to save Zavi's life. That, too, had been a decision to save one life over another.

What then was Hitori's price in all this?

And did she really deserve to die for what she had done?

My head snapped to attention as the door swung open and Rin fumbled into the room. Her arms were burdened with large blankets and cloth sacks.

I rushed to help her.

"Some food to replenish your supplies." She gestured to the sack in my hand, setting a large fur blanket on the floor. "I couldn't carry much, but this should at least make the night more bearable."

She sank into one of the chairs near the table and released a long, drawn-out breath. Her eyes wandered over to Finae, who lay asleep on the bed against the wall.

I cleared my throat, drawing her attention away from my sister.

"Skill Poisoning?"

Rin sighed and dragged her gaze to me.

"Yes, it's the poison that entered your body, as well as…" She glanced over at Finae, and my throat tightened.

"Finae," I supplied for her.

She nodded, averting her dull eyes from me.

Her hesitation in telling me was all I needed to know. I looked away from Rin, my throat was still tight. "There's no cure, is there?"

"The vial I gave you provided temporary relief, though it varies by person how the body handles it."

I watched Finae's slow, rhythmic breathing. Again, I had failed to protect her. How long did we both have before the poison resurfaced? Others in Vaiyene had consumed the wheat. I stood in front of the fire, leaning my hand upon the rough stones for support. How many people suffered back home? Or was the poison dormant in their veins?

"Finae consumed the wheat in Vaiyene?"

I stilled my mind. "How do you know about the wheat?"

Rin hesitated. "I was the one who poisoned the wheat."

I drew my dagger and lunged across the table, scattering papers across the floor as I set the blade against Rin's neck. "You poisoned an entire village! They were innocent!"

Rin didn't flinch against my blade. Her green eyes met mine. Her fighting spirit seemed broken, beaten down—lost. Her lack of emotion made me hesitate more than anything. Did she not feel remorse at what she had done? She had to have known telling me the truth would upset me.

Why had she told me the truth?

"As a former Shadow, you know the consequences of duty." Her eyes stared through me. "We are bound to obey orders we don't agree with."

I removed the dagger and stepped back.

Throughout my years, I had experienced many kinds of missions. During some of those missions, I had questioned my Phantom. If I'd lived in Magoto instead of Vaiyene, my position would have been no different than Rin's, but I would rather have died than obey such an order.

Rin drew back her left sleeve to expose a gruesome scar. It ran the length of her arm, with tiny fingers of pink running along the edges. Whoever had inflicted the wound had not done so with a sharp blade.

"I broke all the vials, save one. I did what I could despite the reprimands I knew I would face." Rin dropped the sleeve of her cloak. "It's your choice what you decide to do with the information I give you today, Phantom. I don't have the strength to stand against Hitori. Maybe you do." Her voice grew soft, but there was an edge to it. A tone of finality. "If I had the strength to stop her, I would have a long time ago."

Her words aligned with the Shadow's Creed.

Despite poisoning Finae and the people of Vaiyene, Rin's attitude was Shadow-like in a way. Her situation was more extreme than any of my own struggles. I wanted to hate her because of her hand in Finae's poisoning, but Finae's fate was a consequence on a much grander scale. Rin had saved my life in Leiko and had prevented the entire population of Vaiyene from being poisoned. Her actions were full of contradictions. Her deeds were courageous, inherently good, but she had been forced to hurt and kill innocent people. How did she deal with the guilt?

And what did that make her?

Finae rustled in the corner, and I glanced over to see her watching us. She had likely awoken at my outburst. I pressed my fingers against my temples. I didn't meet Finae's eyes when I made my request. "If you wouldn't mind recording this, Finae?"

Finae crossed the room and sat cross-legged on the floor. I handed her the journal from my tunic. Her unbiased opinion of our conversation would give me clarity later.

I had left Vaiyene, but I still needed to act like a Phantom.

I brushed aside my residual impression of Rin and gathered my thoughts. This could be my one chance to get the answers I needed.

"What are the Skills? Where do they come from?" I hesitated, not sure of my terminology.

Rin stood and leaned against the window frame, regarding me with calculating eyes. "How much do you know?"

I shook my head. "Not much. There was a False Shadow, Ikaru, who gave me some answers, but—" I stopped speaking at the surprise on her face. As if she had caught her lapse, the emotion then vanished. If she expected me to let it slide, she was wrong.

"Who's Ikaru to you?"

She let out an exasperated breath. "My brother."

It all made sense now. Hitori had ensnared two siblings to do her bidding, winding her grasp around each of them. It was logical but cruel. Each would follow orders, so nothing happened to the other; their failures would result in direct consequence to the other.

The information intrigued me, but time remained limited. I came back to the first question, prodding Rin to continue.

"What are the Skills?"

Ikaru had told me his version, but I wanted Rin's explanation. She seemed to be wiser and more in tune with the world than her brother was. She didn't fear Hitori. Instead, she fought against Hitori in a way that would not endanger her brother.

How would that affect the way she viewed the Skills?

She thought for a moment, then began speaking.

"It's the manipulation of our world and its perception. The basic theory is the transfer and manipulation of energy, but the applications and ways to control the Skills are near limitless." She shrugged, her words becoming bitter. "At least, Hitori has not found one."

I'd seen the Skills and fought against them. My staff rested against the edge of the mantel; the end was still cut from one of Hitori's men wielding the Skills. What else could the Skills affect?

Were they really "limitless"?

"Hitori and her group of followers discovered the Skills while off exploring ruins in the west. They found an almost-destroyed book containing the theory. The rest of the application and how to use them, they improvised."

I shook my head. It was both awe-inspiring and terrifying. "That's extraordinary."

"Unfortunately, Hitori's chosen to use the Skills to scare our people. She's experimenting with the Skills and what they can do with them. It's why she's trying to keep you away from Magoto.

She knows the Phantoms are people of justice and have the power to stop her."

Her gaze drifted to the street outside. "I know you found Hitori's victims in the Kinsaan Forest. Torture cannot recreate the screams of her experiments."

I fisted my hand at my side, remembering the sacks hidden in the forest and the memory tied to the gnarled tree. I narrowed my focus on what was most important: the Skills.

"How long has Hitori possessed this power?"

"Earlier this year, Hitori discovered the book on the Skills. She started her experiments in the summer."

I inhaled sharply. For having the Skills less than a turn of the seasons, Hitori's control over them already seemed beyond our ability to take her head on. We needed to know the weaknesses of the Skills and if there was a way to counteract the power.

"Is the copy of the book here, in Magoto?"

Rin stood and inspected the silver repair on my staff. "Yes, but—"

"It's guarded and impossible to get to." I finished her words with an exasperated sigh, waving her off with an impatient hand. It was a dumb question. Rin's information saved me the trouble of spying on the False Shadows and gleaning what little information I could obtain. I needed to be patient to execute this plan without being too hasty.

I glanced at Finae, who listened with rapt attention, scribbling as we spoke. Rin looked worn, her eyes red from too little sleep, but she seemed willing to answer more.

"How much do you know of Hitori's true plan? What does she want? What are her plans for Magoto? Does she intend to spread the Skills across all of Kiriku?"

"Due to my disobedience," Rin said, stumbling over the word, "Hitori no longer trusts me with her intentions. Much of what I've learned I've gleaned from eavesdropping and bribing the few who are disloyal to her." She rubbed her eyes, her voice betraying her exhaustion. "I was only able to meet you here because Hitori is convinced I am with her loyal followers."

I had not expected her to know what Hitori's plans were, but what little hope I carried, faded a little. Our best option was to find a way to counteract her Skills. If her contacts had known of Hitori's motives, Rin would have known them already. Questioning them would be a waste of time. If Hitori had found one book containing information on the Skills, was it possible there was another? Finding information about the Skills ourselves, without any bias, would be beneficial.

"Where are the ruins where Hitori found the book located?"

"I can give you a general direction, but Hitori's not plotted the exact location on any map."

"Can we go?" Finae asked, her voice quiet.

I glanced at her, surprised.

She never spoke in front of strangers. There was a slim chance Hitori had left anything in the ruins of use to us, but I was interested enough to consider it.

Rin frowned. "It's not an easy place to reach, nor will the route be unwatched. Hitori's spies span the entire lower portion of Kiriku. I can try to throw off her spies, but—"

I held up my hand and glanced at Finae.

"We will make the journey."

"If that's what you want, I won't stop you." Rin walked to the window and glanced outside, then came back, pulling out a rolled-up scroll from the inside of her boot. She laid the map out on the table and pointed to the center. Finae began tracing the triangular peaks of the mountain ranges. The Ranfour Ridges. Hidden somewhere in them could be the answers we sought.

There would most likely be snow. It would slow our travel, but it would also hide us from Hitori's spies.

"I would come with you if I could, but…" Rin crossed her arms as she continued to gaze out the window. "Somehow I have to figure out how to save lives without losing my own."

I studied Rin.

Her words were reflected in the dark circles under her eyes. She dropped her guard for the first time. Her position was a difficult one, as was mine. I couldn't tell if she was too tired to mask her emotions any longer, or if the stark reality of her position made it impossible for her to do so. What must she feel toward me? She sought out my help, but I imagined she envied the freedom my position and title held. My loss of title, as well as my loss of position and influence, could change her desire and willingness to help me. Until I knew I could trust her, she didn't need to know.

Helping Rin fell in line with my mission to find Hitori and put a stop to the False Shadows. Rin needed to be free to prevent as many of the False Shadows' deeds as she could, but was letting her commit crimes, a betrayal of my Phantom oath? Her actions hurt people—killed them even—but without her, more people would die.

Were her actions justified?

Rin rolled her map back up and returned it to her boot, She withdrew a tiny wooden sword on a leather rope. She held it out to me. Small letters were carved into the blade's edge.

We do what we must.

It was good advice for our situation.

"This will get you back into the town. Enter from the western gate. Follow the river that runs from the mountains behind the town. You'll find horses you can borrow there. After dusk, approach the Magoto gate and knock five times. Show the guard the knife, and you'll be able to enter."

I curled my fingers around the wooden knife. "Where are you headed?"

"It's best you don't know."

She held out a leather pouch for me. I untied the drawstring to reveal five glass vials.

I met Rin's gaze. "Are these—?"

Rin nodded. "Use them only when the symptoms are too much to bear. I don't know when I'll be able to make more."

"Thank you," I said. The words were genuine despite the path Rin straddled. She was the cause of Finae's illness and the illnesses of an unknown number of people in Vaiyene. As someone duty-bound, I could not blame her for what she had done, or what she continued to do. She lived with the guilt and fought to make amends where she could. It was admirable in a way, though in a twisted sense.

Rin gave me a short nod before leaving. I tucked the leather pouch into my robe and turned to meet Finae's cold gaze.

"Are you going to let her go?"

I began sorting through the provisions Rin had brought us. I did not like it, but there was no better option. People were going to die either way.

Rin could prevent some of the deaths.

Finae handed me the journal and began packing her bag. "We leave in the morning then?"

"At first light."

chapter twenty-five
ZENKAIKO

I inhaled fresh pine as we meandered through the dense forest of the Ranfour Ridges. It reminded me of home, of the Miyota Mountains, and of Vaiyene. I stifled a twinge of homesickness. I hoped Syrane and Shenrae were managing.

A flake of snow settled onto my eyelashes, and I blinked it away. Snow fluttered through the pine needles and disappeared into the forest floor. I glanced over at Finae, who had burrowed into a blanket on top of her horse.

"Are you warm enough?" I waved my hand over my pack on my borrowed horse. We had been traveling for three days, and today was by far the coldest. Most of the problematic places to navigate seemed out of the way, our path leveling out to a flat alpine valley.

"There's another blanket here if you need it."

She shook her head. "I'm fine."

Her gaze lingered on the ground.

"Do you see something?"

"I'm not sure. Every once in a while, I catch a glimpse of these rock pillars."

I reined in my horse and slowed his walk, veering to the right and bumping against Finae's horse. Dead pine needles lined the forest floor, covering broken twigs, rocks, and decaying leaves. I caught nothing of interest, but it did not mean Finae hadn't seen something. Venturing too far made me hesitate. If we got lost, it would not be easy to find our way back to Magoto, even with the map Finae had copied. The damp air meant more snow would fall. My training in navigation was decent, but snow would disorient any sense of direction.

I drew my staff and pushed back branches of a large pine tree, making it easier for my horse to pass. I glimpsed Finae's white horse through the pine branches, veering into the trees. Tree branches snagged my long fur cloak, and I held my forearm up to fend off the brunt of the attacks. I pulled back on the reins, spotting Finae. When my horse slowed next to her, she pointed to a broken rock structure on the ground. Could this be something from the ruins? I dismounted and inspected the rocks, noticing the clean cut of the stones—too clean to be organic. Judging from the large flat pedestal beside it, the top had broken off from the base. I picked off a layer of moss with my fingers, revealing intricate loops carved into stone.

Finae dismounted and knelt next to something before she motioned me over. It was another piece of the formation, this one round on the top, with a hole in the center. Inside, a discolored stone lay wedged between three thin slices of silver metal.

It seemed like a marker of some sort.

Finae brushed her hand along the silver threading. "It almost looks like your bond."

She rubbed the silver with her fingers, removing a layer of dirt from the surface. The was a slight similarity. Finae wiped her hand over the opaque stone. At her touch, a white, almost smoke-like mist cascaded, from the rock and rolled across the forest floor. It was like the gnarled tree in the Kinsaan Forest.

"Be careful. That stone is imbued with the Skills." I tensed as she gave me a quick glance, her eyes wide with excitement, ignoring my warning. My words had drawn a different reaction than anticipated—excitement rather than caution.

I sighed.

My own excitement lay buried deep inside, locked beneath the thoughts of innocents killed by the False Shadows. The Skills had taken hold of me after I'd touched the tree in the Kinsaan Forest. Finae didn't react the same as I had, with the other tree. Was this a different type of enchantment?

When the mist dissipated, and I relaxed.

"Let's keep going," I said. We had to get going before the snow made it impossible to return.

We mounted our horses and pressed on through the forest, keeping a close watch on the edge of the trees. When Finae found another pillar some distance away, we adjusted our path between the two markers. The horses' hooves clopped against stone.

A road lay under a thin layer of snow.

Finae grinned from ear to ear. When we had left Magoto, I'd not thought we would find the ruins. It hadn't even taken us long to find traces of the Skills here.

It was a promising start.

The pine trees surrounding us began to thin. Giant steps, wide enough for the horses to traverse without trouble, led upward. An archway presided over the top of the stairs, made from the same stone pillars we had seen earlier. Between the two posts, decorative silver tendrils swayed from a suspended metal cord. As we passed under the stone archway, a sense of calm settled over me, like the caress of the wind.

Finae and I slowed our horses.

Weeds sprouted through broken tiles that covered the ground. Dead, twisted vines sprawled across them without reason. In the springtime, wildflowers might have popped up through the cracks instead. Scattered around the area, were piles of weathered boards, slats of rock, and other rubble that rested under the brown vines.

I stared in amazement, my imagination building the fallen stones and wooden boards into buildings.

What kind of people once called this home?

I exchanged a glance with Finae, my excitement reflected in her eyes. We dismounted, and I made my way over to a large, twisted tree, the reins of the horses in my hands. Roots disrupted the cobblestone at the base of the tree, dislodging the stone into uneven angles. I nicked one root with my dagger and found the inside dry, almost soot-like, similar to logs left in a fireplace before they fractured into embers. A fire could have weakened the tree's structure. I didn't know too much about trees, but it didn't seem normal for a tree to appear this way—even if it had contracted a disease or been exposed to fire.

Could the Skills have caused this?

"Kilo, look!"

Finae pushed a thin sheet of rock from a pile of rubble and held up a stone mug. The mound on which she stood had, at one point, been a dwelling. Finae bounced away, digging into another pile of rubble.

"Remember to look out for anything concerning the Skills! Papers, carvings, odd marks, and designs."

I called to her, but she didn't look back. Once she was invested in something, it was hard to reach her. Even away from home didn't make her mind me better. I shook my head and tied the horses' reins around a sturdy tree branch before I continued my search.

I kept Finae within eyesight.

I treaded lightly across snow-covered rubble, being mindful of the people who had once called this home. Their dwellings lay as if a giant earthquake had shaken the entire village except that it seemed too orderly. Nature did not create order; something else had destroyed this place. I clambered up the loose dirt of a small cliff to see better. Large, lush fields kissed by winter spread out as far as my eye could see. In the distance, an emerald lake with dark, deep waters glimmered, with ice around the edges. Rusty hues spilled across the pebbled rocks lining the lake's shore. Between the peaks, something glinted.

Rocks shifted behind me, and my hand reached for my staff. I glanced over my shoulder and relaxed.

"It's only me," Finae said, a smile playing at her lips. "No need to be jumpy. We haven't seen anyone since Magoto."

That didn't mean we were alone.

I extended my hand to her and pulled her up over the edge.

"It's beautiful," she said, taking in the view. I could already imagine the painting she would create. I pointed to the silver object wedged among the rocks.

"I'm going to see what's over there. Don't fall in."

She rolled her eyes at my concern. I jumped onto a large rock below, climbing down to the lake's shore. Finae followed after me. We shadowed the edge of the shoreline until the overgrown brush forced us to change our path. My Shadow garb allowed me to travel without worry. Durable and weather resistant, it could withstand the elements and terrain. I stole a glance at Finae.

She glared at me. "I'm doing fine."

I resisted the urge to say anything more, finding comfort and happiness in her quiet company. I squinted at the glint of silver I'd seen earlier, making out the form of what looked to be a rather large sword. A few snowflakes meandered before my eyes, sticking to my hair and fur cloak. What was a sword doing at the edge of the lake?

I stepped onto a bundle of overgrown weeds. Frost clung to the vines, crystallizing them. They crunched underfoot.

"Kilo…"

Finae was on her hands and knees. I rushed over to her and put my hand upon her back. Her breath rattled in her lungs, and her skin was a pale hue. She coughed, and I rubbed her back until the spasms passed. Was this the Skill Poisoning acting up, or was it something else? I reached down and placed my shoulder under her arm.

Should I use the vials or wait?

"It's a little farther. Can you continue, or do you want to stop?"

She looked ahead. "I can make it."

She leaned on me, and we continued at a slow pace, her breathing heavy but sustainable. The brush dissipated, making our struggle easier and the path more visible. At the base of the sword, stones were arranged randomly to hold it in place.

The sword's outline blurred, and the world swayed.

Finae slumped against me, and I struggled to keep her upright, fighting off a wave of dizziness myself. The edges of my vision blurred and shapes melded together, becoming one. I closed my eyes and lowered Finae onto the ground.

"I'll wait here," Finae said. "You go ahead."

I nodded, trying to push through the dizziness. I struggled ahead, biting back a wave of nausea. If I squinted, I could see a thin strap of leather fluttering off the sword's hilt. I fell to my knees beside the sword, inspecting the blade, letting my breath return to a less labored rhythm. Carved into the edge of the blade were tiny rivets shaped like mountain ridges. It was beautiful craftsmanship. The sword's purpose was most likely ceremonial, but why was it here?

Why had Hitori not removed it?

I reached out to touch the sword and snatched my hand back. A surge of energy flowed through my body. My vision cleared. I wrapped my fingers around the hilt. A flood of energy warmed my fingertips and spread to my hands, racing through my veins as the sensation enveloped me. I lifted my head to see an image of a town sitting on shimmering waters of a lake warmed by a summer sun. The snow and cold had vanished. The base of each building was created from stone, and the top portions were built from wood paneling. I stepped closer to the vision, admiring the architecture and the uncanny sense of home.

Was this sword tied to a vision created by the Skills?

A hand on my arm jerked me back to the present. I blinked and teetered on the edge of the lake, one foot hovered over the ice. The vision of the town vanished from my view, and I glanced back at the sword.

Powerful magic infused this blade.

I shook the vision from my eyes. If Finae had not stopped me, I would have walked out onto the half-frozen lake.

"I saw the town floating upon the lake," I said, explaining my foolish action. Finae stepped closer to the ice, and I held out my arm to stop her. "You're not going out there."

Her eyes narrowed, and she strode away, her back rigid. Her fingers caressed the sword's hilt.

"There's something out there."

A smile twitched at my lips. I could almost see the defiant child from our younger years. This journey had rekindled her spirit. I let my fingers brush the sword's hilt to regain the vision. The town reappeared on the ice. A strange glow rested in the center on top of a stone pillar—the same posts that had led us here. I took the staff from my back and placed it against the ice, pushing against the surface.

The ice held.

"Let me go first," Finae said. From her set jaw, she seemed determined to be the one to walk onto the lake.

I had always protected her; this was her way of protecting me. I needed to trust she could take care of herself, or I was no better than our parents. With reluctance, I nodded and softened my knees, ready to spring into action should I need to dive in after her. Finae shifted her weight, and the thin layer creaked under her feet. I held my breath as she tested the ice. She moved her supporting foot and brought her other foot onto the ice.

The ice held.

I released my pent-up breath, assuring myself the ice was thicker than I had initially believed.

A gust of wind blew across the lake, kicking up snow and obscuring my vision of Finae. When I could again see her, she stood in the center of the lake, her hands outstretched. Her fingers closed around a white stone, similar to the ones that rested atop the stone pillar we had seen before. Her hands glowed as she lifted the rock from the post, her face cast in light. White tendrils swooped around the orb, encompassing both Finae and the sphere. The white glow subsided, the mist disappeared, and all at once, the frozen lake's surface fell away.

"Finae!"

I ran onto the lake.

My foot broke through the ice, and a brief sensation flipped my stomach. It was as if I'd jumped from a cliff, yet somehow, I was suspended halfway inside the frozen lake. The lake's bedrock was underfoot. The same mountain peaks surrounded me, and the same oversized sword lay on the shore. It was as if I could see two realities reflected into one another.

Was I inside the lake now or in the town's memory?

Or both?

Buildings from the past, the same ones I'd seen in the vision, were on either side of me—the same as the mountain peaks. It looked as it seemed: we were somehow inside a memory, with ties to the present.

Finae rushed toward me, the white stone in her hands. It emanated light, though it seemed much subtler now than what I had glimpsed from across the lake.

"There's something you need to see," she said with a wide-toothed grin, sweeping her hand out in front of her. "This is Zenkaiko, as it used to be, before the tragedy."

I glanced at her sharply.

How did she know?

I opened my mouth to ask but lost all words as the town came to life around me. The same stone-and-wood buildings ruptured into color on either side. Color seeped from lifeless banners, and they began to flutter overhead. Each flag was held in place by a rope draped from the second story.

The vision had not been this vivid when I glimpsed it before.

Was this Finae's influence or the stone's?

Finae put her hand on my shoulder, then stepped into the vision. It held, and she walked down the road. I followed her, with a quick glance over my shoulder at the lake we left behind.

Whatever these Skills were, they were a powerful force—if that was indeed what this was. The similarity to the Skill memory in the Kinsaan Forest was uncanny. Those memories of the young girl had been tainted with pain. This place, this memory of

Zenkaiko as Finae had called it, was preserved with a different emotion: warmth and belonging.

Whoever had left the sword at the edge of the lake wanted us to be able to step back into the past, before whatever tragedy had happened here.

We needed to find out why.

Integrated into the town's design were stone soldiers, nestled into the nooks of buildings. They stood on either side, watching over all who lived in this place. The carved stone soldiers wore clothing similar to mine: two-toed boots, close-fitting pants tucked into shin guards, an inner robe, an overcoat that hung down to the knees, leather armor affixed to the shoulder, and— I stopped walking—a bond on the forearm. Thick tendrils were cut in relief from the stone, winding around each soldier's forearm with clear purpose and design. I inspected all the statues.

A bond encircled the arm of each one.

"They're Shadows," I whispered.

Finae nodded and kept walking as if my observation were trivial. Perhaps it was different for someone who was also a Shadow. More than the bonds on their arms though, what interested me most was the unknown connection. This town was old, much older than Vaiyene. If these people also wore bonds, how were the two places related? We stopped outside a building with the same U-shaped design as the Phantoms' house, but it was bigger, with beautiful spirals and stained glass.

The edges of my vision went dark again, and my lungs constricted. I pushed my hand against my chest, and I failed to suppress a fit of coughing. I pulled my hand away, wiping away specks of blood.

Finae spun about, her eyebrows knit in concern.

"I'm fine." I gave her a reassuring smile. "The cold air is irritating my throat."

She seemed doubtful of my answer, but she began walking up a long flight of steps despite her hesitation. It was not a complete lie. The cold air did make it harder to breathe, but she didn't need to know the extent of my symptoms. Until I knew about the effects of the Skill Poisoning, I did not want to worry her.

We stopped at the top of the steps under the reflection of the stained glass. A sword identical to the one at the lake's edge floated over a white pedestal. Finae touched the hilt, and it pulsated. Wind burst forth and raced past us. I closed my eyes against the onslaught of dirt. Finae withdrew the white stone from her pocket. A snaking white light whirled around her hand. The thin light split into two, then three, carving and etching into the rock Finae held. When the light disappeared, Finae held it up for me to see. I took the stone from her, turning it over in my hands while I inspected the impressions. It almost looked like a map, but of what, I did not know.

I handed the orb to Finae and fingered through my journal and the copies Finae had made of Rin's maps.

None reflected the markings.

Finae shuffled beside me. "What do you think it means?"

I shook my head. "I'm not sure. Maybe it has something to do with the memory."

I looked back across the frozen lake, and the image of the town deteriorated before my eyes. Reality began to phase out the town's memory as I coughed into my sleeve, fighting dizziness. My desire to hold out and not take Rin's suppressant ate away at my pride.

We had come all this way.

I couldn't be the one to cause us to go back.

Something about this place affected me, but I could not quite put my finger on it. Finae seemed, for the most part, unaffected.

My fingers shook as I gripped one vial. I placed the bottle to my lips and drank half of the contents, feeling an immediate warmth race through me. My hands regained their steadiness, and my chest relaxed. I wasn't aware of the full extent of my pain until my lungs opened and I drew in an unrestrained breath.

I caught up to Finae and held the vial out to her. "Something to help with the cold." She didn't question me, and I suppressed the guilt.

I needed to tell her soon.

The town's memory returned in full force, and I stood beside Finae, next to the building resembling the Phantoms' house. I trailed my fingers over the building's rocky exterior. The vision appeared so real, yet I could not feel the coolness of stone nor the texture of the rock. I left the sword, and the white pedestal, and Finae walked toward the foot of one of the giant Shadow statues. Intense pain shot through my body as I brushed against the base with my shoulder, starting at the point of contact and spreading through my body. Another pain sparked in my chest, and I doubled over.

Finae's hand touched my back. "What's wrong?"

I swayed, and her hands steadied me. Her voice receded into the distance, and my knees made contact with the damp earth. The ground beneath me swallowed my consciousness.

———

I stood upright, my head sloshing to attention. The stone and wood features of Zenkaiko surrounded me. Finae's presence replaced by a stream of people. They walked past me, not making eye contact as I stood on the side of the street.

I looked around for Finae, but she was not with me.

High overhead, the sun shone, beating down with intense, hot rays. The air was fresh and clean, and the warmth of the sun wrapped me in a welcome. A group of young adults wandered past, their clothing loose and colorful. Silver threads wound around each of their forearms. Across the street, another group of people wore bonds upon their arms. Instincts urged me to intervene, but my mind already knew it was nothing more than a memory. This time, it seemed I'd been transported farther back in time.

I kept to the shadows and away from the center of the road. I didn't want to disturb the memory of the people who walked through the town. After all, I was a guest here, and whatever story this memory had to tell, I would wait without interrupting. My meanderings led me to a central area, where trees pushed around layers of cobblestone. Every bush, tree, and flower was allowed to flourish at will. Unlike the cold stone of Magoto, the imperfections of nature were incorporated into the design. Metal lampposts, with the same silver threading and motifs in the stone pillars, framed the courtyard. They illuminated: a soft glow cascaded down from a round orb hung suspended inside the lantern-like top.

Three people entered the courtyard from different directions. They were dressed in long, white decorative robes. Each wore a bond on their arms. One wore a bond on each arm. On the ground, an insignia had been carved into the stone—twin vines twisting to form a sapling. There were five points to the emblem, each leading down one of the five corridors of Zenkaiko.

The crowd finished gathering, and the three leaders began to speak. I crept closer, bracing myself as the ground shifted—fractured—around me. The group disappeared, but the three leaders remained. Their positions shifted in time. Two knelt in the center of the courtyard with their heads bowed and their swords stuck in the ground at their feet. The man with the two bonds stood, his body facing me. He gripped his giant broadswords and paused for a moment before he thrust the blade into the ground. Together, the three leaders and their swords created a triangular perimeter. The two kneeling figures placed their hands on the cobblestone. The moment their palms hit the stone, the ground shook, and I braced myself to keep my eyes fixed on the spectacle. A white mist began to swirl around the courtyard, growing in intensity around the swords positioned in the ground. Their bonds began to glow. At first, it was subtle, and then a white light engulfed the silver threads. This was the Skills at their full potential.

This was what Hitori could harness.

I stood but a few feet from the leaders. Their bonds blazed, and the flesh beneath the silver threads had begun to blacken. A sickening scent of iron and flesh filled the air. No emotion showed on their faces. Their eyes were closed; their muscles relaxed. They were in a state beyond the moment.

The two-bonded man raised his blazing sword into the air. He swung it crosswise, and a giant crack reverberated behind me. Stones shattered against the ground, and more fissures erupted as a white mist blew across the town. I watched in horror as another tower fell. It split as it hit the road, unearthing a wave of dust and rock. Panic overwhelmed me as a crowd of people ran from the dust cloud, emerging from the town around me. Their screams echoed in my ears, cutting into me as if my own people's lives were at stake.

I drew my staff and spun around. "Stop!"

The two-bonded leader opened his eyes, and his gaze met mine. His eyes focused on me as a single tear spilled down his cheek. Raw emotion hit me.

He could see me.

My heart quickened. "Why are you doing this?"

Hands landed on my shoulder, and I lurched awake. Finae stood before me, shaking me, her eyes wide with terror.

"Kilo!"

I shrugged her hands off and jerked away from her. I had been so close to finding answers! I drew in a breath and regained my bearings, cooling my temper.

I stood in the courtyard. The collapsed buildings were still in the same position as the memory. I dropped to the ground and brushed the snow away, uncovering the insignia below.

"Kilo?"

I heard her, but I didn't want to lose the memory's touch on my mind. Why would the leaders have destroyed the town? For what purpose? And what had happened to the people I'd seen? They couldn't have all died. There were no bones.

"The three leaders if this town were the ones who destroyed this place," I said, walking away from the courtyard.

There had to be a reason.

Finae followed at my heels. "What else did you see?"

"There is a price to the Skills we do not yet understand."

By now, the streets were almost hidden under snow: deep enough that our footprints had vanished. Soon, the snow would hide the ruins from sight—and along with them our way back to Magoto.

I looked out over the ruins and glanced back at Finae.

"We should leave."

She crossed her arms and shivered from the chill. She made no complaint as I turned to go. As much as I wanted to stay and find the memory again, there was no telling how long it would take. And I wasn't even sure I understood what had triggered it.

This was where Hitori had discovered the book about the Skills. Had she also seen the same visions, or was the memory tied to the desire of the leaders who had created the memory? I didn't even know if the leaders were the ones who had created the vision. In the distance, an enormous tree stood tall and stark against the mountain peaks. I led us in that direction, drawn to the familiarity of it. I looked back over my shoulder, sure we were headed toward the horses, but uncertain we were. I frowned and resumed our path, unsure of what I was seeing.

Weapons circled the base of the tree in rows. Each sword, axe, and staff with silver threading around the hilt.

Shadow weapons.

I kicked at the snow, uncovering stone beneath my feet. The weapons were uniformly placed, but every so often, there were spaces in the rings circling the tree. I took a step back and joined Finae. If you took away the stone buildings and banners, it was almost as if we were looking at an ancient Vaiyene.

Finae held the stone in her hand, the silver etchings that had been carved into it now illuminated. Whatever secrets the sphere protected remained a mystery. Who had the leaders of this ancient town been, and had they really killed their own people?

I slipped my arm around Finae's shoulder and drew her to my side as I led her away from the tree and the Shadow weapons.

Snow had begun to collect on my shoulders at an alarming rate. We needed to get warm. As much as I wanted to stay, there were too many variables. Survival was more important than seeking knowledge. We would head back to Magoto, and if we could, it would be beneficial to return, but I didn't know if that would be an option anytime soon.

The memory showed the power of the Skills, and I had a feeling it was only the beginning of what we would discover.

chapter twenty-six
ANSWERS

I hung the wooden knife on the door of Magoto's gate and knocked five times. Finae glanced up at me, and I gave her a reassuring smile. "They'll come.

Our tracks were disappearing too quickly to think otherwise.

Finae's teeth chattered behind me.

The metal latch clicked, and I breathed a sigh of relief as the door swung inward. A tall man with a long, dark fur robe ushered us inside. Next to the gate, a blazing fire burned in a stone pillar. Warmth rushed over our frozen bodies. He didn't acknowledge us or speak; but escorted us to the outer tunnels of Magoto and held out his hand, the wooden knife resting in his palm.

"The horses?" I asked as an afterthought, wrapping my fingers around the wooden trinket.

"I'll see to them."

I nodded and bowed in the Shadow way, thanking the man before we turned the corner. A sinking weight wedged itself into my chest. It was a chill that came not from the freezing temperatures but from the sensation of walls closing in around me. I slid my arm around Finae's shoulder to steady myself against the annoyance. When we reached an intersection of stone walls, we turned right. Smoke spouted from the chimney of the same house we had stayed in earlier. I drew my staff. Finae stopped close to the house, and I crept toward the window to peer inside.

Rin knelt beside the hearth.

I let out a breath and motioned for Finae to follow me.

"My guards told me you were coming," Rin said, turning to acknowledge us before she stoked the fire. "I feared the snow claimed you. Not many could survive in these conditions."

I placed my heavy pack on the ground and began shedding my clothing. We had camped for three nights after leaving Zenkaiko. It had not been pleasant, but we had survived.

The adverse conditions had kept Hitori's spies at bay.

I threw Finae a blanket from the bedside. When I was bare-chested and stripped down to my loose pants, I inched closer to the fire's warmth. Rin threw another log onto the flames, and I reveled in the renewed heat. I could sense Rin's gaze. A disfigurement spanned my back; one that had been made worse in my attempt to save Zavi's life at the cliffside.

I held out the wooden knife to Rin, dangling it from the leather cord. *We do what we must.*

"Keep it," she said.

I tucked the trinket away into my pocket.

Rin placed an iron kettle on a rod and hung it above the fire.

"Did you find the ruins?"

"They were incredible," Finae said. She plopped herself down next to the fire beside me, the blanket draped over her head. She held the folds closed with hands inside the fabric.

Finae glanced at me, and I nodded for her to continue. She liked Rin, and I saw no reason not to share what we had found out. If anything, it would give me a better sense of who she was.

"There were giant buildings with colorful banners." Finae spread her arms up over her head before she shrank back into her blankets. "It felt so much like home. I wish I could have seen it before it was destroyed."

"That sounds like quite the sight," Rin said, a slight smile upon her lips. She glanced at me. "Any information on the Skills?"

"Not precisely. We both saw visions while we were within the ruins: one of the town in its grand state, the other as it was being destroyed by their own leaders."

Rin's eyes widened. "They destroyed their own town?"

I pressed my hands against my temples. "From what I saw, the leaders used the Skills against their own people."

Rin let out a long breath and folded her knees to her chest, sitting inside the window frame.

"Maybe," Finae said, her voice a whisper, "it was necessary."

I glanced at her. "What makes you say that?"

"I'm not sure; I felt maybe it was unavoidable."

I, too, had felt the weight of responsibility, a sense of regret and duty, as the white-clad leaders had taken to the center of the courtyard. The image of the two-bonded man and the tear that had trailed down his cheek resurfaced from my memory, but I dismissed it. There was no justification for killing one's own people.

Rin's expression was withdrawn, but she seemed to be listening. A bruise discolored her left cheek. It hadn't been there before we left.

"How did your mission go?" I asked.

Rin kept her gaze focused outside. "I did what I needed to."

I bit back any further questions. Rin did neither right nor wrong. It was one step above wrong, but still not acceptable. I had always thought the Phantoms embodied justice. Yet here I was, questioning everything.

Finae dug out the stone from her pocket.

"We found something in Zenkaiko," I said to Rin, trying to steer her thoughts to a more positive light. "It came out of a memory left by the Skills."

Rin moved to Finae's side and cradled the stone between her fingers as if it were a delicate piece of glass.

"Such distinct markings."

"It was much brighter when we originally received it," Finae said, watching Rin.

"Is that so?" Rin held the stone out at arm's length, moving it into the moonlight. She glanced at Finae, grinning. "Would you like to try using the Skills?"

Finae's eyes widened. "Yes!"

My heart beat faster, and Rin gave me a sidelong gaze. I didn't bother to hide my interest in the Skills. It was, after all, why we were here.

"I will teach both of you, but not together. The first time can be a little overwhelming. It requires careful observation from someone on the outside."

I nodded as if I understood her meaning.

I couldn't even guess how the Skills worked.

Rin took Finae's hand in her own. "You must first be aware of your senses. Close your eyes and feel where the edges of your fingers end. Feel their reach and gain awareness of your hand and your arm."

Rin brought Finae's hand closer to the stone.

"Do you feel the coolness of the rock beneath your touch? How does your hand feel against it? Where do your fingers end? Can you feel the divots in the stone? Now, I want you to find the source of light within yourself—somewhere there is warmth, someplace that can spare a little light. Try and take this warmth and move it to your fingertips. Push it across the network of pathways inside you and direct it to where you'd like it to live."

Rin fixed her gaze upon the stone beneath Finae's fingertips. My lungs constricted in my chest, and I forced myself to let out my breath.

After a few moments, Rin placed her hand on Finae's shoulder.

"Relax and come back to yourself."

Finae opened her eyes. She blinked, and her brow furrowed, a slight pout on her face. "Nothing happened."

I stifled my laughter. Finae glanced over at me and glared.

Rin's fingers brushed the stone's surface. "Don't be discouraged. It takes time."

Rin enveloped the stone in her hands, took a deep breath, and exhaled. The markings came alive. As Rin dragged her fingers across the surface, the lines redrew themselves as silver light.

"The markings must have a meaning, but I do not recognize them." She handed the stone back to Finae. "I can look through the scrolls within the main building to see if I can find any old maps or an indication of what the inscription might mean."

Rin looked out the window, up to the top of the circular tower that loomed in the distance. "Hitori should be heading out on a mission soon to Leiko. We may be able to sneak inside, depending on who is left in the tower and where their loyalties lie."

"Do you have another mission soon?"

"No, but we best make use of the time we have. The sooner we learn more about the Skills, the quicker we can find a way to kill Hitori, and the more deaths we can prevent."

I cringed at the thought, trying not to wonder if Rin had killed on her mission. When this was all over, who knew if I would even be allowed back into Vaiyene. I tried to find humor in picturing Asdar's reaction to my helping the False Shadows. My amusement didn't last long, and soon my thoughts turned back to Vaiyene, to those I had left behind: to Shenrae and Syrane. Asdar and Lunia would have come up with some sort of story to cover my disappearance. I could only hope they would not turn the Shadows, or the people of Vaiyene, against me.

Rin was speaking, and I forced myself to focus my attention on her words. I could do nothing for Syrane and Shenrae at this distance. Except to accomplish what I had set out to do: prevent the Skills from destroying Vaiyene.

"I have a few trustworthy people inside the castle," Rin said, crossing her arms and pacing the room. "For now, let's focus on teaching one of you to use the Skills. I won't always be around to illuminate the marks."

Rin dug into the satchel at her hip and then patted the table, indicating I should sit across from her. She placed a small metal ball, no bigger than a pebble, on the wooden surface.

"Let's start small. I'll walk you through how to use the Skills like I did with Finae, and we'll see if we can unlock your power."

I grinned at Finae and sank down into the chair, my stomach lurching with anticipation.

"Close your eyes and focus your attention on your fingertips."

I took a deep breath and calmed my mind of wandering thoughts, letting Rin's voice guide me as I settled into a meditative state.

"Let your mind focus on the cool metal. Do you notice the texture? What does it feel like against your fingers?"

The stone felt cool, and unlike what my eyes showed me, the surface was not smooth. There were tiny bumps. They were not uniform, but as I rolled the stone with my finger, I noticed there were divots of various size on the surface.

"Now, try and find somewhere where it's warm, close to your chest perhaps or your palm, and find that warmth inside of you. An internal light that is your own."

I tried to search inside of me, but finding my "inner light" proved easier said than done. My heart beat faster as I concentrated on the rhythm; my awareness of each individual pulse grew. It was warm, was that what Rin meant?

As for light, I could only see darkness.

"Don't search for it, feel it. Let it reveal itself to you. Push it and guide it through your hand, releasing it against that pressure of skin. Allow it to live there and caress it. Don't abandon it, guide it to its purpose."

The only "warmth" building was my anger and frustration. I struggled against the sensation, trying to stay calm and not force whatever was supposed to be happening to happen. But my concentration was broken. I suppressed a groan and opened my eyes. Rin placed her forefinger to her lips.

In the corner of the stone house, Finae sat on the bed.

The white stone illuminated in her palms.

She stood and held out her hands. Then she swayed. Rin almost tripped as she lunged to catch Finae.

The stone hit the floor with a loud clunk.

I shook off my meditative state and rushed to Finae as Rin lowered her to the ground. This journey would be the death of us.

"This is normal." Rin glanced at me and gave me a reassuring smile. "She was overcome by the Skills. It almost happened to me, and it happened to my brother as well."

Rin's hand rested on top of Finae's head. Her eyes were closed, and every so often, her lips would move, as if she were speaking, but no sound came from her lips. The slightest outline of color around Rin's fingertips pulsed as if she were sending waves of energy through the air. Caution of the Skills stirred inside me. Not only could the Skills wipe out an entire village, but they were also dangerous to those who wielded the power.

Finae's eyes opened, and she found my gaze. I took her hands in mine and gave her a smile. "You've cost me a year of my life."

Finae smiled, exhaustion deadening her emotion.

I glanced up at Rin. "What did you do to bring her back?"

"It's no different than the way Finae made the stone's carvings light up." Rin stood and looked out the window. "Once you grasp the basic concept of the Skills, you're able to see possibilities of using them in other regards. It works on everything, but some objects and people are easier to affect."

I opened my mouth for clarification, but Finae spoke. "I saw a village with a huge dome-shaped building. A tree grew around it, with roots wrapping around the outside. Inside there was a library as tall as the ceiling."

A strange vision.

Were we supposed to go to this place?

I didn't know of any village with a large dome-shaped building and large roots at the base.

I helped Finae stand. Some color had come back to her face, but she must have been exhausted. Neither of us slept much on the return journey. My body was used to the strain; hers was not.

"Get some rest," I said, pushing her back onto the bed.

Finae opened her mouth to protest but thought better of it.

"You can listen until you fall asleep." ·

Finae nodded. Her eyelids already drooped.

I pulled the chair closer to the fire and sank down into it, my focus fixed on Rin. "How did you learn all this?"

"We started learning the Skills to avoid Hitori's anger. As she grew in strength, we began to see it as our chance to stop her."

I sensed her hesitation. While I understood her desire to withhold information, neither of us could afford privacy.

"I need to know, Rin."

She sighed and rubbed her arm that had the bond on it. "I have not told you the whole story, and for that, I'm sorry, but I needed you to trust me before I disclosed everything."

She crossed the room and grabbed a couple of mugs from the mantel, fetching the kettle from above the fire. "As you know, there's much to the depth of deceit and power that Hitori holds. What you suspect about Leiko is true. There are crimes being commited by Hitori. It did not start that way, but after a time, she became obsessed with the Skills and turned her meanderings to much fouler uses. Leiko is a testing ground."

Rin poured out the kettle, handing me one of two mugs. I took a sip, detecting a mead of some sort. There were no words of comfort for what she had been through. Even if I had wanted to say something, comfort was not what Rin needed. What she needed was for someone to make what she had done worthwhile.

Rin downed a gulp of the mead. "Hitori is subjecting the people to various tests regarding the Skills. In exchange for her protection against raiders and bandits, the townspeople of Leiko play along with her games. They hope they make it through the trials they must endure to protect themselves from raiders. It's a sickening abuse of trust."

The face of the young child I'd dug up surfaced in my memory. I looked down at my mug, wishing there was some way to forget the image.

"I can see why Hitori does not think fondly of me."

Rin snorted. "You've become her new obsession. She needs the people of Leiko compliant. She knows someone is poking around for the truth." Rin fixed me with a pointed stare. "She knows it's a Phantom of Vaiyene."

Phantom Kural had started the cycle. By getting involved, he had put our people in danger. By continuing to pursue the Skills, I was putting Vaiyene in danger—like Asdar and Lunia had warned. I brushed the guilt aside. I had made my decision, and I still believed it to be the right one.

"When will Hitori strike again?"

"Spring."

I let out a long, deep breath and set the mug down onto the table. Asdar was preparing a new group of Shadows, but they wouldn't know how to fight against the Skills. It would take someone who knew the Skills to train the Shadows against it. My eyes wandered. Someone like Rin. Eventually, someone needed to teach the Shadows how to defend against the Skills—or all those in Kiriku would suffer. I stood, pacing the room from window to hearth and back again. I retrieved the staff laid against the wall, holding the wood in hand. The motion calmed me.

"If we know our enemy well enough, perhaps we can come up with some way to stop her before this elevates into a war."

Rin studied me, her hand upon the sword at her side. "I know where Hitori's notes are. I can get you inside."

Her words stopped my movement. "When?"

"Soon."

Rin left the window and held her palm out toward me, the round metal ball in her palm. "Until then, you need to learn how to use the Skills. Anyone can learn, but with your focus, you should be able to grasp the concept without too much trouble."

I took a breath and nodded, glancing over at my sister. She was asleep. My hand closed around the metal ball, and I sunk into a meditative state. Whatever these Skills were, I needed to figure out the truth behind them.

R in burst through the door, bringing with her a gust of wind. Papers flew off the table and scattered about, whipping around the stone house. Rin was out of breath and held the door open.

"Hitori has left. We need to go now."

Finae smashed the maps against the table to keep them in place. I bent over to pick up the papers from the floor, but at Rin's pointed glare, I left them as they were.

"Kilo, now."

I nodded and looked at Finae. If I took her with me, she would be in danger. But leaving her here seemed as dangerous. Finae glared at me. She knew what I was thinking.

"If you leave me here, I'll follow."

I was torn between praising her for taking a stand or cursing her for her stubbornness. Like most decisions of late, the right choice eluded me. Either could lead to Finae's death.

"Let's go."

It was Finae's decision. And if she came with me, at least I could protect her. I would rather have the chance to defend her than worry something would happen when she was alone.

We followed Rin into the maze of Magoto's white streets. I left my staff fixed on my back. We were not known to the enemy, and even if it were in hand, my dislike for the misshapen town around me would not lessen. There was one main thoroughfare in Magoto. A few side streets sprouted off from the main road, but the town was designed to only have one entry and one exit.

I didn't like this place.

Too many uncertainties.

My sense of direction was as disoriented. Houses butted up against one another, creating a massive wall of stone houses. They were separated into individual buildings and marked by plain wooden doors. Arches connected the homes, with staircases leading onto stone terraces. Overhead, ladders draped from building to building. It created a network of aerial pathways which one could traverse Magoto's different levels.

When we reached the castle, Rin paused at the base of a towering iron door. The gate was strengthened with black metal bars that crisscrossed from edge to edge. To some, it might have looked decorative, magnificent even, but it reminded me of imprisonment.

It was no wonder Rin felt trapped here.

What the town lacked was individuality. Everything was white stone and brown wood. I hadn't seen any of the townspeople, but judging from the state of things, they would be as suppressed. My eyes lingered on the iron bars. Unlike the Phantoms' house in Vaiyene, people were not welcome here. The Phantoms tried to involve the people and nurture a sense of community. All I felt from this place was isolation. Had Magoto always been this desolate, or was it because of Hitori's influence?

I was interested to know more about Magoto's history.

It would help me understand Hitori's disposition.

Two guards shifted to attention. They made no move to draw their swords on us. I replied in kind, keeping my muscles as relaxed as I could. Finae stayed behind me. Her breathing rate escalated, but otherwise, she seemed to be doing well.

Rin met one of the guards, and they led us around the gate to reveal a hidden doorway. The guard whispered something to Rin as she passed through the door, his voice too quiet for my ears. The exchange unsettled me. I put my hand on Finae's shoulder and guided her between Rin and me.

Something felt off. It was too easy.

Light from the outside world disappeared as the guard closed the door behind us. I forced the rising panic down, choking back the constriction of my chest. This was a risk we had to take, but it didn't need to be foolishly taken. I caught up to Rin and kept my voice low.

"How long have you been working with that guard?"

Rin frowned. "Quite some time. I trust him with my life."

I nodded, though her simple assurance did little to alleviate my unease. I didn't know anything about the castle we entered, nor did I have a good sense of how to escape Magoto.

It was risky, but I was desperate for answers.

I let Rin and the guard take the lead, walking behind Finae. "Stay close. If something happens, I will protect you."

The words were both for Finae's sake and my own. Bringing Finae on this mission meant her life came before learning about the Skills, before protecting Rin's life, and before my own. It was Rin and Finae's duty to find information on the Skills and my duty to ensure they both survived.

Like the town, the castle was a desolate place, though a blue rug did span the hallway. It was the only color in sight. There were no paintings. No decorations. Even the high ceiling and the wide hallways imposed a sense of powerlessness. My spirit stirred against the walls closing in around me. The noose settled around my neck.

This was no way to live.

Rin led us up a broad staircase, her shoulders drawn back. What kind of person would she have been if she had been raised in Vaiyene? I had a guess she would have joined the Shadows.

Our footsteps echoed in the hollow stone hallway. The layout of the castle was simple enough—two turns and then a long hallway. One exit. All the corridors fed into the main hall. If we needed to escape, a fight would be inevitable. None walked the inside of the castle except for us. I kept my hand tight around my staff, keeping it close at my side. We came to a halt at the end of the hall. A dull, wooden door lay at the end.

Rin bent down and dug out a long silver pick from the inside of her sleeve, inserting the end into the keyhole. "Not even the guards have a key to this room."

That meant we were in the right place.

Finae fidgeted beside me as I stood with the door to my back. I didn't know how to comfort her, except to be ready. We were targets in this emptiness. Rin fumbled with the lock behind me. It clicked, and e stood. I put my hand out to stop Finae, allowing Rin to enter first. I scanned the room in one sweep, looking for any guards or signs of anyone hiding in the shadows.

Bookcases lined the edges of the room. Each organized meticulously by color and book height. A small, dull black table was placed in front of three enormous windows. The only source of light inside of the castle. I crossed the room to the windows and looked over Magoto. We were high enough to see over the walls. I breathed easy seeing out across the plains.

Finae spoke from across the room. "This is it! It has to be."

Had she found something so soon?

Finae held a large black book with gold-leafed pages. It was in good condition except for the burnt corners at the top. Rin's shadowed figure didn't move. I could not make out any expression on her face. She had grown quiet since we had entered.

I moved to my sister's side.

Finae placed her hand on the cover and with great care opened the book to reveal a blank page. A tiny note had been scribbled quite crudely in the bottom corner.

"To those who live in the coming age: I pray you have better foresight," Rin recited. Her voice was void of any emotional reflection and echoed off the walls in a hollow tone. She joined us at the table, her footsteps dragging across the stone floor. Finae moved out of the way as Rin began flipping through the yellowed pages.

"The rest is quite straightforward," Rin said, continuing to flip through the pages. "There's some theory on how to use the Skills but no written instructions or rules."

The bulk of what was written was text, but there were a few diagrams. One caught my attention. My hand shot out to stop Rin from turning the page. It was a drawing of a bond, the same silver threading the Shadows of Vaiyene wore.

"That diagram drove Hitori crazy." Rin sat on the windowsill, holding up her forearm, her gaze fixed on the metal threads. "She searched for a metalsmith who would be able to recreate it to the exact specifications. Each of us under Hitori's power has an identical metal casing."

My eyes shifted to Rin's bond. I had not picked up on that detail. It would help distinguish the False Shadows from the real ones.

"After weeks of searching," Rin said, her gaze now fixed outside the window, "Hitori found someone with the talents in an outland town. With enough coin, he agreed to move to Leiko and produce the metal bonds. I'd be surprised if you didn't meet him while you were there. He's a hard person to forget."

I thought back to Leiko and the marketplace. The old craftsman who had rambled nonsense. I looked down at my bond. We had seen statues of the Shadows in Zenkaiko with bonds on their arms. The bonds were a part of our history and culture.

Did the bonds originate in Zenkaiko then?

Rin crossed her arms. "Despite what Hitori originally thought, however, the bonds are not the key to using the Skills. Finae is better at the Skills than you, Kilo, and she has no bond."

Out of the corner of my eye, I saw Finae light up at the praise. I wasn't sure being adept at the Skills was a good thing. If Hitori found out, Finae would become a target. She would want her— to study her and find out why she possessed such a natural tendency.

"Hitori's desperation for the authentic material your bond is made from has led her into sickening territory."

I narrowed my eyes. "What do you mean?"

"This metal came from a tainted source. It was taken from the ruins you went to visit. Every day I wear this, it makes me sick to think Hitori will not stop at nothing to pursue the Skills."

Tainted metal? What was she talking about?

Finae stepped back, her skin pale. "He took the weapons of the ancient Shadows."

The missing weapons in Zenkaiko.

"I saw him when he first arrived," Rin said, confirming Finae's realization. "He carried the old weapons and threw them into a furnace to melt them down."

The memory of Zavi's and Mia's swords under the Reikon Tree rose in my mind. I could not imagine taking their weapons, their protection, and purpose, from Vaiyene. Not every person held the same morals as the Shadows, but disturbing the dead was not something most people were comfortable with. From Rin's adverse reaction, her beliefs were similar to our own.

"Why would the metal from the weapons be any different than iron or silver?" I asked.

Why go to such lengths?

Rin looked from Finae to me. "The bond on your arm serves more of a purpose than you realize. *That* is why Hitori is obsessed with finding the secret behind creating an authentic bond. She tried silver, iron, and brass—everything she could get her hands on."

Rin pushed the table and bent down to the floor. "The more a person uses the Skills, the more the body suffers. The bond counteracts this imbalance in some way."

My heart beat faster. How had we not known? In Vaiyene, the bonds were a symbol of becoming a Shadow.

They were ceremonial, nothing more.

Rin drew a small dagger from inside her boot and wedged it into a crack between a couple of stones on the floor. She pried the hidden compartment open to reveal a tidy collection of journals.

"Every experiment Hitori has performed has been documented and compiled in these notes, detailing all of the outcomes and instructions of each technique attempted on the subjects. Somewhere within those papers are statistics of the usage of the Skills by the participants. Those without a bond reported feeling sick, and their body deteriorated much faster than those who had a bond to counteract the Skill Poisoning."

I stopped searching through the papers and lifted my head. I hadn't told Finae yet. I glanced over at her. She was leafing through the book on the Skills.

She seemed occupied with other thoughts.

"Your symptoms align with those who have used the Skills. Hitori somehow managed to take those effects and turn them into something that could poison a person's body without them using the Skills."

Already, Hitori had found the deadliest part of the Skills and used it to harm others. Finae didn't wear a bond, which meant the harmful effects of using the Skills were not being counteracted by a bond..

"Would being near the Skills, or someone using the Skills, make the poison react?"

Rin chewed on her lip. "Maybe."

That would explain our symptoms back in Zenkaiko. If Finae was to continue using the Skills, or be near those who were using them, she needed a bond.

The door burst open. A man wearing the same iron-clad suit as the guards appeared in the doorframe. "Hitori has been spotted with her group of subordinates. They are headed back."

Rin's eyes widened, the color draining from her face. "Hitori must have gotten word about something being amiss here, or her mission failed. If she finds you here, there will be no mercy for any of us."

I watched the guard.

Or we had been betrayed.

Rin scooped up the box with the research notes and thrust it against my chest. "I couldn't stomach it all myself, but if you want to get an edge on Hitori, you need to know what she's planning."

I fumbled with the box, trying to hold it and my staff. "If Hitori finds out this is gone—"

Rin grabbed my arm. Her fingers dug into my skin, and her gaze locked onto mine. "I will deal with Hitori should the time come. I've been living without hope for far too long. Don't let the blood on my hands be for nothing."

She released me, and I passed the box to Finae.

Rin led us out of the room. Unless there was another way out, we would be funneled down a singular corridor toward the main entrance. If we made it in time, we could escape. If not, we would be battling Hitori and those loyal to her in very close quarters.

Rin ran down the stone hallway, stopping midway. She placed her hand on the wall. With a gentle push, a hidden doorway opened. "Take Finae and get as far away from Magoto as you can."

I frowned. "We're not leaving you."

Rin glanced behind her. "I can't abandon the guards who helped me."

I admired her integrity for wanting to look after her people, but she knew better than I that Hitori would not let her live. I needed her alive—to help Vaiyene.

Rin's fingers twitched at her side, and she met my gaze. "I'll meet you on the outskirts of town, in the same house. If I don't make it there by the time the sun goes down, leave without me."

Her hand grasped the hilt of her sword, and she ran down the stone hallway. The guard who had warned us trailed after her. I pushed Finae through the doorway as voices began to echo throughout the corridor.

I put my hands on Finae's shoulder. "Get out of here. I can't worry about protecting you and Rin." I glanced down at the box in her hands. "Make sure these get to Vaiyene if..."

Finae's eyes widened, and I trailed off, wrapping her in my arms. She needed my assurance. I held her at arm's length as tears rolled down her cheeks. "This is something I have to do. Rin is indispensable, though she does not realize it herself. I promise I'll return."

"If you die, there will be no hope for us." Finae's voice did not waver. Even though she trembled, her voice was full of truth that shook my conviction.

I closed my eyes.

The shouts grew louder in the distance.

Would I ever be able to stop leaving the ones who needed my protection the most? My decision to protect one person, one thing, over another was never an easy choice. I should have been used to it, but each time it became harder to choose. Being with Finae and Rin—as short of time as it had been—had rekindled the feelings of being a Shadow and enduring hardships alongside Zavi and Mia. Rin had risked her life to save mine. I believed she meant well and had tried her best given her circumstances. She didn't deserve to be abandoned.

And I couldn't let her die.

"Please, Finae. Can you stay hidden here?"

Tears stained her cheeks, but she nodded. Her hands tightened around the chest containing Hitori's notes. Even as I closed the door to the secret passage, sickness washed over me. I was choosing Rin over Finae. I shook off the weight from my shoulders, holding onto the single thought: Finae would be safe.

She alone remained unknown to Hitori.

I needed to save Rin from her own foolhardy ways. Finae's words had rattled my resolve, but I couldn't lose the one person who could teach us how to use the Skills. Notes meant nothing without application.

Rin shouted in the distance, and I readied my staff.

Swords clashed, and I scanned the disarray before me. The guards wore the same uniform, which meant I couldn't distinguish friend from foe. Rin's dark cloak appeared in the fray, and I thrust my staff out to intercept a blow to Rin's side. She pushed off the guard in front of her, slicing the blade against his knee. He crumpled to the ground, and Rin whirled to face me.

"I told you to leave!"

"Sorry, I didn't hear you." I moved to cover her back; a smile played on my lips.

Rin exhaled heavily, almost growling at my response. "Most of the guards have turned against me. Their loyalty is not worth much when Hitori is around. I should have known."

I lashed out with my staff. I should have trusted my instincts about entering the castle, but if we could escape…

The guard dodged to the left, and I twisted my staff to hit the side of his head. He fell to the ground, and I stepped to intercept another guard's sword. We had to find some way—The hairs on the back of my neck stood up. It was a strange sensation as if the air seemed charged with energy, and it slowed my movement.

Rin froze. "Hitori."

I glanced around for some way to blend in. Rin snatched a helmet from one of the fallen guards and thrust it into my hands. I shoved it onto my head. The cloak Rin had given me when we first arrived was the same as the ones two of the guards wore. Would Hitori notice there were now three cloaked guards?

"You are now a guard of Magoto," Rin said, her voice quiet. "Let the other guards speak and keep your identity concealed."

She bit off the last of her words, trying to inspire her so-called-allies to at least protect me in the situation. It was in their best interest to do so, but I doubted they cared about Rin's emotions any longer. Hitori's control over her people seemed absolute.

They would even betray a friend.

I caught Rin's arm. "I won't abandon you."

"You're no match for Hitori."

The air around me shifted, and I hid my staff in the folds of my cloak. The False Shadows held swords. Three swords lay on the ground within easy reach.

I needed to remain patient and wait for the advantage.

The guards parted in the hallway, allowing a shorter woman to approach. She wore a cloak around her narrow shoulders, the hood spilling to reveal a bright red hue. Her nose and features were sharp, but there was a soft edge to them. Dark eyeliner exaggerated her emerald eyes, making them appear slimmer than they were. Her blonde hair hung to her shoulders, and a thin silver headband crowned her head. Neither her skin nor her gait showed any signs of age.

The leader of the False Shadows and not a scar on her.

A white mist enveloped the bond around Hitori's arm. A sneer spread across her lips as her gaze locked onto Rin. She raised her hand. The guards pressed themselves against the walls as Rin slashed her sword in front of her. Hitori crossed the distance faster than expected, swinging her sword. Rin blocked the attack with her own sword. They were matched in strength, but not with the Skills. The white tendrils around Hitori's sword shimmered a subtle red.

I'd seen that aspect before.

Hitori's blade cut through Rin's sword as if it were not metal. Hitori crushed her other hand against Rin's throat, pinning her against the wall. The skin where she touched turned a sickly black.

I fisted my hand at my side.

Patience.

"I didn't think you were so naïve." Hitori's voice was velvet, her words dripping with triumph. She took a step closer, cutting off Rin's air, her gaze fixed solely on Rin. Her hatred blinded her to my presence. I almost smiled. If only she knew. Hitori removed her hand, and Rin slid to the floor, her knees buckling under her. She gasped for breath, coughed violently, and met my eye.

Not yet.

"Bring Rin and restrain her."

A group of seven False Shadows surrounded Rin and me. I let the guards lead the way but grabbed onto Rin's arm myself. It was shocking Rin had survived this long. Hitori's hatred emanated from her very being. Did Hitori fear rebellion from her own people if she killed Rin? No, Rin's allies had never been true allies. The guards' finicky loyalty lay with whomever they feared the most. There would be no rebellion at Rin's death. If I could find a way to use Hitori's hatred to blind her to our escape, it might be possible to save Rin's life. The element of surprise would be my advantage.

I needed to use it at the right time.

Guards flanked the sides of the room. Hitori walked inside, her hands behind her back and paused beside the table. Sweat beaded my forehead. If she found out we had taken her research, we wouldn't even get a chance. The door creaked to a close, and Hitori's sneer returned. Her soft features transformed into a quiet rage in the harsh lighting. Her gaze fixed on Rin.

I led Rin forward, as close as I dared to Hitori, keeping her hands clasped behind her back.

"Tell me, Rin, why is it that I keep you alive? Failure after failure, you always seem to disappoint me. Do you not care about your brother's safety?"

Rin's hands twitched in my grasp, but she said nothing.

If Ikaru had stayed in my care, we would not have needed to worry about his safety. Though if he were here, would he have already been killed?

I peered through the helmet's narrow eyeholes at the guards who stood beside me. If I gave them cause to believe we could win against Hitori, would they choose our side? Two of the guards glanced at Rin and me as if watching to see what we would do. Were they also holding out for the opportune time as well? A third guard's hand was clenched so tightly I could see the whites of his knuckles. Three potential allies, leaving four to defeat.

And Hitori.

While her knowledge of the skills were rumored to be unmatched, she had one fatal weakness: her guards' loyalty would never be hers. Phantoms earned the people's respect, doing what we could to preserve life. It sickened me that a ruler, with the potential to inspire people, used their power to evoke fear.

Hitori's eyes narrowed; she circled around Rin and me, peering at the blackened skin around Rin's neck. The scent of rose wafted from her hair. She was so close.

"Tell me, why should I not kill you?"

I squeezed Rin's hand and released my hold on her, grabbing the dagger belted at my knee. I flipped the blade and moved to drive it into Hitori's neck—but the dagger stopped a finger's width away from her skin. My wrist jolted at the impact of some opposing force, and I grimaced, keeping the emotion from my face.

I released the blade and moved back.

The dagger fell to the ground. It was like an invisible force or shield of some kind prevented me from hurting Hitori.

All emotion faded from Hitori's face. "It's been a while since someone's tried to kill me." Her eyes flashed, and flames erupted inside the room, growing in strength and number. I knew the trick from Rin; I had seen this use of the Skills before. The fire was not real. I threw back my cloak and pulled the staff from my back, slamming the end at Hitori's chest. She managed to block me. Her sword half-drawn from its sheath. The sharp edge of the blade began to glow red.

She was going to try and cut my staff.

I lashed out with my staff, crushing the back of her hand. She dropped the sword, and the edge seared through the sword's sheath, falling to the ground where it split the stone floor.

She wielded great power, but she was no warrior.

Rin caught my staff and shoved me away, enunciating each word as she said, "Get. Out. Of. Here."

On the edge of the room, a white mist seeped from the stone floors, and the air became heavy and hard to breathe. Several of the guards pulled at their armor near their necks. The mist floated about the room, almost knee height. My legs grew numb, and I tried to pick up my feet, startled when they refused to move. Rin swore at my side, and the bond on her arm began to glow. Tendrils of light swept from her bond and snaked around her body, her waist, and her legs, all the way to her feet. The mist recoiled from her, and she dropped to the ground, touching and unbinding my legs in the same fashion. Each of the guards remained rigid. I exchanged a glance with Rin, who drew her sword and rushed Hitori. I followed, the tendrils of light repelling the paralyzing mist.

Rin slashed at Hitori's arm, connecting with her bond. Her sword skated off the metal surface as Hitori drew back and lunged. I smashed her hand with my staff, stepping closer to Hitori. Her gaze met mine. The mist flared up around her, growing so thick that I could see nothing other than Hitori's face.

Her emerald eyes widened as she realized who I was.

"It's you—the Phantom!"

The air became thin, and I drew in a deep breath, shifting my weight to my back leg. I remembered the guards who were sympathetic to our cause, and I dug into my Phantom strength.

"I'm not afraid of you."

Hitori grinned and flicked her hand to the side. The mist parted to reveal a guard holding a dagger to Rin's neck. A trickle of blood dripped from the tip of the blade.

"That's only because you don't know me." She shifted her attention to Rin and the guard. "There's so much I can teach you of ruling, *Phantom*."

A flare of anger spread through me. "Fear will never gain the loyalty of the people you serve."

Another of the guards came forward, his helmet covering his eyes. His movements were almost unnatural as if he stirred against his will. I watched Hitori's intense gaze, studying her features. The muscles near her eyes twitched as the mist around her bond snaked across the ground.

I gripped my staff and thrust it at Hitori's neck.

Like before, it slammed against some invisible force.

"Tools," I said aloud, in a low voice, finding new meaning in the words Rin had spoken in her introduction. The people of Magoto were puppets to Hitori—whether they chose to be or not. It was not the guard who had pricked Rin's neck. It was Hitori. Her actions were nothing but those of a spoiled child: obey me, or I will make you.

A pain shot through my right arm as I withdrew my staff from Hitori's barrier. Once I figured out how to fight against her Skills, she would fall.

I would make sure of it.

I took a step back and dragged my staff against the ground, thrusting at Hitori with my full strength. My staff shattered at the force of my impact, and I scrambled across the floor to where Hitori's sword lay. The sword's hilt burned me, furious at my touch, but I refused to let go. My fingers still possessed strength. Until I no longer could hold a weapon, I would fight. When I'd begun Shadow training, the sword had been my weapon of choice. Over the years, my experience had demanded a less formidable weapon, one I did not have to hold back with. One that made it easier to restrain my strength. Even the staff that had shattered had been made of thin wood. There was a time when too many had been hurt by my hand—with the excuse of saving people.

But...

I needed to take the threat of the Skills and Hitori seriously. I couldn't keep holding back when so many were counting on me to defend them. Maybe with Hitori, I could make an exception to the Shadow's Creed.

"Feel your fingertips and the surface beneath them."

I spun about, my breath catching in my chest. The guard still held the dagger at Rin's neck.

"Feel the coolness of the blade, the texture." Rin didn't flinch as blood ran down her neck. "Feel the length of your arm and the extension that lies at the end of your grasp."

She was telling me how to defeat Hitori, knowing that in doing so—I choked off the thought, sinking deep inside myself, finding a fire that had been rekindled. I pushed that warmth to the edge of my sword, and a sliver of light appeared at the edge of the blade. I swung at Hitori, my sword piercing her side. When I removed my sword, a line of blood stained the blade.

Rin's scream broke my concentration.

I almost dropped the sword, pulling back my consciousness from the Skills. Hitori's hand was on the bond on Rin's forearm. In one movement, Hitori pulled the bond from Rin's arm and threw it across the room. Blood splattered across the stone floor, and Rin crumpled to the ground. Hitori's blood-coated hand hung at her side. A gash was cut into her side, where my blade had sliced her, yet it seemed she had not reacted to the injury.

Had I lost consciousness while using the Skills?

Was there some lapse in time?

My heart constricted, and I coughed, nausea overwhelming my senses. I was unused to using the Skills. I adjusted my grip on the sword as Hitori turned to me, her hands sweeping outward. The remaining mist on the ground glistened red before flames erupted and swirled in the air.

This time I could feel the heat of the fire.

Hitori's eyes focused on me. "Kill Rin."

The words echoed across the room, and the guards converged on Rin's crumpled form.

By using the Skills, I had penetrated Hitori's barrier. Without the Skills, I could not harm her. But I was weakened; my use of the power had sapped my strength. I didn't know if I could summon the power to use the Skills again.

I chuckled inwardly. I had no idea what I'd even done.

With a steadying breath, I split my attention between keeping Hitori at a distance and guarding Rin against the seven guards, positioning myself between the two. Rin's fingers twitched closer to a piece of my broken staff. I took a step to the left, then another, keeping Hitori ahead but moving in Rin's direction. Whatever Rin had planned, it was better than the idea I was still trying to come up with.

Hitori's gaze flickered down to Rin.

"How very noble of you to want to save her. I do wonder how you can trust her. After all she's done to poison Vaiyene and sabotage your people, it seems a rather odd relationship, don't you think?"

I, too, had once thought that, but the world was not drawn in absolutes. Rin did what she must, as did I.

"Rin is an ally of Vaiyene and a friend of mine." Unlike Hitori, I saw Rin as more than a tool; she was someone fighting for a better future for herself and for her homeland.

"She does what she must because you have forced her to."

Hitori smiled and clenched her fists. The flames grew in size. "And unfortunately, I am done with her."

Rin lunged for the staff and jammed it into the ground. The tiny piece of silver—the one she had used to mend my staff back in Leiko—hit the stone floor, and the flames snuffed out. Hitori drew a short sword from inside her cloak and swung at me, but I met her blade with the sword in my hand, pushing against her.

The guards surrounded Rin, and she tried to push herself onto all fours. I tried to move, but the mist held me in place.

Moving as one, the guards raised their blades.

Hitori grinned. "Finish it."

The guards swung their swords as the door to the room burst open. Their blades clanged and echoed through the room, flashing against what looked to be a line drawn in the air. I squinted against the bright light as the force from the guards' attack swept the mist to the sides of the room. The hold on my feet released, and I slashed at Hitori's head, feeling the sword slice through her skin. She screamed and recoiled from me, her hand over her face.

I spun around.

Finae stood in front of Rin, her hands clasped around the stone of Zenkaiko. The bright line in the air around Rin and Finae flickered and withdrew back into the rock.

A barrier of some sort?

Finae's eyes were glazed over from the Skills. The remaining mist on the ground had dissipated, and I moved to stand between Hitori and my companions. Hitori's breathing was ragged. A trickle of blood seeped from her hand that was still clasped to her face. I offered my hand to Rin and pulled her up. She stumbled to her feet, and I turned my attention to Finae. Her eyes were vacant. She took one step, and Rin grasped her arm. Finae blinked, and awareness returned to her eyes.

Rin let out a pained breath, her hand closing around the piece of staff. She closed her eyes and mumbled something under her breath. The silver around the staff sprang to life and jerked across the ground toward Hitori.

Rin turned to me. "I know you don't like listening to me, but this will only buy us a short amount of time."

I took one last glance at Hitori and at the blood dripping to the floor. Whatever damage I had done was not much, but she would not soon forget me. I nodded, and Finae and I ran from the room. The guards had not yet come to their senses. Rin snatched something from the ground and caught up to us. She pressed her bloodied hand to the wall to reveal the hidden passage.

I stumbled inside and grasped Finae's shoulders. "You are unbelievable," I said. She grinned at me, and I took a steadying breath. "How did you know how to create a barrier?"

Finae shrugged, her eyes drooping from exhaustion. "I asked if there was a way to help, and the stone did the rest."

Her answer unsettled me. Did the stone have a will of its own?

"You need to be careful, Finae," Rin said, using the wall for support. "The stone you carry is dangerous. The Skills are not something to be taken lightly, though I do appreciate you saving my life."

A sliver of a smile crossed Finae's face, and I ushered her down the dark passageway after Rin. I reached into my pocket and fumbled with the light canteen at my side, illuminating the tunnel.

While we had not defeated Hitori, we now knew she was not not without weakness. If there was a way to mix the Skills with the Shadows' combat abilities, we stood a good chance against her. After today, though, she would also have a measure of what I and the other Shadows were capable of.

It would spur her to grow stronger.

At the end of the tunnel, lying against the wall, was the box of research notes. Finae must have placed them there before coming to rescue us. Pride swelled within me. Rin held out her hand to stop us as muffled shouting penetrated our hiding place. She closed her eyes, digging her fingers into the wall to stay upright. I moved to catch her, but she pushed me away.

I handed Hitori's sword to Finae. She flinched as I offered it to her. "Hold it for me, will you?"

Finae's gaze followed mine to Rin's arm, and I moved to shield her from seeing the extent of the damage.

Rin sighed. "We don't have time."

I snatched Rin's forearm, and she hissed in pain. She flinched as I peeled the blood-soaked cloak from the wound. Even in the dim lighting, it looked bad. It was a testament to her strength she was still able to stand. I assessed the damage, separating my emotions from the moment. The silver threading of her bond was no more. In its place was a makeshift bond, carved into the skin with deep, bloody cuts. My stomach churned. From out of the corner of my eye, I saw Finae sink onto the ground. Her knees bent under. She clasped the sword with white knuckles.

Tears fell freely from her eyes.

I dug out a roll of cloth from the pack at my waist and retrieved a thin vial of medicinal herbs from the inner pouch of my robe. I raised the bottle to my teeth and pulled out the stopper. It contained a potent healing tonic. While I didn't have the means to clean the wound, this would at least keep infection away and provide some level of pain relief. I poured a few drops onto Rin's forearm. She hissed through the pain, and I let the abrasions air before I wrapped the bandage around her arm.

When the wound was concealed, I touched Finae's shoulder. "Rin will survive. It's nothing but a scratch."

Finae raised her head and stared blankly up at me. She had seen enough of battle. When I extended my hand, she hesitated, her eyes fixed on the blisters marking my palms. I bent down and offered her my arm instead, pulling her to her feet and taking the sword from her hands.

Finae held the box of research notes close against her chest.

A group of guards ran past the exit, their footsteps clanging across the stone floor. I met Rin's gaze. "Can you make it?"

Her hand touching the edge of a stone. "I've never heard of anyone dying from a scratch. Have you?"

She pushed open the door, and I adjusted the sword in my hand. I smiled to myself.

I was beginning to really like her.

chapter twenty-nine
TO FIGHT ANOTHER DAY

Finae's breathing grew shallow beside me. Her hair draped over her face, and her eyes remained fixed on the ground. I bent down and gave her a small smile. "We'll be away from Magoto in no time. Hang on a little longer."

She returned a feeble smile, and I patted her on the back, peering around the corner of Magoto's white walls. Rin slipped back from the western gate. "The guards stationed are sympathetic to our cause."

The people here knew nothing about loyalty. A comrade was a comrade, no matter how difficult a situation might be. I didn't voice my thoughts, however, fearing Finae's courage would break if I did. If Rin had felt betrayed back in the castle, I hadn't been able to tell. She might have resigned herself to it, but to me, it was unforgivable.

Somewhere behind us, people shouted.

We didn't have time to find an alternative.

There were three men stationed at the gate. Even though I was angry at the guards back at the castle, one of these guards had let Finae and me in during the blizzard.

I could at least make sure Hitori did not kill them.

"We need to make it look like there was a struggle."

Rin considered this, then nodded. "Let me talk to them first."

She led us toward the guards, and I followed, my hand grasping the hilt of the sword at my side. They were older than most of the False Shadows I'd met so far, a little older than Rin or me. Forty summers or so. Scars on their faces told of battle experience, and age had weathered their skin.

"I'm Kilo, one of—" I caught myself and fumbled with the words. I was no longer a Phantom. "Thank you for your help."

I bowed at the waist with my right hand over my chest. When I straightened, I blinked in surprise to find the guards bowing in return to me. A knot formed in my chest thinking as I thought about how I would never have the opportunity to lead the Shadows. Despite the consequences that might come to them, these guards stood defiant against Hitori.

They held onto the hope we had brought.

One of the men went into the open door of the watchtower. When he returned, he handed me a long pike with a blade affixed to the end. "I believe this will suit you better."

I narrowed my eyes at Rin to see if she had tipped the guards off. She shrugged and looked away, but not before I caught the smile on her lips.

"There are whispers about you, about someone who fights without the intent of killing. I didn't think such a man could exist in these times."

I took the pike from him and gave him a small bow. At the time, when facing Hitori, the sword had felt right in my hand. However right it had felt, it was not who I was anymore. I looked around at the men gathered before me, men who did not know me except for whispers that had spread across Kiriku.

I wanted to be the man they believed me to be.

Using the sword, I cut the point from the pike, removing the killing edge. I handed the sword to the guard. "Your efforts will not be wasted. I will make sure of it. We'll be calling on you before this is over."

The guards stood a little taller, their warrior spirit rekindled at my words. I had nothing to offer but my gratitude and a vague promise that Hitori would be stopped. Until then, these men would be the last link to Magoto. Their support was irreplaceable.

Finae pulled on my sleeve, drawing my attention to the people drawing closer. "We should hurry."

Rin fixed the three guards with her gaze. "We need to make it look like there was a struggle."

"We will face Hitori when she comes," one guard said, his voice escalating as he spoke. "We don't need any tricks to defend ourselves."

I understood the sentiment, but, sometimes the best option was to live to fight another day. Loyal men were what we needed the most. We might only have the three men standing here now, but the potential to spread their courage needed time to grow.

I fingered the pill sewn into the pocket in my sleeve, an idea coming to me. "Do you have any spirits?"

My words were met with blank stares.

One of the guards shook off his surprise. "We have some."

"Bring some to me," I said, fishing out the pill and breaking it into three sections with my fingers. When untampered with, the medicine would grant a person renewed energy. When taken with alcohol, a much different effect was achieved. In my younger Shadow training days, Zavi and I had spent the night at a tavern after a difficult mission. We had both taken pills earlier in the day, but when we had gotten to the tavern, the effects had not yet worn off before we indulged in the local sake. It was Mia who had found us on the tavern floor. She had thought we were poisoned. I smiled at the memory. Until now, I had never considered the information anything but a foolish mistake.

When the guard returned, he handed me a flask. "This will knock you unconscious long enough for Hitori to find your bodies."

Finae looked at me curiously, but I ignored her. Some things she didn't need to know about my past. I handed each of the guards a piece of the pill. They eyed it before swallowing it with the alcohol.

"Good luck, Rin. Kilo."

I nodded, and one by one the guards lay down as if defeated in battle, falling unconscious soon after. I removed a dagger from one of the men and ran it across my arm, cutting into my skin to smear the blade with my blood.

"Let's make this a little more convincing."

Using the same dagger, I cut a few places in the guards' clothing. Finae and Rin arranged the bodies and smeared dirt across the men's faces. I mixed my blood with dirt, putting the paste into the makeshift wounds. I squeezed a few splatters of blood around the scene and took the guards' weapons, throwing them across the cobblestones. I handed a bow and a quiver to Rin, slinging a pair over my own shoulder. I stuffed my new staff into the holder at my back. It would have to do.

"That should be more than enough," Rin said, strapping a sword around her waist. I pushed open the gate and scanned the horizon. Snow covered the ground still, but fresh flakes had begun to fall. It would help cover our tracks.

I pulled the gate closed behind our small company, the door creaking to a close. I drew in a breath, guiding Finae ahead of me.

Rin walked past us and headed southeast. "There's a small village to the south, hidden away in the ravines. I don't believe Hitori knows of it, and I doubt she would think to send people all the way out there."

Something scuffled on the wall behind us, and I spun around. Standing upon the wall at our back was a tall, looming figure. His hand drew back; an arrow nocked in his bow. I darted in front of Finae, and the arrow pierced the leather armor on my shoulder. I unslung the bow from my back and nocked an arrow.

"Go!" I shouted, taking aim at the man.

Finae and Rin shuffled behind me, but the man on the wall aimed at them, not at me. I released the hold on my arrow and nocked another one, shouting a warning to Rin. The archer let loose, dodging my own arrow. I let Finae's and Rin's safety fade from my mind, trusting Rin would be able to get herself and

Finae away. I pulled two arrows from the quiver and nocked them both, spacing them out against the string. I knelt to the ground and turned the bow. I released the arrows, and the man on the wall dropped the arrow he prepared. He managed to evade one of mine, but the other struck his shoulder.

I turned and ran after Finae and Rin, feeling no shame in doing so. Back in my Shadow training days, we had been astounded to learn that sometimes the best strategy was to flee. As my father had explained it: "The best strategy is the one that allows you to continue to draw breath."

It was an easy lesson to forget.

Courage sometimes meant swallowing your pride.

An arrow hit the ground next to me, and I pushed myself harder, up and over the hill, into the cover of the trees. After a short time, the fallen trees and stone cavern that created the horses' pen came into view.

"Kilo, over here!" I spun and saw Rin propped against a tree. Finae leaned over her, wrapping a bandage around Rin's left arm.

I knelt beside them. "What happened?"

Rin pointed to a man lying on the ground. Blood dripped from his head, and underneath him, the snow turning red. "He was waiting for us when we arrived at the stables. Hitori must have found out about the horses and sent someone to catch us off guard."

I glanced back at Finae, who gaped at me. "You have an arrow in your shoulder."

It was nothing fatal. More of an annoyance and a dull pain. I was more worried about her. I had thought she would be more scared after being attacked. With a quick motion, I yanked the shaft and dislodged the arrow from my leather armor.

I offered my hand to Rin and pulled her to her feet.

We needed to get away from Magoto before our adrenaline wore off and weakness set in.

Rin brought over a tall, broad gelding like the one Finae had ridden to Zenkaiko. It was a well-suited choice. His stature would make the ride smooth. With Rin's help, I loaded the saddle packs from inside the cavern onto the horses and secured Hitori's research notes in my horse's pack. Finae swung her leg over the horse's girth, and she nudged its flanks with her heels, her movement in sync with the animal.

I mounted my own horse, watching Finae.

What she lacked in fighting prowess, she made up for in the saddle. Finae's unexpected courage and action had surprised even me. She would make a good Shadow. She possessed courage I had not seen from her before, and I found myself smiling.

While we hadn't put an end to Hitori, but we had gained invaluable experience fighting against the Skills. Her box of research notes would undoubtedly lead to a way to defeat her.

I clicked my heels against my horse.

Next time, I would put an end to Hitori.

S he was not going to make it. I spurred my horse forward,
next to Finae's and braced my sister in the saddle. The quick
movement threw my balance off, but somehow, I managed
to stay upright as the horses slowed their pace. I glanced up at
Rin, who was leading the way, her head bent against the chill. Her
hand pinned her oversized hood down to keep the wind out.

"Wait, Rin!" I called.

Rin turned to look back. She dismounted and shifted the
saddlebags from one horse to another. "This stallion can carry
the both of you. He does have a bit of a temper, but he seems to
be in a good mood today."

"I'll keep an eye on him," I said, working together with Rin to
move Finae over to the new horse. I climbed up behind Finae
and wrapped my arms around her. Her head drooped onto my
shoulder.

Rin handed me the brown stallion's reins, and I shifted my
arm to support Finae's head.

"How much longer?"

"Not too much farther." Rin pointed up the mountain to a dip between peaks. She mounted her horse and retook the lead. "We should arrive before the sun sets. We'll find help there."

I nodded and balanced Finae's warm body tight in the curve of my arm. The horse stumbled, and my stomach plummeted. I cursed as we fell, holding onto the reins and gripping the saddle to remain upright. The stallion scrambled and found a foothold in the rocks. We followed no path, as white blinded us in every direction. Snow covered our tracks and hid us from Hitori, but we would be lucky to make it up the mountain in one piece. Whitestar I trusted, Nightwind as well, but I didn't know Rin's horse.

I squinted my eyes against the onslaught of snow, adjusting the scarf around my neck.

Rin had lost a lot of blood—too much blood—but she persisted and showed no signs of exhaustion. Was her fear of Hitori driving her to continue? I offered to break camp more than once, but she refused. Fire could alert Hitori of our whereabouts, but the risk, to me, was worth it. Every moment we spent out in the storm prolonged our exposure to the cold. Rin seemed to think Hitori would send her False Shadows after us in the snow, but I wasn't convinced. Although, from what I'd gathered, she didn't mind expending her resources.

Even if those resources were human lives.

As we crested the mountain, we maneuvered our way through a thick barrier of hearty evergreens. I held out my arm, pine needles brushing against it as I pushed the branches away from Finae. Small cottages lay ahead with thick snow covering the rooftops. Lanterns dangled from iron holders affixed to their stone exteriors. Hearty puffs of smoke trailed from each stone chimney.

Rin came to a stop, and I slowed my horse. Finae stirred as if sensing our arrival.

"We've made it to the village, Finae." I rubbed her shoulder. We all needed a good meal and a warm place to rest. Rin slid off her mare and approached the first cottage. The door swung open; a man with a longbow in his hands approached.

"Who are you, and why have you come here?" The man tugged on a string next to his doorframe, and a bell chimed. The doors of the other cottages opened, and people emerged, weapons in their hands. My heart sank, and I pulled Finae close.

These people seemed prepared for a fight.

Rin held up her hands, and the first man nocked an arrow to his bow, keeping it trained on her. "Where's Jaanae? I ask for refuge from an old friend."

The man's expression didn't change. His bushy brown beard hid most of his face. "Jaanae is dead."

Rin's shoulders slumped. "I didn't know."

At this elevation, the temperature would drop too far to make camp. With the harsh weather, making the journey down would be even riskier than our ascent.

"Jaanae and I were good friends," Rin said, keeping her movements slow. "We used to play together in the fields of Phia years ago. We kept in touch through letters. My name is Rin."

The man lowered his bow, pointing the arrow at the ground. "I remember Jaanae coming home late because she had gone out for a ride on her horse. She always came from Magoto and told us stories about her friend she met there."

A woman with stark white hair appeared next to the man in the doorway. She placed her hand on the man's shoulder and pressed an arm over her chest. "Rin? Is that you? You helped Jaanae back to the village when she fell from her horse. I never got the chance to thank you for helping my daughter home."

Rin nodded and returned her gaze to the bearded man. "Jaanae asked I keep it a secret because she knew her father would be angry if she returned home injured."

The man opened his mouth to speak, but his wife cut him off. "Thank you. We are in your debt. Without your help, we would have lost Jaanae much sooner."

"I wish I would have known of her death sooner. She was a dear friend." Rin glanced back at us. "I hate to be a burden, but we need shelter for the night. Somewhere safe. We've had a long journey."

The woman looked past Rin, her eyes resting on Finae. She stepped away from the doorway and extended her arm in a sweeping motion. I held onto Finae's arm as she dismounted, then slid off the horse behind her.

I let Finae and Rin go first, gripping the reins of the horses before following. Before I made it to their side, the bearded man grabbed my arm and slammed me against the stone house. I grimaced at the impact of stone against my back. Instincts flared, but I suppressed the fight inside me.

The bearded man towered over me, his eyes piercing into mine as his stale breath wafted over me. His gaze dropped to my arm, and he tightened his grasp on me.

"Is that one of those metal pieces they wear in Magoto?"

His hand pressed harder against me, making it difficult to breathe.

"I'm from Vaiyene. I am no threat to you."

"I'm the one from Magoto," Rin said, holding up her right arm as she moved to intercede. "Beneath these bandages is the same silver threading. I've forsaken Hitori, and one day I will return to liberate the people of Magoto."

Rin no longer wore a bond—Hitori had ripped it from her arm hours prior, but her declaration was no less compelling. Rin's spirit was strong. She didn't need me to intervene. I did not doubt that if she had taken up arms against Hitori, the men she needed would have fought alongside her.

Rin pried the man's hand from my chest. The bandage around her forearm was stained with crusted blood. "This is Kilo, one of the Phantoms of Vaiyene, and his sister, Finae. They've offered their aid to put an end to Hitori."

The bearded man took a step back, drawing his shoulders back as he surveyed me with new eyes. "If you are against Hitori, then you are welcome here. Her people took our daughter's life."

Hitori's reach stretched this far?

I followed the man inside the cottage, grateful for the fire that sputtered against the cold air. Heat stung the skin on my face. I led Finae close to the fireplace and pushed her into a wooden rocking chair. Kneeling close to the stone mantle, I knelt before Finae and stripped off both our gloves. I rubbed my hands against her fingers to warm them.

"I hope you're not tired of adventure, Finae."

A faint smile crossed her lips. "Never."

I smiled and ruffled my hand in her hair before glancing around the stone cabin. While the space was close-quartered, it did not seem small. Intricate quilts of greens and blues decorated the walls. Their palettes hinted at cozy nights spent by the fire with a needle in hand. It made the stone walls feel more like home. Set upon the mantel were two wooden toys. One was a horse with frayed white hair, and the other was a worn wooden doll. A family had once lived here—but no more. I sighed, my mind flitting back to the days after our parents had died. How empty the house had felt without their presence.

The woman darted in and out of view as she shuffled about the cottage. She opened pantries, stuffing her arms with this and that, bustling about while muttering under her breath. Then, as if remembering something important, she stopped and stormed toward me, dragging a chair from the table.

"You'll catch a draft on the floor if you stay like that, son."

It had been a long time since anyone had fussed over me. I lifted myself into the chair, a smile on my face. The woman threw a dusty woolen blanket on top of me and shoved a mug of hot liquid into my hands, nearly spilling the contents in her haste.

Rin covered her mouth and stifled a laugh, watching the woman scurry away. "Full of motherly energy, isn't she?"

I shook my head. How had Jaanae dealt with the constant fretting?

And I thought my mother had been fussy.

The scent of lemon, chamomile, and honey drifted from the cup, and I took a sip. Warm liquid and herbs soothed my throat. The woman returned with another two cups of tea, shoving them with the same enthusiasm into Finae's and Rin's hands.

The husband shook his head at our wide-eyed stare. "She gets a little worked up about guests."

I smiled. "Please, think nothing of it."

I took another sip of tea, my eyes finding the painting above the mantel. Jaanae and her parents.

The man followed my gaze.

"I hate to drag up the memories, but would you mind sharing the circumstances of your daughter's death? You said she was killed by Hitori's people?"

Jaanae's father growled, his temper quick to rise. "She went into town, to Aventon, to trade for wool and dried meat. When Jaanae left town, a group of Hitori's people demanded she give them what she purchased." His eyes flicked to the painting, and his brows furrowed. "She refused, and they made an example out of her."

Jaanae's mother paused in the doorway, the fire casting dark shadows across her face. I lowered my gaze to the tea in my hands. The False Shadows were growing bolder and more reckless in their hate. Hitori's control over them distorted their grasp on morality, making them little more than common thugs with a lust for power. Nothing had been gained by Jaanae's death except spreading fear.

Finae breathed deeply in the chair next to the fire. I took the mug from her hand and draped the blanket the woman had given me over Finae's sleeping body.

I had become a Shadow to protect and provide for her. I'd given up being a Phantom for the same reason. In my mind, there was no question of my purpose anymore. Hitori must be stopped, no matter the cost to myself.

I would kill her if I needed to.

I stood and placed the mug on the mantel, drawing my new staff from the holder on my back. I'd left Vaiyene to find a way to save my people. Finae, Shenrae, and Syrane were at the forefront of my mind, always, but they no longer were the only ones who needed my strength. There were people like Rin who would not fight for themselves, and villagers without anyone to defend them.

I crossed the room to Jaanae's parents, holding my staff across my palms. I knelt before them and extended my staff as a Shadow would pledge themselves to a Phantom.

"Hitori has taken the lives of my people, as well as countless innocent lives across Kiriku. With this staff, I will bring justice to all those she has hurt. I will fight for Jaanae's justice."

And I would fight for all those across Kiriku.

A hand touched my shoulder, and I looked up to see Rin standing next to me. The man held his wife and rocked her, her head buried in his chest. I couldn't see her face, but the man's eyes were damp with tears. I stood and held my staff in my hand. Hitori's lust for power had consumed her and endangered more lives than the False Shadows.

Rin would not stand against Hitori.

The people of Magoto would not stand against Hitori.

Vaiyene would not stand against Hitori.

In Shadow training, we had been taught that our weapons were an extension of ourselves, but a weapon served as more than a physical extension. It was an extension of one's intentions—an extension of who a person was. Hitori used the Skills to distance people. Where she would spread fear, I would become the sword to break her hold. I would draw the people around me and be their strength. For the people who could not fight, I would fight for them.

Rin stood to my right, framed by the firelight. Her eyes pierced mine, and she drew the sword at her side. "I will fight with you, Phantom Kilo until I no longer draw breath."

I sensed her fighting spirit return at last. When I first met her, she had seemed a broken person, resigned to her fate. But she had found her strength and will at last.

Kiriku needed both of us to return peace to the lands.

I smiled to myself. I'd found the beginning of strength in unlikely places. Who would have known one of the False Shadows would become one of my greatest allies? I touched Rin's blade and nodded to her. The resemblance of her vow to that of the Shadows humbled me.

"I accept your service. Although…" I pushed her blade away and gave her a wry smile. "You didn't give me a choice in the matter."

Rin chuckled and sheathed her sword. "We both know you were born for this."

Instincts had always guided my path. If Rin had not sought me out, I would have chosen the same regardless of her involvement. Zavi and Mia had always said that I would become a great Phantom. I could see them beside me, their smiles were as clear as reality.

I rested my staff against the wall, next to Finae's chair, meeting her gaze and smile. I fixed her with a pointed stare. "We should all get some rest. We have a long journey ahead of us."

"Thank you," the man said softly from the corner.

I gave him a small bow.

"There are plenty of blankets for you to make a bed." The woman waved to a pile of linens and furs in the corner, her eyes red from emotion. "I'm sorry we can't offer more."

I shook my head. "This is more than enough."

She nodded, and the man shepherded her away.

We sorted through the pile of furs and thick, woolen blankets. Pulling out a large sheepskin, Rin lay down next to the hearth. I laid a thick pelt down beside Finae's cot.

I drew in a contented breath, letting my chest expand to full capacity before releasing the air. Leaving Vaiyene had torn me apart, but now pieces of my old life fell around me. A person's resolve and their beliefs made them who they were. I no longer needed to cling to the title of Phantom or Shadow.

For now, I was content.

I knew who I served.

chapter thirty-one
HOPE RETURNS

A scraping noise pulled me from sleep's deep reaches. I opened my eyes and squinted through a blinding light until my eyes focused. Finae sat in the corner of the room with a woolen blanket on top of her head. It fell down around her petite frame and sprawled out around her on the stone floor.

The stone from Zenkaiko illuminated in her hands.

I pushed myself up onto my elbows, irritation building inside me. "You shouldn't be using the Skills."

Finae turned the stone over in her hands; the silver etchings glinted to life at her fingertips. I stretched out my hand to take it from her, but she moved it out of reach.

"I knew the risks of coming on this mission, Kilo."

I frowned.

I should have explained the Skill Poisoning to her earlier.

"Using the Skills poisons the user. It's a side effect of using the power."

"I know. I heard you and Rin talking about it. Besides, I can feel it running through my body." Finae grew quiet, shifting the stone in her hand. How could she feel the Skill Poisoning? The way she had worded it made me believe it was more than the nausea and side effects we had experienced before.

Finae scooted closer to me and held the stone out. "Put your hand on top. There's something I want you to see."

I glared at her, not wanting to indulge her, but I was curious about her mischief. I settled on a dramatic sigh to show my displeasure. When my fingertips brushed the rough surface, a surge of energy rushed through me as my stomach dropped.

My eyes unfocused and refocused into the memory.

I stood in Zenkaiko before its destruction.

Finae ran down the streets of the town. Her figure was small against the towering buildings. She stopped and waited for me to follow her. I obliged, savoring the bittersweet experience with her. Finae was happy, but I couldn't forget that for every moment we spent in this memory, time was taken from Finae's life. She wanted to help us, but she didn't need to risk herself for us. As someone who had served others all my life, I understood the desire, the need.

I would not stop her.

She was young, but she knew her actions held consequences. If she persisted in using the Skills—and I knew she would not give them up—she needed a bond to negate the effects. Would it be possible for the stone to show us how the ancient Shadows of Zenkaiko had created the bonds?

Or did the stone contain only select memories?

"Hurry, Kilo!" Finae disappeared down a corridor.

I ran to catch up with her.

Her black-dyed hair bounced as she turned a corner, leaving the flagstone and town behind. I followed her into an expansive garden. Stone tiles mingled with green grasses and wildflowers. Those who lived here had done little to deter nature from working its way into the designs. I walked in awe under the wooden archway, touching the intricate silver carvings on the surface. My fingertips tingled with energy as I dragged them across the arch. A sense of calm descended over me as I passed the wooden arch.

The Skills were alive here.

Large maple trees caught the sunlight overhead, casting dappled shadows across the stone tiles and grass. Finae stood next to one of them. Her hand rested on the trunk. I moved beside her, noticing a thick line of silver wedged into the bark. It glinted as I tilted my head to get a straight-on view.

"This tree was struck by lightning. One of the Phantoms saved it by infusing this metal into the bark."

I ran my finger over the metal, and the familiar sensation of energy climbed over my fingertips. Was it somehow reacting to my bond, or could anyone feel this energy? If this magic could be infused into life, how had we not felt its presence before?

Finae rocked onto her heels, bouncing beside me.

"Interesting, isn't it? There's some sort of memory world linked to this stone. The leaders here are called Phantoms as well, and this material"—she ran her finger over the silver riveting in the tree—"is the same as your bond."

Unbelievable. I shook my head in awe. "I didn't know the Skills could be used in such a way."

The Skills *did* seem endless. Rin had said as much, but the concept of infinity was hard to grasp.

Finae skipped away and bent down between two stone tiles. She cupped her hand around a small violet flower. At a distance, it looked no different than an ordinary flower, so why was she taking extra care? I dropped onto one knee and waited for Finae to show me what she had found. Even after witnessing death, and being injured, her spirit remained the artist. Finae would always see the world filled with wonder, even in times like these.

Her kindness and heart astounded me.

As a Shadow—and once a Phantom—my duty lay in finding danger and preventing it. Our worldviews would never be the same. Her view gave me hope more than my own.

Finae caressed the edge of the flower's petals, letting her fingers trail over the outlines as softly and as sweetly as a lover's caress. The Skills answered Finae, and the petals' veins illuminated. The light spread through the stem and into the roots. Through the stone tiles, the network of roots webbed out into the soil as clear as if Finae had drawn the details with a pen's edge. The flower pulsed, and she moved her hand away.

The light disappeared.

Finae stood and glanced around her, taking in every tree, branch, and blade of grass before her eyes returned to me. "There's more to these Skills than Hitori's use. I wanted to show you before you decided what to do about them. We can use the Skills for good too, to help people and the world around us."

Her words were so like her; kind, honest, and filled with hope. My experiences of late had shown me nothing but darkness, with a few glimmers of light. The Skills were dangerous, undeniably so, but as Finae had shown me, they could also be used for good.

There would always be people like Hitori who abused power.

Did the good outweigh the bad?

Finae led us farther into the gardens. The stone tiles, the archways, the flora—everything here—exuded magic as deep and ancient as the land. The world and the Skills were one and the same. If the Skills were a part of the world, why had we lost this magic? Why had we forgotten who we were?

It was a thought I could not shake.

I followed Finae under another wooden archway. Her fingers trailed over the delicate details. The same calm settled over me as before. Then my momentary wonder fell away to reason.

"You can't keep using the Skills, Finae. You'll…"

I couldn't finish.

Finae glanced back at me and sighed. "I know, but I've never been allowed to do anything meaningful before. I want to find out as much information as I can about the Skills and help you and Rin."

She flipped her palm over, and a tiny orb of light extended from her hand. She walked to the archway and touched the wooden structure, sending silver light running along the outline of the wood. Her energy had become light.

Finae removed her hand, and the light faded.

The world seemed a little darker.

As stubborn as I wanted to be, I couldn't deny the beauty of Finae's use of the Skills, or of the future, she believed in. I wanted her to live, and her dream of the future—I wanted that, too.

Finae kept her eyes averted, gazing longingly at a future I couldn't see. "There's so much potential with the Skills. We can help grow food for the winter, purify the lands, and heal wounds. Vaiyene is my home too, but more than that, I want to save Rin and you." Finae's voice caught, and she swallowed her emotion; tears threatened to break her composure. "You've always protected me. Why can't I do the same?"

Gone were the days of coming home with paintbrushes and hoping Finae would be content. She'd become someone who thought about the world and acted on her desires. Finae's talent lay in using the Skills, a feat I had not yet mastered. She could use the Skills without effort, and her kind heart painted the world in a way I desperately needed to see.

I should have never left her in Vaiyene for all those years.

I cleared my throat, drawing in a deep breath to calm my rising emotions. This was Finae's chance to make a difference. Here and now, as the world waited on the dawn of change. Her choices would define not only herself but those who lived in these lands.

"If this is what you want, Finae, I will stand with you."

Finae grinned.

Instincts aside, the Skills excited me. They were a beautiful, dangerous force, and it was time I pursued a brighter future. One where I not only prevented war, but where I took into account how I wanted the world to be. I looked around at Finae's vision of Zenkaiko, returning my gaze to my sister.

"I am quite curious about this side of the Skills."

Finae smiled; her eyes filled with tears. "I don't know how far I can go with you on this journey, but I will do my best to be there for you as long as I can."

The implications of her words cut into me, but I tried my best to brush them off. None of our lives were guaranteed any more. It was a reality better accepted than denied. I stood beside Finae and wrapped my arm around her shoulders, drawing her to my side. For the first time, we were equals: fighting for the same purpose and with the same weight of responsibility on our shoulders.

"I am proud to be your brother."

Finae sniffed beside me. I had never told her before, and our parents had been too hard to impress to have ever said anything. Even as a Shadow I never had received their recognition. I grabbed Finae's hand and knelt before her—to see on her level. Finae's eyes brimmed with tears. She tried to hold them back, but one by one, they fell down her cheeks. I turned her hand over, and from within the folds of my cloak, I withdrew a paintbrush, pushing it into her palm. I'd carried it with me since the day I'd become a Shadow.

"Create the world as you want to see it."

Finae curled her fingers around the brush, and I stood, ruffling her hair. I took one last glance around and fixed the memory in my mind. I would remember the vision and the promise it held.

"I think it's time to leave."

Tears still stained Finae's eyes, but she nodded and held out the white stone. I brushed my fingers over it, and Finae took a breath before the memory fell apart. The stone walls of Jaanae's parents' house fell into place around us. The fire dwindled in the hearth, and I grabbed a new log, throwing it onto the spent logs. I turned to find Rin's gaze on me. She sat cross-legged on the wooden floor. She held something in her lap. Her eyes drifted to Finae, who sat on the bed beside me.

She was anxious, but why?

Rin stood and handed the bundle to me. I untied the makeshift sack and snatched my hand back. Inside, silver threads wound around an invisible forearm.

It was Rin's bond.

She must have taken it before we escaped.

"What is it?" Finae stood up so she could see. I glanced back as Finae peeked over my shoulder, my mind too slow to shield her view. The color drained from her cheeks.

"For Finae," Rin whispered. "I know it's unsettling, but, Kilo, she needs it more than I do. If she's going to be using the Skills, she needs a bond. I made sure I didn't leave without it."

Rin had cleaned the silver threading, but I could still see the blood staining the bond in my mind. I glanced at Finae.

It would filter the Skill Poisoning and prolong her life.

We needed to find the man in Leiko who created the False Shadows' bonds. Neither Rin nor Finae should use the Skills without one. Sneaking into Vaiyene wouldn't be possible. We would have to convince the crazy old man in Leiko to make one, or...we would have to take a bond from a False Shadow.

Even the thought tasted foul in my mouth.

There were the dead buried in the forest outside of Leiko, as well as the bodies I had burned in Mashin. Even Kefnir might have kept the bonds of the False Shadows who had taken their lives in Tarahn. I glanced between Finae and Rin. It was a matter of who needed it more.

Finae stared at the bond in my hands. "But, don't you need it, Rin? The poison will affect you as well."

Rin shook her head, fixing her eyes on the fire. She leaned against the mantel with one arm. "It will take some time before the poison will take hold of me. Because of me, the poison was already in your veins, even before you used the Skills. It seems fair I try and lessen the damage I've done."

Repentance.

Finae chewed on her lip, deep in thought. "I'll take it."

Without Rin's admission of guilt, Finae would likely not have agreed. She always tried to lessen the pain of others. None of our options sat well with me, but what other choice did we have? I pressed my fingers against the bridge of my nose.

"Do you know how to affix it?"

"I have a theory." Rin gave Finae a reassuring smile. "Don't worry; it won't hurt."

Rin took the bond from my hands and sat down in front of Finae's bedside. I sat beside Finae and placed a hand on her shoulder. I hoped Rin knew what she was doing. Rin closed her eyes, and her fingers traced over the bond in her hands. She ran her fingertips over the tendrils until they shuddered under her touch. The silver threads squirmed into life—first one, then another—until they snaked up and over Rin's hand. She reached out and took Finae's hand, and the silver coils wrapped around her arm.

It was the same as what had happened back in Leiko when I first met Rin. She had fixed my staff with the Skills, willing a silver thread from her bond into the crack in my staff. The silver tendrils split from one coil into many, winding around Finae's arm. The bond wasn't like the diagram in Hitori's book. The pattern belonged to Rin's will as she guided the metal onto Finae's arm. Rin wavered, and I caught her as she fell backward. She startled awake as if she had been fast asleep.

"Thank you," I said, grateful for her sacrifice and for prolonging the time I had with my sister.

Rays of light peeked through the windows of Jaanae's parents' humble stone cottage. I shifted and turned onto my side. My hand reached for the dagger beside the fireplace, but my eye caught Rin watching me from the corner.

In her hands, she held the stone of Zenkaiko.

I bolted upright as Finae stirred beside me. I kept my voice low to not awaken our hosts.

"What are you doing?"

Rin ignored me, or rather, she didn't hear me. Her mind and existence lay inside the stone, in whatever memory she sorted through. If it wasn't Finae, it was Rin. I kicked off the furs and made to storm over to Rin, but Finae grabbed my arm.

"I don't think you should disturb her while she's not here."

Finae was right. I still didn't understand how the Skills worked—except that using them took a great deal of focus. I crossed my arms, shaking off the restlessness in my body. What was Rin thinking? I drummed my fingers on my arm and then focused on reviving the fire. I stoked the embers with my dagger, blowing on fragmented pieces of wood until it blazed red hot.

Rin was as reckless as I was.

When I straightened, a sly smile crept onto Finae's face. She raised her eyebrows and looked toward Rin. I followed her gaze. Rin remained inside the stone's memory.

"You're worried about her."

"Of course I am. Who knows how long Rin's been inside the stone? And she doesn't have a bond, which means she's poisoning herself."

Finae remained silent. Her smile widened.

I narrowed my eyes. "You're not worried?"

Finae shrugged. "Of course, I am. Just not as much as you."

Cloth rustled behind me, and I turned to see the light from the stone fading as Rin withdrew from the stone. I held my tongue for a few moments before glaring at Rin until she noticed me.

"You know, people say I'm reckless. Both of you"—I spun to include Finae— "are as thoughtless, if not more so. We're never going to get the chance to face Hitori if both of you continue pushing your bodies to the limits."

Rin and Finae exchanged a glance and laughed. I returned my attention back to the fire and sighed.

They were no longer taking me seriously.

"I found out where the markings are leading us."

As upset as I was, and as much as I wanted not to care, whatever Rin had found out would be helpful. I followed Finae over to where Rin had placed the stone on the floor. She held out a fingertip and touched the edge of the rock, drawing out the silver markings across the surface.

"It is a map like we thought, but it's written in code."

She pointed to a triangular-shaped mass. "The mountains are oceans, and the water's edges are landforms. If you invert the two and take into account Zenkaiko's location and our current knowledge of Kiriku, we need to head to a village called Konro."

As Rin pointed out the location on the stone's surface, I noticed that the tips of her fingers were blackened. She handed the stone to Finae, who had already dug out a pen from her bag. Rin noticed my gaze and slid her hands into her pockets.

The Skill Poisoning already affected her.

I pushed the thought aside.

We needed to make our sacrifices worthwhile.

I watched over Finae's shoulder as she transcribed the map, filling in the blank spaces with my knowledge of the land. If my estimations were correct, the village of Konro was closer to Vaiyene, somewhere in the Orem Cliffs. It wouldn't be an easy location to travel to. With it being more north than Magoto, would we even be able to make it there in the dead of winter?

Finae drew a placeholder for Konro village on her map. I crossed to the window and pulled back the sheer curtains. Sunny skies lay to the north. The sun's warmth would melt the ice and lessen the risk of descending the mountain. Out of the three of us, Rin's injuries were the worst, but judging from her stamina in using the Skills, she would be able to ride.

The sooner we left the lower regions of Phia, the better.

I wanted to put as much distance between Hitori and us as we could. We had her notes and a direction. All we had left to do was connect the pieces and follow the trail.

———

My foot slid out from underneath me, and I fell. I grabbed onto a tree branch and dug my heels into the ground to stop myself from falling over the cliff. My heart pounded in my ears, and I drew in deep, steadying breaths. I'd known traversing the Orem Cliffs in winter was a bad idea. We had been traveling a couple weeks since leaving Magoto. Progress had been slow due to the weather, but our lives had not been in danger.

Until now.

Rin and Finae called out from behind me. I waved my hand to acknowledge them. My quick reflexes had saved me from falling over the cliff. I scooted backward and pulled myself up, using my horse's packs to steady myself. From the height we were at, the rock formations and maze of peaks spread out without an end in sight. The mountains were strange, seemingly chiseled by a dull blade with deep rivets.

Rin and Finae tested their way down to me, sinking one foot in the snow to assure a secure step. My near fall had given them caution in their descent, but I still held my breath. Finae joined me at my side, looking out over the thin slates of mountains.

"Breathtaking," Finae said.

Dangerous.

"Looks like that thin pathway is our way down." Rin pointed to a small trail that was wide enough for a single horse and rider. I eyed the pathway. It faced the south, which meant the ice would have melted. That also suggested it would be slippery.

I voiced my concerns first. "Should we turn around?"

If we chose not to risk climbing down into the valley, we would lose an opportunity to find information on the Skills. Hitori's notes would help, but if the stone held memories of the ancient Shadows and their use of the Skills, would we be able to unlock that knowledge in Konro village?

Was it worth risking our lives over?

Rin met my gaze and sucked in a breath. "That's a steep drop."

"Finae, what do you think?" I asked.

"Konro village is close," Finae said, her voice unwavering. "We've come so far; it would be hard to turn back."

I led my horse over to the narrow pathway and sank down onto my heels. The path, for the most part, was covered in a light dusting of snow. Good for traction. I shifted my position but did not see the sheen of ice.

I mounted my horse. "Let's not think too much about it. The mountain we scaled to escape from Magoto was no different. These only look intimidating."

Rin and Finae mounted behind me. I glanced back at Finae. "Keep your weight centered with your horse and spread out along the pathway."

They nodded their understanding.

Snow crunched under the horses' hooves. I kept my eyes ahead of me, on the obstacles in front of my path, leaning and keeping in line with each movement. My eyes wandered over the edge every so often. The chiseled peaks looked as spectacular, if not more so, from this angle. I doubted many people dared descend this path, which did make it the perfect place for a hidden village.

We took our time as we descended, putting caution above speed. By midday, we'd made it to the bottom and were traversing the base of the chiseled mountains. There seemed to be little flora. What little vegetation did grow, hung onto the steep sides. Their lanky limbs spread far overhead to reach every ray of sunlight. A thick layer of mist rolled over the ground, creeping closer to us. I dug into my saddle pack and pulled out an extra light canteen. I lit the inside with a flick of flint and handed it to Rin. At my side, my own light canteen glowed. Finae followed my lead and shifted hers around from her belt.

"Keep each other in sight," I said as the fog engulfed us. I shivered from the crisp air and held my hand out in the thick mist. There had been a candy in Vaiyene with the same molasses consistency. I couldn't even make out the ground.

I glanced around, then above us, noticing the small patches of sky through the vegetation. I almost wished it were nighttime so the stars could shine over us. Through the fog, we would not have been able to see them, but in my mind, twinkling lights dotted the sky. The same glistening lights winked at us from either side.

I paused.

Had I imagined it, or had I seen an actual glimmer?

I leaned closer to the rock, my nose a hand span away from the surface. A tiny silver channel ran from the bottom all the way to the top. The shape and purity of the silver seemed unnatural— like the material my bond was made of. I dragged my hand along the surface, my fingers scraping against the jagged stone.

Rin had always described warmth within the body when trying to project the Skills into an object. The rock was cool, and my hand was warm. It was simple enough. I imagined the heat moving into the cold stones. The rock grew warm under my fingertips. My concentration almost broke at my excitement, but I forced myself to remain calm and level-headed. A soft glow emitted from my bond and pulsed in time with the silver crack within the stone.

"The light will illuminate the way to Konro village."

I jumped at Finae's voice. I'd been so focused on using the Skills that I had not heard her approach.

"I saw the Phantoms of old using something similar to this, in one of their memories," Finae said with a shrug. "The Skills illuminate the silver threading, and it creates a pathway for those who know where to look."

I ran my fingers over the silver rivet in the rock.

"Now we have our direction."

Rin scowled at the mist and the rock formations. "There's still the problem of finding our way through this fog."

I snorted, urging my horse along the path.

"Quite the optimist, aren't you?"

Rin gave no response as she nudged her horse ahead of mine.

Fog rolled off in waves from the sheer mountain peaks, dropping to the ground. Our light canteens allowed me to keep Rin and Finae in sight, but the thickness of the mist kept my vision limited. The horses' hooves echoed through the maze, distorting any sense of space. On the edge of my mind, I felt something. Since connecting myself to the Skill markers and the pathway to Konro, my awareness seemed to span farther than my own body. Somewhere, distantly—I could sense the drip of water as it ran over the rocks and slid down the mountainside.

I could *feel* it.

Had I somehow linked with the Skills in the mountains?

In my mind, the Skills were a river of color. My awareness swept down the currents and rising rapids of the landscape. Once I reached the end of one channel, my consciousness spread farther downstream to light up the pathways. I tried to keep my awareness short-lived and touch only the slivers of bond-material in the rocks nearest us, but the effort strained my mind. Light illuminated the small rivets in the rock formations that towered around us. They glimmered in the mist, creating a calming haze that refracted the Skills' blue light with a rainbow edge. Against the fog, and without the light from the sun, it glowed and pulsed with life, creating a clear pathway to the edge of the peaks. I leaned my hand against the last of the rock formations and broke off my consciousness, withdrawing my energy from the rocks.

Exhaustion drained me.

I felt as if I'd been training for days when all I had done was use the Skills for moments.

I dismounted and led my horse forward, straining my eyes to gain my bearings. Fog continued to roll at our feet, but it seemed less thick here. I inhaled, savoring the clean air and the heavy scent of damp, decaying wood. A forest. Through the mist, now that I knew what to look for, the soft outlines of trees came into focus.

"Can you sense any more pillars or markings?" Finae called from behind.

I shook my head, though the mist obscured the gesture. I responded verbally instead. "It seems this is the last of the markers. The pathway ends here."

From inside my cloak, I withdrew my journal to make a note of the area around Konro and my use of the Skills. With as much detail as I could, I drew a quick sketch of the landscape and path we took. They were brief notes, and I doubted I would forget the experience, but the act of documenting was important.

Rin walked beside me, her horse bumping its muzzle against her shoulder. "Do you have a weapon, Finae?"

Finae's eyes widened, and she shook her head as she dismounted beside us. Rin reached into a saddlebag and withdrew a dagger. It was longer than a normal dagger, with gold leaf set into the hilt. She handed it to Finae.

"Even if you have no formal training, you should have some sort of a way to protect yourself. Don't think yourself incapable of saving your own life if the circumstance demands it."

I turned my attention to the forest, daring to hope. Maybe now Finae would finally take a blade.

"I don't want to kill anyone."

"Its purpose is to empower, nothing more."

Finae glanced at me, but I kept my eyes fixed on the forest's outline. I'd tried to teach Finae how to defend herself on countless occasions, but each time, she had refused.

But she had now been in battle.

Finae took the blade, running her fingers over the sheath.

I put my hand on her shoulder before leading the way into the forest. The mist retreated at my steps, gliding away and recoiling at my approach. Immense power hung in the air. If there was a place where the Skills were alive, this was it. Birds fluttered overhead, disturbed by our presence, and in the distance, a deer and her fawn raised their heads at our approach. A large tree broke the faint trail in two. The circumference of it akin to a small hill.

Vaiyene's forest was an infant compared to this elder forest.

We proceeded, humbled by the giants that guarded this place. I was content to listen to the creaking of the trees. My gait relaxed until a light ahead caught my attention.

It glowed silver for an instant, then vanished.

I glanced back at Rin and Finae. "Did you see that?"

Finae shook her head.

Rin glanced at me. "It disappeared too quick."

It was like whoever carried the light had snuffed it out.

"Be on the lookout," I said, scanning the trees on either side of the trail. "We do not know what we are up against or how we will be received."

No movement caught my eye. I paused and bent down, examining the ground. There were no footprints on the forest floor, except for ours, but the snow and wind could have swept them away. Or the person could have come from a different direction.

From Konro?

I resisted the instinct to grab my staff. It was imperative we did not appear threatening. Though we came on peaceful terms, a hidden village would be cautious of outsiders. I always desired peace, but the desire was not always met in kind.

If it came down to it, we would be ready to fight.

The pathway we followed opened into a broader, more pronounced indentation on the forest floor. If we had been coming for other reasons, I would have left the path, but we were not on a secretive mission. Something shifted in the forest ahead. Silver light and the shadow of a figure emerged from the forest. I raised my arm against the sudden flash, trying to shield my eyes enough to assess the threat.

"You wear a bond upon your arm," a deep voice said, sounding as wise and as old as the ancient trees. I kept still. I didn't know for sure he was a threat. I stepped ahead of Finae and Rin, slowly, to separate myself.

It would give them an instant of time if there were a fight.

"I do," I said, keeping my voice as neutral as the stranger's.

"Where are you from, travelers?"

The voice was kind but authoritative. My eyes burned at the light. It was hard to judge who we were up against by a voice, but honesty seemed the wisest course.

"My sister and I are from Vaiyene, our friend from Magoto. We come seeking answers."

The light abated, but white blocks of light remained in my eyes. I blinked, trying to dislodge them. The man's feet crunched in the snow. A blade, thin as grass, pressed against my neck. I stared ahead, the watering of my eyes blurring my vision.

"Kilo!" I heard a scuffle behind me and the slight ting of metal.

I held my hand out at my side to stop Rin. My vision began to clear. I didn't sense any ill will from the man before me. The blade at my throat was firm but not painful.

"With whom does your allegiance lie?"

I could make out the basic shapes of the man's face now. I blinked again, and my eyesight became clearer. He pressed his lips into a thin line, and his gaze wandered over me. He was trying to figure out who I was, and what my purpose was here.

I knew better than to lie to this man.

"I used to be a Phantom of Vaiyene, but now I am a servant of Kiriku and those who suffer at the hands of the False Shadows."

"And your intentions here?"

"A seeker of knowledge and of strength. My companions share the same ideals." I held his gaze. My arms relaxed at my sides. There was nothing to fear from this man.

"We were led here by a stone bestowed to us in the ruins of Zenkaiko." Finae's voice was steady as she walked to my side and drew the white stone from her pocket. She held it up for the man to see, and he lowered the blade from my neck.

"We have been following your progress since you activated the markers," the man said, turning his gaze away from me. "A daring thing you did, entering the ravine. It took a lot of strength to keep the pathway illuminated." The man shifted his gaze to Rin. "You're from Magoto?"

Rin nodded.

"And your allegiance to Hitori?"

"None."

The man remained silent for a few moments, then spread his hands out to his side, welcoming us. "I will lead you the rest of the way to Konro. The Guardian is already aware of your presence and is most eager to meet you."

The man slipped his blade back into the folds of his sleeve and turned. We grabbed the reins of our horses and followed him. We had almost made it. Here, I hoped to find the advantage and strength needed to defeat Hitori and her False Shadows.

What would such a village look like?

An image of Vaiyene came to my mind. Was Konro a similar place? Would we find solace as well as answers?

As my mind drifted, so, too, did my grasp on time.

I treasured rare moments like these, where I could let my mind wander and my spirit renew. At present, none of our small company was in danger. Vaiyene would be impassable to the False Shadows, and the False Shadows lay beyond our control.

The world brightened around me as the forest's canopy thinned out. We climbed the remaining length of the hill as the sun peeked out from thick cloud cover. Large snowflakes fell. One landed upon my nose, and I brushed it aside. A winding path snaked down into the valley, with tall grasses frozen into place.

Snow fell from trees in the distance, warmed by the sun, the flakes catching and shimmering in the all-white field. A dome-shaped building dominated the village landscape. Gnarled roots from a giant tree wrapped around the building, hiding it almost from view.

"Welcome to Konro," a wise voice said.

An elderly woman ambled over from the forest's edge, her white robes dragging in the snow. Her hand rested upon a man's outstretched arm. Deep creases ran across her forehead, and her eyes were sharp, though they were touched with age. Her robe gleamed the purest white, with elegant spirals of silver that faded seamlessly into white.

"I always hoped in my lifetime someone of purpose and good intentions would come." She gazed at us with a warm, welcoming smile. "It seems it was fated to be."

Bending my arm over my chest, I knelt on one knee, my head bowed. I executed the fullest, most respectful gesture one gave to the Phantoms. "It is our greatest pleasure to be welcomed by you, Guardian of Konro."

The woman's smile faded. There was a touch of moisture in her eyes. "The Phantoms of old used to bow that way. I never thought to see it again. We have guarded this village—and the remaining knowledge of the Skills—since the day Zenkaiko was destroyed. We hoped one day we would give the knowledge back to the land. It's been many years, and I've waited a very long time to meet you."

She held out her hand, sweeping her palm toward me, and I stood. Her eyes washed over me with approval. "Once you enter Konro and unearth the Skills, they can never be subdued again."

I glanced at Finae. Her eyes were shining with wonder and a future she believed we could achieve with the Skills. She had found her purpose and freedom. She smiled at me. Rin gave me a nod, drawing in a breath. Her carved wooden dagger was still in the folds of my robe. *We do what we must.* Hitori would never allow her to live. Her fate was now entwined with Hitori's. I had uncovered the truth about the False Shadows and discovered a power, the Skills, too dangerous to ignore. For my belief in stopping the False Shadows, I'd been exiled. I had left Vaiyene to protect those I loved, but I now fought for all those in Kiriku. It seemed we had all come to the same conclusion.

I returned my gaze to the Guardian and smiled, my heart at peace with the decision. "We are prepared for whatever will come."

part four
SHENRAE

chapter thirty-three
AMBUSH

Long brown grass swayed in the wind, backlit by the moon's glow. I waited in the brush and settled against a large rock overlooking the open field. It was a cloudless night. The weather couldn't have been better.

It would only be a little while longer.

I drew my fur-lined cloak around my shoulders and rubbed my hands together, breathing on them with hot breath. Snow crunched as I shifted my weight. My hands rested on the light canteen at my side, waiting.

Many weeks had passed since I had come under General Mirai's care, and still, their rowdy nature drained me. It was not that the general's men were unkind to me, but their lifestyle was sometimes too much for me. Shadow ways were rooted in quiet solitude, with an emphasis on tradition and reflection. These men knew how to celebrate a hard day's work. They were, however, efficient and deadly. Every movement made by the group, and the strengths of each person, were taken into account. That was very like the Shadows, and as Asdar had said, they seemed to uphold the ideal to not kill.

At least, they had yet to kill in my presence.

A change in the wind drew my focus, carrying a damp undertone from a nearby lake. I adjusted my gaze to the east, across the Plains of Phia, as snow fell lightly around me. My breath rose from my mouth as I tried to still the racing of my heart. I blew out another long breath, then another. A shadow broke from the distant tree line. The pounding of horse hooves became louder as the rider adjusted his path. I unstoppered the flask inside my canteen and flicked a small rock against my wedge of flint. The flame ignited, and I placed the canteen on the stones behind me.

I positioned myself to watch both the rider and the western plains. General Mirai's men waited there. From the hidden pocket inside my boot, I withdrew a tiny reflective piece of glass. General Mirai had taught me how to catch the light and translate information through a series of flashes.

I hadn't thought I would, but I actually enjoyed the strategy my position in General Mirai's ranks gave me.

The rider's cloak billowed behind him. He leaned close to his horse's neck, his hands tight on the reins as he spurred his horse on. A white puff of snow trailed after the rider. Every so often, a flake of snow would reflect the moon and sparkle against the night. I gripped the mirror in my hand and aligned it to catch the moonlight, flicking it twice. Two short bursts meant "yes." One long reflection was "no."

The first message to convey was if the rider was alone.

Yes.

The next answer was trickier than the first. I had to indicate in which direction the rider headed. General Mirai's men knew the number of flashes assigned to each direction.

A single flash in the distance responded. They had received the first message. The rider headed west, across the plains. I flashed the mirror four times, indicating the rider came from the south. There was a quick flash in response, and General Mirai's men moved into action. I remained crouched, hidden in the brush, and waited. The rider's silver bond glinted. I swallowed, my thoughts turning sour. Hopefully, wherever he had come from, he hadn't killed anyone.

The rider's horse reared, and the man struggled to remain seated. One of General Mirai's men must have released the first arrow. General Mirai and his riders swooped in from all directions and surrounded the man. Ropes fell over the stallion's neck.

The rider didn't attempt to resist.

I tucked the mirror back into my boot and left my vantage point, glancing over my shoulder. For a False Shadow, he seemed somewhat complacent. General Mirai's men outnumbered him, but still, it seemed convenient one of them was in his grasp. We'd been after the False Shadows for a long while.

Now we would finally have some answers.

———

I leaned against a tree, cast in shadow. The rough wood poked into my back as I shifted farther into the darkness to hide the emotions from my face. Even though I'd been around General Mirai's men for some time, I still was uncomfortable letting down my guard. I couldn't show weakness—not in front of them. Unlike Asdar, General Mirai didn't owe me anything. If I caused a mission to fail or lacked strength, I could be disposed of, and I refused to let that happen.

Thus far, the men had taken me seriously.

None of the men expected me to be on the same level as them, which was a relief, but I didn't want to lose face with them. I represented the Shadows and needed to maintain a good relationship.

I had to keep their faith in the Shadows.

I needed to remain indifferent to this False Shadow, even if my anger stirred looking at him. He didn't appear any different than a normal person, and I wouldn't have been able to pick him out of the crowd as a False Shadow. His hands were tied behind his back, and there was a blankness to his face that suggested his mind was on other matters. His shoulders slumped forward, and his gaze fixed on the ground. Now that they had captured him, what did they intend to do with him? I swallowed and found my throat tight.

They wouldn't kill him, would they?

General Mirai reined in his horse and dismounted, handing his stallion off to one of his men and heading toward the prisoner.

"Are you one of the False Shadows?"

I held my breath and waited, my eyes fixed on the man.

General Mirai already knew. It was a trick question.

Would he be honest?

The man didn't answer. He raised his head and stared down the men surrounding him, his eyes finding me in the shadows. I tensed as he fixed his gaze on me, unable to look away. He was one of the False Shadows—part of the group that had killed my parents. My heart pounded in my ears.

What if he was the one who had killed my parents?

The man looked away and his gaze returned to General Mirai. "Yes."

General Mirai nodded. Questions were a mere formality at this point. This much I knew, but was finding answers the sole reason we captured him? Before leaving me with, Asdar had reassured me of the general's character. Would General Mirai spare this man's life though? The False Shadow had killed innocent people—like my parents. I took a step closer, straining to hear, wanting desperately to understand. Why did the False Shadows kill and parade as the Shadows? What good came from killing my parents?

I waited as General Mirai continued his interrogation.

"Where are you headed, False Shadow?"

The man didn't say anything. General Mirai began pacing around him, looking him over, inspecting his resolve and demeanor. Even from this distance, I could see that the man's hands trembled, tied behind the back. He dug his nails into his palms.

"What's your name, boy?"

The False Shadow was scared. Was that why he didn't answer? He was unsure, like me. An unsure person was not capable of killing two very capable Shadows. This man couldn't have killed my parents; he didn't have the resolve.

General Mirai drew his sword. As he circled, he shifted it in his hands. The ropes tying the False Shadow's hands were cut, and he was handed a sword. "If I win, you tell me what I want to know." Mirai cracked his back and shook out his sword arm. "If you win, you are free to leave as you are."

The general then stood, his sword arm at his side.

"Do we have a deal?"

The False Shadow nodded and shifted between both feet. His hands wrapped around the blade in his hands. Without warning, the man sprang and slashed at the general's side, but the general blocked his sword, and both disengaged. The False Shadow's eyes darted to either side.

He was going to try to escape.

I moved from the shadow of the tree and removed the staff from my back. The False Shadow threw the sword to the ground and bolted in my direction. General Mirai's men sprang into action, crossing their swords to block his path. Gripping my staff, the False Shadow's eyes met mine. Fear swirled in his emerald eyes. Two more men grabbed his shoulders and dragged him back, tying ropes around his wrists once more. The men held him while they drove a wooden post between his back and his wrists.

Like before, he didn't struggle.

It seemed foolish he had even tried to escape.

General Mirai sheathed his sword and picked the blade up from the ground. "Why did you try and run when you knew you had no chance of escape?"

Again, the man said nothing.

The general's men were not so silent.

"You're lucky our general doesn't string you up," Takai said, breaking from the ranks. His long straight beard and bald head stopped inches away from the False Shadow. He leaned in with a blade, his teeth baring in a wicked grin.

His brother, Sakai, stepped beside him, also drawing a blade. "If he doesn't want to cooperate, why should we show him the courtesy of our hospitality?"

My heart quickened at their approach. Out of all of the men, these two were the fiercest. Their tempers were short and hot. They thrived on fear, working off each other to intimidate and break people. I understood the need for answers, but something about this False Shadow made me sympathize with him. His hands still shook, and no matter how much he dug his nails into his palms, he couldn't steady himself. Back on my first Shadow mission, my fear had taken hold of me, stalling my actions. I'd almost died at the hands of one of the False Shadows. I'd buried the truth from Syrane and Torey, but I remembered the fear of death.

How paralyzing it could be…

Takai and Sakai jeered in front of him. Takai, the older, bald one, took a thin blade from the pocket at his hip and pressed the sharp edge to the man's cheek.

"Something wrong with your tongue?"

The False Shadow closed his eyes. I could see the panicked rise and fall of his chest. His fingers on his right hand inched up, drawing the sleeve of his robe down, exposing the silver bond on his arm. The movement was subtle and seemed desperate.

What was he trying to reach?

Takai removed the blade, revealing a thin line of blood on the False Shadow's cheek. His brother spat in the False Shadow's face and drew his sword. Sakai grabbed the False Shadow's hair and yanked his head back. My hand tightened around my staff. We didn't even know if this man was guilty of anything, except of being a False Shadow.

"Speak, or I will make you!"

I winced and took a half-step toward them, then shrank back. Was it my place to intervene? He was one of the False Shadows, but did he deserve to be tortured, made fun of, and spat upon? I averted my eyes, unsure. It was then that I noticed General Mirai's eyes were focused on me. I loosened the grip on my staff, and the general's eyes narrowed. He spun around to address his men.

"Leave him. If he does not wish to talk, we will not force him. My brother, Kefnir, and Phantom Kilo have already told me everything about this particular man. His name is Ikaru, and he is not our enemy."

I stared in shock, forgetting how to breathe. General Mirai knew he was an ally and had said nothing? He strode to my side, his quiet anger evident in his stiff posture.

I didn't meet his eye.

"Next time you wish to intervene, don't hesitate."

I froze at his words. It'd been a test.

The general had wanted to assess if I would act on my instincts, my own sense of justice, and I'd failed. Shadows followed the Shadow's Creed, no matter what. It defined who we were and made us strong. My morals had waned at the fear of being berated.

How far would I have let Takai and Sakai go?

I gritted my teeth. Kilo would have acted.

My heart pounded in my ears, and I checked the amount of firewood at the edge of the camp. It would give me an excuse to leave, but... I shifted my attention to General Mirai's back.

What was my duty to General Mirai?

Was there any?

My duty was to my Phantom, and my Phantom had entrusted the general with my training. But Asdar had never told me the purpose. General Mirai seemed disappointed in my lack of action. Had he expected me to disobey him? Gathering firewood would let me escape. I would be serving a purpose, and I could brush off what had happened. No one would call me out for it. I could slink away, withdraw and be content with scouting and gathering information. It was what I was expected to do here anyway.

But something stayed my feet from heading into the woods: General Mirai's assumption I would have stopped the two men from hurting the False Shadow.

It would have been the honorable thing to do.

Why then had I not done it?

I dragged my fingers through my hair, groaning. I needed to speak with the general. I should have clarified my place under his command when I arrived. So far, all I felt was uncertain, and my own self-doubt had grown. The pressure to be perfect made me question every action and thought. And today my front had failed. I stormed through the camp, ignoring the attention I drew. Most prepared for the night watch or tended to chores around camp, but there was an air of curiosity that followed me. I didn't care. I needed to see General Mirai before I descended into crippling self-loathing. I'd spent too long unsure. Asdar had never answered my questions, but maybe General Mirai would.

Standing outside his tent, with his back to me, the general talked to one of his men. At my approach, they both glanced over at me before the man nodded and headed back into camp. Before the general had his full attention on me, I blurted out the words that plagued my mind.

"What do you want from me?"

The words were a collection of frustrations. Ever since the day I'd asked the Phantoms to sponsor me as a Shadow, I felt unsure. I needed to know. I didn't even care that I was questioning his authority or that I was angry.

General Mirai laughed. It was not a chuckle, but a full belly laugh. His usual demeanor fell before me. The emotional mask he and the Phantoms often wore, vanished.

"I forget what it's like to work with someone so young," General Mirai said after he recovered. "There are not many who dare disobey orders, let alone raise their voice to me."

I groaned inwardly.

I should have gone to get firewood.

General Mirai took a breath and studied me, regaining hold of his amusement. "Did Asdar tell you why he asked me to mentor you?"

"He never tells me anything."

The general smiled. "Asdar has good reasons for what he does, but he often fails to communicate those reasons." A smile remained on General Mirai's face as he ushered me back through camp. Unease settled upon me, and he stopped.

"Why are you anxious?"

Heat rose in my cheeks. Was the general that aware of my emotions? Shadow duty demanded my honesty, even as I withered under General Mirai's gaze. I'd already humiliated myself once by telling off my superior; it mattered little now.

"I'm not comfortable around your men."

General Mirai nodded. My words drew neither a snicker nor outrage. "And why is that, Shenrae? They're not so different than you. They have experienced more and are older, but our ideals are the same as the Shadows'."

He settled back on his heels. His dark eyes were kind.

"Takai and Sakai would not have acted on their threats, as they knew I wouldn't allow it. Outwardly, my men may seem tough, but I assure you each of them is a good man. They wouldn't be in my ranks if I didn't trust them."

The scare tactic, as General Mirai had called it, bothered me, but that wasn't the core of it. I tired of looking weak, being weak. I should have acted, but once again, I'd hesitated. General Mirai still waited for my answer, and I floundered to put words to the feeling.

"I can't allow myself to be weak in front of them. I don't..."

I sighed. "I don't trust them."

It wasn't the most articulate answer, but it was the truth.

"The Shadows rely on trust and camaraderie. To be taken from that environment, I'm not surprised. However, the best way to train to be a Shadow is to not train with the Shadows."

My heart sank. He sounded like Phantom Asdar.

General Mirai led me to the edge of the camp, where he stopped and addressed me. "Let me ease your mind regarding my men. It was my idea for Takai and Sakai to intimidate Ikaru."

My assumption about it being a test had been correct, but it didn't make me feel any better. In fact, I felt worse knowing that no matter how hard I tried, I failed to progress.

Time and time again, all I could do was fail.

"Shenrae, listen to me."

I dragged myself from my thoughts and met Mirai's gaze.

"Asdar is a weapons master, and his strength lies in combat. What he lacks is the instinct of right and wrong and the moral conviction that comes with it."

General Mirai motioned for me to follow him, leading us away from the camp and into the trees. He bent over and grabbed a fallen branch from the forest floor. "I set out to scare you into action today. This time, it was in an environment I controlled. Next time, you will have to live with whatever choice you make."

He held the tree branch out to me. "Choose wisely."

I took the branch, and General Mirai gave me a short bow before he left me alone. I adjusted the piece of wood into the crook of my arm and bent to pick up another.

The general believed I could be a better person.

The test hadn't been to prove I was weak, but to prove that I was capable of more. Was this what Asdar had seen in me when he sponsored me?

I steadied another log against my arm.

Asdar had told my brother and me that he didn't want the Shadows to blindly follow him. He'd given me extra training, but he'd also told me I would never be a warrior in the same sense as Kilo or Syrane. Neither Phantom Asdar nor the general saw my lack of combat skills as a weakness. They saw something else in me, and maybe, I was beginning to understand.

I drew in a breath and glanced back toward camp.

Tomorrow, I would no longer hesitate.

chapter thirty-four
AKIO

This was not going to go well. I tried to swallow my apprehension, but my stomach hurt too much to pretend I was anything but anxious. The other Shadow trainees had laughed at me during training. Losing the false front of seeming like I knew what I was doing—in front of trained mercenaries—made my skin crawl. I'd refused all invitations to attend the training sessions.

Today, I decided to take part.

General Mirai walked me onto the field with a smile on his face. I didn't share his enthusiasm as four of his men followed us and spread out in a circle. Taking a breath, I tried to calm my nerves. I hoped Phantom Asdar's training had prepared me to not look like too much of a fool.

The general's voice came from beside me. "Have you fought against more than one opponent before, Shenrae?"

I gripped my staff tighter, to keep my hands from shaking. There was no sense in denying it.

"I never made it that far in my training."

To my surprise, the men around me didn't laugh or sneer. Were they waiting to see how I reacted in battle before they judged my skills?

General Mirai nodded, looking around at his men as they came into position. "Your staff is the perfect weapon to keep your opponent at a distance. My men will try to get close. Keep them away."

With no additional words of instruction or advice, the men tightened their circle. Their advance made my heart pound. A flash of a memory stalled me. A blade pressing against my neck during my first mission. I shook the memory from my mind.

I was no longer that scared girl.

General Mirai's men closed in, and I eyed their blades. How was I supposed to fight all of them? There were four of them, and I only had two ends to my staff.

My heartbeat rose.

"Analyze the situation. Look around and figure out who is closest and most threatening."

General Mirai's voice broke through my haze. He stood beside me and gave me a reassuring smile. In his hand, he held a staff. He bent his knees, ready to spring into action. Asdar had taught me to keep myself loose, agile. I drew in a breath and forced myself to relax, loosening my grip and bouncing lightly between both feet. General Mirai made the first strike, lashing out at one of his men in a simple thrust. His man retreated to dodge the blow. The general crossed the staff in front of himself and dipped low, making another man withdraw. He kept this up, moving around the circle, picking his target by nothing more than proximity. It was a subtle dance, the steps of which were foreign to me. Asdar had taught me ten fundamental strikes, with a focus on defense.

A man at General Mirai's back crept closer, and I swung at him. His sword clashed against my staff, and I twirled the staff, aiming for the side of his head. He ducked and stepped back, giving me a small smile. During Shadow training, the pressure of competing and rising in the ranks had weighed on my mind. Here, General Mirai's men tried to better themselves as a group. They genuinely wanted to help me improve.

I fell into an uneasy rhythm, watching one half of the circle while Mirai took the other. The sun's light and the world's distractions dimmed around me. Every breath fell in line with my strikes. Time was no longer a factor. The focus on preventing our opponents from coming closer became my single priority.

One of the men raised his sword from the ground, and I held out my staff with both hands to block him.

"Halt."

Everyone froze.

I paused and let out a long breath.

General Mirai stepped outside the circle. "For your first attempt, that was well done."

The general nodded to his men, dismissing the four who had sparred with us. A small crowd had gathered in the distance. I scanned their faces, trying to pinpoint any signs of mockery at my novice abilities. I found none. Most regarded me with a mild curiosity. Some, catching my gaze, gave me a small nod and a slight smile. I'd made excuses not to train before, and General Mirai had never forced me to participate. I expected ridicule, but these men seemed happy I had decided to train with them.

Like I was one of them.

Before I could analyze their gazes further, a young man stepped out from the crowd and joined General Mirai and me. In his hand, he gripped a dark-wooded staff as tall as he was. The color of his staff matched his dark skin and black hair. He was the youngest of General Mirai's men. His frame was thin and toned—long and lean—like the weapon he wielded.

"Akio is my most talented staff master," General Mirai said by way of an introduction. I'd seen him around camp and on our journey, but as with the rest of the general's men, we hadn't spoken.

"I've asked him to show you combinations, as well as address any of the issues he sees in your form."

I bowed to Akio. "Thank you for your help."

Akio dropped his gaze, a slight touch of red on his cheeks. He twirled his staff and nodded to General Mirai before the two of us broke off from the others. We stood face-to-face, and I expected to begin doing drills from that angle, but Akio crossed the distance between us and stood next to me. Our height difference was apparent. He held out his staff and glanced down over his shoulder at me.

"Let's do some simple combinations. Watch my form and try and mimic the movement. It's all about finding a rhythm."

I tried to maintain focus with Akio being so near.

Around us, the men broke off into pairs and began sparring. General Mirai gave the two of us a slight smile before he paired up with Takai and Sakai.

"Shenrae?"

I snapped to attention, floundering the staff in my hand and knocking my shin with the heel of the wood. I clamped my mouth shut to stifle the pain. Akio laughed and eyed me, an odd expression on his face.

He adjusted the staff in his hands.

"Remember to split the staff into thirds. This is the position you always return to."

He turned to the side so I could mirror his movement and position, shifting his weight as he brought his arm outward in a smooth gesture. His turned his head and glanced over his shoulder to see if I followed him. I watched his movement, but I wasn't focused. My stomach tightened with nerves. As if sensing my lack of focus, he rested his staff on the ground before he kicked it up with his feet. He then proceeded into a flurry of twirls and spins, adding in a few kicks for show. For the finale, he twirled the staff over his head and slammed it into the ground.

His technique and movement were…dazzling.

Akio returned to a standing position and rested the staff over his shoulders, a smile spread across his face. The men in the area were pretending to be training, but I'd caught a few of them watching Akio's display.

"You do realize they're watching us," I said.

It made my skin crawl.

Akio shrugged and waved his hand at me, pointing to the ground in front of him. "Come here."

I stilled the unease of my stomach and stood in front of him. I raised my staff and held it in my hands, making sure to cut the length into three equal sections. Akio reached around and put his hands on mine.

I stiffened, my heart pounding.

"Relax," Akio said, "You're too mechanical in your movements. The staff is a dance."

I tried to relax, but I felt the heat in my cheeks and grew even more nervous. My breathing was out of sync, and my self-doubt nearly overwhelmed me.

Akio was going to think I was terrible.

"Give me a chance."

Despite my nerves, I gave in and nodded. I had vowed to stop hesitating. "A Shadow always finishes what he starts." My father's words came back to me. It'd been my father's motto as a Shadow and the ideal he had upheld. Though he was no longer here to tell me himself, I knew it was the advice he would have given me at the moment.

I'd wasted too much time being nervous and unsure around General Mirai and his men. They wanted to help me become a better warrior. I'd been too afraid to look foolish.

But no longer.

I let Akio guide the staff in my hand, sweeping it up and over, around and under in every direction. Instead of counting and executing steps, he pivoted and glided, moving his arms as much as his feet. He released my hands and picked up his own staff. I followed his movement. Instead of feeling the eyes of the people around us, I focused on creating the most beautiful curves and arches I could. I drew in a deep breath, calming my heart.

Out of the corner of my eye, I saw a crowd gathering.

My heart pounded, but I pushed them from my mind. I cared about what people thought of me and how I looked, but the rhythm we fell into, the beauty and poise, soothed my fears. Being ashamed of my abilities and my unique talents were my burdens to overcome. Akio lived his talent, reveling in the delight and joy of being who he was and being seen for it. I could worry and fret about people's judgement, or I could do the best I could and try and find the potential both General Mirai and Asdar saw in me.

My parents might have been able to take time to find themselves in the Shadow ranks, but they had never had to face the threat of the False Shadows. I couldn't afford to flounder and resist the training Phantom Asdar believed would help me become a better warrior.

I'd asked him to help me.

Being here was his answer.

I twirled my staff up and over my head. Akio's staff collided with my own, and he bowed to me, spreading his arms out to the side. General Mirai's men whooped and clapped their hands at our display. Heat rose to my cheeks, but I didn't shrink away from their praise. Instead, I raised my staff, and they cheered louder.

Akio met my eye, and I grinned.

chapter thirty-five
A NEW DANCE

I pulled back the tent flap and ducked under the entryway. The stale air assaulted my determination. I'd come for answers about my parents and the False Shadows, but my courage wavered. Would I find the answers I sought here? Would Ikaru even talk to me? The glint from the False Shadow's bond caught the light from the sun.

Maybe I shouldn't have come.

I steadied my breath and tied the tent flap open, letting in light and fresh air. When my eyes adjusted, my gaze locked with Ikaru's. His hands were tied around a wooden post to keep him in place. I swallowed against the lump in my throat. I didn't understand the False Shadows, and I didn't understand the man tied before me. I crossed my legs and dropped down in front of him, ignoring my instincts to leave. I needed answers, and I was tired of being afraid to pursue them.

"Why are you a part of the False Shadows?"

The man called Ikaru let out a long breath, seeming irritated by the question. General Mirai had probably already asked the same thing. Irritation crept into the back of my own mind. The general had said Ikaru was an ally, but he didn't act like one.

That also didn't make sense.

I cleared my throat. "You know, if you were more sociable, you wouldn't be tied up."

Ikaru's mouth opened. Then he clamped it shut as I grinned. "You met Kilo?"

Ikaru narrowed his eyes and nodded. He must have found the question harmless enough to answer. Had Ikaru talked more with Kilo? I chewed on the thought for a while. Maybe I could trick him into telling me what I wanted to know.

"Did he seem well?"

Ikaru's eyes were steady on me. I glanced around the tent and pulled a dagger from the sheath at my thigh. I turned the blade in my hand, playing with the sun's reflection.

"Phantom Kilo. Did he seem well?"

Ikaru scowled at me, then nodded.

"They're taking good care of your horse." I pushed a piece of grass off my pant leg with the dagger's tip. "I snuck her an apple this morning."

Ikaru's lips twitched at the corners.

"I know what you're trying to do."

"And what's that?"

"You're trying to get me to talk."

I let a grin spread across my face. "It worked, didn't it?"

He shook his head, rolling his eyes. "I suppose it did."

"I'm sure General Mirai would loosen the ropes if—"

The general rushed in, dislodging dirt at his entrance. "I see you've found your voice, Ikaru. Do me the favor of retaining it a few moments longer. I require your advice on a particular matter."

The general dropped to one knee beside Ikaru. "There's a False Shadow group heading east. Where are they headed?" They stared at one another. Neither blinked. "I'd like to remind you that people's lives are at stake. We're both trying to prevent innocent lives from being taken."

I stared back and forth between General Mirai and Ikaru.

Ikaru was trying to save people?

After a tense silence, Ikaru spoke. "They're heading to Leiko, under orders to cause a scene to mask Hitori's presence. There's been a particular…breakthrough with her research."

General Mirai swore and scuffled onto his feet. His hand wrapped around the hilt of the sword at his side. "I feared it would not take long."

The general glanced down at me.

"Unbind him and meet me at my tent."

He stopped at the tent flap, his eye fixed on Ikaru. "If you run away again, we will not be able to protect you. Rin is with Phantom Kilo and no longer under Hitori's grasp. You are free to make your own decision now. I would advise you to stay with the people who can protect you."

Ikaru stiffened at the general's words. "I understand."

I waited until General Mirai left before rounding on Ikaru. "What is going on? What did General Mirai mean? Who are you?"

Ikaru raised his eyebrows. "Untie me first?"

I glared, suppressing the urge to yell at him for answers. I stood and cut the ropes binding his wrists. They hadn't been tight. If he'd wanted to, he could have escaped. Ikaru stretched his arms out and rolled his shoulder blades. He groaned as he worked the stiffness from his muscles. I ducked under the tent opening and shielded my eyes from the sun.

Ikaru followed.

"You're not going to run, are you?"

I eyed him, though even if he did, it sounded like the general would not stop him.

Ikaru inhaled and let out a deep breath. "No, I'm not going to. Nothing is forcing me to stay loyal to the False Shadows any longer."

Takai's bald head bobbed through the commotion of the men breaking down camp. He stepped over a doused fire and upon spotting us made his way over. Ikaru stiffened beside me and averted his gaze, but Takai didn't bother to glance over at him.

"General Mirai asked me to ready your horses. I've left them on the south side of camp for you."

I nodded, looking south. Greymoon stood with two other horses. Who else was coming with us?

One of General Mirai's men moved the tent behind us, dislodging the poles and folding the canvas. I elbowed Ikaru and kept to the outside of the encampment, trying to stay out of the way as someone threw a bucket of water over hissing coals. Next to his tent, the general exchanged hushed words with someone clad in all black. The person next to the general wore a hood and mask, revealing nothing of their identity. A letter was exchanged before they whistled for their horse.

I'd seen similar people before.

They were part of General Mirai's spy network.

Had Phantom Asdar sent me to be under the general's care to observe how he controlled the people under him? To realize how important the alliance with the general was? As far as I knew, the Phantoms didn't possess any network of their own. Although Kilo seemed to be using the general's to stay informed with what was happening.

General Mirai turned to address Ikaru and me. "You will not be coming with my men. I've made arrangements for you to deliver this letter to the Kinshi Post instead."

He extended the letter toward me, his eyes fixated over my head. I took the folded-up paper and glanced over my shoulder. Akio appeared, a smile spreading across his face. He carried a staff at his side—or what looked to be one. A thick cloth bound with rope covered the triangular edge. It was not a staff, but a spear.

He expected a battle.

"I've entrusted your safety to Akio," the general continued. "He will escort the two of you to the Kinshi Post."

After training with Akio, I knew how to work with him, and I trusted him. Ikaru, I wasn't sure of yet.

I nodded. "I understand."

General Mirai bent next to a tree stump, rifling through layers of papers. He pulled out a worn sheet from the bottom of the pile and handed it to me. "This is a map of the southern region of Kiriku, centered on Phia. If you get separated, head to Tarahn. My brother will be able to provide you shelter and protection."

I folded the map into neat squares before I tucked it inside my tunic. General Mirai straightened, and his chin tilted upward as he looked down at Ikaru. "Shenrae is training to become a Shadow. Fill her in on the details—all the details, Ikaru. I know what power you and Hitori possess."

Ikaru held up his hands before him. He seemed small under General Mirai's gaze.

"I will share as much as I know."

General Mirai nodded, though his eyes lingered on Ikaru as he addressed Akio. "I'll expect a full report of the details. If the word 'Skills' is not written, there will be consequences."

Ikaru bristled and glared at me as if it were my fault.

General Mirai tucked the remaining pages into a small box and handed it off to one of his men. "Look after one another. I will make contact as soon as I can."

Akio shifted the spear in his grip, laying it against his chest as he crossed his arms. "General, how long should we wait before we head to Tarahn?"

I swallowed, my throat dry at the implications.

"Standard procedures."

Akio planted his staff into the ground and gave a short bow to General Mirai. "We'll see you soon."

I bowed in Shadow fashion. The general gave a short bow in return, and our small company headed toward our horses.

"We'll travel light," Akio said, glancing first at me, then to Ikaru. "There are a few hours left in the day, and I'd like to make some headway to the Kinshi Post."

Men shouted on either side of us, untying ropes and continuing to break down tents. They stuffed the lines, metal anchors, and hammers into sacks, creating a pile of completed packs. We'd been camped for over three weeks: the longest we had ever stayed in the same location. To the north, horses and riders lined up.

General Mirai swung his leg over his horse.

"Move out!"

The general clicked his heels against his horse's side, and the first wave set out to Leiko. The second wave would follow with the rest of their supplies. It cut down the time needed to take action. This ensured the mercenary group was well equipped and prepared at all times. As their horses carried them off into the distance, my heart sank a little. They were not Shadows, but in a short amount of time, they had become almost a second family to me.

I hoped I would see them again.

Akio split away from our group and exchanged words with a man taking inventory of the weapons. He picked up a cherry-colored staff from the pile and returned to my side.

"It's our custom for the master to give their students a gift, once they're ready," Akio said. His eyes had a sparkle in them.

I smiled and took the gift. Asdar had given me Kilo's old staff as a necessity. This one was a bit shorter than the one I trained with, and the wood seemed harder and more durable.

I swung it to test the balance.

"Thank you.. I will make sure to take good care of it."

Akio gave a slight bow. "It's an honor." His attention passed to Ikaru. "The general had your sword returned, as well as your horse. Do you need anything else?"

Ikaru shook his head, his eyes on the horizon. "Swords will do little to help us if the False Shadows come after us."

The happiness I felt at Akio's gift faded.

What did Ikaru know we didn't?

Greymoon whinnied at my approach, and I raised my hand to stroke his muzzle, gently cooing to him.

Akio moved ahead of me, his head turning to the east. "Let's head out and distance ourselves from this location."

―――――

We stopped well before the sun went down, leaving ample time to set up camp. Water trickled under the ice at the edge of a thick grove of pine trees.

I inhaled. How I'd missed the smell of pine.

Ikaru and Akio returned from gathering firewood, stacking an ample amount of wood under the trees to prevent it from getting wetter. I knelt on the ground in front of the small fire, tending to it with care. If not for the small amount of dry wood we had found, starting a fire would have been a more difficult process.

I fed another piece of dry wood and blew on the growing fire.

Ikaru sank down onto a rock that surrounded our meager campsite. He drew up one knee, letting the other leg hang over the edge. "So, what is it that you want to know?"

Akio moved to the edge of the camp. His spear rested against his chest as he turned his back to us. The blade at the end of his staff remained wrapped in cloth.

I returned my attention to Ikaru. He was a False Shadow. Would he know who killed my parents?

"Have you ever been to Vaiyene?"

"No, but my sister has. I don't know what happened there, except for vague details."

I remembered Kilo saying a False Shadow had tried to save my mother. Could it have been Ikaru's sister? Not that it really mattered. Even if I had a name, it would not bring back my parents. Better I didn't know.

I needed to focus on what could be done; not what had been.

I continued, thinking back to General Mirai's words. "How do the False Shadows save lives?"

"I joined the False Shadows to save lives."

I narrowed my eyes at him. The difference in his response to my question was minuscule. "This is serious."

Ikaru pushed himself off the rock. "I *am* being serious. My sister and I are both in the False Shadows so that we can save lives. We're doing what we can to make sure the missions fail."

He pushed back the sleeve of his robe to reveal his silver bond. If he'd been a Shadow, he would have received it after completing Shadow training. I smothered a twinge of jealousy. It hadn't even been a full turn of the seasons since I started training. I wouldn't be receiving mine for many years.

The bond on Ikaru's arm began to glow, and I recoiled. All my previous questions vanished from my mind, and a million more sprung up in their place. He bent down and swiped his hand over the ground.

Flames rose from the snow.

"It's what General Mirai wanted me to tell you. This is what the leader of the False Shadows is trying to hide—a power that will influence our world." Ikaru stood back and stared at the flames. He seemed lost in thought. "Hitori wants time to figure out the limitations of the Skills, without your Phantoms interfering."

The flames swayed in the air and flickered like normal flames, but they remained where Ikaru had placed them—on the snow. These were not normal flames. I bent to the ground and stuck my hand into the fire. Akio made to stop me, but when the flames did nothing to my skin, he resumed his post.

The flames were cool.

"How?" I looked up and met Ikaru's stare.

He shrugged. "It's like an extension of yourself, but it requires complete thought until you can summon it from memory." He waved his hand in front of his face, glancing around as if he were hesitant to give further details. His eyes rested on Akio, and he groaned. When Ikaru's eyes returned to mine, a ghost of a smile touched Akio's lips.

At least Ikaru feared General Mirai enough to cooperate.

"To summon the flames, I first had to picture them and push some of my energy into the vision to make it come alive. It drains the mind the same as battle."

The flames vanished from the snow.

"Is this power called the Skills?"

Ikaru nodded.

"Can anyone use the Skills?"

"Yes, but there's no basic theory. My sister and I can use it, and so can a handful of the False Shadows."

Akio returned from the edge of camp, taking a seat on a rock next to where I knelt. He placed a large log onto the fire, and I moved back, sitting on a vacant rock.

Akio laid his spear at his feet. "And Hitori is the leader of the False Shadows?"

"Yes."

"Do you plan on going back to Magoto, to Hitori?" Akio leaned forward, resting his elbows on his knees. He watched Ikaru without blinking. Ikaru shifted under Akio's gaze. Tension settled between them. Akio was not only waiting for an answer but also a reaction.

Finally, Ikaru looked away. "I don't know yet."

Akio nodded, seemingly satisfied by the answer.

At least he was honest.

When neither Ikaru nor I said anything more, Akio prompted the conversation. "What does Hitori hold over you?"

Ikaru drew in a deep breath. "My sister's life and my own."

I didn't like that his involvement with the False Shadows hurt people, but I understood. I would do anything to help Syrane. Killing was against the Shadow's Creed. But would I kill to save Syrane's life? I stared at the place where the fire had disappeared from the snow, my mind churning. What else could this power do? The flames were an illusion, but was that all they were?

Illusions didn't seem life-threatening.

"Is there more the Skills can do?"

Ikaru sat back down on the rock and rubbed the back of his neck. "Thus far, we've not found a limitation. Once someone has a basic understanding of the Skills, they can experiment with the power in countless ways."

Akio stood and retrieved another log, adding it to the now roaring fire. He picked up a branch and stoked the flames, scattering embers into the sky.

His focus turned back to Ikaru. "Can you give an example of how a person can use the Skills? How does Hitori use them? Who is 'we'?"

"My sister and I have experimented with the Skills since Hitori taught us how to use them. We saw it as an advantage. Blades are no match for the Skills. It's like"—he stumbled, searching for a suitable comparison— "fighting fire with water. The Skills can cut through metal. No blade can withstand it."

I eyed the bond on Ikaru's hand, not sure if I'd drawn the right conclusion. "The only way to defeat the Skills is to use the Skills?"

Ikaru snorted. "Don't think we haven't thought of that. Hitori is too powerful. No one stands a chance."

I stood and brushed embers from my boots. "Teach me."

"No."

I glared at Ikaru until he elaborated.

"It's not something you can pick up, like a sword."

I laughed. If he only knew. "I don't expect it to be easy."

When Ikaru remained silent, I tried one of General Mirai's tactics: reasoning. "We need to gather strength where we can. What's the harm in trying to teach me?"

Ikaru's eyebrows raised. "I'll consider it."

"You'll teach me, or I'll figure out how to use the Skills myself. Think of all the danger I'll be putting us all in if things go wrong."

Akio coughed and turned away to hide his smile.

Ikaru let out a noise somewhere between a groan and a sigh, pushing himself up from the rock and stepping out of the firelight. "Fine, I'll try to teach you how to use the Skills."

I grinned as Ikaru paced around the campfire. "But, I'm not responsible for what happens."

"I've failed more than once in my life. It's nothing new."

Ikaru looked me over as if my words surprised him. "It's not physical wounds that concern me."

I'd already made up my mind. General Mirai's words about not hesitating ran through my mind. I had to know if I was capable of using the Skills.

I stilled my thoughts. "I can handle it."

Akio eyed Ikaru. "Explain what the risks are."

Ikaru's gaze met mine as he answered Akio's question. "If you lose your focus, you could lose yourself in your mind. There's also the fun side effect of being poisoned as you use the Skills. You'll need to have one of these"—he held up his arm, twisting his bond in the firelight— "to absorb the effects of the poison, so you don't die." He turned back to Akio as if expecting him to say something to dissuade me.

Akio turned to me. "Do you still want to learn the Skills?"

I nodded. I had to.

Ikaru paused for some time before he retrieved his bag his horse's saddle pack. His movements were slow and deliberate. He fumbled with the latch to a green satchel for some time before his hands steadied enough to open it. He was hesitant.

Did he fear the Skills that much?

Or was it Hitori's use of the Skills that scared him?

After some digging, he withdrew a silver strand of metal about the same width and length as a finger. He stared at the piece of metal, twisting it in his hands as if deciding what to say next.

"The easiest way to become aware of the Skills, or to figure out how to channel them, is to use something metallic. For some reason, metal reacts to the power, especially if it's the same material as this silver encasing."

He held up his forearm with the bond on it.

"Where did you get that?"

I made to take it, but Ikaru moved it out of my reach.

He sighed. "I can only explain one thing at a time, and if you keep distracting me, you're never going to learn. What you don't want to do is lose focus when learning the Skills. Keep your mind trained on one thing."

I pushed down my irritation. It was one thing to be scolded by Phantom Asdar or General Mirai, another entirely to be reprimanded by someone like Ikaru. He handed me the silver bar, and I held it between my thumb and index finger.

"We're still learning how to use the Skills, but I've found a method that works well for me. Everyone's method evolves."

I nodded.

Everyone had their own method of fighting; that made sense.

"I like to think of it as relating to hot and cold."

He ran his fingers over the bond on his arm as he spoke. "If you want to create light or fire, that's a warm sensation, right? So, the trick is to find that same warmth or coolness inside you and transfer it into something else. Not forcing it but exerting a gentle push to make it move."

Ikaru's bond glowed as he spoke.

Was the warmth from his fingers transferring to the bond? It seemed simple yet complicated at the same time. How did you find "warm" and "cool" inside yourself?

The light died from Ikaru's bond, and he looked expectantly at me. Like I would somehow have grasped the concept already.

"That's it?" I blurted out, then flushed. Akio laughed, and I felt the heat deepen in my cheeks. It was a childish outburst, but it was the least bit of explanation I'd ever been given.

"Like I said, we're still figuring out how the Skills work. There are no manuals or steps on how to do it. There's freedom in how you approach it. I've already given you my theory."

"I know you can do it." Akio gave me an encouraging nod before he left Ikaru and me alone. He stood at the edge of the firelight.

I appreciated him giving me space.

I stared at the silver bar.

The Shadows learned by being shown step-by-step how to do something. Creative freedom was new to me. If I could get the basics down, maybe it would not seem as abstract of a concept.

"I can walk you through the sensation if you'd like?" Ikaru asked. I raised my eyes, and he gave me a lopsided smile. "It's how I learned how to do it. You'll have a basis on how it works at least."

"That would help."

I spread out a fur next to the fire and sat on the ground cross-legged, the silver thread in my palms. I let out a long breath and waited for Ikaru to start.

"Close your eyes and push away all other thoughts. Focus on nothing but being present in this current moment. Breathe and relax. Nothing else matters. Don't mind anything else."

I tried to focus on Ikaru's words, but thoughts of Kilo, General Mirai, Akio, and my friends slipped through my peace. Were General Mirai and his men in Leiko yet? Were they fighting against the False Shadows already? Had they encountered the

Skills? Was it too late to help them? Did Ikaru think I was weak? What did Akio feel about me? How were Syrane and Torey doing? Did they miss me in Shadow training?

"Stop, stop, stop. You're distracted."

I opened my eyes and frowned, realizing that my foot had been bouncing with the thoughts.

"Sorry, it's hard for me to stop thinking."

"Clearly."

Ikaru crossed to the other side of camp. He untied a pile of blankets from his horse and set them on the ground near the fire.

"When you can calm your mind, let me know."

"Let me try again." I pushed myself onto my feet.

Ikaru glanced at me, his lips pressed thin. "No. Stray thoughts are deadly. It's not a bruise or an injury you can grit your teeth through. You're ignoring my warnings."

I bit back my words and attempted to relax. I was being impatient. Asdar had said as much to me in training.

He had also said I let things distract me too much.

I walked over to Greymoon and put my hands on my blankets. The black stallion brought his face next to mine and nuzzled my neck. He'd been such a good friend, and I didn't even have a treat for him. His deep brown eyes met mine, and I tried to let go of my frustration. I left my blankets and instead grabbed the staff Akio had given to me. I glanced over my shoulder at Ikaru. He had buried himself underneath a pile of furs and blankets.

Would I be able to learn the Skills?

Or were they too much for me?

To stop my thoughts, I twirled the staff. The balance differed from the others I'd used, but it seemed a worthwhile trade. I brought the staff up and over my head, keeping my moves deliberate as I glided through a combination. I swayed and turned around, catching myself at an odd angle.

Akio ducked under my staff, his spear in hand.

His blue eyes caught the firelight. "Care to dance?"

I lowered my staff and regained my stance, a smile creeping against my composure. I struggled to contain my smile, biting my lips to not seem *too* happy to practice with him. We moved away from the camp and into the moonlight. Akio stood beside me, holding his spear with both hands. He crouched down, and I mirrored his stance. My muscles protested, but I fell into a rhythm, and the pain soon disappeared. Nothing mattered but the mindless repetition and sway of action.

I was no weapons master, but the flow—the dance Akio taught me—eased my mind. I needed to stop caring what others thought and learn how to focus on one thing at a time. I smiled to myself. If experience had taught me anything, it was that concepts like these took time.

A lot of time.

I pivoted on my feet and focused on the movement. I was making progress, and for now, that would have to do.

"Whatever you do, don't think about anything else."
It was the fifth time Ikaru had warned me, and for the fifth time, I reassured him I wouldn't think about anything else but using the Skills.

"I know."

"If you lose yourself in the Skills—"

"I understand. Really. I do." I folded my hands in my lap and twisted the metal between my fingers as I drew in a deep, exaggerated breath and waited.

We'd been traveling for a few days, keeping to the dense areas of the Kiren Forest. Rain pattered against the shelter Akio had created from fallen branches and fur pelts. He kept watch outside, ensuring we wouldn't be disturbed. Nothing was around to distract me. It was me, Ikaru, and the Skills.

I breathed in, then out, in and out.

Finally, Ikaru spoke.

His voice startled me, and I almost fell out of my meditation, but somehow, I remained calm and focused.

"Feel the weight of the metal between your fingers. Do you notice how cool the metal is against the warmth of your fingers?"

The metal bar was cool against my fingers. I rubbed it idly with my thumb. The more I did so, the warmer it became.

But that was because I was warming it with my hands...

I pushed the thought away. I couldn't think logically. This was theory, not fact. Creativity, not logic.

Ikaru stopped talking as if he sensed my mind wandering.

Breathe in. Breathe out. Breathe in.

He resumed after a few moments.

"The metal is warm, warmed by your own touch. Think back to how it felt before and push the coolness you have taken into yourself back to the metal."

I caught myself before I rationalized his words, breathing in, then out, and feeling the metal at my fingertips.

Cold metal.

Warm fingers.

"Now think of the cold and remember how the metal felt against your hands. Push that feeling where you want it. Remember, the Skills are an extension of yourself. Whatever you touch can be considered a part of yourself."

I bit my lip against Ikaru's nonsensical words.

None of this made sense.

I tried to push my thoughts away and focus on the cold air around me. It rippled the back of my cloak and weaved in and out of the cloth keeping me warm. I imagined the silver thread in my fingers experiencing that same coolness, the wind rushing over it and stealing the heat—sucking the warmth from my hands. The metal against my fingertips felt cold, actually cold.

I opened my eyes and looked down at the frost on the silver thread. I'd used the Skills!

I looked up to see Ikaru's eyes focused on me.

He shared none of my excitement.

"Now that you've managed to use the Skills, you need to be more conscious of your thoughts."

I nodded, vaguely hearing him speak. Was it possible to create something more substantial? To engulf the metal and freeze it solid? I stared down at the thread, recalling the sense of cold I'd harnessed earlier. The cool breeze and the caress of the wind against metal removed any warmth. The frost on the metal spread.

My grin reflected my success.

I forgot about the logistics of my hands against the metal. The unnatural frost grew in a flurry, climbing onto my fingers with surprising speed. I dropped the metal. Ice crystals expanded and leaped into the air, freezing one of the poles holding our shelter in place. I scrambled away, and Ikaru touched the silver bar with his hands.

The ice crystals melted.

Ikaru relaxed, and I took a step back.

If I had not seen and felt it for myself, I would not have believed it. The Skills held such power.

I glanced over at Ikaru. "Do the flames you create feel warm to you?" I had thought it was an illusion, but the Skills I called forth had burned my fingers with their icy touch.

Ikaru shook his head. "I don't know why your use of the Skills was real. Hitori's use of the Skills is real as well. Perhaps mine is different because I intended it to be nothing more than an illusion."

My stomach turned over. What I wielded could have spiraled out of control. I hadn't known I needed to set my intention of real or fake ice. It seemed an important thing to specify.

"Now you understand why Hitori's exploration of the Skills needs to be stopped." Ikaru stared at the silver thread on the ground. "We don't know what she's capable of."

My eyes were focused on the metal thread. What was I capable of? I pushed the thought away and disciplined my mind. I took a deep breath and leaned back onto my hands, peering through the wooden branches of our makeshift shelter. I couldn't see much, but Akio still stood watch.

He hadn't rushed over to see what had happened.

Ikaru stood and brushed off his pants before he made toward the exit of the shelter.

"Thank y—" I swallowed the sentiment. Ikaru had already left. He wasn't the most pleasant of companions. I glanced down at the metal thread in my hands. The Skills *were* more dangerous than I'd expected.

I sighed and rocked onto my feet, leaving the shelter.

Akio's gaze followed me. "How did it go?"

His gaze returned to the forest. Even though he was watching for danger, I knew I had his full attention.

"I used the Skills."

Akio turned his head toward me, a smile on his face.

Before he could say anything, I amended the statement. "I used the Skills and could have gotten us killed."

Akio gave me a crooked grin. "That dangerous?"

"Apparently so." I drew my cloak closer around me, not wanting to discuss it further. I wasn't afraid of using the Skills, but I was cautious about what I didn't know about them.

The forest was quiet, laden with snow. Overhead, a group of birds fluttered from tree to tree, but little sound reached my ears.

It was peaceful.

If only I could be as quiet as the snow.

I glanced over at Akio. "Have you always been this focused?"

He crossed his arms around his spear, leaning it against his chest. "It came with time."

He grew quiet, and I watched a bird catch its balance on a thin tree branch. Snow dislodged from the tree and splattered to the ground. The bird bounced up and down while the limb steadied under the weight.

"When the world doesn't care about you, you tend not to think too much. Idle thoughts are nothing but a burden."

I hadn't expected his answer to be so serious.

Akio kept his gaze ahead. I stayed silent for a moment, hoping he would continue. His eyes seemed fixed on something; he was too serious for bird watching. What was it that he saw? When he didn't say anything further, I cleared my throat and kept my tone light.

"I wish my mind were as calm."

Akio chuckled and looked down at me. A smile returned to his face. "If you keep watch as often as I do, you'll grow tired of thinking. Better to be present at the moment than worry yourself to death."

"Maybe I should help you keep watch then."

Akio returned his gaze to the forest. "I'd like that."

chapter thirty-seven
SHENRAE'S CHOICE

Our group stopped before an immense, haphazardly thrown-together building. The Kinshi Post sat crooked upon a foundation of pavers. The building leaned first to the left, then to the right, and finally straightened out with a long, spiral tower. Rickety metal stairs thrust out from the sides of the building. It looked like a handful of builders had come together, but none could agree on a single plan for construction. It looked unstable, but the people who walked near the base didn't seem to share my fear of the building collapsing.

I dismounted and moved closer, keeping my horse close.

Akio led us through the crowd of people gathered outside the make-shift marketplace. I side-stepped a large group of people, pulling Greymoon after me. My mouth watered, and I peered between heads, trying to find the source of the sweet-cinnamon aroma.

We passed under a doorway, with metal gates bent open. The metal between the doors was as thick as my hand. It would take an ox and many strong men to push the doors closed.

I didn't imagine them being used regularly.

Inside, decorative stained-glass panels lined the building, casting light across the walls. Little nooks and crannies were set into the walls. Scrolls and small boxes had been stuffed into the holes, with names scribbled at the bottoms designating the recipients.

"Quite a spectacle, isn't it?"

Akio's infectious smile spread across his face.

"I never knew something like this existed," I admitted, looking around. "Who are all these people?"

"People who need information from other locations. Instead of having a rider go and deliver messages, this is a way to shorten the distance from one area to the other."

He winked at me and scurried ahead, pausing at the base of the rickety staircase.

"I'll show you where my nook is."

I hesitated at the bottom of the steps. The metalwork seemed no stronger up close. I glanced over my shoulder to Ikaru walking in the opposite direction.

"Aren't you worried about him?" I asked.

Akio followed my gaze and grabbed the railing of the staircase, leaning over the edge. "The general told me not to interfere."

General Mirai did have more experience dealing with people, but letting Ikaru go in such a public place seemed risky, even with my inexperience.

What if he sent a letter to Hitori and betrayed us?

"I don't think he's a bad person," Akio continued, "but he's run from help before. I think he feels trapped in his circumstances. Letting him choose what he wants to do may work against us, but the general has always fought for free will."

Ikaru climbed a staircase on the opposite side of the building. Akio touched my shoulder and redirected my attention. "Don't forget, you have to deliver General Mirai's letter."

He was right; there was nothing we could do about Ikaru.

I placed one unsure foot on the staircase, relieved the metal didn't creak or shift under my weight. After a few steps, I began to relax and admire the construction of the stairs. Like the outside of the building, they had been thrown together in a somewhat unconventional way, but the design work was intricate. Akio stopped and pulled a key from around his neck, sliding it into the slot below the nook. He pulled out a few letters. I shook my head in disbelief. The staircase wound around the entirety of the building. There must have been hundreds, if not thousands, of messages waiting for their recipients' arrival.

As we descended, my gaze wandered the wall. I reached inside my inner robe and pulled out the letter entrusted to me by General Mirai.

"How do we find out where to mail this?"

I couldn't decipher the scribbles written on the back of the letter. Akio glanced back before he took the remaining steps to the ground level.

"Drop-offs are sorted by region." Akio moved to the center of the building. "See the markings on the wall? It's a little abstract, but if you look close enough, there's a map in the ceiling. It'll give you a general idea of where to start."

I tilted my head. "I don't see anything."

"Once you see the pattern, it's hard to forget. Here, I'll show you how I learned to see it."

Akio laid down on the floor, not caring about the people walking around him. He looked up at me. "I guarantee at one point, or another everyone here has done the same thing."

I glanced around the room and returned my gaze to Akio.

His eyebrows were raised at my hesitation.

"Trust me," he said, and I relented, lying down parallel to him. I followed the direction of Akio's finger. I squinted, finding the tiny cracks of light that outlined the landscape of Kiriku. The outline of the Miyota Mountains came to me. I scanned the mountain range, my eyes settling in the centera a bright star—Vaiyene.

Home.

Once the snow melted, I could return, but thinking about it stirred a strange feeling. I missed Syrane and Torey, but now that I had left, I wasn't sure I wanted to return. Maybe my feelings would change when winter was over. I pushed the thoughts away and kept my eyes on the Miyota Mountains etched into the walls. Akio stood and offered his hand to me. I hesitated, then let him pull me up. "Now, look around at the walls and see if you can figure out where Vaiyene's drop-off would be."

I moved my focus to the walls, remembering the secret of the light. The cracks moved across the ceiling in a deliberate pattern. I pointed out the white star of Vaiyene.

Akio nodded. "Good eye. Where does the letter to General Mirai need to go?"

I handed the letter to Akio. "I can't read it."

He spent a moment looking at the scribbly text and then glanced around, his eyes resting on Ikaru. "While I doubt our friend will run off, I would rather he not know where this letter is being sent."

Akio gave a casual glance across the way, and I nodded my agreement. Ikaru had yet to prove his loyalty to anyone.

"Here, Shenrae." Akio held out a letter addressed to me. "This came for you."

For me?

"I'll be right back. Keep an eye on Ikaru while you read."

I nodded and flipped the letter over. In familiar handwriting, Kilo had penned my name. I stared at it, skeptical.

How had he known I would receive it?

Shenrae,

I hope this letter finds you well. So much has happened; I fear I won't be able to convey the gravity of the situation through words alone.

First, congratulations on your sponsorship! I am proud of you, as your parents would have been. I hope your experience during training is as rewarding and meaningful as it was for me. I am fighting hard to ensure that the lives of you and your brother will not be controlled by war.

General Mirai's informed me of Asdar's decision to have you trained under him. He is a great man and a powerful ally—one who would have become Phantom if born in Vaiyene. He can teach you many things about being a Shadow.

Finae and I are with a False Shadow, learning to combat the power they wield. We hope to find a solution to a peaceful end.

From what General Mirai tells me, you are with one yourself. I don't believe he means harm, but be cautious who you trust. Hitori's spies are everywhere.

Stay strong. You're more capable than you believe.

Kilo

I sensed Ikaru's presence before I looked up from the letter. He'd paused a respectful distance behind me, but he said nothing while I reread the letter and tucked it into my robe.

Kilo was still protecting us. It eased my mind.

When I looked up, I noticed that Ikaru's face had drained of color. He crumpled the letter in his own hands and gritted his teeth.

"I have to go back."

I cringed, already fearing I knew the answer. "Where?"

"With my sister gone, there is no one left to hinder Hitori's plans. Anything she demands the False Shadows to do—killing, poisoning, blackmailing—all of it will go according to plan."

"Won't Hitori kill you if you go back?"

"I have to."

His voice was hollow as he spoke.

I sighed and tried to find some other option. I inhaled and held my breath. Ikaru believed deterring the False Shadows' movement was more important than anything, but what if learning how to wield the Skills would help more?

Kilo was studying the Skills. He must have thought the same.

I let my breath out and looked down at my hand. At the blisters and calluses left by my staff. No matter how hard I trained, I couldn't defeat the False Shadows with this staff.

Ikaru had already confirmed this.

I drew in another deep breath and held it.

If I could figure out how to use the Skills, would I be able to stand against Hitori alongside Kilo? To do that, I first needed Ikaru to teach me the Skills. I let out my breath, feeling more centered. The Shadows had grounded me after my parents' deaths, but training with Phantom Asdar, General Mirai, and Akio had given me a purpose and a sense of direction.

"You can't. You have to teach me how to use the Skills."

Ikaru blinked, his mind returning from wandering around the area. His eyes focused on me.

"Please, it's the only way I'll be able to help. I can't wield this staff, except to defend my own life." And so far, I'd been lucky with the opponents I'd faced.

I tried to keep the emotion from my voice. "I have to find some way to help Kilo and save my friends from the Skills. I don't know if I can, but I have to try."

Ikaru continued to stare at me.

My thoughts returned to the day Syrane was almost killed when Phantom Asdar saved his life. Syrane's eyes had been empty then. Like Syrane back in Koto, Ikaru couldn't hear me, but unlike my brother, I didn't know if he would listen to me, or if he would come around.

Akio appeared behind us.

He put a hand on my shoulder and one on Ikaru's and pushed us toward the exit. "This is no place for these discussions."

I bit my bottom lip. I hadn't even thought about it.

Akio's eyes scanned the crowd as we untied the horses and moved into the forest. After Akio scouted the woods for others, he joined us.

"*Now* it is safe to discuss matters."

Akio's reproach seemed unimportant in comparison to Ikaru's demeanor. His eyes retained their vacancy. Was he really considering going back?

Akio narrowed his eyes. "What happened?"

"Ikaru is going back to Hitori."

"You can't be serious." Akio placed his hands on Ikaru's shoulders and shook him roughly. "You'll be killed."

When Ikaru didn't react, Akio's tone deepened. "Ikaru!"

Ikaru's head jerked, snapping him from his melancholy. He sighed and turned his attention to me. I needed his help, but more than that, it would keep Ikaru from leaving.

Akio let go of Ikaru, and I stepped forward.

"Ikaru, will you continue to help me learn how to use the Skills?" I held my breath and waited.

Ikaru sighed again, acting as if even words pained him. "I will continue to teach you. At least for a while."

"That will be enough." I placed my right hand over my chest and bowed in Shadow fashion. It seemed the best decision for us, but to Ikaru, I was sure it remained complicated. He'd spent his life believing what he was doing was necessary.

Now he didn't know whether it had done any good.

Akio watched Ikaru with interest, then glanced over at me. "All we can do is try."

A Shadow does what he is capable of; no

more can be asked of him.

I wasn't a Shadow yet, but the ideals guided who I wanted to be. All we could do now was learn how to wield the Skills and hope to come up with a way to combat Hitori's knowledge of the Skills. Ikaru didn't believe in me, but I would learn how to wield them. I would help Kilo defeat the False Shadows and save the lives of Syrane and Torey. They trained under Asdar, but if they fought against them, they would not stand a chance.

I drew in a breath.

I didn't know what strength lay inside me, or what General Mirai and Asdar thought they saw in me, but I would do what I could to save my friends.

part five
HITORI

chapter thirty-eight
GRUDGES

I should have killed her when I had the chance.

Now she and her precious Phantom were dissecting my notes. The research I'd meticulously been compiling for months. I dragged my fingers across the spines of my books, pulling out a hefty, pristine tome. My notes were copied by one loyal to me, but the resentment of losing the original notes maddened me.

What if Saitou had not transcribed the methods precisely? Even the slightest error could upset the delicate process.

I shouldn't have trusted him with such an important task.

How foolish of me.

My hands caressed the cover of the book, and I opened it as a mist rolled over the edges. The black ink shone against the moonlight, and I extended my will into the pages. The black words shifted to gray, revealing the true copy and diagram of the procedure. I ran my fingers over the lines, making sure the records Saitou had inscribed were correct.

This entry seemed to be.

I let go of the Skills, and the words reshuffled themselves. If she managed to break the seal on my experimentations, there was a slim possibility she and her Phantom friend could find equal footing against me. I curled my lips back in disgust at her name.

Rin.

I had let my feelings get in the way of killing her. She might have been a friend once, but she was no longer. The opportunity for her to make amends was gone. I'd trusted her, and she had betrayed me. Because of my weakness, she had wounded me again.

Next time, she and her Phantom friend would not survive.

I would make sure of it.

To you, dear reader,

I hope this story inspires you to find your own strength. Never stop questioning who you are. You are capable—strong enough—to fight whatever journey lies before you.

Thank you for taking a chance on a humble author,

Noelle

www.noellenichols.com

acknowledgements

When I first started this series a decade ago, I lacked the confidence in the story inside me. It takes a great deal of strength and courage to follow a dream, a confidence that's taken me many years to discover.

This book wouldn't be possible without the people:

To Mr. Sherman, the first person who saw the author inside me and allowed me to write the beginnings of this story in class: Thank you for believing in me. I wandered a bit in life, but I found my way back to writing.

To my first beta reader, Dankia Hinz, who read the entirety of this story when it was a complete mess: I hope you're surprised (and delighted) with how this story has taken on its own life. I sure am!

To my editor, Katie Phillips, who read my manuscript and told me my story didn't start until the last couple of chapters: I thought I would die that day, but your much-needed honesty gave me the push I needed to re-evaluate (and salvage) the beginning of this story. Ha! :)

To my proofreaders, Emily Cargile and Kate Allen, who helped me iron out the last nuances in this book. Thank you! I can finally breathe again.

To my wonderful beta reader, Amy Vanhorn, who spent much time leaving me with thoughtful insights and questions to deepen my story world after many revisions, and to all the countless other beta readers who have shared their thoughts and given their time to make this book the best it could be: Thank you!

To the amazing #amwriting and #amediting communities on Twitter: The friendships I have made have sustained me through editing hell. There is a light at the end of the tunnel, even if at times the tunnel seems impossibly far. You can do it!

To my friends and family, too many to name here, who kept asking about my progress—this book is who I am. I hope you can see a part of my life in these characters.

To my dad: Thank you for thinking I'm crazy and calling me to make sure I'm okay. It's been one heck of a journey.

To my brother, Nathan, for his support: I'm going to write those hundred books—just watch. I hope you like reading all of them!

To my husband, Jamey, for keeping me fed and understanding when all I could do was write: Your encouragement and support have given me the push to make this book as I envisioned it. I couldn't have done it without you.

Noelle lives in the mountains of Colorado with her husband and their three border collies. When she's not dreaming of fantasy worlds and contemplating life, she's creating art and doing as many things as she can.

Made in the USA
Monee, IL
05 July 2020